REDEMPTION

Redeemed
Trilogy
1

REDEMPTION

DONNA M. YOUNG

Published by Donna M. Young
P O Box 76, Lawton, IA 51030
dmywriting@wiatel.net

Author photo by Elizabeth Rose Kahl

Published in the United States of America
ISBN: 978-1-947143-04-3
Fiction / General
Fiction / Christian General

Acknowledgments

First and foremost, I want to thank my Lord Jesus for pursuing me, for loving me, for saving me, and for teaching me about the gift of His Grace.

I would also like to thank my husband Marty, my rock and my best friend; and all our children for being inspirations to me and for believing in me even when I had a hard time believing in myself: Aaron, Elizabeth, Jarrod, David, and Alicia. God bless you. I pray that you will realize every one of your hopes and dreams through Christ.

To Robin, Bobbi, and Richard. We've made it through so much by the Grace of God and His merciful hand. Always remember how much He loves you.

And last but certainly not least, my Aunt Barbara. Thank you for being like a mother to me when I really needed one; and my Uncles Floyd and Allen for your godly guidance.

PART 1

Prelude

HEART POUNDING HARD in her chest, she rounded a boulder at the base of the mountain and spied the ruins of a dilapidated farm just ahead. Limping, she crossed the barren yard to reach a hulking, rusted silo on the far side of the deserted homestead. Stepping quickly into the murky interior, she simultaneously grabbed the edge of the twisted metal door and pulled it with both hands, scraping and screeching across the cracked, up-heaved cement of the entryway threshold. She could only hope no one heard the squeal of the door being dragged shut, resonating through the still afternoon air.

With the entry nearly closed, the echoing interior swam in darkness. Jana was never known as a particularly patient person, and the stress she felt as she waited for her eyes to adjust in the inky blackness caused her to examine her own level of anxiety. "Calm down, girl," she murmured under her breath, clenching her fists and fighting to control her breathing.

A stench strong enough to cause spontaneous gagging filled the musty air of the structure, and assaulted Jana with a force sufficient to churn the acids in her otherwise empty and already nauseated gut. Wondering what in the world the awful smell could be, she covered her nose with her dirty coat sleeve and battled the urge to retch. Her recently well-honed survival instincts leapt into overdrive as she caught the sound of light scratching on the other side of the unlit chamber. Instinctively, her right hand dropped to the hilt of the hunting knife sheathed securely on her slim thigh.

Sliding her lithe body slowly against the cold galvanized steel of her shelter, she lowered her profile and made ready for anything. Partial vision returned by the time she inched her way to the cause of the noise and source of the dreadful odor. A large, currently unrecognizable, animal had wandered into the gloomy, vacant hulk to die, and a pack of emaciated rats, grateful for the easy meal, were busily feasting on its rotting carcass. Initially, the vermin didn't notice the petite girl decked out in survival gear standing behind them. Then, one curious beady-eyed creature with yellow and bloody incisors got a little too close to her hiking boot. Her kick, spontaneous and prompted by revulsion, sent it sailing into the nearby wall.

A high-pitched shriek followed by a hollow thud and silence told her this one wouldn't be bothering her again. Jana, conscious of the noise made by her impulsive action, suddenly became aware she'd been holding her breath. Giving herself a moment, she leaned against the cold steel wall to compose her thoughts and quiet her shaking frame. Oddly, she realized she'd quickly become somewhat immune to the offensive odor.

Watching the grizzly feast with wearied detachment, she lowered her heightened defenses just long enough to allow a hint of despair, which had been lurking just out of thought's reach, to stab deeply into her anguished soul, causing her usually squared shoulders to droop forward in exhausted resignation.

How long had she been running? It was more acknowledgment than question as she knew full well the extent of her recent travels. Days and weeks melded together. Feeling temporarily overwhelmed by the events affecting her life, her slumped shoulders folded even further inward for the emotional weight they carried. But then she wondered had her life ever really been normal? Well, except for her years with Josh, which were conventional according to the world's standards, she supposed she'd never really known a normal life. Those unspeakable things which happened long ago in her childhood came back to her now, thankfully and regretfully, only while she slept. So much ugliness in that tortured past. She'd gladly pluck those thoughts permanently from her wounded mind if she could. Shocked awake more often than she'd like to admit, with faces and horrors she'd thought long forgotten; the only redeeming piece of this life on the run was the guaranteed fatigue which accompanied her harried existence. This breakneck pace often meant weariness so extreme it allowed her to sleep most nights without being wakened by bad dreams and the loneliness which plagued her so often in the quiet of the night.

Jana halted her contemplation long enough to wonder how close her pursuers were. Had she left them far enough behind to allow for these few stolen moments of respite, or had she overstayed already? She wouldn't let them catch her, couldn't. Deaths of so many would have been in vain and lives of so many others at risk if she didn't see this through. Suddenly, the wall of the silo where she rested began to vibrate ever so slightly against her back. Realizing she could hear it as well as feel it, a helicopter was drawing close to her refuge. Noise from the engine getting louder; letting her know without question she was trapped, like one of those foul rodents, in this cold metal tomb.

The copter landed in the desolate barnyard, and immediately, the earth outside the silo thundered with the sound of boots hitting the dry cracked ground. Its engine's spinning rotor picked up dirt and gravel from the farmstead and hurled it, pelting everything in the vicinity including the shelter where Jana hid. She dropped to the cold cement floor. Through the sound of pebbles raining on metal, she heard a deep voice shouting orders and her eyes grew huge with terror as she watched the steel door to her sanctuary begin its screeching trek across the broken cement threshold.

1

Just last year

Josh stuck his head in the room one last time. "Hey, Jana, you sure you don't wanna come? I'm just about ready to go."

"Joshua! You do this to me every week! Sunday is my only day to sleep in. I am not getting out of this bed! Now go away."

"Okay, okay. I'll see you later. Maybe we can go get lunch?"

"Not if you're going with your nut job friends!"

"Well, I'll see you late this afternoon then?"

"Sure, Josh, fine! Sleeping now! Go!"

Blowing her a kiss, Josh quietly closed the bedroom door. She heard him rummage through the hall closet for his jacket and then the sound of their bright red front door opening and closing. Soon his small, gas efficient, conservative blue car backed down the driveway, and he sped off to spend the day with his, in her opinion, infinitely weird group of friends at their useless little church. "Great, some peace and quiet at last," she sighed, as she rolled to Josh's side of the plush mattress. Inhaling the fresh, masculine scent of him, Jana smiled knowing she could never stay angry with Josh for longer than a minute.

Her husband was the sweetest, gentlest man she'd ever known. At a little over six foot three with strawberry blond hair, impossibly deep dimples, cleft chin, and mischievous green eyes, which lit up when he smiled, he had a way of making people feel at ease wherever he went. Also in surprisingly good physical shape for someone who spent his working hours behind a desk in a small church office; his mere appearance, as he walked through their bedroom in a towel, could still excite her. Even the thought of him caused her to blush a little. No, she couldn't stay angry with him, but she did have to admit she was glad to have a little time to herself. Life had become tremendously hectic since her latest promotion at the store, and Sunday really was the only day she could relax a little and maybe even sleep in if the universe would just allow her to do so.

Snuggling deep under her cozy, down comforter, she was determined to get a little more shut eye before getting up for the day, but after lying with her eyes squeezed shut for a few more minutes, she gave up, knowing there would be no going back to sleep today. Instead she stretched, enjoying the feel of the cool, silk sheets against her skin. Gazing sleepily toward the window, where beams of sunlight were doing their best to sneak through a slim opening in the cream-colored drapes, she paused, sighed, and then turned her head to survey her richly appointed bedroom suite.

This was her sanctuary. Decorating the room herself, she'd used a calming palette of soft earth tones. Jana's California king-size bed, which was the focal point of the room, was big enough for two to sleep without touching if you didn't want to, though that certainly wasn't its only purpose. Smiling, she savored lingering memories of last night, which caused her to feel instantly warm inside.

All her life she'd wanted a massive, comfortable bed with lots of pillows and fluffy covers, an effect she'd accomplished marvelously! Though it was a bit of an annoyance to take all the pillows off the bed at night and put them back on in the morning, it achieved the look she craved, so she tolerated the bit of extra work required. Much of her youth had been spent sleeping wherever she was allotted some small space, so she'd decided long ago she would choose her own sleeping assignments from now on, thank you very much!

Jana's entire adult existence, so far, revolved around empty perceptions. She cared a great deal about how things looked to others though she wouldn't have admitted that out loud to anyone, and she had a driving desire to achieve more, gain more, and have more at all costs. For appearance's sake, she endeavored toward a standard of living which was admittedly above their combined income and then presented that false life to people who were of absolutely no importance to her, or Josh, at all.

America's economy had taken an ever more frightening nosedive in these past few years, and she was in a constant state of distress about how the changes in the nation's financial misery might affect her own personal style of living. With tens of millions of people jobless now and more added every day, she was forced to be even more diligent than she'd ever had to be previously, in her efforts to get ahead and stay there.

Josh didn't understand. He didn't care about things, and he got a little upset with her constant need to "keep up with the Joneses" as he put it. Actually, she was more interested in leaving the Joneses in the dust on her way to the top. But she worked hard! They both did. Why shouldn't they have something to show for all their combined efforts? And if it made the neighbors a little jealous, well then, that was an extra added bonus and even kind of made her smile a bit on the inside.

Life at this moment, in her mind, was pretty close to perfect. If others were having a hard time, that wasn't any concern of hers, no matter how much Josh desired to save the world. She'd imagined her way of thinking would have had a bigger impact on him by now. His "do good" attitude never got them anywhere! Well, she would continue to work on that one and perhaps, if he had any sense at all, he would come around eventually!

It was kind of funny how some of the most significant things about his values, which had drawn her to Josh when their friendship first began; his compassionate attitude toward the unfortunate and his aspiration to change the world for his god were the very things that caused her the most aggravation about him now.

They'd met just a couple of years after college. He'd been working as a teen counselor in a local Christian ministry and was excited about the opportunity to make a difference. She was a hungry, junior buyer at the local department store then, aiming for a quickly ascending and profitable career. The biggest difference between them then and now was that she was willing to do anything to achieve her professional goals and he had his precious "ethics."

Their meeting was etched in her memory as one of the best moments of her life and happened on a beautiful, sunny day in their favorite park by the river. A Memorial Day picnic sponsored by her work was the venue. He was Mark's friend; Mark being one of the junior accountants at the department store where Jana had been an assistant buyer for over a year.

She noticed Josh right away. How could she help it? He was playing volleyball with a group of guys; laughing, green eyes sparkling, strawberry blond hair blowing in the breeze. Jana was amazed at how agile he was for someone so tall, and she was enjoying the sight of him. He hadn't seen her at first, but when he did finally look in her direction and she realized she'd been staring, her face blushed red. Annoyed at being caught looking, she turned the other way to watch a group of kids playing Frisbee in the grass, surprised and bothered by her own shy behavior.

Believing herself to have overcome all bashfulness long ago, she was always the aggressor, the ruthless pursuer, in every situation and relationship of her life until that single defining moment in the park.

All of Jana's previous relationships with men—well, since the adult controlled relationships of her childhood passed into painful memories—were initiated or manipulated by her. Never wasting much time on people who didn't interest her, or who didn't appear to be in a position to further her life or career goals, she was very particular about who she admitted into her private world. Through college, and until she met Josh, she'd been in and out of a long series of affairs which were profitable for her, at least for a period of time; either for sex or for the advancement of her ever growing professional agenda. Each affair though had left her feeling emptier than the one before, and she'd become almost unbearable even to herself.

Not a fan of failure, this continual fiasco involving men had begun to be a problem for her, even to the point of imagining she might need to revamp her life's agenda a bit. Though, mind you, this was an agenda she'd plotted out many long years ago in her childhood. She had to admit, looking back, she'd been woefully lacking in the "meeting Mr. Right" department before getting together with her Josh, but meeting him had changed all that.

Later in the afternoon, at that same Memorial Day picnic, Josh approached Jana for an introduction, and her heart did a series of small flips in her chest causing her severe discomfort and embarrassment. He smiled, which deepened his dimples all the more, and try as she might, she couldn't stop a small grin from creeping across her own usually preset, stern, and composed features. He reached out to shake her hand, and upon their fingers touching, she felt a jolt of electricity rip through her body filling her stomach with butterflies and leaving her knees weak. A small gasp caught even her by surprise and caused a glint of amusement to dance in Josh's, impish, emerald eyes. She wanted to kick him, or at least hate him for his mischievous beaming smile, but she was much too smitten for that to be possible.

Quickly an item, seeing one meant you could count on seeing the other. Josh brought out something in Jana she hadn't known was there. Laughing for the first time in memory, she had to admit no one had ever tried so hard to amuse her, or make her smile; and they discovered together she had a natural, wry sense of humor. He also brought out a softer side in her nature—a side which was hidden behind the professional bravado, self loathing, and sense of unworthiness which filled her to the point of pushing people away the moment they began to get too close; a secret side which longed more than anything to be loved and accepted. Josh made her feel as though she belonged; and not just belonged, but belonged with him.

Every aspect of their lives meshed completely until Josh began inviting her to attend church with him. Jana made it very clear to him that church wasn't in any of her immediate plans. So after several well-intentioned offers, he stopped pestering her and seemed only sad and distant over the whole Sunday morning subject.

Regardless of their differing opinions on religion or church, their relationship grew due to that special something Josh saw in Jana, which no one else had recognized and the goodness Jana recognized in this special guy. And, as time went by without sexual advances from Josh, Jana began to aggressively pursue the idea of intimacy with him. Experiences with men in her past always led to sex long before this phase in the relationship. Though, if she was honest, Jana would have to admit none of her previous relationships ever lasted anywhere near this long.

Josh made it clear to her that intimacy was not in his immediate plans, and he intended to wait until he was married to the right girl before allowing himself that kind of relationship. His conservative way of thinking was foreign to Jana and confused her all the more. In fact, on several occasions during their months of dating, Josh left Jana's apartment early after a nice meal, a movie, and some cuddling got to be a little more than he thought he could handle. This concept was bizarre to her, and when she couldn't understand his lack of interest, she felt incredibly insecure, though she also wondered if perhaps somehow he was the one who was right in his naive, old-fashioned sensibilities.

Jana knew she was falling for Josh in a big way and couldn't seem to stop herself from caring what he thought no matter how hard she tried. He was different from any man she'd ever dated, and though she found him quaint, she also thought him handsome, intelligent, strong, infinitely adorable, kind, and compassionate. He was the man of her dreams!

If truth be told, the idea of him trying to protect her innocence, however misplaced, made her feel strangely respected and valued somehow, a feeling she'd never known before. She'd manipulated men for years, and this strange turn of events made her feel a bit powerless for once. She really didn't like the idea of waiting at all—or of not being the one in control of the situation—but Josh was adamant and ever so convincing. He claimed it had something to do with his Christian morals. She learned to deal with it.

After their courtship had advanced for a time, Josh came to her with the idea that he would like her to meet his parents. She'd never met any man's parents and knew he must finally be feeling as serious about her as she'd felt about him for quite some time. Though she was nervous about the meeting, her heart soared, and she couldn't wait for the upcoming weekend to arrive. This would be her chance to see where this quirky, wonderful man came from, and it would give her an opportunity to get to know him even better.

They left the city on a cool autumn Friday afternoon. Jana wore stonewashed jeans and a burgundy, soft wool sweater. Her excitement was palpable and her eyes wide as they drove toward the hills, ever farther from the bustle of the urban experience. Overcome by a feeling of peace in her surroundings, her very features softened and relaxed, and Josh watched her face transform from the hard edges of Jana the businesswoman to the easy wonder of childlike innocence as each new scenic marvel moved her.

With eyes like those of a kid experiencing birthday presents for the first time, she was seeing the fall season's bounty in all its Crayola box glory. She knew deep inside it couldn't be practical to live in the country, not if she wanted to actively pursue her "fashion buying" career to its fullest, but the colors of the changing leaves and the soft autumn cast of the sun in the sky were enthralling, and for just a moment, she had visions of a life out here in the verdant hills surrounded by nature. Her heart beat fast at the sight of a majestic, antler-crowned deer on the edge of the tree line as they entered the rolling hills, and she experienced the delight of watching flocks of geese begin their flight south for the upcoming winter. What could be more awe inspiring than those V-shaped miracles which seemed to have their own miniature built-in GPS systems?

Josh looked over at her. "Are you nervous?"

"Why would I be nervous, Josh? Well, I-I don't know, truthfully, maybe a little. Do you think they'll like me?"

"They'll love you. I love you and I have good taste, so they won't be able to help themselves."

"I've never met anyone's parents before. I'm not really sure what to say."

"I thought you always knew what to say, baby."

"Not always smart aleck! I just want to make a good impression, okay?"

"I get it, Jana. Don't worry, they're going to love you. If it will make you more comfortable, you can follow my lead."

"All right, I'll just listen for a bit."

"I love you."

"I know."

As they drove up the lane to Josh's childhood home, he watched Jana's face change yet again. She was mesmerized by the beauty and wonder of this magical place. The house was an ancient, but well-maintained farmstead, which had been in the Conyers family for four generations; it was two stories tall, with shutters at the windows, flower boxes bursting with summer color, a wide front porch, a grand entry door, and a new coat of white paint. The yard was well manicured and surrounded by a picket fence of the same bright white as the house. An antique white wrought iron arbor, still abounding with red, velvet roses covered the gate for the flagstone walkway to the front door.

Left of the house, a gargantuan garden was surrounded by wire fencing, necessary to keep the deer and rabbits out of the easy dining opportunity they would have found there. Rows and rows of every vegetable kind imaginable, most of which were ready, or on the verge of harvest filled every available space; and the whole thing was guarded by a large smiling scarecrow wearing a straw fedora which, laughingly, seemed to be more of a crow perch than the hat of a scary, vegetable garden guard.

Right of the house, a clothesline filled with bedsheets of purest white fluttered in the breeze. Behind the house and far beyond, in a sizeable orchard with several varieties of fruit trees, Jana saw bright red apples even from this distance. The sight brought a huge smile to her face, and she looked excitedly over at Josh. He saw a twinkle in her eye he'd never witnessed before and could tell she already wanted to get out of the car to investigate. *Who was this enchanting creature?* he wondered, as he watched her. He'd always known there was an actual feeling person, who could connect with pure joy, under all of her "business as usual" demeanor. Josh truly believed in Jana with all his heart, and seeing her this way was giving him reason to believe he'd been right about her all along.

Farther yet, out past the orchard, wheat fields rolled off into the distance as far as the eye could see; filled with crops ready for the ingathering. In the other direction, left and behind the vegetable garden, was the biggest, reddest barn imaginable with a large brightly colored, wooden quilt hanging high on one side, a rooster wind vane adorning the top peak, and a sixteen-by-six-foot sign with the name Conyers' Farms, fashioned from bent rebar and painted white, hanging over its front doors.

Pulling up close to the house, Jana witnessed a small woman wearing a ruffled, gingham apron rushing from the side door to the steps. She stood waiting anxiously, wiping her hands on her smock; her smile growing as she watched her son emerge from the car. Josh ran to his mom, lifted her high in the air, and then hugged her tight. With mixed emotions, Jana watched the affectionate display.

The obvious loving relationship between mother and son warmed her heart, but it also caused her an uncomfortable sense of something akin to jealousy. This was an emotion previously unfamiliar to her. She'd not formerly cared enough about any man to be jealous of his relationships no matter who they might include, so putting a cap on her confused feelings, she exited the car and walked forward with her hand out. Mrs. Conyers walked right past Jana's outstretched hand and pulled her into a warm embrace. Jana, not used to open displays of affection from strangers, stiffened in self-defense. Her defenses soon lowered though as she was made to feel at home and welcomed immediately.

"So this is our Josh's, Jana," Mrs. Conyers exclaimed. "Welcome to our home, Jana. You're probably tired, so let's get you settled in."

"Thank you, Mrs. Conyers. I'm actually not tired, but I'd love a place to freshen up and I'm excited to look around if that's okay."

"I'm sure Josh would be happy to show you around tomorrow. It will be dark soon and we'll be sitting down for supper shortly. I'll finish up in the kitchen, but first we'll get your things put away, okay?"

Mrs. Conyers showed Jana to her room. The space was homey and comfortable. Antique quilts in hand worked wooden frames were displayed on the walls;

crisp white curtains bordered in ruffled lace hung at the windows; pictures of Josh's family, including several of Josh as a baby and as a small boy were placed around the room, and the bed was covered with the most beautiful handmade quilt Jana had ever seen. Mrs. Conyers even took the effort to fill a vase by the bed with fresh flowers from her garden and soft, clean towels sat folded in a neat stack on the old rocker by her door.

Supper that night was crispy fried chicken with piles of whipped, creamy, mashed potatoes and gravy, roasted corn on the cob with hand churned butter, sautéed vegetables; the lightest biscuits Jana ever tasted smothered in more of that amazing hand churned butter and honey, sweet and golden, from Mrs. Conyers's own hives. Homemade apple pie—made from the fruit in their orchard—and homemade vanilla ice cream for dessert left her feeling as if she might burst at the seams. "Mrs. Conyers, thank you. That was the most delicious meal I've ever eaten. I'm sure if I ate like that all the time, I'd weigh two hundred pounds easily!"

"Thank you, Jana. I assure you we stay pretty busy around here, so busy in fact that we don't have a problem burning the calories. We eat like this every day, and we have for all the years, we've farmed if you can believe it."

"Well, Mr. Conyers, then I have to say you are a very lucky man!"

"I know I am, Jana, for many reasons, but why don't you call us Chuck and Emma if you're comfortable with that?

"Thank you, I will. And thank you for having me out this weekend. You have a beautiful home and a wonderful farm. I can't wait to look around."

That evening, Jana sat with Josh's family in their living room, near a cozy blaze in the fireplace, hearing wonderful stories of Josh's boyhood. She laughed so hard tears ran in unrelenting rivers down her face. Josh's parents endeavored to find out a bit about Jana and her own childhood, but the minute they attempted to delve into her personal space, her defenses rose. Claiming exhaustion from the trip, she headed off to bed.

Sleeping better than she could remember ever in her life, Jana didn't wake throughout the whole of the night. Nightmares, which usually plagued her when she tried to rest, were remarkably absent. The feather mattress in the guest room was encased in newly washed sheets, which smelled of the warm sun and fresh air that dried them, and combined with the silence of the country night was so comforting, she slept straight through until the knock at her door invited her to breakfast.

Her rest was so deep she'd slept through the resident rooster's crowing and all the sounds of Mr. Conyers and Josh going out together to take care of early morning chores. Jana jumped out of bed refreshed and made herself presentable in jeans and a sky blue cashmere sweater. She pulled her thick, wavy hair back in a short ponytail and dabbed on a bit of blush and lip gloss before heading for the kitchen.

Mrs. Conyers, who'd been up for hours, had Josh's favorite breakfast of waffles, eggs, fried potatoes, and crispy bacon, complete with steaming mugs of hot coffee and freshly squeezed glasses of orange juice ready at their places. The bounty left their huge, antique farm table fairly groaning from the weight of it. Her efforts filled the house with smells that caused Jana's mouth to water in anticipation. Never a breakfast person, usually just downing a double half-caf low-fat mochaccino on her way to the office, she had to admit nothing she could remember had tasted so good this early in the morning!

After breakfast, Jana and Josh walked the property. He showed her his mother's garden up close, pulling up and brushing off a carrot for her to munch on. She'd never seen so many different kinds of vegetables in one place, and there were actually several variations in numerous rainbow colors she couldn't have named if her life depended on it. Walking out to the orchard, they examined different varieties of fruit trees. Josh picked an apple and polished it on his shirt. He offered it to Jana, and she bit into the fragrant, red fruit. It was delightfully crisp, and she was sure she'd never eaten anything so juicy and sweet. Looking up into Josh's eyes, she knew she could live in the glow she found there forever. Sun shone down through the trees as they walked, and the branches above filtered morning light till it danced and twirled in the grass like sparkling fairies. Wandering down by the creek, Josh stooped over and picked a late wildflower, tucked it in her hair over her right ear and gave her a light kiss on the end of her chilly nose.

Jana felt as though she was walking in heaven and thought in another time, after her career was on the right track, possibly they could have a little place in the country like this. It might be nice to get away from the city on weekends to better enjoy their meager time together. She could see them living in a wonderful little house in these autumn hills, playing in the leaves, perhaps a couple of kids and even a big dog romping beside them.

That evening, during another wonderful supper of succulent roast beef, roasted baby red potatoes, glazed carrots, banana muffins, more real butter, and then double chocolate, chocolate cake to top it all off,

Chuck and Emma invited her to come with them to church the next morning. She declined, looking down at her plate uncomfortably. Emma looked surprised and glanced sideways at Josh, who would not meet her gaze, while Chuck, not knowing who he was more embarrassed for, his wife, or Jana, quickly turned away and attempted to change the subject to something less divisive.

Next day, Emma seemed a bit cool. She prepared breakfast, and before they left, she put part of their lunch in the oven to cook while they were gone. While Josh and his parents worshipped, Jana wandered about the house snooping into cupboards and drawers looking at ancient pictures and family artifacts. After the family returned from church, Emma again got busy in the kitchen, and soon, she'd produced a delicious dinner of roast chicken, stuffing, sweet potato casserole, fresh peas with pearl onions, yeast rolls and fruit salad. Stuffed, but satisfied once again, Jana went to her room to get her things together for their trip back to the city.

She had to admit she'd miss Emma's fabulous cooking along with the peace and quiet of this idyllic place, though she couldn't seem to rid herself of the feeling she had caused an uncomfortable rift in future relationships with her refusal to attend church with the family. She was in awe of this diminutive woman who seemed able to handle so much with her vast talents, and she wanted them to be friends if at all possible.

Packing her belongings in the quiet of the guest room, Jana overheard a knock on a door and a conversation between Josh and his mother. He was breaking the news to her that he planned to ask Jana to marry him in the upcoming week. Jana suspected his intent from the moment he'd asked her to come home with him for the weekend and her heart leapt for joy, until she heard Mrs. Conyers's reply. "How well do you know this girl, Josh? You have always been taught not to be unequally yoked. She doesn't even go to church. How much do you really even know about her beliefs and background?"

"Mom, I realize you don't know her the way I do. I believe in Jana. I know her heart will soften. She'll come around. I trust it with everything I am. I love her Mom, and I want to ask her to marry me."

"Josh, I've never made your decisions for you. You and Jana will be the ones most affected by your choices in this, but I can't give my blessing. I love you, Josh, but I can't in good conscience give my approval for you to marry this girl who is clearly not a Christian."

"I love you too, Mom, but with or without your blessing, I will be asking Jana to marry me. I hope you'll change your mind, but I have to do what my heart tells me is true, and I know Jana is the only woman who is right for me."

From that day forward, Jana kept her emotional distance from Mrs. Conyers. Eventually, over time, her mother-in-law began to warm up to her in spite of their obvious differences, but Jana would not put herself in a position to be hurt by this woman who obviously felt superior to her in some way.

Jana didn't even know what "unequally yoked" meant! Well, she thought, that's just one more person I'll have to prove something to! She'll see. Once I'm rich and successful, she'll be sorry she ever thought she was better than me. I'll show her. I'll show them all!

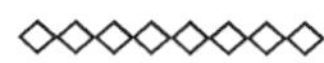

On a starry fall evening, following a lovely dinner of pasta, salad, and warm crusty bread at their favorite Italian restaurant, Josh drove Jana out to the park by the river where they'd met just the previous spring. Though the night was chilly, the stars were bright and the fresh air was glorious. Jana's sweater proved to be too light, and Josh wrapped his jacket around her shoulders. It draped around her down to her knees and they both laughed.

After a nice stroll on the walking path near the water, he directed her to their bench and dropped suddenly to one knee. Taking her small hand in his large one, he said, "Jana, obviously, I can't be your joy, but I cherish you and I would love to be your husband. Would you do me the honor of marrying me and making me the happiest man on earth? I promise you, Jana, I will do everything in my power to be the husband you deserve." Her heart felt ready to burst in her chest, and her eyes filled with tears of delight as she leaned forward to wrap her arms around his strong neck, giving him her answer with a long, enthusiastic kiss.

Their wedding was lovely. The day was beautiful, and Jana had never been happier. Since she'd no family remaining alive and wasn't keen on making friends, her side of the church held only a few work chums and their significant others. Josh's side of the sanctuary, however, was packed to overflowing with family and lots of friends from his church and the local community.

Taking the same care in her appearance for the wedding, as she did in everything she considered for public viewing, Jana went all out. Her dress was an elegant though scanty number especially designed for her. Form fitting from bodice to thighs and opened above the knee to a long train, which swept the floor as she made her slow and deliberate way to the altar; it certainly made a statement. The audacious neckline boasted thousands of tiny hand sewn pearls, bare shoulders and exposed cleavage. Jana, however, didn't care what others thought and wasn't afraid to flaunt what she considered to be her assets.

She'd chosen not to wear a veil. After the fortune she'd spent on upswept hair with sprays of tiny pearls throughout her shining, auburn locks, she wasn't about to cover it up. Pastor Mike blushed when he saw her décolleté dress. A young pastor, this was his first wedding since taking over the church. Her new mother-in-law looked a bit scandalized over her appearance, much to Jana's amusement, when she witnessed exposed legs and the daringly low cut gown. But her husband-to-be beamed at her as she walked without an escort down the wide center aisle of the small church. In her expertly manicured hands, she held a chic, fragrant bouquet of white orchids surrounded by a cloud of baby's breath.

Her reverie broken suddenly by the sound of a neighbor's lawn mower roaring to life, she sat up, snapped back to the present, and with a faint smile still playing on the corners of her lips, reached for her blue silk robe and slippers. As hard as it might be to leave the comfort of her luxurious, cool sheets, she thought she might just get up and make her way to a nice warm bubble bath and a glass of that excellent red wine left over from last night.

"You won't believe what Mark saw on the internet last night," Josh shouted, as he entered the house.

Jana jumped. She was absorbed in the report she'd been laboring over for work and didn't hear his car drive up. "Believe what?"

"Mark. You won't believe what Mark read last night on the internet."

"Are you talking about my Mark? Mark from accounting? When did you see him?"

"Jana, he goes to the same church I go to every week, Pastor Mike's church—the church I invite you to every Sunday." Jana looked up at him with a blank stare. "You know, Jana, the church where we got married?"

"Okay, okay, don't start that again. What did he say? Oh, wait a minute. This isn't a bunch of conspiracy theory stuff again, is it? I don't want to go there. I have a report to finish."

"Jana, you can't work all the time. Life's too short for that. Anyway, what I'm talking about is that Mark has a friend with enough clearance to get him onto a secured website we've been trying to breach for some time now. The website contains sensitive information about the People's Militia. You know, the civilian military group our ever enlightened leader promised us. This is the group which will ultimately report only to the president. I told you about them before. Mark said the information on that site led him to believe the organization of those military forces is much further along operationally and mechanically than we'd ever dreamed it would be by now. The site also showed aerial photos of camps scattered through the mountains filled with battalions of militia soldiers in training. Who knows how long that's been going on or for that matter how many locations and troops are out there?

"The same website had information about the government-run health care program. You know the one that got crammed through congress a few years ago?" Jana looked lost again. "Remember the health care bill they passed in the middle of the night, Jana? People were really up in arms about it, but the administration changed a couple of pieces and without anyone from congress even reading the stupid thing to see what they were signing up for, the whole darned thing got passed anyway." Jana's face still held nothing but a vacant stare. "Jana, it's the health care plan we use now. The one you were griping was more expensive than our old one; the one that was supposed to save us money?"

"Oh, that. You're always complaining about insurance, Josh. Prices go up that's all."

"Well, the last I heard you were the one complaining, but that doesn't matter now. All I can say is, as far as our government is concerned, they might as well have put up a sign and declared, to heck with 'of the people, by the people, and for the people', huh? Nobody really thought much about the hundreds of pages of that bill which weren't being implemented right after they rushed the legislation through. Only recently have obscure bits and pieces of the bill begun to be put in place. Now folks are seeing the rewards of their ignorance. It was weird how the president thought he had to get that program through right now, but then didn't begin executing parts of the plan until after he was reelected. I think the administration knew how angry people were about the whole idea of forced health care, and they were right. And I believe the president knew he'd better let the noise die down before he showed us the rest of the story."

"Josh! What is your point? You're rambling again, and I am so tired of hearing all the crazy theories from your weirdo friends! I told you I have a report to finish!"

"Well, hold on, I'm getting to the point, Jana! From information available on the site, it seems that participation in this new health care plan will include some details no one had discussed before. There's plenty we, as voters, are not being told and are not allowed to view, starting with the fact that our illustrious government will be requiring all citizens to have a chip implanted in their hand for identification and storage of medical and financial info, you know, to save on paperwork and to track individual stats, or some crazy lame excuse like that. In other words, Jana, we won't have a choice to opt out of the implants at all. We already knew we wouldn't have the choice to opt out of health care without stiff fines and penalties, but the implants? If this healthcare deal is so great, why is it that none of the government officials are being forced to participate in it and are also not being made to comply with chip implantation for their own families?"

"Oh, for crying out loud, Josh, what site? Who are they? I can't figure you out sometimes! How can you be so gullible? You believe everything Pastor Mike and his crazy bunch from the church tell you! And what is Mark doing on a top secret site anyway? I'm beginning to wonder who the bad guys really are here, Josh!"

"No, don't say that, Jana, you're wrong. We are not now, nor have we ever been the bad guys! How can you even think that? Mark was getting information for us that the government has been keeping secret from American citizens. Information we have the right to know! And just so you're aware, I don't believe anything just because people at my church say so. I read things. I see the direction this country is headed and where the leaders are trying to take us. I see changes in our freedoms and potential threats which are becoming more than just threats these days. Many of these threats and worse case scenarios have begun to manifest in ways which are subverting our very way of life. I also hear plenty of things in the news."

"On the news, what do you hear on the news, Josh? Oh, that's right you watch the news on that other channel. Josh, haven't you learned by now you can't believe everything you hear. Especially the stuff you hear from those people?"

"Those people, Jana? Most of them are conservative, God-fearing patriots, and they believe the same things I believe."

"I know, Josh. But not the same things most people believe. Most of those people are so conservative and right wing crazy they believe we're all going to hell just for disagreeing with them. Well, I'm not going to hell, if there is one, just because some religious nut says I am."

"What has to happen for you to believe what many of us already know, Jana? Do the militia thugs have to come in here and drag us off to inject us with microchips? Well, I won't go. I will not allow myself to be marked for their regime! Besides, once they tell us what kind of health care we have to use and plant us with their tracking chips, who knows what could come next. Are they going to tell us what to eat, what to read, and what to believe? What if they start telling us who to worship and who we can and can't pray to, what are you going to say then?"

"Oh, for Pete sake, Josh, you are so melodramatic! Okay, I will remember no one gets to mark you for their regime, all right? Besides, I don't care who anybody prays too. I've told you before that your god, if He exists, never cared about me. They can do whatever they want to with Him. As far as I'm concerned, He can go to hell if anyone ever does find Him. Now, leave me alone I need to get back to work!"

Josh and Jana didn't speak for the rest of the evening. At bedtime, Josh quietly brushed his teeth and crawled under the big down comforter on the giant, California king-size bed. He crossed his arms under his head, looked over at Jana and said, "I love you, Jana, you are my heart, but I will do the right thing no matter the consequences. I hope you will follow me, but I will do what needs to be done regardless of whether you do or not. A bunch of guys from the church are getting together for some meetings later on this week, and I want you to know I'm going to go. Good night."

Jana didn't know what to make of his last bold statement. She wasn't used to Josh confronting her in so contrary a manner. He was usually a peace loving and accommodating man who did everything within his power to avoid conflict in their relationship. Jana knew without question her husband was intelligent, though she rarely bothered to tell him that. And, actually, who was she kidding? Thinking back, she doubted she'd ever told him that at all. He told her quite often how smart and beautiful she was and how much he loved her. He gave her a great many compliments, whether or not she really deserved them, but she couldn't recall ever returning any of those compliments. Maybe she should try to give in a bit more, at least on the things that didn't really matter to her. After all, what could it hurt? If he wanted to hang out with the nut jobs from the church a couple times a week, what difference would that make to her?

Tomorrow she'd let him know he had her permission to go to his foolish little meetings if he wanted to.

Laying in the dark, Jana waited until she heard Josh's breathing become slow and regular. Rolling to her side she watched his chest rise and fall. Drawing close she pressed her body against his warm powerful frame. He was handsome, rugged, and strong, but tender too. She traced his face with her finger, ending up in the small clef of his chin. As if on cue, his muscular arm encircled her and the tense look on his sleeping face disappeared.

No one had ever loved her in the way Josh did. She was safe in his arms and knew he would never leave her. She didn't know if she had the capacity to love anyone the way he loved her. It was a scary love, a self-sacrificing love, an unconditional love she'd never experienced from anyone in her life until she met her husband.

To open up to that kind of raw emotion might be more than she could deal with. Suddenly, tears sprang to her eyes, and she was overwhelmed by feelings she couldn't explain. She loved Josh and was grateful he'd chosen her to be his wife, grateful he'd asked her to marry him in spite of his mother's misgivings, grateful for his big loving heart. But before tears could make their way from her eyes, she pulled away and commanded her sentiments be calm.

She'd only come this close to crying a few times in her life, and she wouldn't become one of those weak-willed women who give in to useless emotion! If she was ever going to cry, it would certainly take an event much more significant than a brush with emotion.

2

MONDAYS WERE MURDER! Jana's position as principle buyer for the clothing store was a situation she'd worked hard to attain, very hard indeed. However, when she arrived on Monday morning and found her usual pile of messages and a long list of monotonous meetings she'd be expected to attend, she groaned and wondered anew how to make it through another week of mundane repetition. There was a time when her romantic vision of her current career contained more moments of creative genius coupled with travel and adventure and fewer of these administrative nightmares, but she supposed someone had to do it.

Looking around her workplace, she had to admit she was rather proud of her achievements here at the store. Her office wasn't the largest in the administrative wing, but it wasn't the smallest either. Positioned on the tenth floor with opportunities to make it as far as the twelfth if she remained diligent, she'd moved up the ladder even more quickly than she'd anticipated she would when it all began. The room boasted a huge tinted window with a nice view of the downtown area and a large Amish style desk made of light oak paired with an elegant, though comfortable, brown leather chair. Her status even rated her own beautifully appointed bathroom; a personal secretary outside her door; and walls which sported various pictures, plaques, and awards attesting to her innate ability to sell important people on ideas which were significant to her.

Jana's sales ability, in the fashion world, was legendary. She could convince almost anyone to trust in virtually anything she believed, and her ability to change your mind for you, even if you'd been firm in your opinions your entire life, was uncanny. Buyer extraordinaire and highly respected in her chosen field, well, maybe respected wasn't the word most people would use referring to Jana, she was invaluable to those who came to her for advice on new trends and styles. Her employers loved her, other buyers wanted to be her, and other store owners wanted to steal her away. But her bosses knew her loyalties were more about money and whatever acclaim she might garner for her ever growing ego than any other factors, so they kept her highly compensated, highly praised, and wanting for nothing.

Rita, her secretary, was loyal to her, or so she believed. And she kept Jana abreast of the goings-on in the office building, a nice plus since Jana wasn't much of a work buddy to anyone and missed most of the water-cooler gossip.

For a short while, recently, Jana wondered if all the cutbacks at the store would result in the loss of her job as well. Many employees had been let go with very little warning and no prospects in this crazy economy. But she'd been assured of her personal value by the "powers that be," and her position seemed secure, at least for now. Jana was sure her willingness to follow commands from the top, even when those commands nudged her conscience and caused her husband to question her morals and motives more than a little, probably had a great deal to do with that. "Oh well, we do what we have to do to get ahead," she reasoned with herself. Getting ahead was her ultimate goal and had been most of her life.

Ambition had always been her drug of choice. "So what, at least it's a legal drug that can't hurt anyone," she lied to her own shallow sense of morals. It's hard to be "tough enough," she thought, if your sense of ethics is very deep, and tough she was. She'd always needed to be.

Jana was only four years old when her parents were killed in a tragic car accident. They walked out the door one morning for church, leaving her with Grandmother Anna, because she was too ill with the flu to go along, and they just never came home again.

Grandmother tried to explain to her what had happened. She told Jana that her parents had gone to live with Jesus in heaven. Well, Jana was quite sure she didn't want them to live with Jesus in heaven. She wanted them to live right here with her, and for that matter, right now!

For years and years afterward, she asked Jesus, begged Him in fact, to send her parents back to her; after all, she needed them much more than He did. But no matter how much she begged, pleaded, and prayed, He didn't answer; and as her hope slowly faded and died, her heart grew harder and ever colder toward an, in her estimation, unfeeling, faraway god.

Jana's parents were warm and kind, gentle and loving people who'd made her feel important and cared for in the four short years she knew them. When the cathedral doors were open, they were there. And they were greatly loved in the church and the community where they served and volunteered. Jana was much too young at that time to comprehend the commitment they'd made to their God, but when they didn't come home to her that terrible day, a jealousy sprouted up in her heart against Him that would not be quenched. To think He would be so unfeeling, or that He wouldn't do anything at all to help her be reunited with her family and insisted instead on keeping them to Himself. It was positively unthinkable in her young, tortured mind and she hated Him for it.

Over time, the memories of her parents began to grow dim, their faces fading in her child's mind; but she lived with her grandmother now, who missed Mama and Daddy as much as she did, and Grandmother tried to share as much as she could remember about them every day. Grandma gave Jana an old picture of her parents, taken on their wedding day, to put in her new bedroom. As a girl, she'd looked at that old picture every single day and memorized the details of their magical long-ago wedding.

Jana still had that old picture and looking at it always made her feel a little sad. How different her life might have been if they hadn't left her the way they did. But looking at the picture also stirred up old, angry emotions. Where was their God with His miracles when they needed Him anyway? As far as she was concerned, Josh could talk about Jesus until he was blue in the face, but he hadn't been deserted by the guy like she and her family had been!

Grandmother, though Jana was sure she loved her in her own way, was a card-carrying, Bible-thumping

"Jesus freak" too, so much worse than Jana remembered of her parents. Grandmother prayed out loud, making a spectacle of herself several times every day, in ways and places where she would be heard by not only Jana, but by anyone else who might be near. It was embarrassing, and frustrating, as she quoted Scriptures until Jana wanted to scream and tear her own hair out, often using them as ammunition to prove a point or to get her way. She was a hard old taskmaster too; tough and demanding in what she expected of her young ward. Jana worked so eagerly to measure up, so intently to be the perfect, angelic little girl her grandmother wanted her; seemingly, needed her, to be, at least at first, but she always managed to disappoint and mess up somehow.

Eventually, it was all she could do to keep her mind closed to the guilt trip her grandmother tried to unload on her. All the commandments and rules she was expected to follow to be good enough, and her complete inability to do so, no matter how hard she tried, seemed to make her grandmother angrier by the minute. After a while, she simply decided she would be very sure none of that nonsense crept into her mind to make her feel worse about herself than she already did, and she definitely did feel the weight of guilt she was forced to carry, so she stopped listening altogether.

Sunday school and church with Grandmother Anna every week, at the old woman's insistence, was mandatory from the age of four until she was ten, but what good did it do? Trying her hardest and doing her best hadn't protected her when she was four, nor did it help when she was ten, and this Jesus guy hadn't protected her either. His track record in her life was pretty bleak and hadn't gotten any better in recent memory. What had He ever done for her? If He truly cared wouldn't He, at the very least, have kept all the crazies out of her life, or perhaps kept her parents alive for her?

Then, one Sunday morning, almost nineteen years ago, when Jana was ten years old, Grandmother hollered up the stairs for her to: "get a move on, Jana! We need to eat quickly or we'll be late for Sunday school!" Jana came ever so slowly, dragging her feet down the stairs (she would rather have slept in even then) to find her grandmother pale and motionless on the kitchen floor.

Dr. Bloom said a heart attack. Pastor told her grandmother Anna had gone to live with Jesus, and Jana decided then and there, this Jesus person, if He was even real, never had time for her, so she wouldn't waste one moment of what remained of her life, or time on Him either. If this was how He wanted to play the game, she could play it too!

Relegated to foster care at ten years old, Jana didn't have much to remind her of her prior existence— a few pieces of worn clothing, an old pair of shoes, hairbrush, toothbrush, and that old picture of her parents taken on their wedding day. Looking at the old picture eventually became a comfort, the only consolation she had, giving her a sense of belonging to someone, or something greater than herself, even though she now felt more alone than she'd ever been in her short life.

School, she'd hated school! The other kids made fun of her timeworn clothing, and they never let up on the orphan thing, calling her "little orphan Jannie." As a youngster, her hair was a brighter, redder red than the dark auburn locks she was blessed with now. Additionally, she'd been cursed with just enough natural curl to help her fit that horrid nickname right down to the large, vacant eyes and freckled nose.

Authorities despised her, as she'd developed a very bad habit in the eyes of those in power, of trying to defend against the attacks from grown-ups put in charge of her interests. Officials don't like to hear of their appointed foster care individuals or school administrators acting in ways which could be frowned upon or considered inappropriate, so they often protected those appointed individuals until a solution for their replacement could be found. Jana decided early on she would be her own solution.

Whether in school or in a foster care situation, she decided she wouldn't take abuse from anyone anymore without a fight. It didn't take long then before she was deemed "incorrigible" by both the school and the foster care system. Soon no one in control listened to her reports of abuse and instead took the word of those caregivers over hers without question.

Making the rounds through a series of terrible and frightening placements, her reputation for rebellion grew and followed her doggedly every step of her painful way, giving any and all new foster care givers a pass to treat her in whatever manner they deemed fit. She was hopelessly lost in the system.

In her eleventh appointed foster family, in what remained of her eleventh year of life, her foster dad came to her bed in the middle of the night. Waking terrified with his fat, sweaty hand clamped tight over her small face, she fought. His hand was so large it covered her mouth and nose, cutting off her screams for help and her air at the same time. As she battled for breath, through the putrid smell of his alcohol-drenched kisses, he brutally raped her. She tried to tell but no one listened. She was the troublemaker, the problem child, and for the next year of her life, his visits were a nightly horror. After eight months of trying to fight him off and being beaten down for her efforts, she surrendered, in hopeless resignation, deciding it would be safer for her to lay motionless while he did his nasty business.

Though she'd previously given up on the idea of God, she decided to give the faceless deity one more chance. She prayed and prayed, begging Him to save her from her circumstances. Didn't He see? Didn't He care? She wondered why she ever bothered to pray at all and even to whom she was pleading. In His obvious absence, she decided once and for all there was no god! In her mind, the answer had already come.

When stomach problems, which she'd developed shortly after arriving in their household, became progressively more serious, her foster mother wondered. The girl tried to tell her hateful things about her husband shortly after her arrival, had pleaded with her in fact, but she knew the man she married would never do those disgusting things. As far as she knew, he'd never done anything like that with any of their other foster girls they'd taken in, had he? He certainly didn't try those things with her. Pretty soon, the accusations stopped. For goodness' sake, they'd fostered dozens of girls before this willful twit came along, and they'd never had a problem like this.

However, the woman began to notice more bruises on the slight girl, and she perceived Jana fighting harder and harder to avoid bedtime each night, so her suspicions grew. Finally, she became concerned enough about her husband's obsession with the tiny wisp of a girl that she determined the child must be enticing her husband in some way. After fourteen months of unthinkable torture, her foster mom finally made arrangements for Jana's removal.

Another day, another house; she wasn't even sure she remembered this new family's names. Why bother? She sat alone in the small attic space they'd assigned her, looking at the old, faded picture of her parents; useless tears glistening in her eyes. She was cold, and the only blanket she'd been given was wrapped around her shoulders. But wouldn't you know it was scratchy and stiff, and not nearly enough to keep her warm.

For eight long years, the foster system remained a revolving door of families who used Jana's legal captivity for maid service, babysitting, and perversion. Finally and understandably, they'd all become a blur of faces and places in her mind. She grew colder and learned, over and over throughout her formative years, not to trust anyone, swearing to herself that someday it would all be different.

One day, they would all wish they'd treated Jana Brown right! No! Someday, they would all wish they were Jana Brown as she became rich and famous and left them to their pitiful, miserable little lives.

For that reason, when Jana married Josh, she kept her maiden name instead of becoming Mrs. Josh Conyers. She was determined that when she finally "made it," she could be sure they all knew who she was. They would remember her! The name Jana Brown would mean something!

Examining the image of her mother now, she could see she was a great deal like her—petite and slim, just barely five feet tall with dark auburn hair and large brown eyes fringed with long thick lashes. Dad's contribution to the gene pool was the nose she'd always thought a little too big for her face. Josh told her it was a fine Roman nose, whatever that meant, and it gave her face character. She felt she could do with a little less character, so a bit of shading when applying her makeup in the mornings helped some. Her tiny frame made it difficult to buy clothing off the rack which looked both stylish and mature. But she insisted on dressing the part and employed a seamstress to create business suits which were elegant and beautifully tailored, as was befitting her position as head buyer.

Josh's background was as different from hers as day from night. His degree in psychology was from Oral Roberts University. Jana attended a small community college as a poor ward of the state. He probably never missed a Sunday church service in his life. Jana quit wasting her time in church the day her grandmother died and would have preferred if it'd been sooner. His parents were there for him, supporting him, every step of the way; she learned to manipulate and use people to get what she needed, and she had to admit she had become rather good at it.

Josh's parents, as she'd discovered, still lived in his childhood home and gave away practically everything they earned. They said it made them "happy" to give their things and their money away. Sadly, as far as Jana was concerned, they'd passed that deplorable trait down to their bighearted son. Jana and Josh butted heads on more occasions than she could keep track of about the money he gave to his "charity cases." She advised him frequently he should change careers. The poor dear didn't make nearly as much money as she did. But what could he expect working for the church counseling troubled teens?

With his talent and background, he could be working for any number of large firms in a human relations capacity. She put his name out on the market during the first year of their marriage, and he received several job offers. When Jana brought the offers to him, he shook his head and said to her, "You just don't understand, Jana." What she did understand is, they would never get ahead as quickly as she'd planned, if he wouldn't cooperate.

Recent conversations sounded like reruns of previous arguments, and Jana hated that they wasted their time and energy on nonsense. He truly didn't get her. When you grow up as a foster child, you learn a couple of things. You learn you can't depend on the state, and you definitely can't depend on the foster parents; at least not the foster parents to whom she'd been assigned.

Those folks in particular had been the kind of foster parents who were in it for the monthly check; the foster parents who force you to work like Cinderella and babysit their brats while they partied and slept in; the foster parents who eat steak while they feed you hot dogs; the foster parents who assign you some small space to sleep and then invade that place with their sickness and perversions, causing you to never feel safe again.

Jana, though, was very self-sufficient now, very proud of her achievements, and very, very serious. She knew what she wanted from this world and what she was willing to do to get it. Josh teased her sometimes about her lack of a sense of humor and overly logical nature. "Well, sometimes we become who we are out of self-defense and self-preservation. One of us has to have some idea of how we're progressing toward our goals, Josh." She often felt a need to defend her selfish desires, perhaps to convince her husband of their soundness, but maybe sometimes to convince her.

"Your goals, Jana, your goals. My goal is to be a good husband and a great dad. I want to spend time with you. We talked about seeing the world together. We planned trips and talked about babies."

"Josh! I won't go there again! We've discussed this over and over! We are not having kids until we have enough money to give them the kind of life we want them to have. And the trips can wait until I've achieved my career goals. There will always be time for that later."

"What life, Jana? What kind of life do we want them to have? I know what kind of life I want them to have. But right now, that doesn't seem to be where we're heading. We seem to live just to buy stuff. Who are we buying the stuff for? You know, they say if we all waited till we could afford it before we had kids, the population of the world would have been extinguished soon after it started and you never know if there will be a later, Jana. We don't spend time together anymore. When is the last time we were camping, or even hiking? We used to go every weekend."

She hated to fight with him, and this topic of discussion never accomplished anything new. But she'd planned her life out long ago and being poor wasn't part of it. Not anymore! If having children figured in to the equation at some point later, she would consider it.

For now, she knew she didn't want any kid to go through things she'd endured in her childhood. If she ever had children, they would have a sense of belonging and they would lack for nothing. They would never have to feel like they were an imposition to anyone. Besides, all the best financial experts in the country were predicting trillions, and trillions, of dollars of debt for the next generation due to policies being put in place by the government. She was actually kind of doing all those children a favor by not conceiving them, wasn't she?

3

JANA WAS BECOMING uneasy over the recent unpredictable behavior of her husband. Josh's meetings with the crazies at his church were occurring more frequently over these past weeks, and his demeanor changed drastically. Strangely secretive and nervous, anxiously looking over his shoulder at every little noise, this erratic man didn't remotely resemble the easygoing Josh she'd married and come to know. Overtime hours had become an integral part of her schedule in the last couple of years, as she found herself ever striving for that next rung on the promotion ladder, so she hadn't picked up on the obvious changes in Josh's personality and actions until quite recently.

Since she'd begun to notice the difference though, she found it disturbing and hard to justify. Of late, Josh would arrive home long after his office closed, slink cautiously away to his study and quietly do whatever strange things he did in there now. She could hear him chatting softly, whether on the phone or just talking to himself, she wasn't sure. When Jana asked what was going on, he guaranteed her all was well and that he was taking care of everything. "Don't worry, baby," he assured her. "I've got it all covered. You don't need to worry about a thing." But she was unconvinced. Jana knew her husband well enough to know he was up to something big, probably huge, and she didn't like it at all.

Things were going on she couldn't rationalize, such as: the house phone would ring, but if she answered it, the caller would hang up, and then Josh's cell phone would ring soon after. If, however, Josh got to the phone first, he would sidle away to speak privately to the caller. If Jana didn't know the character of the man she was married to as well as she did, she might have suspected he was having an affair, but that was ludicrous, wasn't it?

"Jana, do you believe this?" Josh yelled, as he stormed into the house.

"I don't know, Josh, believe what?"

"Mark brought a letter to the meeting tonight. It's ordering him to bring his family to the Global Health Organization (GHO) office to have their healthcare microchips implanted next week!"

"What? Surely, he just misunderstood the letter? You guys are so hyped up by all this conspiracy theory stuff he's probably just assuming things that aren't there."

"No, Jana! I have a copy of the letter right here. Read it for yourself if you don't believe me!" He thrust the letter at her.

Taking the letter from Josh, as he stomped past, she began to read. Josh was right. The letter was indeed telling the Randal family where and when to be at the local GHO office on Monday. "But, Josh, this doesn't say anything about microchips. Do we know for sure this is about implanting microchips?"

"Jana, several of the guys in our group have friends and family members in other parts of the country who've already been implanted. They got letters just like this one, and when they showed up at the GHO and were confronted with the fact they were there to be implanted most of them were afraid not to comply for fear of retribution from the government. Many of them contacted their friends and families afterward to warn them of the letters they'd be receiving. We've calculated that somewhere from a fourth to a third of the country is implanted already. We don't know how to help the ones who've already received chips, at least not yet since the little buggers seem to have a fail-safe which is triggered by attempted removal, but we hope we might be able to help some others who just don't want to be led like sheep to the slaughter!"

"Josh, be reasonable, no one in the administration ever said anything about mandatory implantation of chips being part of eligibility for the government health care program. Our president is just trying to take care of us and be sure we all have adequate health coverage. This wasn't a part of the plan from the beginning."

"Oh, Jana, no one in the administration ever talked about the bands of People's Militia roaming the streets, which would be trained to keep American citizens under government control either! All the random executive orders that our president has strategically put in place have given this man more power than any before him, and the power we've unwittingly allowed him to grab has come back to bite us all in the rear! Mark and some of the others have absolute proof of the existence of those military groups now, just like I told you! Mark's cousin refused to go to the GHO after he got his letter. On the day his family was scheduled to be implanted, they stayed home. The next day, a People's Militia squad came and arrested them. Did you hear me, Jana? They arrested them, for endangering the health of the community by not complying with a governmental health order. No one has seen them or heard from them since that day. Mark and his family won't be going to their scheduled appointment on Monday! We will be getting our letter soon and you already know how I feel. I can't keep you from doing whatever you decide to do, but I will not be going."

"I don't know what to say, Josh. This all sounds insane. Has Mark really not heard anything from his cousin? How do we know this hasn't just been some huge misunderstanding! If we don't listen to the government and we get ourselves into some kind of trouble, Josh, I've worked so hard for this promotion. I just can't get into any trouble and risk my future. What do you want me to do?"

"Jana, you have to do what your heart and your conscience tells you to do. I'm your husband. I love you. I would hope your heart would have you follow me and trust my instincts, but I won't force you to do anything. I'm going to bed now. Our group has another meeting tomorrow night after work, and I'm going to listen to what Mark and his family are planning to do before Monday rolls around."

Jana arrived at work with her usual armload of samples and projects. Rita caught her attention, and from the look on her face, Jana could tell something was amiss. Jana indicated that Rita should follow her into her office, and once they were alone, her secretary quickly spilled her guts. She told Jana the store received a call from a government entity who claimed to be part of Homeland Security. They were asking questions about Mark and Josh. "What kinds of questions?" Jana asked her.

"Well, mostly ones we didn't answer. I couldn't figure out if we had the answers they needed anyway. What's going on, Jana?"

"I don't know for sure. Josh and Mark have been meeting with a bunch of guys from their church about all of the government health care issues. I guess Mark got a letter from the GHO telling him that he needs to bring his family in to be implanted with microchips."

"Yeah, we got our letter a couple of weeks ago and went in for our chips. It's just a small chip in the hand, what about it?"

"So, it really is a microchip? The government is really demanding everyone get an implant? No one ever talked about anything like that during the campaign, or at any time after in reference to the mandatory health care bill. How can they expect everyone to be on board with something like that?"

"What's the big deal, Jana? How do you expect them to keep track of everyone's medical stats without using some sort of advanced computer technology? It sounds like you have a problem with all of this. Haven't you and Josh gotten your letter yet? What's all this stuff about Josh and Mark having meetings at the church?"

Call it a hunch, or just the overly suspicious look on Rita's face, but Jana suddenly knew, in her heart, she shouldn't say anything else to Rita. Memories of a not-too-distant past when the government began asking citizens to step forward and report anyone who was speaking negatively about the administration, or the health care plan; with eight hundred numbers to call advertised on television and plastered over billboards around the city, came flooding back to her. Wondering how many concerned citizens might have become government snitches in the past few years; or worse, how many others ended up on the wrong end of negative reports after they became the victim of someone's wacky sense of duty or angry retribution? Would this turn out to be the Salem witch hunts all over again?

"Oh, I don't know, you know those guys when they all get together. I'm sure they were coming up with answers to all the world's problems or something. Hey, you want to go grab me the marketing results from last week? I've got tons of work to do." It could have been all the stress lately starting to get to her, but she found herself beginning to have thoughts bordering on conspiracy theory stuff. She was sure she felt Rita's stare boring a hole in her back as she turned, and quickly walked away.

When Jana arrived home later, she received a disturbing phone call from her neighbor, the one who lived directly across the street, asking her if everything was okay. It seemed she too had received an odd call from a government entity asking questions about Josh. She was pretty sure the gal didn't care about them a single bit and was only digging up fodder for her local gossip channels, so she played it off as nothing.

Very unnerved, she mentioned the calls to Josh when he came in. He shrugged it off, but turned and hurried to his study, where she could hear him through the door talking rapidly to someone in hushed tones. What could all this mean? She knew people at work regarded her strangely all day, or was it just her imagination? Well, at the very least, the neighbors would think they were nuts!

"That's it!" she groused. "Doesn't he understand he could ruin everything for me, everything I've worked so hard for?" Marching to his study door, she was poised to knock when Josh opened the door and rushed past her, giving her a quick peck on the cheek.

"Be back later, baby, love you!"

Jana fumed, "What in the heck is going on here?" Pacing back and forth in the hallway, she contemplated calling Josh's parents, but knew they subscribed to most of the same conspiracy theories as the bunch of crazies from the church. What could she do? "Well, he can just go jump in a lake for all I care. He is not going to mess up my chances with his crazy ideas and weirdo friends!" She marched across the room to her paperwork, frustrated and angry, but well aware she was powerless in this situation.

Calming herself as best she could, she turned back to her work. "Well, there are always more reports to work on. At least I can count on that!" She exclaimed out loud. Nagging fear in the back of her mind continued to interrupt her thoughts and interfere with her ability to concentrate for the rest of the afternoon, and to her dismay, she got little done.

Obviously, Josh was up to something, but she couldn't figure out what could be so secret that he wouldn't want to share it with her. They'd always shared everything, hadn't they? Well, maybe not so much lately with her newest promotion and his meetings at the church. Come to think of it, did she really know anything about her husband's current life at all? And if she was honest, with all the mystery, did she really want to know?

A phone ringing somewhere in the distance irritated Jana back to consciousness. It took a moment for her to get her bearings and then she realized with a jolt it was very late, and she'd fallen asleep on the sofa working on her reports again. Tumbling sideways off the couch as she reached for the phone, her mind raced in dizzy confusion. Why hadn't Josh wakened her when he came in? Had he come in? She didn't remember hearing anything. Fumbling, dropping the phone, picking it up, "Hello?"

"Mrs. Conyers?"

"This is Jana Brown, or well yes, Jana Conyers. Who is this?"

"Mrs. Conyers, this is St. Mary's Hospital. Your husband has been brought into our emergency room, and we found your number with his identification."

"Josh? You have Josh in the hospital? What happened?"

"Mrs. Conyers, we can't release any information over the phone. Do you have someone who can come with you to the hospital?"

"Oh god, no, please tell me what's going on! I, I don't know who to call. Please just tell me!"

"Mrs. Conyers, we also found another number. I believe it is your husband's parents. May we call them for you?"

"Yes, yes, someone just tell me what's going on, please!"

Before Jana knew what hit her, Josh's parents were at the front door of the house and whisking her away to the hospital. Away to who knows what? How bad was it? Would the doctors have insisted they come to the hospital if this situation was not serious? Maybe Josh was gravely injured, even paralyzed, what if he was paralyzed? What would she do then? This could be a truly horrible state of affairs. Her mind raced with questions and possible scenarios. Could she handle it if his injury was something serious? How would she take care of him and work too, if he was gravely hurt? Then, even in the midst of her fear, she realized how selfish her line of thinking had become. Why did her mind always go there? She assumed she constantly reverted to self-preservation mode out of shear necessity. Taking a deep breath she tried, for once, to make this not about her. "Please let him be all right," Jana sighed, pleading to the open universe.

Never had she been this frightened. Nothing she'd endured as a child or in the dog-eat-dog frenetic business world could compare with the terror of not knowing what to expect on her ride to St. Mary's. Her mother-in-law talked somewhere in the background endlessly in motherly soothing tones, but nothing penetrated the self-imposed fog. She wasn't sure she even wanted to hear the reassuring drivel. Josh was fine, she'd decided. She was sure of it. Nothing else would make sense.

Street lights, synchronized guardians of the night, creating small islands of faux day, flashed by in a rhythmic parade. This would register in her mind at some point as the strangest and most frightening ride of her life. As the hospital—huge and black against the night sky—loomed ahead, Jana's chest tightened, and she thought she might never be able to take a normal breath again. Inside the doors of St. Mary's, Mr. Conyers walked to the information desk, and soon they were all ushered off to a private conference room. "Why are we in here?" Jana demanded to know. "Why aren't they taking us to Josh?"

"I don't know, Jana. The nurse told us the doctor would be in to talk to us in a minute. We just need to keep praying and know that Jesus is with us." Josh's mom comforted.

"Okay, okay," Jana said, thinking if their Jesus could come through on this one, perhaps she might give Him one more chance. "We'll see about that," she said to no one in particular.

Staring, devoid of meaningful thought, at a large poster on the door depicting a cartoon stick character coughing into the crook of his arm; she recalled it as an old reminder of well-publicized precautions advised during the last big H1N8 pandemic—the pandemic which killed tens and tens of thousands as it ravaged the land. When the door opened and the harried doctor entered, Jana knew from the look on his face that the news was worse than any of them imagined. She backed toward the wall.

Mark's family was at the hospital too. His wife, what was her name? was sobbing and begging to see her Mark. The hospital wouldn't allow it. "Too much damage to the bodies, too badly burned," she heard the doctor tell Mr. Conyers. He didn't think the ladies could handle seeing that amount of carnage, and he didn't want to be responsible. The conversation sounded so very clinical and unemotional. Her head swam in a jumble of unconnected and less than rational ideas, not allowing for her usual degree of analytical thought. Numb, she felt totally and completely anesthetized, as if she was on the outside looking in, frozen in time. No one seemed to have any information about how this unthinkable thing happened, and worst of all, no one was answering any of her questions. Jana wasn't a crier, but they wouldn't let her see Josh either, and she felt very small, insignificant, and terribly, terribly lost.

Having a hard time accepting what the doctors were telling her without some sort of proof that this was unquestionably Josh in the hospital's holding room, she watched Mr. Conyers leave the conference area hesitantly and stiffly following the doctor to make identification. He came back to the room changed, ashen faced, eyes filled with grief, to hold and comfort his anguished wife. "The body was so badly burned I couldn't tell, but he was wearing Josh's watch, and his wedding ring too. It had to be him," Mr. Conyers choked.

There was, however, no one to comfort Jana. They tried to draw her into their wet, tearful, messy hug, but she pulled away, shaking them off. "No, this is not possible," she said. "You must have made a mistake. He's not dead, he can't be." She knew if this horror were true, things would never be the same, could never be the same. How could she ever be comforted again when there were no longer any strong arms to hold her tight; when there was no one left that she could trust, no soft voice to quiet her, no more sanity, no more Josh? He was the only real thing in her life, the only one that mattered.

Sitting down hard on the pleather couch in the consultation room, her mind reeling in manic circles, she tried to reason. Dead. Her one true love was dead. Her miserable life was done…the only person who had ever, just, loved her. The only person who could make her smile, or laugh, or feel anything.

Josh's parents wanted to stay at her house with her, or take her home with them, so she wouldn't be alone. She didn't want them. She didn't want anyone. No one but Josh and, now, that part of her life was gone forever. How could she survive without him? Every selfish thought she'd ever entertained as she went along her self-absorbed way; every "me" moment she'd ever experienced, all the years of expecting his world to revolve around her egocentric planetoid suddenly slapped her in the face so hard she felt as though she couldn't breathe, and none of it was of consequence anymore. Without him, absolutely none of it mattered.

The morning of her husband's funeral dawned bright and sunny. The air was fairly saturated with birdsong and cotton candy clouds filling a sky of incredible robin's egg blue. The beautiful weather seemed obscene and wretched under the circumstances, which caused this day to be even more nightmarish, if that was at all possible. How dare the sun shine, birds sing, or people live their ridiculous, happy little lives when Josh was no longer here? Her emotions shut down the day He died and part of her—the best part—died with him.

Josh's parents would be picking her up shortly. She hadn't done anything with herself yet. What was the point? It was three days since that fateful day at St. Mary's, and so far, the fog hadn't lifted. Not sure she wanted the fog to lift, causing her to have to face the reality of this day and the inevitable sentence of being alone forever; she sat wrapped in Josh's throw with her feet tucked securely under her bottom.

They—Josh's parents, Mark's family, and her—were still in the dark. No one had any answers for them about the accident. According to the authorities, Josh and Mark randomly went through a road barrier and over an embankment, but how? Why? Josh's dad went to the site of the accident and could find no evidence of skid marks, or anything which would indicate they'd tried, even minimally, to keep from going through the rather substantial guard rail and over the clearly protected embankment.

Chuck did tell her, in hushed tones, he'd found small pieces of taillight material in the taller grass next to the edge of the road. He also told her the road had all the earmarks of having been swept clean, and perhaps those pieces were missed in the hasty attempt to mislead? Were the bits of taillight material proof that Josh's vehicle had been hit hard enough from the rear to push them over the edge? If they'd gone over the embankment unaided, what would explain those telltale bits of taillight glass on the side of the road? Why would the area need to be swept clean at all if not in an effort to cover something up?

Authorities seemed to have no information which would tie together what they knew with what Mr. Conyers found, and they were all treating him now as if he were crazy, or worse, a subversive. This administration didn't like subversives; not one little bit. He was going so far as to believe the police knew something more than they were sharing. Was this another one of his crazy conspiracy theories, or was there more to this whole event than met the eye?

Jana's brain couldn't process the information yet, or perhaps it was too much to think about so soon. Why would the police withhold information? What could they gain by covering up the cause of Josh and Mark's accident? Mr. Conyers seemed sure it was no accident. But who would have benefited from Josh's death? Everyone loved Josh, everyone!

She couldn't fathom why Mr. Conyers was so certain there must be some evil afoot, and she couldn't deal with the stress his implications created in her own mind; the suspicions and fears that trauma birthed. These people wanted to turn everything into a plot by the government, and she was sick of it. Maybe if she just stayed here wrapped in Josh's chenille throw, she could pretend nothing of these last several days had happened.

Longing to lie down and sleep, to pretend everything was as it had been last week, she buried her face in the heady aroma of his cologne. Her head ached, and her eyes burned to shed the gallons of tears stored behind them; yet she knew if she let loose those tears she might never be able to stop the flow.

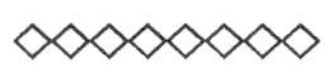

The ride to her in-law's country cemetery, where Josh would be laid to rest, seemed infinitely longer than the ride to St. Mary's had been a few nights before. After all, she had only empty eternity before her now. She wasn't ready to say good-bye. Had she told him she loved him that last day? No, she most certainly hadn't. He was always so quick to tell her the things she needed to hear, and she was always so busy taking care of her big plans, her promotions, and her future that she never returned the love he showered on her. Now, none of it made a difference. Nothing was important if Josh wouldn't be here to share it with her. He'd wanted so desperately to be a dad. She'd denied him that one too and now.

She'd never have the opportunity to tell him he was the best thing to ever happen to her. There would be no babies, no trips to see the world, and no one to grow old with. What did any of her big plans matter now?

So many people at the cemetery; the throng caused her to feel trapped, angry, mobbed by their condolences. Did she know this many people? But, of course not, they were here for Josh and his parents. He'd touched so many lives with his wisdom, kindness, and compassion, just as he'd touched hers. So many hordes of milling, apologetic, weepy, damned people.

His parents handled all the preparations. There was no viewing, for obvious reasons. Walking slowly through rows and rows of ancient headstones to get to Josh's gravesite in the family's plot, centuries of life and death and loss, felt surreal. Could this place be where Josh would spend all of eternity? Where was his damned Jesus now?

As sad as she was, she found she was also filled with deep reservoirs of barely contained rage. Irate with the idea of living without him, livid at him for leaving her, irritated at the rest of humanity for having someone to love, annoyed at the world for smiling and laughing on this day in which she would bury her husband, and most of all, angry with God! If He was real, this God of theirs, how could He let this happen to someone who'd been so overwhelmingly on His side? Perhaps this was just one more way to punish her? She had an overwhelming urge to punch something hard, but hadn't the energy to proceed with that act or anything else.

Wanting only to leave this place of finality before the proceedings could make everything absolute in the eyes of all who watched, thereby forcing her to be done. Done with what? Done with grieving? Would she ever be done grieving? Or better yet, maybe she should be done with life. Without Josh, there was no life.

The casket—Josh's casket—of beautifully polished cherry wood glowed red in the morning sun. Fragrant arrangements of red roses, carnations, and ferns filled the air around the gravesite with wonderful, stimulating, sweet smells of life.

Shivering with grief, Jana stood within the canvass tent, trying without success to contain the shaking of her body. The bright green canopy set to cover the chairs where Josh's loved ones would sit and watch as he was lowered into the hard, cold ground, flapped above her.

Josh's parents urged her to sit in one of those designated chairs, but she pulled away and stood as far to the side of the enclosure as she could manage, without being bathed in the vulgar, midmorning sunlight. Jana had no desire to be seated in a chair and watch her husband lowered into the dirt. She didn't want to be here at all. How on earth could any of this be happening? Wasn't it just yesterday that she and Josh met in the park by the river? Fighting the desire to run screaming from this offensive place, she felt her agitated blood pressure pounding in her aching temples. Legs, which felt like gelatin, protested as the pastor—maybe her in-law's pastor, or perhaps supplied by the mortuary, she wasn't sure—droned on about green pastures and the love of God and blah, blah, blah…

As the service ended, the casket was lowered slowly into a hole dug in the earth by unknown men and covered with a blanket of fake grass. She wanted nothing more than to crawl in after Josh and let them bury her too. So many hands to shake, so much commiseration, so many useless, sorry people.

Jana wasn't remotely ready to venture back to work yet, but it'd been two weeks since Josh's untimely death and her bosses were getting impatient for her return. Several buying trips and a large marketing deal needed her input, so she agreed to resume her duties on the upcoming Monday morning. Resenting their lack of empathy, but aware she would have reacted the same way toward another's pain only days before, she couldn't fault them. Theirs was after all a business of sudden changes and overnight trends shifting on a whim. That facet of the fashion world used to be one of her favorite challenges, and now was just one more irritation demanding her attention.

None of the frantic striving for promotion and status seemed particularly important to her anymore; it took most of her effort just to breathe, but she would have to pay her bills somehow. And since she'd talked Josh out of purchasing life insurance every year when he mentioned the idea, in order to save money, after all they were both still so young; her savings would only last so long. Perhaps the busyness of work, as unfulfilling as it might currently be, could take her mind from the things which were tearing away at her sanity bit by bit.

For the past two weeks, Jana had done little, but sat alone on the sofa in Josh's study, wrapped in his chenille throw, staring empty eyed at her wedding album, imagining all that could have been and all that would never be. How futile it all seemed. She'd never again know a man as good and kind as Josh, she knew it, and she hated his Jesus more than ever before.

Saturday already, and she wasn't sure how she'd pull herself together enough by Monday to be her usual composed, competent self, but she'd have to try; there was no one else to do her job. Having succeeded in making herself indispensable to those in command, as was her plan from the beginning, she was ultimately stuck with those repercussions. Once again, bundled in Josh's favorite throw, breathing in the fragrance of his cologne and curled up on the big sofa in his study, she was lightly dozing when the phone rang. Who could be calling her? She didn't recognize the number registered on the caller ID and almost didn't answer, but then felt suddenly compelled to do so.

"Jana?"

"Yes, who is this?"

"This is Tina. May I come over to talk to you?"

"Tina? Tina who?"

"I'm Tina Randal, Jana. Do you remember me? I'm Mark's wife."

How terrible she felt that she hadn't remembered Mark's wife's name. Mark was Josh's best friend and the accountant at her store for all these years, and she didn't even know his wife's name! She didn't feel in the slightest like talking with anyone, but something inside softened. "Sure, Tina, you can come. I'm just sitting here in Josh's study, and I probably won't do anything to myself, but come on over anyway." Maybe the company would do her some good, and very probably, the only person in the world who might know how she was feeling at this precise moment would be Tina.

When Tina arrived, she looked as terrible as Jana felt, and the moment she saw Jana, she burst into a torrent of tears falling on Jana and trembling like a frightened child. Jana wasn't a hugger, but she put her arms tentatively around Tina, patting her back and doing her best to comfort the young woman. "How will we live, Jana? How will we survive? I don't know what to do without him. He was my life. I've sent the kids to my sister's, but I just can't seem to get it together."

"I don't know, Tina. I guess I'm not doing very well either, if I have to be honest, and I don't know what to imagine anymore. Josh's dad doesn't think this was an accident, but I don't know who to believe. I can tell you one thing though, no one is listening."

"Jana, you can't talk to anyone." Tina said, sniffling and wiping at her nose with her jacket sleeve. "I'm sure this was no accident! We don't know yet who we can trust, or if we can trust anyone. I know I won't be going in for implantation, and the authorities are already looking for me, so I haven't gone home at all. I won't be able to go back there ever again."

Jana handed the girl a box of tissues. "Tina, you can't be serious. Do you think the authorities would force you to get the implant? They can't make you do anything you don't want to do. They work for us! This is America, remember?" It seemed Jana was still living in a world of delusion even after all that had happened.

"All I know, Jana, is that we still haven't been able to contact Mark's cousin, and there are people all over the nation who are rebelling against the implantation idea. We've heard of other families disappearing after the president's death squads showed up in cities in their part of the country. We believe there's something very big going down, even bigger than the microchips. We just haven't quite figured it all out yet. And really, Jana, do you think anyone out there in our government has been working for us, or for our benefit, for a long time now? Every one of them is more interested in keeping the lobbyists happy and adding pork to every bill that gets passed, in order to get their payoffs and bonuses. They don't care about how the economy is affecting the average Joe, because they'll just keep voting themselves more raises and watch the prices rise for the rest of us!"

"It's hard to believe any of this, Tina. It all feels like a bad dream. I can't wrap my mind around the scope of it yet. And I don't know if I want to try."

"Jana, we can't allow Mark and Josh's deaths to be for nothing. This whole mission meant enough to them that they were willing to die trying to warn others. They discovered proof the government has been slowly gaining control over just about every aspect of our society since the new administration took over—finance, health care, education, social programs, military, education, jobs, and even our religious freedoms. You know, they think we're too stupid to govern ourselves, or make decisions concerning our own lives.

The czars who've been added to the president's White House team are answerable to no one but that administration. Tell me, how is that constitutional? Yet, who challenges him? His executive orders continue to cancel out every venue for due process. No, we've known for quite some time that things are not right. The president's people have been able to manipulate the media enough to cover it up until now, but the guys were uncovering some pretty scary stuff, and they were about to blow the whistle on some of their schemes! Some of the areas which have already been maneuvered into socialist realms are pretty frightening."

"I know Josh was coming up with some pretty bizarre assumptions, but I don't think he could prove any of it. I just figured it was a bunch more of his conspiracy theory stuff."

"You want proof? There is plenty of proof! Some of the facts, which Mark and Josh uncovered, started a few years back with the last H1N8 pandemic. One of the guys at our church is a doctor who used to work in a university research department where they handled several yearly contracts for the government. I'm referring to some very major contracts such as the government's annual top secret development of flu virus."

"You mean a yearly flu vaccine?"

"No, I'm talking about a virus, Jana. His department developed a new strain of flu each year. Our beloved government practices something called 'selective cleansing' many societies around the world do the same thing. After a new strain is created each year, they introduce the virus into the population by creating two sets of vaccines. The first batch is produced with a live virus, and when it infiltrates the populace, it immediately begins to dispatch the very old, very young, immune compromised, and sickly. Then they bring out the real vaccine commonly made with a dead virus and begin immunizing the remaining population. Jana, that's just part of the story! Our government has had their dirty hands in everything from public health to finances and societal issues for more years than you can imagine! We're nothing but lab rats to them."

"This is a bit hard to swallow. Are you trying to tell me our elected officials are involved with a program that would kill their own citizens?"

"You can't possibly be that naive, Jana! Our government, along with those of other countries, has been involved in some of the most insidious plots ever executed in order to gain control of certain factions, or to thin out their own populations, for all sorts of reasons.

Remember, these are people who care more about developing welfare give away programs we can't afford; securing money for polar bear breeding programs and sending billions to countries who want nothing more in this world than to destroy America and everything it stands for than they do about their own hardworking citizens.

"They'll bring their own ideologies to bear no matter the cost. All you have to do is look at world history for other examples, Jana. Benito Mussolini, Pol Pot,

Hitler, Joseph Stalin, and my all-time favorite, Mao Zedong, boy what a guy. He did away with seventy million of his own Chinese citizens. Do you really think this kind of thing doesn't happen here, Jana? I could show you example after example of experimental programs designed to thin out the ranks of our poor and minorities. Don't even get me started on Margaret Sanger and her proabortion and euthanasia ideas to do away with so-called undesirables—blacks, Hispanics, and those with mental handicaps! She worked right along with our own government clear up till the end.

"The current administration isn't any different. How many in our government are proabortion and pro-euthanasia? Tell me, Jana, how is killing a baby, an elderly person, or a disabled person any different than killing healthy individuals our age? A person is a person, who are they to decide the worth of a human being? There's significant proof our administration has been working closely with other world authorities to develop a one-world government and one-world financial system. Many of those plans are much farther along than you might believe, and it is all beginning to fit together."

"Well, what does this have to do with the H1N8 pandemic? That flu killed multiple tens of thousands of people in this country alone, but eighty percent of those who died were ages twenty to twenty-eight. If they were trying to thin out the old and diseased, they didn't do a very good job of it, did they?"

"For that very reason, Dr. Rose quit the university research program. The year that particular H1N8 flu was created, something in the research went horribly wrong, and it caused a killer mutation in the virus. He'd always felt at least a twinge of guilt about creating diseases which caused so many deaths each year, but he soothed his remorse by remembering his actions were sanctioned by our government. Figuring he was simply thinning out pieces of the population which were the biggest drain on our economy. You know, those that the socialists hate because they are consuming more than they produce, he tried not to dwell on the losses. When he became a Christian, his views on things began to change. Well, when that pandemic swept through the population, he finally realized he was doing nothing less than taking part in mass murder, and he couldn't make excuses anymore. He tried talking to the 'powers that be' in the grant program, but he was told, in no uncertain terms, to drop it. The FBI paid him a visit shortly thereafter and threatened him with imprisonment for treason and harm to his family if he pursued any action.

"They left him with a broken leg and two broken ribs as a reminder of their visit. He was seriously frightened, so he lived with his guilt, moved far away from the university where he'd done research, and went on with his life until he began to see where our country has been heading lately. By then, enough time had passed that his 'personal bodyguards' didn't seem to be following him quite so closely anymore. He couldn't just stand by, knowing who was behind all of the socialist agenda and militia activity, so he started attending meetings at the church. For all we know, his attendance may have been the reason our boys were being watched.

"After his second meeting with us and after sharing much of his past at that meeting, he brought some top secret papers which were tied to the programs in which he'd been involved. These were papers the government believed destroyed long ago. He'd managed to keep those proofs all these years, knowing he might need them some day as insurance. He turned them over to Josh and Mark. Then, one night, when he and his family were on their way into the protective custody of ARM from a meeting at the church, he delivered his family to Mark and Josh and turned around to go back home for something he'd forgotten. Nobody ever saw him again. He simply disappeared."

"Disappeared? How long ago was that? And what in the heck is ARM, Tina?"

"About a week before Mark and Josh were killed. And ARM stands for America's Resistance Movement. We are a group formed in direct opposition to the government's People's Militia, a group, which has been growing like wildfire."

"I remember that night, Tina. Josh ran out of here and was gone till all hours."

"Yeah, I know. He and Mark were taking Dr. Rose's family to an assigned safe house, for holding before transport after his disappearance. It seems they'd received their implantation letter already, and it was only a matter of time before the president's People's Militia would be coming after them anyway. They've gone into permanent hiding."

"Hiding, where are they hiding? Are there more of these people who've run away from the government?"

"Jana, when Mark and Josh were murdered, it was the same night they'd come back from making arrangements for our family, and for you if you wanted to come, to go under protection as well. We were to leave here last weekend. Josh knew the authorities were already following many of us, and he wanted to be sure we could get out safely and also, that you would be taken care of if anything happened to him. Then, when his parents were almost run off the road, he got a call from his dad. Well, he and Mark were on their way back from talking to Josh's parents when they were forced off the road and killed."

"Wait a minute. Are you telling me Josh's parents were almost murdered too? His dad never told me. No wonder he was so sure there was foul play involved. So, they were pretty darned sure then that Josh and Mark were intentionally killed by the government?"

"We are absolutely certain they were murdered, and your in-laws will be going into hiding as well. I'm here to see if you will come with me. I'm going to be sending for my kids to follow me too, I miss them so much, and I won't be able to communicate with you anymore. Will you come? I know it's what Josh would want."

"Tina, I can't. I'm still not absolutely sure what I believe, but I have things I need to clear up here first before I could go anywhere. I'll have to see what happens next. Besides, Josh and I never even got a letter from the GHO, so it's hard for me to believe certain parts of this conspiracy theory stuff without some kind of proof."

"Gosh, Jana, I don't know how much more 'proof' you need to see after the death of your husband, but I can't force you to do anything. I know Josh loved you more than anything on this earth, and I know he is with Jesus now, just like my Mark. I hope everything works out for you, but more than that, I hope you will let the Lord into your life. Josh would have wanted that too. He always said he believed in you. If you do that, if you begin trusting Jesus, many more things will begin to become clear to you."

A little incensed that Tina had mentioned allowing the Jesus, who so recently allowed her husband to die a horrible, fiery death into her life, Jana stood stiffly and held out her hand. "Be safe, Tina. I wish you and your children all the best." Tina took a quick step forward and gave Jana a hasty hug.

After walking Tina out to the foyer and closing up behind her, she leaned into the door and rested her aching forehead against the smooth, cool surface for a long moment. For all she knew, Tina might have all the facts correct, but it was so far-fetched and hard to believe. This was stuff a good science fiction writer would scarcely have come up with. It couldn't be true, could it? She felt bad Josh's folks hadn't told her about their near miss, but the three of them weren't exactly close, and she hadn't been very open to anything they'd had to say to her in the past, so why would they confide in her now and risk their own safety? She supposed she could understand.

Jana ached with loss and confusion, and the chilly panel felt good against her head. Not sure yet what she'd do; she only knew she was tired, and if she was going to be able to work on Monday, she'd better get some much needed rest.

Turning around slowly and surveying the large pile of mail on the table in the entryway, she walked toward it and suddenly felt completely overwhelmed again. Knowing she didn't have the strength to deal with all that it implied today, especially knowing some of that mail would be addressed to Josh, she turned and walked to the study. Monday when she returned from work would be soon enough.

Arriving at work after a sad and lonely weekend, Jana felt strangely uncomfortable coming up the elevator. This store had been a second home to her for years now, so why this odd feeling? Her usual aggressive, in-your-face sales style didn't seem appropriate anymore, not after everything which had transpired recently. When the lift opened on the tenth floor, Jana sensed every gaze in the place on her. Glancing into the stares of several coworkers, she saw the barrage of questions in their momentary looks and the pity on their faces.

Hot mist rising to her eyes, she quickly turned away and headed down the empty hall to her office. Approaching Rita's desk, she was surprised and a little thrown by Rita's comment. "Hi, Jana, glad to have you back. Wasn't it sad about Tina?"

"Tina?"

"Yeah, Jana, You know, Mark's wife, Tina?"

"Rita, I know who Tina is. What's sad about her?"

"Sad about her dying that's all I meant. It must be horrible for her kids, especially after losing their dad just a couple weeks ago."

"Whoa, Rita, What are you talking about? Tina is dead?"

"I got a call this morning from her sister. She tried to call Tina's cell phone last night and couldn't reach her. I guess the kids wanted to talk to their mom. She finally got pretty worried, called the police and asked them to go by and check on her. Tina was found hanging from the ceiling in her bedroom. It looks like suicide. Mark's death must have been too much for her. Rachel, Tina's sister, didn't know who else to call here and thought she might have friends where Mark had worked. Boy, when it rains, it pours, huh?"

Jana felt as if she'd been punched in the gut. She knew Tina would never, could never, have killed herself. She was fine just two days ago, strong and fine. She had children for crying out loud—children who were coming to join her—and she was going to carry out Mark's wishes to get his kids out of harm's way. There was no way she would have dishonored the memory of her husband that way. Arrangements for escape, all of them, were made. Jana tried to take a step forward and almost collapsed; her head swimming.

Tina specifically told her she was not going back to her house. She knew the authorities were looking for her, so she wouldn't have been that careless. None of this made any sense and the whole setup was just too convenient as far as Jana was concerned.

Without a doubt and with no second thought required, Jana knew Tina had been murdered. Did they know Tina had been over to see her too? Were the authorities watching her? She desperately needed to call Josh's parents! Her stomach twisted in knots as she turned back to Rita, "I don't think I was ready to be back here, Rita. Tell whoever you need to. I'm going home."

"Are you okay, Jana? Do you need me to call the nurse? You're white as a ghost!"

"I'll be okay, Rita. No, I don't want the nurse. I just need to go home and lay down. I'll let you know what's going on later."

Heading back through the long hallway, all eyes again on her, down the elevator and out to her car, Jana's mind raced with the implications of this latest news. As she drove, she dialed her in-law's number and got their answering machine. "You've reached the Conyers, we can't come to the phone right now, but leave us a detailed message, and we'll get back to you as soon as possible. God loves you, have a great day."

"Okay, Jana, don't get paranoid now," she muttered, as she tried to decide what to do. "They could be anywhere. Maybe they've even gone into hiding already?" Jana decided she only wanted to get home. There, she would figure out what her next step would be. A red light stopped her progress, so she took a moment to reflect and calm down. Her moment obviously overstayed its welcome, because a prolonged honk from the car behind shook her from her introspection. Stepping on the gas, she headed into the intersection on a light, which had once again turned red. Horns blared from all sides causing panic to rise up and bringing tears of confusion to her eyes. Driving home, reeling from the tragic news about Tina, she had little doubt now there was something sinister going on. She just had to figure out what that evil something was.

On her way home through massive morning traffic, Jana tried her in-law's number several more times with no results.

Making her approach up the driveway, the suspicious black sedan she'd been watching in her rearview mirror all the way home moving slowly by; she tried looking through its dark tinted windows using her rearview mirror to no avail. Had they been following her? Was she just imagining things? Perhaps she was even buying into the whole conspiracy theory idea? Jana didn't know if she was going insane, or just feeling that way? She couldn't believe Tina was gone and didn't believe for a minute the woman had taken her own life; not when she was just about to go into hiding with her kids. Suddenly, out of the corner of her eye, she saw the nose of the dark sedan poke back around the corner and then slowly back away. The driver had merely driven around the block and come back. Were they spying on her? She got out of her car and walked to her front door; the eerie feeling of inquisitive eyes heavy on the back of her head.

4

PEEKING THROUGH THE stained glass panel beside her front door, Jana scanned the road to see if the mysterious black sedan might reappear. Seeing nothing, she began again to wonder if she was indeed going crazy or imagining things. What was she to believe? Were Josh and Mark murdered? Where was the evidence? At this point, all she'd heard was speculation, but now with Tina's death added to the mix, things were more confusing. Even the pieces of broken taillight on the side of the road weren't definitive proof, were they? Mr. Conyers was always seeing a conspiracy, even where none existed. She didn't believe for one minute Tina had committed suicide, but who could possibly want to hurt her?

And, she wondered, where were her in-laws? Had they been taken, or were they in hiding? Should she call the police, or were they also in on this whole state of affairs? Would things be made worse if she let them know her worst fears? She must try to get a grip on herself. No matter what was going on, nothing would be best served by her doing anything in haste. Perhaps she would have a bite to eat and try to calm down, and then she would be less likely to do anything which might come back to haunt her later. Sliding the dead bolt home and latching the door handle, she checked the entry one more time and nodded her silent approval.

Walking past the granite-topped vestibule table, Jana picked up her long neglected pile of mail. The house seemed hollow and empty as she heard her own footsteps echo off the marble floor on her way to the kitchen. Walking to the back door, she checked to be sure it was secured as well, then paused and took a deep shaky breath.

Josh hadn't always been here when she'd arrived home from work, but whenever he wasn't around, she knew it wouldn't be long before he'd come crashing through the door with a funny story and a cheerful laugh. He could always be counted on to liven up a room with his bigger-than-life personality. A warm tear slid down her cheek and dropped slowly to the marble floor by her foot. Heart aching with the fact that her Josh would never again explode into a room wearing his mischievous grin, she had to acknowledge finally that she'd never see his handsome, dimpled face again, aside from her dreams.

Walking to the sink, she turned the hot water lever all the way to the left and washed her hands as the fresh scent of green apple soap wafted to her nose. Her skin shone bright red before she realized she was burning her hands, so she shook them semidry and turned off the steaming water. Looking indifferently out her kitchen window she stood for hours, how many she wasn't sure; but, observing the last of a blazing sunset as it colored the sky with pinks, oranges, and reds; she watched the waning light. Out of the blue, Jana realized all she could see through her ruffled white curtains was her own miserable reflection in the glass as darkness claimed the night. She didn't know what happened to the time, but emotionally exhausted, she decided she wasn't hungry after all.

The beautiful sunset had reminded her of walks with Josh at their place by the river as their relationship blossomed and of their first years of marriage when they'd spent weekend upon weekend hiking, fishing, hunting, camping, and planning their future together. Josh brought out something human and special in her, which she'd never known existed. He was her hero and her hope, and he caused her to want to be a better person; she just hadn't completely laid claim to what that concept meant yet. She knew though that he believed in her as no one in her life ever had. The memory of their time at the park was so crystal clear she imagined she could still smell the aroma of freshly mown grass in the air and could hear the sounds of children laughing as dogs barked and they played together at the close of day.

Abruptly, the utter exhaustion, which had been stealing slowly over her mind and body throughout this terrible day, settled in with a vengeance, and she realized she had no energy left even to stand. Walking shakily across the room, she made her way to a padded leather dinette chair. Sitting sullenly at her glass-topped art deco table (the one she believed she had to have, no matter the cost, or Josh's opinion), she sighed and began dismally to sort the mail in three stacks; one for her, one for Josh, and an additional one for the trash bin.

"Wait a minute," she murmured, "what's this?" A letter addressed to her from the Global Health Organization; glaringly, not addressed to both her and her husband, as she would have expected, but only to Jana Conyers. Digging through the still unsorted pile of mail, she looked but couldn't find a GHO letter for Josh!

She held the communiqué turning it over and over and then noticed with a jolt it was postmarked on the same day Josh had died. She was almost afraid to open it, almost afraid to have her worst fears con-firmed. Finally allowing herself to tear open one end, she tapped the envelope on her hand and pulled the letter out. Unfolding the heavy, official looking paper, she saw it was indeed addressed to only her. Why was Josh's name not on the GHO letter? The Randal's notification letter had listed all family members.

This letter was written and dated on the day before Josh's death and then mailed on the very day he was killed. How could the government officials responsible for population notification have known she would be alone; unless they were all somehow involved with Josh's death? The date for her GHO implant appointment was set for the upcoming Friday.

Jana tried calling her in-laws one more time, with no success. When she couldn't reach them, she began to cry, softly at first, then sinking to the floor and folding in on herself, she sobbed uncontrollably, choking on her tears. Crying for the loss of her Josh, for her parents and her grandmother, for Mark and Tina, for her purposeless life, and for the full, wonderful future she would never know but admittedly didn't deserve to have. And probably most of all, she cried for all the years she'd never allowed herself to cry while she tried to portray herself as a strong, able woman when in fact she was nothing but a scared, insecure, wounded little girl. She'd never felt so alone. Nothing, since her parent's terrible death and the loss of her grand-mother, had left her feeling so impotent and scattered. She hated not being in control, she hated her circumstances, and most of all, she hated God.

Though the world viewed her as an independent, confident, businesswoman, she'd grown accustomed to having Josh in her life, and she'd come to the conclusion she didn't like being alone one single bit. She'd created her own prison of isolation; she knew that now and probably deserved every bit of the hell she was enduring as a result. Her whole body racked with grief and violent weeping, she began to plead, "I don't even know if you're real, or if there's anybody out there. But if you're there, God, please help me. Please help me know what to do, where to go, I'm so lost, so lost."

Wiping away mascara stained tears with the sleeve of her white silk blouse, leaving black smudges on the fabric and on her swollen face, she pulled herself up unsteadily by the glass-topped kitchen table. Utterly spent, totally empty, and lacking the desire to fight, or even live at this point, she walked slowly to Josh's study, kicked off her shoes, and curled up in a fetal position on his big leather sofa. Covering up with his brown, chenille throw, inhaling the scent of his familiar cologne and shutting her eyes tight against the insufferable pain of loss, a persistent, growing migraine which began at the crown of her head and wrapped around her skull to the base of her neck threatened to undo her. She managed to drift off to sleep even while plagued with stuffed sinuses and painful, hiccupping sobs.

5

JANA WOKE WITH a start, disoriented, and inexplicably frightened in the blackness of Josh's closed study. She was twisted up in his throw and had a moment of panic as she wrestled her way out of her self-imposed chenille snare.

A cloudy night kept even minimal moonlight from filtering in through the house's back windows. Quick to get her bearings though, she pulled her cell phone from her pocket to check the time. Two in the morning was all. *Strange*, she thought, as she wondered for a moment what could have awakened her. Then, she heard it. "What the," she murmured lightly, a soft scratching noise at her back door. With no idea what caused the sound, she decided to investigate. Rising silently and sliding her stocking feet over first the den carpet and then the marble kitchen floor, quietly to the rear door on the far side of the room, she peered out, being careful not to trip on or bump into anything between here and there.

What she saw caused her heart to skip a beat and the hair on the back of her neck to stand on end. Two men dressed in black, the closest one attempting to jimmy her back door lock. She thought about screaming to scare them off, but something stopped her. What? Clouds shifted and moonlight glinted off the barrel of a large revolver in the hand of the second man. Jana knew instinctively this wasn't a mere burglary. These men wouldn't be afraid to break the door down if they realized they'd been prematurely discovered.

Dashing soundlessly across the room, she stopped and turned around. She might be at an advantage here. They thought they were catching her unaware. Running as hurriedly as she could to the front door, she was about to open it for a rapid retreat when she noticed the black sedan, the same black sedan from earlier that day with its lights off, parked in front of her house. A third man sat on guard in the driver's seat. This wouldn't be the way. She'd be detected whether she tried to leave by the front or the back. Thoughts of calling the police quickly fled her mind; she knew if these men were who she suspected them to be, making a call like that would just confirm to all parties concerned she was indeed inside her house.

Jana had another advantage. She knew of a place to conceal herself in Josh's study. A panel at the bottom of the bookcase could be moved enough to squeeze through and would give her a place, though somewhat tight, where she believed she might be safe. Scurrying rapidly to her hiding place, she waited, concealed from sight. Soon, she heard the men who'd now successfully broken into her home walking through the kitchen, whispering; their shoes making soft slapping sounds on the smooth marble floor.

Their whispers grew louder, and her heart pounded so hard and fast in her chest that she feared her pursuers might hear it beating, even from deep within her shelter. These horrible strangers moved from room to room, slowly and quietly at first, but when the house proved to be empty, to the best of their estimation, loud and systematic destroying everything in sight in an all-out attempt to find whatever object it was they sought. It seemed as if they were somehow angry, they hadn't found her at home and felt cheated at not having a victim to torture. A shiver ran the length of her spine, and nausea nearly overwhelmed as her imagination ran wild with fear.

Would they discover her secret nook? She began again to pray, "Josh, please don't let them find me," under her breath. From her seclusion, she heard what sounded like drawers crashing to the fl oor, closets being emptied, and furniture being overturned in the next room, she felt she might be physically sick from terror as they ventured nearer her refuge. What could they be looking for? When the two men entered, demolished, and left the study, she heard what seemed to be the same method of search taking place in every other room of her rather large house.

After hours of destruction, she heard one of the men make a call. She listened as he reported in to, what sounded like, his superior. "No, sir, we didn't find them. We turned the place upside down. No, sir, she never came back. No, her car is here, but…I don't know, sir. Maybe she got wind of something going down. No, sir, we didn't leave any prints, but we'll check things over again before we leave. Yes, sir, we're outa here now."

Hearing noises then that led her to believe the men might indeed be leaving, she speculated on whether or not to depart her hidey hole. Terribly cramped and in much pain, balled up in her tight quarters the way she was, she was equally petrified to leave the safety of her sanctuary. What if they were still lurking about? Maybe they were just being quiet to lure her out of her hiding place?

Remaining in the confined space for another hour before kicking stiffly at the wooden screened panel by her feet, she finally crept slowly out into the light. Perhaps the men had been frightened by that very approaching daylight? The false front on the bottom of the bookshelves had proved to be her safe haven, but it would take a while to work all the kinks out of her twisted and sore body. Stretching her petite frame, Jana surveyed the damage to Josh's study. Feeling anger rise up, she kicked at a pile of rubble in the middle of the room. This study, his stuff, was all she had left of Josh and it was destroyed, totally ruined. Relief and rage instantly vied for the emotional forefront of her psyche.

Straightening damage caused by her persecutor's search of her home for over an hour, she finally decided the effort was a waste of time. The destruction they'd caused reached far past any physical damage of mere possessions, and she knew that no amount of picking up or cleaning could fix that. It would prove as useless as trying to pick up the metaphorical pieces of her bankrupt and broken life.

Desecrated, she felt sullied in the wake of these men's degradation, as humiliated as she'd felt in the hands of her former foster families when she'd been raped, tortured, and treated worse than an animal. It infuriated her to know anyone could still wield this kind of emotional power over her and could still cause in her such feelings of raw hatred. Distance would now, could now, be her only defense against this new threat.

6

DECISIONS WOULD HAVE to be made quickly. Jana knew without a doubt she couldn't stay in her home now. She wanted to be out and as far away as possible before dark, in case the "men in black" came back for another look. She also knew from the conversation she'd overheard that they hadn't found what they were looking for the first time around. If the men did come back and find her here, they would more than likely believe she was in possession of the information they wanted, what else could they think?

At a complete disadvantage not knowing what they were after, she was also pretty darned sure they wouldn't believe her if she told them that. And who knew what they were capable of? Well, all she had to do was look around her at the destruction they'd created to get some idea of what they might be capable. What frightening measures might they be willing to take in recovering their information? She wouldn't give them a chance to show her.

Jana might not have any idea who the men represented, or what they were tearing her house apart to find, but she was convinced it had something to do with the intense conversation she'd had with Tina the day before she was killed. Josh and Mark most certainly uncovered some very controversial material, which actually might be hidden somewhere in her house. She vacillated between anger at Josh that he would have put her in this kind of danger and fury at the government that their lies and policies were causing so many problems for honest, taxpaying citizens.

Not wanting to think about what the thugs who broke into her home might be skilled at doing, she was sure they could take her out of the way in the same manner they'd disposed of Tina, the doctor, Mark, and her husband. Jana knew it was necessary for her to get going, but didn't have any idea where she might go.

Facing the fact she hadn't exactly spent her life winning popularity contests, there were no friends and no family left for her. She didn't know any of the people at Josh's church well enough to feel comfortable calling them even if she'd known their names and phone numbers. No, she didn't think even her secretary Rita was an option, not after the recent conversation at work and Rita's confrontational questions, so her choices were practically nonexistent. Well, this wouldn't be the first time in her life she'd had to make some tough decisions. And it certainly wouldn't be the first time she'd had to depend solely on herself. She was going to have to stay out of populated areas, but her destination? She would figure that out once she cleared the city; it would be too dangerous to stay here now.

When she didn't show up for her scheduled appointment at the GHO on Friday, the PM thugs would more than likely come after her anyway, and she wanted to be completely off their radar by that time. She'd decided for sure she was not going to that appointment, nor would she comply in any way with any other government requests! Josh was right after all. She was sure of it now, and that was one more thing in which she'd questioned his intelligence and leadership. If she had it to do over, things would be much different. Why couldn't she have listened to her husband? Why had she spent their marriage disagreeing with everything he said and arguing about nothing? But, realistically, she was never going to get the chance to undo what she'd done. That would not be an option ever again and that thought again caused angry, frustrated tears to roll unchecked down her cheeks. Kicking an already shattered coffee table, she sent a wooden leg flying across the demolished room and into the far wall.

Double-timing it down the stairs to the basement, almost tripping on items strewn about from the search, she hoped to find all she needed in her well-stocked workout/supply room. All their camping, hiking, and sports equipment was stored in the walk-in closet on the south wall.

Trying very hard not to be enraged all over again when she was confronted by the decimation of the basement, she went about the task of readying for her trip. Now though instead of searching the closet as she'd planned, she would have to dig through mounds of items covering the floor to accomplish the same end.

In her rummaging through piles of their belongings, she spotted several things which might come in handy: a large hiking backpack, canteen and water purifying bottle with extra filters, first aid kit, hand cranked flashlight, and a survival packet with assorted items including: purification tablets, flint and steel, fishing supplies, cooking and eating utensils, freeze dried soup and seasoning packets, and some travel size personal hygiene items. The kit included a survival book listing instructions for many emergency scenarios with pictures of plants and trees used for medicinal purposes, which might be helpful. Additionally, she found a portable hand cranked radio and included it in the pack. Locating Josh's large hunting knife and sheath, Jana snatched it up and added it to her collection of survival gear.

The gun safe was empty of course. How she wished she had access to the weapons she and Josh used to practice with at the range. Flashing back to times Josh had taken her out and how much fun they'd had together honing skills she'd never known she possessed was bittersweet. How ridiculous she felt the first time she shot a gun; the recoil snapping her arm back so hard she landed squarely on her bottom. It all seemed so very long ago now. She'd managed to get quite good with Josh's handgun and was giving him a run for his money by her fourth visit to the range, surprising even herself.

Josh was right about that too; right about laws which were passed shortly after the mandatory health care bill was rammed through; laws which forced all gun owners to register their arms, including shotguns and rifles.

He'd warned her that the government was trying to disarm its populace; that the forefathers intended the second amendment for a purpose and that purpose was to keep American citizens in a position to defend themselves against even the tyranny of their own government. Ridiculing him again, of course;

she'd thought herself very wise and progressive not so long ago.

It hadn't taken long after mandatory gun registration for new laws to be passed wherein citizens were ordered to turn over all their weapons. It was foolish to think you might be able to hide a weapon once it was registered, which had obviously been the administration's intent all along. Of course, there were still plenty of arms out there; since only law-abiding citizens complied with the newly instituted laws, so the bad guys had all the firepower now, including the bad guys who were right there in the government's organizations. Of course, Jana wished she still had their handguns, but she'd have to make do. In their excursions to the range, she'd become quite proficient with bow and arrow as well.

Smiling at the memories these thoughts invoked, Jana wished she'd continued to accompany Josh on his trips to the archery range, knowing she was probably rusty by now. They'd had so much fun together in those outings to the countryside. Also learning much from him about "roughing it," she was quite expert now in the art of outdoor survival. For instance, who would have thought a city girl could get so good at starting a campfire, or cooking supper over an open flame? Back in those early times, she'd enjoyed being in the great outdoors with her strong, talented husband, but a couple years ago, she'd exchanged their fun together for something she considered more important at that time—namely, long hours with no free time.

He'd begged her, after that decision, to come along on many different occasions, but she was always too busy perfecting her precious reports in the ever growing desire to be a success. Finally, he'd stopped asking all together. "What a fool I've been!" She thought out loud.

Gathering the lightweight, compact bow and arrows, with additional fletching and arrow heads, in case she might need to do repairs, she loaded all her supplies into the pack and slung that and the bow over her shoulder, hoping soon she might have a chance to brush up on her skills. Spying a sleeping bag and tarp cover half buried in a heap by the north wall, she added them to her finds and toted them along with her up the cluttered stairs.

Entering her bedroom, she was taken aback again by the destruction she saw there. Wondering silently if she should be used to the overwhelming devastation in her life by now, she decided she could never get used to the idea these men felt they'd the right to come in to her home and create this kind of ruin. Mentally throwing her hands in the air, she gave up, fell to her knees, and began digging through piles of clothes and bedroom articles dumped in the middle of the floor to find several pairs of jeans, some sweatshirts and T-shirts along with socks and underwear to stuff into the swelling pack.

Slipping out of her rumpled work clothes and into a clean pair of jeans and T–shirt, it dawned on her that she hadn't dressed this way in a couple of years. The supple jeans were comfortable—more comfortable than she'd remembered—and recalling how her husband used to put his hands in her back pockets and pull her into an embrace caused her to blush, as the fond memory faded to sadness.

Her professional lifestyle lent itself to designer, chic instead of serviceable and comfortable, so jeans for her, unhappily, had become a thing of the past. Stopping long enough to strap the sheath of Josh's hunting knife to her body by tying one leather thong around her slim hips and the other around her thigh until it felt snug; she then stuffed the pile of salvaged clothes into the largest pocket of her backpack, zipped the long, straining zipper and tied the sleeping bag and tarp to the frame's bottom.

In the kitchen, she filled her canteen and water bottles, stowing them away in the netting on the outside of her pack; then grabbed protein bars, several containers of trail mix and nuts, coffee packets, and apples to add to her supplies. She headed for the entry and rummaged through the closet for her hiking boots and old down filled jacket, wishing she'd taken Josh's advice about keeping up with new advancements in outerwear technology. Not long ago, Josh purchased a jacket made from some new space age material and he'd raved about how light it was, while being the warmest jacket he'd ever owned. He wanted to order one for her as well, but she'd made light of it and told him not to bother, how she wished she'd listened to him concerning that subject and so many more. Never would she have believed this could be as important a topic to her as it was now. Well, her old jacket would simply have to do.

Walking back to Josh's study one more time, she looked around at the mess on the floor with a deep and growing frown on her face. Reaching down through the clutter, she picked up a picture hanging from a broken frame. Removing bits of shattered glass and splintered wood from the treasure, she felt her eyes well up again with hot, angry tears as she gazed longingly at a picture of their beautiful, long ago wedding day. Slipping the photo into her pocket, she stood and noticed Josh's Bible tossed against a wall on the other side of the room. Wading through piles of broken memories across the study to retrieve the discarded book, she bent over slowly, lifting it reverently to her heart.

Smoothing the book's pages, she noticed his almost unintelligible scrawl posting personal notes and revelations throughout. This caused another ache in her heart, so severe she had a hard time drawing breath. Then, something caught her eye. A miniscule bit of white poking out from the book's back lining seemed oddly out of place. Jana examined the inside layer, and there was indeed something within, so she looked for Josh's letter opener among piles of litter on the floor. "Here it is!" she exclaimed out loud. "Now let's see what you are, my friend." Running the sharp edge of the letter opener between the lining and leather of the Bible, she released the material enough to remove the item hidden inside; once loosed, she opened the folded paper and gasped. It was a letter from Josh addressed to her.

Jana love,

If you're reading this, they must have managed to put me out of commission. By "they" I mean the current administration. I knew if something happened to me God would manage to direct you to my Bible, so I figured this would be the safest place for a letter.

I've made arrangements with the group ARM (American's Resistance Movement) to take you in if anything happens to me. I will give you directions. They will also receive the information from you that Mark and I collected. Their connections will know what to do with the info and will pass it on through proper channels. I'm going to give you directions to the place where I've hidden the intelligence, but I have to assume you might not be the only one reading this letter, so head to that peaceful place where I first saw your beautiful face. If you sit in our favorite spot, you will be able to figure it out.

I want you to know Jana that you have been the one and only great love of my life. I know things haven't always been easy for you and that made you somewhat bitter and resentful, but I've always known the real you as a loving, capable, kind and remarkable woman. I've seen you smile and laugh and we have experienced true joy together. I treasure the love we've shared. Sadly we allowed life and its trials to creep in and steal away bits of our happiness, but I will always love you!

I cherish you, baby, and I don't want you to worry about me, if I'm not with you I'm safe in the arms of Jesus. Now that you hold the answer to all eternity offers, in your hand, make me a promise, ok? Promise me you will read this Bible and really consider all that it implies, it truly holds the keys of life.

You are my heart, Jana, I love you.

Josh

"I promise I will, Josh, and I love you too," Jana whispered.

Josh had known all along this would happen. Once again, the knowledge made her a little angry—angry that he would put them, her, their life together, in danger. But with all the information she was finally coming to understand, she suspected now he didn't have much choice. And he'd been thinking about her too, clear up until the end. He prepared something in advance for her. Suddenly, she didn't feel quite so alone anymore. Somehow her husband was still looking out for her and there would be others waiting for her along the way. She was resolute, she could do this!

7

JANA LOADED SUPPLIES into the trunk of the car. She'd need transportation to get as far as the park by the river where she and Josh first met. It was imperative she put some distance between herself and her house before dark. At the park, she would make her way to "their bench" (his clues were very clear to her) and search for the intelligence Josh and Mark had hidden so she could pass it along to ARM.

Josh said, in his letter, he would leave instructions for her to find the revolutionaries, so her newly devised plan was to leave her car as deep in the trees as she could manage and set out on foot from there to find the ARM encampment.

Once her gear was stowed in the vehicle, she walked back into the house. She didn't care about the stuff anymore, but she wondered, would it be hard to leave this place filled with memories behind? Knowing she would likely never see her house again, she stopped a moment to reflect. Then, in a flash, she realized it wasn't going to be as hard as she'd imagined leaving her house, her stuff, because the place ceased being a real home when Josh was taken from her. And so, with one more, quick look at his study and the piles of shattered pictures of their life together, she was gone.

Switching on the radio as she left town, Jana tried to calm herself and look as inconspicuous as possible. She'd left her iPhone behind along with anything else she thought might be tracked by satellite or other technology. She would ditch the car as soon as she arrived at the park, sure that the P M soldiers could track her through her on board GPS system. Her music was interrupted by a special report. A nervous-sounding announcer came on the air and began relating news, which caused chills to goosestep the length of her spine. Josh was right again! Soon the president of the United States was speaking to America about the current state of unrest prevailing in major cities nationwide. His tone, as usual, was superior and condescending.

It seemed groups all over America were protesting the mandatory implantation ruling by the government and protesting hard. Marches and rallies had begun in most chief metropolises in the US. The new People's Militia would have their work cut out for them. Did this man think his voice could ever be the voice of reason to the multitudes of people he'd hoodwinked with his mandatory bills and ridiculous executive orders?

Knowing this course of action would give his PM soldiers more power than ever, because now they could move publicly at the behest of the president, she believed she'd escaped just in the nick of time. No more slinking around in the shadows for his death squads. In addition, the Commander in Chief announced he'd removed power from all current military and police organizations until further notice, calling them a threat to society, insurgents, and possible terrorists. Who was he trying to kid? Now that she could finally see more plainly, she realized the administration had at last become more of the transparent organization they'd always promised they'd be. She was seeing their evil very clearly now.

The president was condemning the people's anger, calling the assemblies "riots" and blaming the riots on right-wing extremists and Christian terrorist factions. He was calling for martial law. The news flash further reported that strict curfews would be enforced, city by city, and all citizens would be required to use a check-in process to verify their whereabouts. This was bad news for everyone, but especially terrible news for those trying to flee the city!

A whole fresh set of problems needed consideration. Jana realized now she would be missed much sooner than she'd initially anticipated. Though, she'd just cleared city limits, and the militia might be otherwise occupied taming crowds and quieting riots, at least for awhile. She hoped to be able to get to the park undetected before anyone began searching for her in earnest. With any luck, she could get a good head start on her pursuers, though this news would definitely make it harder to travel. Curfews and mandatory check-ins would be keeping people who didn't want to deal with any drama indoors and movement, or travel by anyone outdoors, would be noticeable and highly suspect.

Arriving at the park, Jana drove immediately to a large stand of maple trees close to the water. Their park was ablaze with fall color—reds, oranges, gold, and yellows. Josh proposed to her on their bench in the fall time; and again memories caused welled up emotion to sting the backs of her eyes. As tears began to fall unchecked and her vision blurred because of them, she hastily swiped the offending wetness away with the back of her hand, angry at her recent frequent bouts of weakness. Unloading her gear, she stowed it hastily in a nearby, shallow ditch, covering it with loose brush and leaves, until which time she would have an opportunity to investigate the area near their bench. Driving her car further into the trees, she covered it liberally with branches and leafy debris. The car wouldn't stay hidden forever, but the camouflage might buy her a little additional time.

Not sure in what type of container Josh's information might be stored, she concluded he would have stowed it in something waterproof. He was after all the most intelligent man she'd ever known, and he seemed to have figured out every other required step in the transfer of intelligence. "Okay, Josh, help me out here, buddy," Jana whispered under her breath. "You've gotta help me do this, Josh."

Scanning the space around their bench, she didn't spot anything out of the ordinary right away. Then, getting down on her hands and knees, she crawled around the vicinity, feeling along the ground for loose earth, or a stone which might be moved, with no results. Inexplicably, she felt drawn to the waste can nearby. Looking inside, she didn't see anything, but had a hunch. Lifting the can, she spied a depression in the dirt beneath. Using Josh's hunting knife to excavate, she made good time moving the previously loosened soil and soon hit something which elicited a hollow "thunk" when struck by her blade. Digging feverishly, aware she was running out of time, she retrieved the hard, plastic, fishing pole container from the freshly dug hole. She began to open the container then thought this might not be the ideal place to look over its contents. "I'd better get my gear and find some good cover. I can look this stuff over when I'm out of sight," she said out loud to no one.

Retrieving her equipment, loading up and sprinting out of sight, Jana made her way to a stand of trees on the opposite side of the park grounds. It would soon be dark, and she wanted to be as far from the square as possible when the park's trail lights snapped on. This way, when her car was discovered, she wouldn't have to worry about being found right along with it.

It'd been a long time since Jana was forced to depend on her physical abilities to the degree this escape was demanding. Back in the days, when she and Josh camped, hiked, fished, and hunted almost every weekend, she'd certainly have been more physically prepared. Sure she did the usual treadmill run and sit-ups to try and stay in shape, but carrying a backpack and running full tilt this way was another story. She knew she'd be sore tomorrow for sure and maybe for many days to come.

The park was flanked by National Forest to the north, and Jana took advantage of that geographical fact for all it was worth as she left the grounds.

Though she certainly wasn't in her best physical shape as of yet, she was aware she'd be running for her life and that knowledge caused her to keep going at a pretty decent clip. Running until she had an undeniable stitch in her side and then until the pain was gone again, she logged a good number of miles before darkness crept in for keeps.

When she knew she had no choice but to stop for the night, she found a hollow at the base of a giant redwood tree and slid the heavy backpack off her shoulders. Digging through her belongings, she pulled out the flashlight she'd stashed there and then untied her ground cover and bedroll from the bottom of the pack. The forest was dense, with a heavy canopy of redwood and various deciduous trees. Jana figured if she was careful enough, she could avoid being detected.

Setting up camp was pretty simple. Her tarp would make good ground cover, and the sleeping bag should be plenty warm enough on this chilly fall night. Covering the lower three quarters of her bed with loose branches and fallen leaves, she placed a pile of debris next to her top quarter in case she needed quick camouflage. Pulling a bag of trail mix and an apple out of the zippered pouch in her pack, she decided that and some cold water from her canteen would have to do for supper tonight. It was okay really; she wasn't feeling particularly hungry anyway, but would eat simply to keep her strength up.

Hauling the sleeping bag over her head just like when she was a kid hiding under the covers from her grandmother in order to read after bedtime, she hunkered down in her comfortable cocoon. Setting her flashlight down at an angle on a fold of fabric, she cracked open the plastic pole container which held the secrets that cost her husband and his friend their lives.

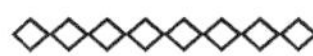

As she unrolled the thick stack of paper, ingeniously enclosed in its protective green carrier, her eyes fell on a note scribbled in that oh so familiar script. It was another note from Josh. A lump formed instantly in her throat making it hard to swallow, but she took a long shaky breath and began reading.

Hey Baby,

I knew you could do it. I promised you directions to ARM and you will find a map included with the papers you found in the canister. If the "PM" has gotten wind of ARM's whereabouts they may have bugged out, but they assured me they will provide a way for you to find them whatever the circumstances.

Materials Mark and I discovered are enclosed as well. Guard them with your life. The papers are proof of the administration's conspiracies against the American people and they detail plans for buildup of the People's Militia, as well as evidence of the government's involvement in the yearly production of a flu strain, for "selective cleansing," which Dr. Rose supplied before he left.

There are pages dealing with plans for nationwide implantation, the president's intent to use Martial Law to gain further control, and the systematic destruction of financial systems in our country.

Feds have been using the "Cloward and Piven" strategy to create one "crisis" after another, so they would be able to step in with, what we would see as "the only solutions" available in each scenario, moving us closer and closer to a Socialist government.

We also found info concerning the "One World Government" plans which are being developed between our government and the European Union. What was it some socialist friend of the administration once said? I think it was, "Don't ever let a good crisis go to waste." So, expect to see scenarios arise in the country, which will rock you to your core!

Needless to say the government has been working their way into every aspect of our lives for years now! No one saw it coming at first, and when we did begin to realize our freedoms were being stripped from us, we didn't want to admit it, or we were too lazy to do anything about it!

Now it will be up to all of you to start over again. You won't be very popular, and it will be very dangerous for those of you making a stand, but someone has to take our country back! I'm only sorry I can't be with you through this difficult time, but in the bottom of the canister you'll find a hand gun and some ammo I was able to hide which will help in the upcoming trials. Though possession of the handgun is illegal I figured if things got so far out of hand you were out here, digging up a plastic container in the park it probably wouldn't matter much anymore and I knew protection would be important for you.

I want you to know Jana that the greatest years of my life have been the ones I spent with you. You are my heart and my one true love. I believe God put us together for a reason and he made you a strong, smart lady for a reason too. I wish I could be there for you now. I know it will be hard to do all that will be required of you, but all our camping trips should have prepared you for most of the essentials.

I love you Jana! I have faith you will do the right thing. You found my Bible and I trust you to open it and begin reading. I know how you feel about religion, but this book contains everything you will ever need to know about relationships; and answers to every question you could ever think to ask. Know that Jesus loves you and that I love you with all my heart and soul.

Good-bye, my sweet baby.

Josh

Through sore, red, tear-filled eyes, Jana glanced at a page of directions Josh had included in the canister and saw a mountain. She turned the canister upside down and the gun and ammunition which had been planted there fell into her cushioned lap. Lifting the gun after she made sure the safety was on, she turned it over in her hands. It had a familiar weight and feel. Examining the holster and ammo, she was deciding where in her bag she would store the items for now. At this juncture, the sound of gunshot would draw too much attention, so she'd bring it into play at some point in the future. Feeling as if her life was filled with too many mountains these days, part of her wanted to give up, dig a hole, and climb in. She knew though that Josh was counting on her to do this thing, and she felt a new resolve fill her as she lay down to sleep clutching the letter, from the only man who had ever really loved her.

8

J ANA WOKE TO plaintive calls of mourning doves in the trees above her. Subtle rays of sunlight danced through branches and up the distant mountain in a kaleidoscope of colors as she watched the display in awe struck wonder. That distant mountain was her destination, unless ARM had been forced to bug out. The ensuing sunrise was more brilliant than any she could remember before, and it filled her with a much needed peace after the pace of yesterday.

She'd fallen asleep last night holding Josh's letter, with more worthless tears in her eyes. Now with the new day crisp and cold, her face was swollen, and her eyes bloodshot and raw. Dawn, however, brought glimpses of brightness; and with the morning came a new clarity and sense of well-being. Hope encased in great gulps of fresh air filled her soul. Exhilaration at the thought of upcoming adventures occupied her mind, and she felt a tingling positivity which had been absent from her life since the loss of her Josh, or perhaps even much longer than that.

Sadly, she'd allowed her life to be about things which didn't matter for a very long time, and she'd dragged her husband right along with her through the futility, which was her existence. Now, though, things were different. Now, she knew a sense of purpose she'd never recognized before. Oh how she wished Josh was here to go through this journey with her, but she would do this for him and for all the times she'd discredited his authority and intelligence. She wasn't sure how, but thought this might in some way make up to him for the times she'd made him feel silly when he tried to warn her about the state of the world around her.

After splashing cold water, from her canteen, on her face and running her fingers through her messy hair, she dug through the front pouch of her pack and brought out a protein bar for breakfast. Folding Josh's letter and putting it in the inside pocket of her coat along with her wedding picture, she patted the wad of paper and smiled a faint longing smile. Hunger sated for the moment, she leafed through the stack of papers she'd taken from the canister.

Scanning each sheet again, there arose in her some inkling of the potential impact this information, which had been entrusted to her, could have. When she reached the last sheet containing her directions to the ARM encampment, she took in the terrain and specifics on the detailed map.

Beginning at last to understand the enormity of the task before her, she wondered, would she be up to that task? Well, she just had to be—for her own sake, for Josh, for all those who'd given their lives, and for all those whose lives were still at risk.

Packing up her gear, she stopped long enough to look around and get her bearings straight. She'd head north toward the mountain and try to put as many miles between herself and the People's Militia as she could before nightfall. From her present location to the mountain was national park, for the most part; first forest and then tall grass land after that, so the chance of running into another human being now was slim. Her biggest problems would be her pursuers and whatever wild animals might make this area their home or hunting grounds. Slinging her pack onto her shoulders, wincing at the soreness she'd known would be there, she headed through the trees.

Jana found she got used to the steady pace much more quickly than she'd imagined she could. Even with a large pack on her back, she was jogging at a pretty respectable rate after only four days.

Up to this point, meals consisted of trail mix for breakfast, an apple for supper, and a stop each day at noon to eat a protein bar and drink plenty of fresh, cold water. Thanks to the purification system in her canteen and the frequently occurring mountain run off streams throughout the forest, she'd been able to keep up with her never exhausted need for fresh water easily enough. She'd lost a little weight, but she was leaner now than she'd ever been. And as she began to feel her body for the first time in her life, she was surprised at the strength and energy surging through her lithe form. At this rate of on the job training, she determined, she'd soon be up to anything they threw at her.

At the end of each day, with evening creeping in to exquisitely transform scattered patches of blue sky into ornate tapestries of pinks, oranges, reds, and purples, she sought out a probable site at the base of a giant tree to set up her modest camp.

As darkness stole in each evening, she crawled into her sleeping bag with a flashlight and Josh's Bible. She'd made a promise to her husband and she meant to keep it. Reading each night until she couldn't keep her eyes open anymore, she was discovering much to keep her questioning mind busy. In her evaluation of the Word, she began to trip over passages she remembered from long ago years with Grandmother Anna. Many of those passages were finally, slowly beginning to make some sense as she viewed them from an adult perspective and studied them out. As she read, she found herself regretting even more the wasted years. Agonizingly, she accused her guilty soul out loud, "If only I'd listened to Josh's wisdom and wishes, gone to church with him, given him, us, a baby. I only wish there wasn't so much to be sorry for."

Jana knew though no matter the future, she was finally doing what she was destined to do. She could feel it. Fading into sleep holding Josh's letters, she kissed the increasingly crumpled picture of him from their wedding day—the wedding day which seemed almost too long ago now to remember.

Josh wanted her to meet his Jesus and trust Him as Savior, but she didn't think she was ready for that yet, who knows, might never be. The pain of all He'd taken from her was still too new and her anger at Him still too raw, but she would read, for Josh, she would read as she'd promised and who could guess what the future might bring?

Another sunup brought cooler temperatures. With each day shorter than the last and her bedroll less able to keep her warm in the night, she grew concerned. The bag's insulating cover helped some, and she was infinitely glad she'd possessed the foresight to raid their equipment closet for that item and others before she left but wondered how much longer she would be on the run and if she had the gear and supplies she needed to get her to her destination before the temperatures dipped dangerously lower.

Perusing her map she saw the forest opened to a span of exposed grasslands beginning at about twenty, or thirty, miles ahead of her current location. The open area of terrain looked to measure about ten to twenty miles, totally devoid of trees, and appeared to cover a slope at least part way up the base of the mountain as well. With such a large area bereft of camouflage up ahead, she would have to adjust her travel somewhat and couldn't be sure how long she'd have the ability to avoid detection. After all, she didn't know how much cover she could count on to find in the grasslands.

Radio broadcasts were off limits since her ride to the park the day of departure, and she wondered at the state of the world, but for now she couldn't be overly concerned with those things she had no control over. She'd put as many miles between herself and "them," in as little time as possible, just to be safe.

Stowing her gear again for travel while munching a handful of her dwindling trail mix supply, she washed her breakfast down with water from her canteen. Splashing more of that same cold water on her face and trying to run her fingers through her hair, her nails caught in the badly tangled tresses. Momentarily disgusted by the condition of her matted mane, she stopped to remove a few of the crunchy leaves she found entwined there.

It was no wonder her head was such a mess after so many days on the run. Her hair was the last thing on her mind these days, and she hadn't spent much time on personal hygiene while on this trip. Heck she hadn't had an opportunity to bathe, or even wash up with more than a splash of water in the mornings since leaving home. She'd have to take care of that as soon as possible.

"Well," she reasoned, "the days of hot soaks and bubble baths are gone, so I need to get used to that!" But she might be able to figure out a way to at least clean herself up a bit, which would also deter tiny hitchhikers. That could wait awhile too. It would have to. For now, she'd best be on her way to keep distance between herself and those who she was sure would soon be following, if they were not already.

That evening, ten days into her escape, as the sun was setting behind her distant mountain, Jana noticed a curious space in a cluster of trees ahead. Approaching the clearing, she spied a stream which sported a wide bend, creating a pool deep enough in which to submerge. In the waning light, she pulled off her ripe clothing and retrieved soap, a towel, and clean garments from her pack. Plunging herself into the frigid water quickly to get the shocking experience over with as soon as possible, she dunked her head under the water and came up sputtering and gasping from the cold.

Scrubbing and rinsing rapidly in hopes she could accomplish the task before her fingers and toes became completely numb, she dunked her head one last time to rid her hair of the days and days of dirt, sweat and leaves, plus any residual soap which had accumulated there. Stepping out of the water, she dried with rough, brisk strokes in an effort to warm herself and deftly stepped into her waiting undergarments, jeans, and sweatshirt, finally attaching her lifesaving weaponry. Then, cleaner than she'd felt in days but chilled to the bone, she tugged her fingers through her snarled hair and pulled her tresses back in a loose, short ponytail. Fastening the pony with elastic, she turned to wash her filthy jeans in the cold stream as she thought back on her trek of the day and began planning her strategy for tomorrow's part of the journey.

Deep in thought, she was startled by a small noise from behind. Freezing in place, tremors of fear running rampant up and down the length of her backbone; her mind went blank. For just a moment, she forgot everything she'd learned over these past days on the run. Forcing the logical, stronger piece of who she'd become to her brain's forefront, she willed herself to think more rationally. That was the sound of a twig snapping, she was sure of it now. Her heart beat almost out of control; then there was another small rustling sound and another twig snapped. Her senses, which had become super attuned to her surroundings during this forced jaunt through the forest, also became fantastically aware. She knew positively that she was being watched by someone.

Without turning around, she didn't need to; she could feel eyes burning through the back of her head, and all the hair on her neck seemed to be standing on end. Not wanting her pursuers to know she was aware of their presence, even though a huge piece of her logical mind was all but jumping out of her skin with anxiety, desperate to run, she tried to remain still, pretending she'd not been alerted to their arrival until she could formulate a plan. Instead she began to whistle lightly while she washed.

Coming up with just a hint of an idea, she determined to chance it. *One, two, three*, she counted mentally. Then dropping deftly and quickly to the ground, she rolled behind the nearby tree where her pack was stashed. She snatched her gear and ran, regretfully leaving her small pile of dirty clothes laying on the water's edge.

Gunshot and the sound of men's voices shouting and cursing erupted from behind her. *How could I have been so stupid?* she thought. *Why didn't I hear them coming? So careless, so damned careless!* She scolded herself mentally. *How could I let my guard down that way?* The self-deprecating thoughts filled her mind. Who knows how long they'd been tailing her as she went her merry way, believing she'd outwitted them. Well, she could only stay low and run for her life now. But Jana had learned things about this forest, things which her pursuers might not know. She would use her newfound knowledge of the past week and a half to her advantage and run for her life.

Dark enough now that she believed her pursuers wouldn't be able to detect her if she was smart, she stayed low and ran quietly. She could hear them crashing through the trees behind her, a bunch of clumsy louts, giving themselves up every step of their bumbling, swearing way. If she'd returned fire at this point, she'd have alerted them to her position and they certainly had more ammunition than she, so she ran. Positive she was outnumbered by the sheer amount of voices she'd heard when they'd surprised her near the water, she had no solid idea how many were attempting to keep up with her rapid pace. *How close are they now?* she wondered under her breath. She knew better than to slow down to assess the situation just yet, so keeping her head down, she continued to run faster than she'd ever sprinted in her life. She may be small, but after all, her recent practice with a pack on her back, she found she could run like the wind.

As she sprinted, her autopilot mode kicked in. Running in a zigzag pattern through the foliage, she heard the intermittent volleys of bullets slowly grow more distant as she added vast amounts of space between herself and the dogging soldiers. Days and days in the forest made her familiar with its diverse terrain and comfortable with its ebb and flow; the troops following seemed confused and easily spooked by every movement and shadow, as evidenced by the distant bursts of wild gunfire which were becoming even more random than before. She could feel the distance growing between pursued and pursuer.

Why hadn't they taken her before? She was vulnerable while she was sleeping, and perhaps even more so while she was bathing. The thought they'd been watching as she washed and dressed made her angry and caused her no small bit of embarrassment. They were only doing their job, probably hoping she wouldn't detect their presence and might lead them all the way to the secret ARM encampment.

She couldn't let those troops catch her now. Not now that she finally had a purpose. She wouldn't allow them to get the papers which Josh and Mark protected with their lives and entrusted to her. Running with everything she had in her, she jogged so fast and so far, she didn't know how far until she came to the end of the forest thickness and saw the sun beginning its daily stunning ascent up the mountain side.

She'd run all night. Jana thought it amazing that though she was breathing hard, she wasn't out of breath. She was exhausted though, both emotionally and physically. Barely recognizing the capable woman she was quickly becoming, she decided she liked the new Jana a great deal in spite of her current circumstances. Rest though, she needed rest and was pretty sure she'd lost her hunters, at least for the moment.

Quickly digging fallen leaves from the sunken root base of a large tree, Jana piled her gear and herself hastily into the hole. Covering her body completely with leaves and debris, she was camouflaged and resolved to wait until dark before setting out again, since her forest cover would now be officially all but gone, she'd be forced to do most of her traveling by night. Over and over throughout the day, she thought she heard sounds in the distance, noises which caused her to want to leap from the leaves and run, but something held her. It was as if a comforting hand reassured her. And though the sounds let her know the militia squad was closer to her than she liked, she stayed.

At about midday, the clamor of searching troops subsided, and by the time darkness fell again, she was able to breathe normally. Calmness returned to the forest and nature resumed her regular ebb and flow, so Jana deftly uncovered herself and prepared to be on her way, shadows hiding her for the time being. If her pursuers had employed dogs for the purpose of seeking her out, she likely wouldn't have had a chance; but again, by the hand of some unknown force, she seemed to be safe for the present.

Somehow she knew Josh, or maybe his God, kept her hidden from her trackers, and she began to contemplate a life after this one as she headed to the forest's edge and started her trudge toward the mountain. Needing to believe Josh was alive somewhere in the universe, she wondered if that didn't open her mind up to the possibility of a heaven and a keeper of that place. Not ready to embrace those thoughts, or ideas, just yet; she would read as she'd promised her husband she would, but as for changing her mind or beliefs, that might take a lot more than words on a page. For the time being, she'd put all such thoughts out of her mind and concentrate only on her immediate quest for the encampment she sought. Following the maps Josh left her, she would get to the distant mountain and, hopefully, find the ARM camp. Beyond caring what happened to her now, she had to do this for Josh.

Daylight dawned on another morning as Jana's trek continued. One additional night without sleep caused her to become more careless than she would be under normal circumstances. Scolding herself silently, knowing she should stay alert and keep her eyes peeled for wild animals as she got nearer the looming monolith, she tried to stay prepared.

Aware the foothills and the upcoming mountain abounded with wolf, mountain lion, and even bear, so far she hadn't seen anything in her examination of the area she was traversing, except the occasional pile of scat that spoke of their close proximity. Having no desire to run headlong into anything bigger, or hungrier than she was, she forced herself to remain extra vigilant in spite of exhaustion.

The forest thinned to a modicum of trees and was soon completely replaced by tall grasses. Jana thought, when she'd initially looked at the map, her journey would get easier once she was clear of the wooded areas, but discovered instead the vegetation at well over nine feet tall blocked her vision in every direction. The region was planted in big bluestem or "Turkey foot" grass many decades ago by pioneers who'd moved in and farmed the area, as fodder for farm animals. And as so often happens when man takes the things of nature into his own hands, it had grown out of control in the fertile soil and temperate climate at the base of the mountain.

Though the grass is excellent forage for horses and cattle and can even be cut and dried for future use, it can also grow up to ten feet tall and develop into dense clumps with very deep roots. When left alone, the clumps obviously increased in size and finally overshadowed naturally occurring vegetation in that area, becoming an invasive cancer in the region and successfully destroying all manner of native flora.

She knew the mountain was still there for it loomed high above her even from so great a distance.

Naturally, she assumed walking straight ahead would get her to her destination eventually, but having her sight blocked became disconcerting.

Each grass clump was made up of tall, well-established stalks and newer, shorter stalks. With each laborious step she took, the grass' seed heads and three spike-like projections, whipped up and around catching in her clothes and lashing at her exposed flesh until her hands and face were a mass of small, bloody, stinging lacerations. Already frayed morale suffered more with each passing minute of torture. Tired, hungry, and sore, she began moving more quickly than safety dictated in an effort to be done with this evil foliage, until she heard a distinct rattling noise to her right and stopped dead in her tracks.

Living in this part of the country and not knowing the sound of a rattlesnake could get you killed pretty quickly. Scared, confused, and trying to decide in which direction to go, she stood without moving. Suddenly, from the corner of her eye, she saw movement; panicking, she sidestepped a large clump of roots catching her foot in the vegetation. Twisting her ankle, she fell hard to the ground. The ensuing pain was excruciating, and she lay rocking back and forth on the earth, tears of agony and frustration filling her eyes as she pounded the dirt with her fist. At that precise moment, a black helicopter flew directly overhead. It seemed the early morning hours brought out more than one kind of snake.

From her position in the waving grass, she was not visible to the pilot or passengers of the aircraft, and though it would not occur to her until later, her fall in the bluestem had kept her from being detected by her pursuers. Jana sat up. Wincing in pain, she looked around and tried to assess her situation. Not hearing anything further from the local rattler population, she tried to make her situation comfortable for the time being. She could outwait the helicopter patrol right where she was as long as she didn't have any slithery company. Lingering here would give her the chance to rest her ankle a bit and come up with a better plan for finding more permanent cover, as long as the rattler had moved on, she'd be fine.

Assuming the chopper held more of the same terrorists, which had chased her through the woods, and that was a pretty good assumption; they had a fair idea she was heading for the mountain. If she could lay low long enough, it might throw them off. The search helicopter made several more sweeps of the area and it seemed, from their intense circling, they'd lost all traces of her trail. Their circles became wider and wider until the chopper finally flew off once again in the direction of the city. Aware they could reappear at any time, she decided to take action as soon as possible, getting herself to a position of better cover and safety.

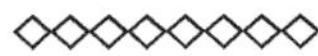

For days upon days, Jana trekked through the tall, razor sharp grass. The going was painstakingly slow as her ankle swelled to more than twice its normal size and became pure anguish to walk upon. First aid supplies, which she'd had the foresight to pack, came in handy; wrapping the injured ankle and throwing back a couple of aspirin now and then helped, though only slightly, with the intense pain.

Rationing became a necessity; the grassland didn't offer as many fresh water supplies as the forested areas, or perhaps their whereabouts were blocked from view by the blasted, hateful grass. Nevertheless, she decided to be proactive and prepare for whatever time she might be stuck in this insufferable situation.

From time to time, she could still hear the distant sound of helicopters, searching for their elusive prey, and when they drew near, she threw herself to the ground, knowing the swaying grass would offer her some protection from their prying eyes. At intervals, when the throbbing of her ankle grew bad enough to warrant it, she rested. It was distressing to have her visuals blocked by the tall grass, not knowing where the next source of danger might lay. And it was difficult to have no earthly idea where she was, but she hoped to soon be through this cursed vegetation. So far, she'd been lucky enough to avoid more contact with her slithery friends, and the rattlers hadn't bothered her again either. The mountain loomed slowly closer as her supply of protein bars and other ready foods became exhausted. Hunger would soon become a major factor in her quest.

9

Fter what seemed like a lifetime battling ten to twenty miles of "Turkey foot" grass and night after night sleeping in the detestable tangled roots, Jana noticed the vegetation beginning finally to thin a little, and she observed as it got steadily shorter that she could see her destination more clearly. This change in circumstances would make her march easier, but would also provide her with less cover. It would be imperative now that she move quickly.

She hadn't heard pursuit helicopters for half a day now and wondered if the militia squad had given up, or if they were watching her from some distant vantage point. Her struggles through the grass had left her more exhausted than ever. In addition, her hands and face throbbed with the after effects of the tiny cuts which covered all her exposed flesh. She washed her skin with fresh water and dabbed at the small wounds with antiseptic cream, but the stinging seemed to be unaffected by her medical ministrations.

Though she'd rested a bit in the grass, she'd not had any measurable amount of good sleep for some time now and knew it was essential to remain alert enough to avoid detection should the need for that arise.

Jana was hoping to make better time now that the weeds were no longer a major impediment, and though she was very hungry, food could, would have to, wait. Adrenaline coursing through her veins at the idea of imminent capture kept her motivated to move and reach the mountain's cover. There'd been too much hard work and risk expended after weeks on the run to give up, or slow down, now!

Heart pounding hard in her chest, she rounded a boulder at the base of the mountain and spied the ruins of a dilapidated farm just ahead. Limping, she crossed the barren yard to reach a hulking, rusted silo on the far side of the deserted homestead. Stepping quickly into the murky interior, she simultaneously grabbed the edge of the twisted metal door and pulled it with both hands, scraping and screeching across the cracked, up-heaved cement of the entry way threshold. She could only hope no one heard the squeal of the door being dragged shut, resonating through the still afternoon air.

With the entry nearly closed, the echoing interior swam in darkness. Jana was never known as a particularly patient person and the stress she felt as she waited for her eyes to adjust in the inky blackness caused her to examine her own level of anxiety. "Calm down, girl," she murmured under her breath, clenching her fists and fighting to control her breathing.

A stench strong enough to cause spontaneous gagging filled the musty air of the structure, and assaulted Jana with a force sufficient to churn the acids in her otherwise empty and already nauseated gut. Wondering what in the world the awful smell could be, she covered her nose with her dirty coat sleeve and battled the urge to retch. Her recently well-honed survival instincts leapt into overdrive, as she caught the sound of light scratching on the other side of the unlit chamber. Instinctively, her right hand dropped to the hilt of the hunting knife sheathed securely on her slim thigh.

Sliding her lithe body slowly against the cold galvanized steel of her shelter, she lowered her profile and made ready for anything. Partial vision returned by the time she inched her way to the cause of the noise and source of the dreadful odor. A large, currently unrecognizable, animal had wandered into the gloomy, vacant hulk to die, and a pack of emaciated rats, grateful for the easy meal, were busily feasting on its rotting carcass. Initially, the vermin didn't notice the petite girl decked out in survival gear standing behind them. Then, one curious beady-eyed creature with yellow and bloody incisors got a little too close to her hiking boot. Her kick, spontaneous and prompted by revulsion, sent it sailing into the nearby wall.

A high-pitched shriek followed by a hollow thud and silence told her this one wouldn't be bothering her again. Jana, conscious of the noise made by her impulsive action, suddenly became aware she'd been holding her breath. Giving herself a moment, she leaned against the cold steel wall to compose her thoughts and quiet her shaking frame. Oddly, she realized, she'd quickly become somewhat immune to the offensive odor.

Watching the grizzly feast with wearied detachment, she lowered her heightened defenses just long enough to allow a hint of despair, which had been lurking just out of thought's reach, to stab deeply into her anguished soul, causing her usually squared shoulders to droop forward in exhausted resignation.

How long had she been running? It was more acknowledgment than question as she knew full well the extent of her recent travels. Days and weeks melded together. Feeling temporarily overwhelmed by the events affecting her life, her slumped shoulders folded even further inward for the emotional weight they carried. But then she wondered, had her life ever really been normal? Well, except for her years with Josh, which were conventional according to the world's standards, she supposed she'd never really known a normal life. Those unspeakable things which happened long ago in her childhood came back to her now, thankfully, and regretfully, only while she slept. So much ugliness in that tortured past. She'd gladly pluck those thoughts permanently from her wounded mind if she could. Shocked awake more often than she'd like to admit, with faces and horrors she'd thought long forgotten, the only redeeming piece of this life on the run was the guaranteed fatigue which accompanied her harried existence. This breakneck pace often meant weariness so extreme it allowed her to sleep most nights without being wakened by bad dreams and the loneliness which plagued her so often in the quiet of the night.

Jana halted her contemplation long enough to wonder how close her pursuers were. Had she left them far enough behind to allow for these few stolen moments of respite, or had she overstayed already? She wouldn't let them catch her, couldn't. Deaths of so many would have been in vain and lives of so many others at risk if she didn't see this through. Suddenly, the wall of the silo where she rested began to vibrate ever so slightly against her back. Realizing she could hear it as well as feel it, a helicopter was drawing close to her refuge. Noise from the engine getting louder, letting her know without question she was trapped, like one of those foul rodents in this cold metal tomb.

The copter landed in the desolate barnyard, and immediately, the earth outside the silo thundered with the sound of boots hitting the dry cracked ground. Its engine's spinning rotor picked up dirt and gravel from the farmstead and hurled it, pelting everything in the vicinity including the shelter where Jana hid. She dropped to the cold cement floor. Through the sound of pebbles raining on metal, she heard a deep voice shouting orders, and her eyes grew huge with terror as she watched the steel door to her sanctuary begin its screeching trek across the broken cement threshold.

<h1 style="text-align:center">10</h1>

JANA HELD HER breath as the twisted, steel door began the journey across its warped concrete opening. The soldier's hand wrapped tightly around the rusted edge of the metal was pushing its way into her sanctuary, and Jana thought momentarily about unsheathing her knife and relieving him of all the fingers on his right hand.

She held back though, knowing he'd not come alone, the sounds of shouted orders and thundering boots rocked the farmyard outside, and this rational would only lead to her immediate discovery, so she stayed hunkered down in the shadows of her prison instead.

He managed to move the door only eight inches or so before he stopped. Witnessing the soldier's profile, framed by brilliant light streaming through the gap in the doorway, she saw his face screw up in disgust. "Phew! Man-o-man, it stinks in here!" He muttered under his breath.

It was ironic, but Jana barely noticed the smell anymore.

"Riley!" the soldier's superior shouted. "What've you got in the silo?"

"Nothing, Sergeant," the soldier lied, she assumed to eliminate the possibility of having to investigate the inside of the unpleasant relic further. "Silo's empty."

"Okay, men, spread out and search every square inch of this place. Scouts said they saw her come in this way, and if she isn't here, she's already up in those mountains. It's going to be a lot harder to find her in the rocks!"

What a stroke of luck that the very odor causing her so much discomfort a short while ago should be the thing to save her now! Somehow she felt again that Josh and maybe even his God were watching over her.

After the young soldier turned and walked away from her shelter, Jana crept carefully to the corroded metal door and peered through its slightly more open space, watching what she could of the scene beyond. A helicopter in the farmyard gleamed like black onyx in the bright sunlight. Its rotating propeller kicked up dirt and gravel, whipping it through the air to pelt everything within fifty feet of its makeshift landing pad, and creating a cloud of dust which would make their hunt a little bit harder. Her cover being somewhat secure, she crept back to the dark side of the space to await the outcome of her pursuer's quest.

Listening to the rhythmic tapping of tiny rocks on the side of her refuge, she watched what she could of the manic goings-on through the small space in the opening of the door from where she rested. Invisible to the soldiers, she could still witness bits and pieces of their nonexistent progress, as the squad of militia searched the premises from top to bottom. She couldn't help wondering if someone would decide to give her safe haven another look-see, so she continued to be ready for anything.

After a thorough examination of all surrounding buildings, which lasted another excruciating hour, the team was ordered to gather at the helicopter. Creeping closer to the door again, Jana listened intently, so as not to lose bits of shouted conversation in the subsequent noise of the copter's running rotor. "Men, looks like the target eluded us again," the sergeant yelled, trying to be heard over the sound of the engine, "but it has been entrusted to us to find her and recover the stolen information; and by god, recover it, we will in whatever way is necessary. I will expect all of you to keep a sharp lookout and report anything you see immediately. We must capture the suspect at all costs. The security of our operation, and of this very nation, is at stake. Now load up and let's get this job done."

Jana was dumbfounded after hearing the officer's speech. Painted by the administration and now by this commanding officer, as some sort of terrorist, she knew now she couldn't put her trust in anyone until she found the ARM encampment.

The packet of intelligence Josh had passed along proved to her positively that the government was engaged in activities which would be understood as, at the very least, extremism and a quick descent into socialism, but in her estimation, terrorism at its most insidious. She was sure they'd stop at nothing to get the information back, and she now felt the full and terrible impact of the power this information wielded.

More determined than ever to ensure the government agents heading up this chaos could no longer implement their cover-up games, she would go to any lengths necessary to get through to the resistance movement. What was it that Josh used to say about people in this country letting the government play them? Oh, yes, "Like sheep to slaughter." Well, no more. Not if she could help it.

She was completely convinced now that for all these years, her husband had been right about everything—absolutely everything! This whole experience really wasn't some obscure conspiracy theory, it was fact at its worst and most frightening. The government really and truly was out to capture her and if they did, would likely kill her; and she knew it was up to her to outwit them. With all Josh had taught her and the things she'd learned on the run, they'd have their hands full, she would see to that. They didn't have any idea with who they were messing!

11

FTER THE PM troops exited the farm, Jana speculated whether she felt safe leaving the protection, if slight, of her silo shelter. Obviously, she couldn't stay in the metal retreat forever. She needed food, and the scavenger rats would likely stay entertained only as long as the meat supplied by the rotted carcass lasted, so she had to make a decision quickly. Resting here comfortably wasn't a viable option, and she desperately needed some sleep, or she concluded, she wouldn't be able to function much longer.

The mountain was so close now, she could feel the power of its presence, and she was sure there must be places to hide in the rocks above. Was she positive the soldiers weren't parked close by, waiting for her to reveal her hiding place? Well, there was just no way to be certain. It was apparent though, with the enemy squads out publically now in full force, that society, or at least American society as she'd known it, must be truly falling apart.

Determined to wait her escape until darkness set in, she knew she'd be able to take advantage of any protection the cover of night might afford. Stomach growling loudly, she willed herself to ignore it once more, because food would again have to wait. The next hours were hard. Anxious to leave this place, she hoped she wouldn't be discovered in a vulnerable state.

As the last hint of sunlight disappeared from view through the narrow opening of the silo doorway, Jana grabbed the rusty edge of the metal opening with both hands. Being vigilant not to cut her fingers on the ragged, corroded edges, she pulled the door slowly open across the cement threshold. The screeching was much louder in the darkness than she'd remembered in the light of day, and her heart began once again to pound uncontrollably. Night seemed to magnify the sounds of her getaway, and she could only hope no one was close enough to hear.

Waiting a few moments longer, she again heard the music of crickets singing and reasoned she'd not been discovered. Feeling a bit better about her prospects of a breakout, she breathed a small sigh of relief. Cold night air flooded the acrid space quickly, bathing her face in cool relief and causing her to be even more aware of how fetid the atmosphere inside her hiding place had been throughout the past hours.

Opening the entrance wide enough to squeeze through, without causing too much bodily injury, Jana stuck her head entirely out of the expanded doorway and looked around intently. When she was fairly sure there was no imminent threat, she loaded up her gear and limped out toward the mountain breathing in the fresh air of the chilly fall evening in great marvelous gulps.

Hoping before this night was done, she would have found shelter and something to eat, especially something to eat, she marched toward her ever closer goal. Her challenge for now would be to keep her focus while she was so very tired and hungry.

Climbing the mountainside's steep rocks at night was risky, but staying out in the open would be profoundly hazardous. As she climbed, Jana's stomach growled and gnawed relentlessly at her middle, but obviously there wouldn't be much food on the sheer side of the mountain so finding cover before dawn had become her new priority. Obtaining something to sustain her hunger would have to take a back seat yet again.

Jana was making pretty good time for a city girl, especially considering she'd never done any rock climbing in her life and hadn't packed any equipment for the task. She'd been at a distinct disadvantage not seeing where Josh's map would lead her until after she'd packed supplies. Fingers and toes were her only mountaineering paraphernalia; her hands were rapidly becoming a bloody, torn mess. The soreness in her hands though was still exceeded greatly by the recurrent throbbing pain in her terribly swollen ankle.

Her only light supplied by a waxing moon, she climbed ever higher on the mountain's face as night declined. Jana could see the going might get a little easier as she maneuvered past jutting rocks and forward to the tree line up ahead. There was bound to be more level ground there and at least some degree of useable cover which she could claim for the night once she reached the ledge. Finally reaching the tree lined ridge she'd spied earlier in the evening, she pulled herself over the rock ledge and onto level ground. Unloading her heavy pack, she stopped to survey her surroundings; breathing deeply to fill her lungs with crisp nighttime air and catching a much needed second wind. With minimal lighting, she could see only the outlines of several rocky outcroppings which might prove to be promising hiding places.

The silence of a cold, still night was suddenly broken by a low rumbling growl from somewhere behind her. Jana whipped around, ducking to the right, just as the crouching mountain lion flew through the air; gleaming eyes, lit by the moon, it's only visible feature in the near blackness of night. Fangs bared and claws extended, the predator clamped down on Jana's shoulder as girl and cat rolled on the ground, a blur of hair and fur in the dimly lit night. Those killer teeth had been aimed at her left jugular, but her instinctive duck to the right saved her life for now. The pain was white hot and her left arm fell immediately, all but useless at her side. Instinctively, her right hand struggled for the hilt of the knife at her hip. Pulling the blade, she thrust up and to the left in one continuous motion. Jerking her arm over, she managed to pull out a rope of feline intestines along with her knife; the cat screamed and collapsed limply on top of her shaking form.

In death, the mountain lion jaws loosened from Jana's shoulder, and as they did, her bleeding began in earnest. She lay for a few moments on the hard ground, in the cold night air, gasping for breath. Blood soaked her jacket as she felt the warmth of it leaving her body; the smell cloying and coppery in her nostrils. How much of the blood was hers and how much belonged to the cat, she couldn't be sure, but she presumed her light head could be a good indicator, and she rationalized if she was losing that much blood, she would need to move quickly to repair her injury. So, pushing the flaccid animal off her small body, Jana grabbed her gear and stumbled, lurching with all her remaining strength to the nearest rock outcropping.

Finding a small opening at the base of the boulders, she pulled out her flashlight and crawled, shaking, through the hole to a tiny interior cave. Inside, she held the flashlight in her mouth and pulled out her first aid kit. Sweating profusely and feeling faint, nauseous, and seriously dizzy, she pulled her shirt over her head and opened her canteen to pour water over the bloody shoulder in an attempt to rinse it clean. She shivered from the combination of cold air and a shocked system.

The area where the lion's teeth had ravaged her shoulder was pumping blood at a fairly steady rate. Jana retrieved a bottle of hydrogen peroxide from her pack and gingerly splashed it over her wounds. Stinging pain sent lightning flashes through her eyes and into her skull. Turning her blood soaked shirt inside out, she used the driest part of the fabric to wipe the wound and to apply pressure staunching at least some of the blood flow.

Digging further through the open first aid kit, she found what she was looking for. Twisting the cap off the vial of yellow powder, she dusted it liberally over the affected area and leaned weakly against the cold rock wall behind her. The sulfur powder began to staunch the bleeding a little more and the panic which had filled her, since she'd turned to see fangs flying through the air at her throat, began to subside at least minimally.

Now that the blood flow had slowed a bit, Jana was determined to properly clean and dress the wound; with that intent in mind, she pulled cotton balls and gauze from her kit. Injuries left behind by the cat were deep puncture wounds, and as far as she could tell, stitches wouldn't be of much use. So, soaking the cotton with water from her canteen, she began the painstaking job of swabbing the blood from her arm and torso to get a better idea of damage done in the attack.

Teeth chattering so hard she feared they might crack, she pulled her bloody jacket up to ward against some of the cold. The cat's fangs had penetrated deep into the muscle, but the sheer bulk of Jana's padded jacket—perhaps she was glad she hadn't purchased the thin microfiber one after all—had lessened the depth of their permeation somewhat. She couldn't detect any broken bones, which was a plus, as she continued to mentally assess her own injuries. Applying more sulfur to the wound, she then wrapped the affected area tightly with sterile gauze from her kit.

Finally, she pulled a clean shirt from her pack and drew it gently over her head and bandaged shoulder. Counting out four aspirin from her depleting stores, she downed them with a long pull on the canteen. As exhaustion overtook her, tears flowed unchecked down her cheeks leaving zigzag tracks through the dirt and remaining traces of blood on her face. She found herself silently thanking Josh that she was alive, still believing he was watching over her. Covering her torso with the bloodstained sticky jacket and wrapping up as well as she was able in her sleeping bag and tarp, she folded herself into a fetal position and drifted off. Curled up like an infant, Jana rocked herself back and forth in the blackness of the cold, dark cave until the sleep, which she had managed to elude for days, finally had its way with her.

Once again, as in so many dark nights of her past, nightmares flooded her restless sleep. In those black dreams, she was a little girl again, hiding from foster parents who'd beaten her and running endlessly, ceaselessly from the man who'd been assigned by the courts as her protector, who instead of defending her used his position to do unspeakable things to her.

In her sleep, she fought the fat, filthy hand which covered her mouth, her nose, and her screams as it all but cut off her air supply. Twisting and turning, she tried in desperation to escape the fetid, alcohol-laden breath which came in grunts and gasps on the back of her neck until its owner collapsed on top of her. In her nightmares, she struggled to go back to her safe place—the place her young mind had created so long ago to cope with life since the untimely death of her grandmother.

Jana woke, flailing, gasping for air, to the sound of her own screams echoing back in the small cave. Clothes, and sleeping bag, drenched in sweat, even in the cold, murky, void; she had no idea how long she'd been asleep. Woozy and disoriented, nausea overwhelmed her as she sat up, causing her to retch. Though, with nothing in her stomach for so long now, the retching became dry heaves and then deep racking sobs. She heard and then smelled the rain falling outside the small cave and was grateful at least she had a roof over her head.

Flipping on her flashlight, she wanted to get a look at her aching shoulder and gently pulled off her shirt. Her arm was stiff and sore. Peeling gauze from the crusty wound, she was struck immediately by the putrid smell emanating from the deep, penetrating injury. Shining her light on the damaged shoulder, she tried to assess the situation as best she could. The angry swollen, red wound was of great concern, as she had no doubt now the area was infected. Getting things under control before contamination could spread, thereby doing even more damage, would be critical. First though, she needed some food and supplies. These needs were things which would cause her to necessarily leave the protection of the small cave.

Loading belongings into her backpack, she rolled up her sleeping bag and tarp and crawled unsteadily out into the semi-light of the mountain ledge. Rain still drizzled from a slate grey sky, and Jana was left not knowing what time of day it might be. The carcass of the marauding cat had been picked almost clean by scavengers, and any blood from the attack had been washed away in the ensuing shower, this all lead her to believe she'd probably been asleep for much more than a day, perhaps even two.

This summation was evidenced by the fact that she suddenly realized she was witnessing a sunrise on her exit from the cavern, and not a sunset. She'd probably never know exactly how long she'd slept, or how much time had elapsed, but she couldn't let her goals be thwarted by the circumstances of her attack and injury, no matter their severity. Her hunger had reached starvation proportions, so something needed to be done about finding food and water before she could adequately take care of anything else.

Once she ventured outside the cave, she realized air temperatures had dipped lower than before her climb up the mountain began. Some of which she was sure could be accredited to the increased elevation, but that wasn't the whole of the situation. Time was slipping away to winter, and as she made her way up the massif, it would get steadily higher, steadily later, and steadily colder.

Her jacket, which was not much protection before her attack, was woefully useless now. Dried blood stiffened the fabric and fl attened the insulating material, so it rubbed and pinched now under and around her wounded shoulder. Pulling a sweatshirt out of her backpack in an effort to make do in a difficult situation, she reasoned she had several more sweatshirts and T-shirts, and perhaps layering them would keep her warmer. Jana's remaining strength was quickly waning for lack of food. She'd lost a substantial amount of blood, and it would take care and nutrition to get her body back to some semblance of normal now.

Rain stopped, and a pair of red squirrels danced down a nearby tree, searching for pine nuts to add to their winter store. Jana's instinct for survival kicked in. She reached slowly and steadily for the hilt of her hunting knife and sent it flying so suddenly, she surprised even herself. Her aim was perfect, and her prey never felt a thing. Years of target practice with her husband had apparently stayed with her, and she evidently wasn't as rusty as she'd thought she might be. Josh always told her she was a natural.

Jana unrolled the tarp that had covered her sleeping bag and began to load pieces of wood for a fire. She knew she should be using dry wood to avoid a smoking fire, which might give her position away to anyone who was still searching for her, but dry wasn't an option after the recent rain.

A small nearby mountain stream would provide water to boil for sterilization and for making a sustaining broth. She made quick work of cleaning the squirrel, something she'd never done before. She wouldn't win any prizes for the neatness of her work, not even rookie prizes; but the fur was removed from the outside and the entrails were removed from the inside so it would do. She'd never tasted squirrel before, but thought, in her current ravenous state, she might eat just about anything which was no longer moving.

Dragging the loaded tarp behind her and erasing her tracks as best she could with the sweeping motions of a fallen pine branch, she examined several potential hiding places. After a minor search, she found a cave which would fit her purposes for now.

Inside the cave, she saw it came furnished with a nice level ledge where she could build a sleeping pallet. When covered with pine boughs, it could gratefully afford a little protection from the colder stone floor. On the far side of the cavern, she noted a hole in the ceiling which would allow excess smoke from her fire to vent out and away from the entrance to her little hiding place. She unloaded her tarp in the cave and set out to get the rest of her safe house in useable order.

Filling her canteen, water bottles, and one of her collapsible cooking pots with water from the nearby small stream, she then gathered enough rocks to make a satisfactory fire ring. Cutting abundant pine boughs to create a comfortable sleeping pallet on the stone ledge and extra to camouflage the entrance of the small cavern, she also took time to shave a large pile of kindling to use in her fire-starting endeavors.

Back inside her hiding place, Jana constructed a stone circle and worked on starting a small fire using her flint and steel with a pile of slightly damp tinder. The process, which she'd achieved over and over in her camping trips with Josh, took much longer than she imagined it would since she was using moist kindling in her efforts, and she was completely exhausted by the time she finally had things well on their way.

As her kindling caught, she added wood until there was a good, though smoky, blaze going. Placing the recently cleaned squirrel into a pot of boiling water along with a good amount of salt, pepper, and dried soup vegetables from her backpack, she moved on to other chores. The smell of food cooking caused her saliva glands to jump into overdrive. Hunger was severely cramping her stomach, so she grew more aware she needed to get some of the soup into her system before she attended to any of her other circumstances.

Jana didn't think she'd ever been so famished. Even as a foster child, she'd been fed at least once a day by the worst of her long line of temporary families. With her ready-made foods exhausted, it'd been days since she'd partaken of even meager rations since she'd had no access to fire and water supplies. When the soup was finished, she pulled pieces of meat off the small bones, savoring each morsel and licking her fingers after every bite. Thirsty as well, she'd been forced to ration her water for several days before ascending the mountain, and now that she had sufficient supplies, she intended to make good use of them. If she'd not been so voracious, the idea of eating squirrel might have been revolting, but at this moment, she would swear nothing ever tasted so wonderful.

After eating her fill, she realized she'd need nourishment for later, so she broke the small cooked bones of the squirrel, exposing the delicate marrow, and put them back in the pot. Then, refilling her pot with extra cold water from the stream and adding some seasonings from her pack, she put the concoction back over the fire to simmer for a future meal. With her broth on the fire, Jana checked to see that she had sufficient liquid in her second pot and then topped off canteens and water bottles with enough of the lifesaving fluid to tide her over for a while. Placing more fuel on the fire, she also piled wood close to her pallet to assure easy access after her emergency surgery procedure was complete.

Stacking fir branches inside, at the cave opening, she stepped back to examine her work and felt she'd now be more protected and even better hidden from the possibility of prying eyes. Then, with dizziness once again engulfing her aching head, she decided things were prepared enough to begin the next essential task; she secured her knife, hydrogen peroxide, alcohol, some additional sulfur powder, a needle and sutures, soap, and aspirin from her supplies. What she planned to do would test her to her limits, but it was also the only thing that might save her from the infection, which would most certainly kill her if not halted.

Getting ready to begin, she put the clean pot of water to heat on the fire and took a roll of gauze from her kit. Soaking the gauze in boiling water, she added powdered soap to the rough material. She put the blade of her knife into the rapidly boiling water to sterilize it, and placing a stick in her mouth, she pulled the clean knife from the pot into the waiting alcohol and then plunged the metal point of her weapon deep into the infected puncture wounds of her shoulder. Making a deep cut between the puncture wounds to assure proper cleaning of the contaminated area, she almost screamed out loud in anguish.

Sweat beaded on her brow as she bit hard on the wood between her teeth. Dropping her knife to the floor of the cave and using that hand now to squeeze the infected area, she was both disgusted and shocked by the amount of puss and pollution which flowed from the swollen, inflamed wound. She found herself on the verge of vomiting, or passing out, on several occasions during the procedure. When she was satisfied with the blood to puss ratio of the discharge, she shakily picked up the soapy gauze and scrubbed her shoulder and surrounding tissues until the hurt caused stinging tears to run freely from her eyes. The whole excruciating procedure made her feel even more nauseous than she'd felt previously.

After rinsing the affected region free of soap, she sewed the wound. Struggling with each thrust of the needle and grimacing in discomfort as she pulled each stitch tight, she realized after her needlework was finished, she'd been holding her breath through most of the process. Taking a series of trembling breaths to steady herself, she used a clean shirt to pat her skin dry and sprinkled a generous amount of first, hydrogen peroxide and then, sulfur powder over the entire area.

With fever still raging through her body and the soreness of her ministrations still fresh in her mind and shoulder, she broke down and cried for a good long time. Then she downed four aspirin with water and escaped into a fevered, fitful slumber. Jana spent the next few days fighting a rampant, high temperature which left her delirious, spinning in and out of the world. She was vaguely aware of throwing wood on the fire and sipping water from her canteen, or tasting small bits of broth, from her semi-prone position. But battling the fever took every bit of the energy left in her body.

Her broth was soon gone, and she would need more nourishment again, but for now, she could only rest. In her weakened state, her body would not allow for anything more.

Waking refreshed for the first time in weeks, Jana knew immediately something was different. The cave was cold, but her eyes felt clear. She realized at once her fever was gone, because her head no longer ached. Attempting to rise, she found she was still weak as a kitten, but all signs of the infection, which had ravaged her body for days, appeared to be gone. Sitting on the edge of her pallet, she looked toward her extinguished fire and decided as soon as she could stand without passing out, she would have to do something about that.

Picking up her canteen told her it was empty, and since water would be essential throughout this healing process, that situation too would need rectifying immediately. Of course, this would require her to venture outside not only to fill her water containers, but to search once again for food. Her journey to find ARM could not continue until her strength was rebuilt, but thankfully, she was growing more resourceful every day and would live, at least for now. She prayed to Josh and thanked him for taking care of her. Perhaps he'd interceded with his God for her. If that was true, then she was truly grateful to both of them.

12

WEEKS ALONE IN her cave sanctuary had flown by so quickly, but Jana managed to keep herself quite comfortable all the while. Definitely feeling better about her ability to take care of her personal needs than she might have believed possible even a couple of months ago, she was actually a bit proud of herself. Looking back on the habits of her previous life, she doubted she would have imagined herself here in this place and doing so well in this rough and rustic setting.

The small cave seemed a bit like home now, safe and familiar. She'd not been discovered by her pursuers, at least as far as she knew, and she'd turned out to be a very good hunter and provider even in spite of all her injuries. Growing more adept each day at using her knife, her bow, and her fishing pole, she had no problems at all filling her soup pot, even managing to bring in enough additional meat (squirrels, rabbits, and fish) to smoke and pack away for future use.

Dried meats would be a great alternative to fresh, if conditions were not safe for hunting or lighting a fire. Jana was also doing quite a bit of reading through her survival book and managed to recognize and dig up many edible roots and tubers. Collecting pine nuts, seeds, herbs, and berries, she'd rounded out her larder nicely. Additionally, the vast treasure of honey she found in a dead log hadn't cost her anything but a few stings, and she filled several of her previously emptied trail mix containers with the liquid gold. She was feeling inordinately delighted about her newfound abilities, and soups had gotten much more interesting with the addition of root vegetables and fresh herbs collected from her environment.

Creatively using a deep depression in the floor on the back side of her cave, she'd lined the space with her waterproof tarp and filled her tub with several pots of boiling water and several more of fresh water until the bathtub's temperature was perfect. Amazed at her own resourcefulness, she washed and rinsed her hair and scrubbed her skin till it was positively pink. Washing her clothing next, she did her best to get blood out of the shirt and jacket she'd been wearing during the cat attack, though her jacket didn't respond well to the attention.

Extensive exercising in the privacy of her shelter continued doing a great deal to rebuild her strength and stamina, and she'd been working on flexibility for her ankle and shoulder. This time, when she left the protection of her sanctuary, she'd be better prepared than she'd felt since leaving civilization.

Temperatures though were getting steadily colder, and she was becoming more aware daily that she needed to head out before snow on the mountain became a bigger threat. During her period of healing in the cave, Jana spent hours reading through Josh's Bible, letters, and the papers which were stored in the green canister. When she first entered the small hiding place weeks ago, she'd been filled with fear, but she felt somehow safer now than she did before, for all the information she'd accumulated. Believing to be far from any curious, listening ears, Jana also began turning on her radio for the first time since leaving the city.

What she heard on the news, once she cleared up most of the static, shook her. The world as she'd known it was indeed in shambles. Martial law was the rule of the land, and the People's Militia was definitely no longer working in the shadows, just as she'd feared would be the case.

The president's goon squads were widely deployed now and accepted, by much of the country's population, as the only acceptable means of policing the general populace. A force to be reckoned with and growing exponentially, the militia answered only to the White House; nullifying any remaining authority of all other police and military organizations, just as Josh had tried to warn her, would be the case from the beginning.

Jana was positive the ruse which was being perpetrated on America was indeed a con. But they were actually getting away with it. How could an entire people be hoodwinked so easily? Well, she had to admit she'd been duped by the same lies until very recently. It was easy to accept the status quo when you didn't have the will to change it for yourself. It angered her though to see an entire nation, other than that small percentage that formed ARM be as gullible as to turn over their very freedoms to an arrogant dictator.

By giving more authority to the militia, the administration was increasing its own vast reserves of power daily. Again, "leading sheep to slaughter" as it were, while also making people feel they were safer and more secure under the thumb of this regime than they'd been before socialism began its evil stranglehold; and all of it happening just as her husband had so often predicted it would. The hoax had been laid out so perfectly no one had seen it coming, except for those in the resistance movement, and no one had been listening to them not even Jana herself, until lately.

Main line media usually tended to ignore stories which didn't agree with their own liberal, political views, but even their collective reports sounded most dire as time went on, and the administration's thugs openly walked the streets now as judge, jury, and enforcement squad. Listening to newscasts, she discovered many pastors of conservative churches around the country had been arrested for hate speech and for inciting unrest among the people.

Their crime seemed to be that they were using Bible scripture in their sermons. Their churches were ultimately taken from them and were now closed, which was causing even more unrest among the people and resulted in even stricter government control. Around and around they go, she thought. "Can't these people see what they are up against? And how they are being manipulated right into the administration's trap?" she wondered out loud. But she hadn't seen it either. Not until she'd been backed into a proverbial corner. Even though she might never be mistaken for one of those all out, Bible thumping, Jesus freaks, she still knew it was wrong to tell people they couldn't pray to whatever god they wanted, or tell them they couldn't quote out of their own holy books. How could any of this be constitutionally right, or even remotely okay in any one's sensibilities? Even liberals had to see that stripping American's rights and freedom wasn't okay, didn't they?

Growing angry with herself for allowing so much time to pass here in her sanctuary before getting back to the task at hand, she was riddled with guilt and condemnation. Conversely though, she reasoned her pursuers might think her long gone or even dead by now, and she would have a greater chance of avoiding detection after such a lengthy absence from their radar. Soon she'd discover the answers to all her questions and more, and she felt a sense of excitement to be on her way.

Reorganizing her supplies, Jana determined to get herself and her backpack ready for tomorrow's departure from the cave. Building up the diminishing fire to warm her small space, she laid freshly washed jeans and shirts on rocks, surrounding the blaze, to dry. She had lots of empty containers, which were previously used to hold her foodstuffs from home; and now those, which didn't hold honey, were filled with dried meats and the assorted nuts, seeds, roots, and dried berries she'd collected throughout her past weeks of isolation and recuperation. It would be getting too cold to forage pretty soon, so the food stuffs would be invaluable for preparation of well-balanced meals. Weather conditions were pushing toward winter. And though she would still find herbs and tubers for a while, most of the berries were past their seasons now.

Newly washed hair, which had grown longer over the past long weeks since her departure from civilization, was tied in a pony tail to keep it up and out of her face. Jana didn't have a mirror, but she'd seen her reflection in the water on occasion, and she was sure no one who'd known her at the store would recognize her if they saw her today. Tanned and toned with a gleam of confidence in her eye, she looked the part of a mountain woman.

Sorting through her first aid kit was a more depressing prospect. No way to replenish the stores of gauze, hydrogen peroxide, sulfur powder, and aspirin, which were almost depleted, she would have to figure out a way to make do. "Well, I'll just have to avoid mountain lions and large, root clumps at all costs," she said with a chuckle, "and join up with ARM soon!"

Slowly sharpening the blade of her knife by firelight brought it back to its previous well-honed state. Her knife had been a blessing, but she knew there might be some situations coming up which would require a different sort of protection. Choosing to be prepared for the worst, she pulled her handgun from the bottom of the pack. Turning it over and over in her hands to remind herself of its weight and dimensions, she knew it was time to add the gun to her daily wear, so digging a box of shells from the front pouch of her backpack, she loaded the gun and filled her front jean pockets with additional shells for easier access in emergency. She donned the gun's shoulder holster and adjusted its strap for maximum comfort and ease of reach. The pistol fit snugly in its holster, and the weight against her chest felt good, safe even.

Her old jacket had certainly seen better days. She'd done her best to clean it up, but nothing revived it. With dried blood matting and flattening the insulation, it was worse than useless and would probably prove to be just one more bulky thing to carry around, so she chose to leave it behind. Several layered sweatshirts and T-shirts could create enough insulation to keep her moderately warm, and she would just have to keep moving to help her metabolism burn hotter until she could build a fire each evening.

Finding shelter each night to set up a camp would continue to be imperative. A shelter would mean she could cook and have some protection from wild animals, precipitation, and wind while she slept. It would also mean she could live without a coat a little longer, at least until the winter snows came. Hoping to save as many of her dried foods as possible for emergency situations, cooking each evening and morning would be the optimal choice. Perhaps she wouldn't need emergency supplies at all, but who could guess what she might run into, she'd prefer to be safe rather than sorry in any case.

Hoping to find the resistance group soon, she'd be able to replenish her supplies then if she needed to. Her map showed the ARM encampment on this side of the mountain, but at an elevation much higher than where she was currently residing.

During her time in the cavern, she'd heard faint pounding noises from somewhere high on the monolith. Noises, which at times reverberated through the very floor and walls of her hiding place; the sounds began early in the day, and she'd been wakened throughout her recovery on several occasions. The thought that her destination might be very close now was reassuring. The sooner the better, so she could be rid of the canister of information which kept her a hunted woman. Just to know she'd completed the task Josh requested of her—to get the data into the right hands—would be a huge weight off her shoulders.

One more meal in the cave and a good night's sleep should prepare her better for the journey ahead. Jana stepped to the opening of her shelter as the sun was beginning its evening descent behind the mountain. A cold twilight sky was stained with the remaining pinks and reds of a stunning sunset. Hidden behind the branches she'd placed there weeks ago to help obscure the cave's opening, she could see without being seen. In a matter of only a few moments, a pair of large rabbits scampered into the clearing just beyond her sanctuary. She threw her knife so skillfully her prey was dead before it hit the ground, and its mate bounded quickly out of sight.

Events of these last weeks had honed her skills under very adverse conditions, and she had her supper skinned, gutted, and skewered in a matter of minutes. Roasted rabbit would be a nice change from the soup, which had been her staple through the long illness, and an added bonus was she wouldn't have to clean and stow the soup pot again.

Scrubbing and peeling several small tubers, she placed them on a flat rock, nearest the blaze, to bake while she seasoned and turned the sizzling rabbit. The aroma of roasting hare caused her mouth to fill with saliva, and she took a drink from her canteen to calm the acids churning in her stomach. She'd steadily grown to enjoy the taste of rabbit and squirrel and even a rattlesnake was a welcome treat, though the latter was becoming harder to find as the temperatures dropped.

Supper crackled on the spit, and while Jana waited, she lifted her shirt and examined her shoulder, checking on the progress of the still healing wound there. The redness was completely gone, as well as the stitches, but she knew the tenderness meant the muscle was still recovering. And though she would have some eternal evidence of her run-in with the lion, all was looking pretty good. Her ankle was still a little swollen and sore, but if she kept it wrapped and remained as careful as possible, she thought it might be okay for the upcoming trek.

Eating every bit of the succulent, roasted rabbit, she licked grease from her fingers one-by-one. The tubers were tender and sweet, and she patted her stomach in satisfaction as she finished eating her final meal in the cave which had been her home through a difficult time. Moving her pack nearer the fire, she could use it as a backrest for reading before getting some shut eye. Staying up late wasn't an option though, as she planned to leave at first light.

Scratching sounds woke her in the night. From her sleeping pallet across the cave, she saw fire reflected in glowing eyes. A wolf, crouching near the cave opening with teeth bared, was close enough to reach her with one powerful lunge if not for the meager barricade. She could hear the low rumbling growl from where she lay, and the hair on her body stood on end.

Pine boughs were a deterrent, but she had no doubt, if the fire had gone out, she would have had a hairy, snarling visitor in the cavern.

Rising to her elbow, she picked up a nearby rock. She knew she'd have only one shot as she hurled the stone. Her aim was true, and she heard a loud crack as the projectile connected with bone. Immediately, the low growl turned to a high-pitched yelp fading to a whimper. Quickly adding more wood to the fire in hopes it would deter her uninvited guest, she pulled her gun from the gear which was already loaded for departure the next morning.

Though she could see several shapes skulking back and forth in front of the cave opening for most of the night, the predators didn't attempt to cross the threshold of her refuge past the barricade of pine boughs and blazing fire.

Lingering aromas from her meal more than likely attracted the wolves, and she made a mental note to bury all her garbage from now on. Only half sleeping, holding the loaded revolver at her chest, the remainder of her night was spent keeping one eye open and her fire burning. By daybreak, the wolf pack had moved on to more promising prey, and as Jana removed the boughs from her doorway, she checked the area thoroughly to be sure she had a clear path from the cave.

13

J ANA'S DESTINATION LOOMED high before her, and now with her health much improved and daylight on her side, she was able to assess the situation more clearly. The incline, from what she was able to deduce, was very steep, but appeared to be comprised of a series of sheer, jagged walls intersected by flat ledges all the way up the side of the mountain at intervals of about 150 to 200 feet. At her current elevation, the side of the mount she could see looked oddly like giant porch steps. Jana knew above her, somewhere, ARM was encamped and would offer her sanctuary, but she would have to find them first. Climbing and hiking all day breaking only to stay hydrated, eat lunch, and get her bearings, she scaled the wall to each successive ledge as it came and as carefully as her injured ankle would allow her.

Water sources she'd depended upon while in the cavern originated somewhere high on the mountain, and she was able to find trickling tributaries all along her arduous path which fed into that same stream. At least she wouldn't be at risk of dehydration on her trek up the behemoth!

Evening came, shadows gathered, and she knew it was time again to find shelter for the oncoming night. Wildlife abounded on the mountain, as she was all too aware, and she should have a fire going before the nighttime predators ventured out. When she located another small cave, which seemed to suit her purposes, she filled her canteen and her cooking pot and quickly gathered enough branches and kindling to get her through the night.

Supper that evening consisted of stew made with dried meat, tubers, and herbs; finished off with reconstituted berries and nuts. After washing her cooking pot, Jana cleaned herself up a bit and laid out her bedroll. The fire was bright enough to read by, and she fell asleep with Josh's Bible in her arms as had become her new nightly custom.

While she slept, Jana dreamed. This time though, for the first time in years, her dreams were not the horrid nightmares she'd come to expect and dread. Her sleeping mind's eye was filled to overflowing with visions of beautiful valleys, vibrant wildflowers of every size and color imaginable. Off in the distance, she made out the figures of two men and knew instinctively one of them was Josh. She ran to catch them, almost skipping through the field, and as her body collided with Josh's larger, more muscular one, he swept her off her feet in his powerful arms, swinging her around and around in a tight embrace. A tear rolling down her glowing face dropped, and she watched it fall to the ground in ultra slow motion. As she looked into her husband's countenance, she knew in her heart she was home.

When he set her on her feet again, she spun around to be introduced to the second man and realized he was no longer there. When she turned questioningly to Josh, he shook his head and said, "The time has not yet come, my love." Jana, wondering what Josh's final remark meant, found herself dragged from her dream to the edge of consciousness. Even in sleep, she knew in her soul she didn't want to wake. Imagining she could still smell his cologne, feel his gentle hands, and his strong arms caused her heart to ache all over again with the pain of missing him.

He'd seemed so alive in her dream and his embrace so comforting. She felt, even as she woke, like the grieving widow from several months ago. When she opened her eyes and confirmed with herself she was still in the same small cave, she lay solemnly watching the flickering firelight against the drop of her stone fire ring until daylight wandered lazily through the cavern opening. Rising, she added more wood to the fire, in preparation for her morning meal, all the while with the tears she'd been crying in her sleep still wet on her cheeks.

Proceeding to roll up her bed and throw together a breakfast of coffee, nuts, and dried berries to calm her stomach, she began packing up her few belongings and crawled out of the small grotto to meet the new day. Immediately, struck by the cold, quiet morning air, she dug through her pack for an additional shirt to add to her layers. Time was running out, if she was going to find ARM before snow began to fly, which would make her journey exponentially more difficult.

Climbing and hiking throughout the day, Jana felt a new and pervading sense of sadness over the loss of her husband and was trying to shake off the disquiet when she noticed the sound of gunfire higher on the mountain. *Is that the ARM encampment?* she wondered under her breath. Those sounds of gunshot appeared to come from a point on the mountain, if one considered her current traveling speed, perhaps a day and a half or two days journey from her present position. Puzzled at the sound, due to her own perceived need for secrecy on behalf of the ARM base, she suddenly had unsettling feelings about what she might find at the top of the mountain after all.

Wouldn't they be subject to being hunted by the same soldiers who'd become the bane of her own existence? But she thought perhaps they were conducting target practice and certainly they must post guards and have a sense of the distance of their enemies. Or, perhaps she'd come farther than she knew; maybe those enemy soldiers had given up on her and gone home by now. If that were the case, ARM would know of their position and would feel comfortable training more openly. She could only hope and pray that was the case.

How odd the word pray would enter her mind, though it seemed to be happening more lately. But she shook her head and dismissed the thought. This was not the time or place to be thinking about anything other than her immediate goal of getting up the mountain to safety.

Another evening and another small cave presented themselves. Jana was so exhausted she didn't bother to try cooking. Some dried meat and water served as a light meal and with her fire built and extra wood sitting by to add throughout the night, she read for a few minutes and fell quickly off to sleep.

Dreaming again, she saw the same beautiful valley filled with flowers of every description. She looked expectantly for Josh and saw, again, two men in the distance. Running, she leapt into her husband's arms and again felt and tasted salty tears running unchecked down her face. Again, Josh swung her round and round as she reveled in the feeling of warmth and safety filling her while she was held secure in his embrace. Once again, she turned to be introduced to the other man, and for a second time, he was gone. Turning to Josh, she questioned, with a look, the disappearance of the man, and once again, Josh spoke saying, "No, my love, the time has not yet come."

Waking again, in time to meet the dawn, she packed more slowly and then opened her Bible. The pages fell open to Psalm 30, and she read:

I will exalt You, Lord, because you have lifted me up and have not allowed my enemies to triumph over me. Lord my God, I cried to You for help, and You healed me. Lord, You brought me up from Sheol; You spared me from among those going down to the Pit. Sing to the Lord, you His faithful ones, and praise His holy name. For His anger lasts only a moment, but His favor, a lifetime. Weeping may spend the night, but there is joy in the morning. When I was secure, I said, "I will never be shaken." Lord, when You showed Your favor, You made me stand like a strong mountain; when You hid Your face, I was terrified. Lord I called to You; I sought favor from my Lord: What gain is there in my death, in my descending to the Pit? Will the dust praise You? Will it proclaim Your truth? Lord, listen and be gracious to me; Lord, be my helper.

You turned my lament into dancing; You removed my sackcloth and clothed me with gladness, so that I can sing to You and not be silent. Lord my God, I will praise You forever.

How marvelous that Josh's Bible opened to that very comforting Psalm! As she read, she felt strengthened, connected somehow in a way she'd never felt before. She could very well have been the author of these verses for the situation which the author described was the very one she faced now. The passages spoke to her, and for the first time in her life, she knew she was on the verge of some eternal truth, something much bigger than any individual person, time, or circumstance. More questions and hopefully, in time, more answers would come to her and help to set her spirit free.

A smile touched her lips, and she found she couldn't contain her gladness as she picked up her belongings and packed her bag. Knowing the world and the People's Militia wasn't going away didn't seem to matter much anymore. She would figure it out, and in some strange way, she knew Josh and maybe even his Jesus would be there to help. And, she thought, for the first time in memory the idea of Jesus being there wasn't so objectionable.

Getting closer now to the source of the noise above her, Jana figured by tomorrow she might reach the ARM camp. Another arduous day left her exhausted and shelter for this night, in lieu of anything better, would be little more than a deep indentation in a large boulder. Darkness might bring unwanted visitors yet she didn't dare light a fire, for fear of drawing undue attention to herself from possible human sources. Knowing the night would get very cold very fast, she layered on every T-shirt and sweatshirt from her bag, wrapping one of the sweatshirts tightly around her head and neck to protect her ears.

Curling into a fetal position in her sleeping bag and holding her Bible and pistol both close to her chest, she fell into a fitful sleep.

Once again, she dreamed, and for the third time, she was in the same lovely valley filled with the identical breathtaking array of flowers. Again she looked in excited anticipation for the figures of the two men, whom she knew would be there in the distance. Once she spied Josh she ran full tilt into her husband's embrace. Eyes filled with tears of joy, she hugged him tightly, imagining once again that she could physically feel his protective loving arms around her. But this time, when she opened the eyes of her dream self and looked up into his face, it wasn't the face of her husband at all. Not in her husband's arms, but securely in the arms of Jesus, she looked awestruck into His wonderful face as He said, "The time has come." As if transported on a bolt of lightning, she was suddenly awake right back on the mountain ledge gasping for air and reaching for, whom? She lay looking at the starry sky for what seemed an eternity before finally drifting off to sleep, until dawn's early light peeked over the nearby ledge.

Waking, shivering in the bitter cold, to faint streaks of pink in a morning sky, Jana faced a new day filled with more courage and resolve than ever. She knew her destiny was laid out before her, and she was about to walk into the plan for her life. Jana wasn't sure what the man in her dream—the man she was sure was Jesus—meant, but she realized deep within her being He loved her and had a design for her existence. No one had told her any of this, but she knew, somehow, He was the God of the universe, and He had everything under control. Jana also knew there was something out there she was meant to figure out, and she would—she knew she would—with His help.

But she also knew now, also without being told, that it was Jesus who'd been watching over her, not Josh. And she knew He wouldn't leave her, not for anything, ever. That knowledge was more filled with life and comfort than anything she'd ever known before. If only Josh were here to share this miracle with her.

14

JANA SPENT THE whole of that day once again climbing and hiking, and while she traversed the mountain, she held a quiet conversation with God. Pleasantly surprised at how easy He was to talk to, she poured her heart out. She'd never known before what a friend and comfort He could be. She couldn't help but notice a gradual change in her own thinking toward a God who had deemed it fit to enter her life through her own unsuspecting dreams. It seemed He was reaching out to her in a way she'd never expected and she had to admit probably the only way her mind would have been entirely opened to Him.

Their conversation was interrupted though as she drew nearer to the place she suspected was the ARM encampment she'd been searching for. As she inched ever closer to her goal, she noticed the noise she'd heard, reverberating through the ground much farther down the mount, was considerably louder as she gained a nearer perspective. At regular intervals now, the ground shook with a deep and persistent pounding in the bedrock which almost took her breath away in its frightening determination. The consistent, hammering noise, which came from probably one, or possibly two, ledges above her now, was broken intermittently with the disquieting sound of rapid gunfire. The gunshots tended to immediately and for a noticeable time afterward silence all natural sounds of life on the great mountainous peak as if birds too were frightened to sing.

Day was wearing on as, exhausted, Jana rounded a clump of scrubby, low growing pine trees in her search for a better way up onto the mountain's next ledge. On the other side of the trees, she was halted in her tracks and shocked to her depths, for standing in her path was a huge, snarling, lone wolf with teeth bared in an eerie foaming grin. Jana tried to take in as much detail as she was able as quickly as possible.

Appearing badly wounded, blood matted the wolf's fur on the right shoulder and side. If it lunged at her, it would most likely lunge left. The whites of its eyes weren't white at all, but deepest bloodshot red and she also noted thick lather dripping from its muzzle, so in all likelihood it was rabid. Never actually having seen a rabid animal before she figured that would likely be a good summation. Trying to remain calm, she took a deep breath as her hand went slowly to the holster snap on her chest. And gently sliding the gun from its pocket, she pointed it at the wolf's head just as the beast crouched down preparing to pounce.

The wolf lunged left as she'd predicted. Her shot rang out loud and echoed throughout the mountainside as the bullet entered the predator's right eye. The animal dropped to the ground still growling, and she followed the first shot with a second to its twitching head. Still shaking, she knew she'd done them both a favor, but wondered how many might have heard her shots. Had she given herself away? Well, she would be arriving at the ARM camp by this evening, so they would meet her soon anyway.

As afternoon wore on and evening approached, the pounding sounds from the elusive encampment slowed down and finally stopped. ARM soldiers must be halting their work day and getting ready for supper. "Good," she said, "I'm starved! And I'm just in time to eat!"

Dusk encroached and the mountainside gave itself up to the darkness of a moonless fall evening. As that last glimmer of light vanished behind clouds, she pulled herself up to the edge of a plateau and saw, on the far side of the highland, the encampment for which she'd been searching. Relief swept over her, and she felt her body go slightly limp with sweet release as realization registered that this was, at last, the end of her journey.

Jana completed her long mission by pulling herself over the lip of the ridge and then stood to wave in the direction of the camp's center. Opening her mouth to shout her arrival to anyone who might hear, she was grabbed roughly from behind. A large hand covered her mouth, making it hard for her to breathe and another hand grabbed her outstretched arm, yanking it down and holding it firmly at her side.

Kicking and struggling to no avail, Jana's heart raced with fear. With her arm held in her assailant's vise-like grip, she couldn't reach her knife. Repeated kicking of her attacker elicited only a few irritated grunts, and her legs, already taxed by the climb, grew so tired she finally gave in to her fatigue. Her mugger, still holding her tightly, proceeded to drag her small body into the vegetation at the right of her ridge access point. As revelation of his probable intent rang through her mind, she fought again with all her strength. A rough hand over her face had, after all, meant only one thing in her past experience.

Turning her face, ever so slightly in his grip, she found the fleshy part of his hand with her mouth and bit hard enough to draw blood, but even though he groaned loudly his grip remained. Panic welled up in her heart until she thought she might burst from the stress, but she had to keep her wits about her in order to have any chance at all of escape.

Once her assailant dragged her fully into the shrubs, he loosened his grip on her arm and her hand shot out and went immediately and instinctively to the hilt of her knife. Grabbing her by the wrist, her attacker twisted her arm till it was numb causing her to drop her knife in the dirt. He pulled her hand and arm with him as he turned his body to crouch over her, ready to lower his knee to her chest. Jana, seeing the opportunity she needed, brought her own knee up fast and very hard, connecting with his groin. As his body, shocked by her attack, crumpled in agony on top of her, she wriggled free and rolled over grabbing her weapon once again. Her knife hand swung up just as he, shakily, achieved his knees.

Wielding her weapon with the speed and precision of one who had honed her skills for months in the wilderness, she slashed deep into his left side, twisting and pulling up as she rolled away. She was set to strike again and quickly run back in the direction of the camp, after her final blow, when she heard her mugger croak her name in a pained whisper, "Jana."

She stopped just short of impaling him a second time while her confused mind tried to make sense of whom, that would know her by name, would be attacking her on this mountainside. It was dark enough now to make identification difficult, but he struggled to pull his hood back, revealing his face, so she could have a better look at him.

"Pastor Mike?" Jana gasped in utter astonishment. "What in the world? How did you, why were you grabbing me, and what are you doing on this mountain?"

"Jana, let me catch my breath" he said through gritted teeth. "Nobody told me you were such a scrapper, and you really took me by surprise," he said between gulps of air. He reached slowly to his side to examine the growing bloodstain there. "Help me get to my cave, Jana. I need to get a better look at this wound."

"I'm so sorry! I had no idea it was you, and when you grabbed me, well, my instincts took over. I've been on my own for a while now. Why don't we just go into the camp here? I'm sure they must have medical supplies."

"No, Jana, we can't go in there. We have to get to my cave."

"Okay, Pastor Mike. Here, let me help you. Show me where you want me to go, and we'll take care of you."

The hiking was difficult and very slow, with Mike leaning heavily on her shoulder and growing weaker by the minute, until they came to his well-hidden sanctuary on the other side of the plateau. His entire side, from chest to shoe, was soaked in blood by the time they arrived, and he was deathly pale. Jana had all she could do by then to hold him up.

After helping him to his sleeping palate, quickly stowing her gear and grabbing her first aid kit, she rushed to get a fire going so they could see. Pastor Mike was ghostly white even in the pink firelight. Looking at his coat and the amount of blood saturating his clothing, she guessed she'd done a pretty good job of defending herself. Quickly locating an empty container, she filled it with water from a wonderful, pure water spring which bubbled up inside the cave and got her pot on the fire to boil. "Gosh, Pastor Mike, I am so sorry. Let's get your coat and shirt off, so we can get a better look at the damage I've done."

"No, Jana, you don't have to apologize," he said, gasping in obvious pain. "It was my fault. I understand you were protecting yourself. I just had no idea you were so good with that thing. Before today, I was afraid for you, but I probably should have been afraid for the goon squad, huh?" He said, chuckling lightly and then grimacing with the effort. "We all kind of thought you'd been taken weeks ago, when we didn't see any sign of you for so long, but when I heard the gunshots earlier and realized they weren't coming from the militia camp—"

As Pastor Mike talked, Jana helped him with his coat and shirt, so she could see his wounded side more clearly. Uncovering the affected area, she saw a gash that was six to eight inches long and very deep. It was bleeding heavily and would need to be staunched and stitched shut. Things could have been worse and would have been if he hadn't been wearing his heavy coat, which appeared to have taken part of the impact of the blade. But when she twisted the knife as she drew it up, some of the fabric from his shirt and coat may have been pushed into the wound by the blade and that could be a problem. Examining the injury more thoroughly, she didn't think she'd hit any vital organs, but for now, cleaning it up and staunching the bleeding would be her focus. "Wait a minute," Jana interjected, "what do you mean the militia camp?"

"The PM, Jana, you were about to walk into their camp when I grabbed you."

"Are you kidding, oh my goodness? I could have ruined everything we've worked for. I was so ready to be done with all this responsibility of these papers I've been carrying. I didn't even look things over first. I was so sure they were the good guys."

"No, Jana, ARM doesn't camp in the open anymore. Not since the president started using bombing runs to keep us in check. Most of the group bugged out when the bad guys moved into the neighborhood. I stayed behind to wait for you. The documents you're carrying are important enough that we wanted to be sure you, and they, were safe. I've been keeping a look out for you since the bigger groups left, but the more time passed, the more I was losing hope of ever seeing you again.

"When I saw you about to announce to the world you arrived, I knew I had to stop you. My new mission has become gathering intelligence from the militia, and I've been spending a great deal of time hiding in the shrubs outside their perimeter. With some of the strange comings and goings I've seen, I've begun to think the administration might be housing some pretty high level prisoners in the caves out there." Mike's voice was nothing but a whisper now, and he was clearly in serious trouble. With all the information he was imparting, it felt almost as if he was briefing her in case he didn't make it.

Jana continued to apply pressure to Pastor Mike's wound and knew she had to get the gash stitched up, so she looked him in the eyes and said, "All I can say is thanks, Pastor Mike, for stepping in and keeping me from destroying everything. I'm so sorry for cutting you open, but now I need to sew you shut and that is probably going to hurt a whole lot more. It's a pretty long wound too, so it's going to take longer to close you than it took for me to open you up, and again, I'm sorry, but it has to be done."

"Just call me Mike, Jana. Glad I was there for you. We all promised Josh you'd be taken care of, even before we knew how dangerous you were (chuckling, and then grimacing again). I know this probably isn't going to feel very good, but I will try to be as still as I can for you."

Mike's whisper had gotten steadily weaker as his wound seeped blood and now his eyelids fluttered as he fought to stay conscious. Jana was worried for him—the amount of blood he'd lost, the less than sterile conditions, the fabric which in all likelihood had found its way into the injury—but she could only do what she had the tools and experience to do.

Helping Mike lay back on his bed, she began in earnest to clean the injured area. Stitching his gaping wound would have to be done in stages, and when she began the first layer, she watched him grimace in pain again, before his face went slack. "Good," she thought out loud as she let loose a big sigh. "It'll be much easier to do this while you're unconscious." When she was done sewing, the pastor shut she cleaned him up and concentrated on tidying the area. It didn't seem she'd cut into any organs or major arteries, much to her relief, so she was able to stop the bleeding, sans a bit of seepage which she would keep a close eye on. Now she could only wait. After washing herself and changing her shirt, she soaked Mike's coat and shirt as well as her own clothing in cold water in hopes of removing the blood which remained from their struggle. She was forced to change the water in her wash basin several times before it started coming back clear.

Jana wasn't particularly hungry, but knew the importance of keeping her strength up so she took some dried squirrel from her pack, and while she chewed, she sat mindlessly staring into the dwindling fire. Her thoughts filled to overflowing with recent dreams, current facts, and old worries until she realized suddenly she didn't know how long she'd been sitting in the semidarkness of the cave in front of an almost extinguished fire.

Moving in what felt like slow motion, she rose to put more wood on the fire. Suddenly overwhelmed with total and complete exhaustion, she crawled under the cover of her recently rolled out bed and dropped into an exhausted and uninterrupted deep sleep.

15

Waking in the dark, it took Jana a moment to remember where she was. The cavern was pitch-black and the fire cold. Wrapped in her sleeping bag, she shivered, stirring the coals, but found no life there. Pulling out her flashlight along with flint and steel, she got a small pile of kindling lit and added wood to the growing fire. The room was so frigid she could see her breath before her and her fingers so numb she could barely operate them long enough to get the menial task done.

Unaware of how long she'd slept, she looked past pine boughs blocking the cave entrance and outside to an inky black night devoid of moon or stars. This couldn't be the night she'd laid down to sleep, she felt too rested for that to be the case. Willing to bet she'd slept through the first night and right on through the next day, she knew she and Pastor Mike had both been exhausted so it wouldn't be hard to believe they'd slept for more than twenty-four hours.

As the fire grew and the room brightened, Jana looked across the chamber to where Mike lay on his palate, shaking and shivering uncontrollably in his sleep. Moving quickly, she reached him and touched his face with the back of her hand. Terribly feverish and clammy, his blanket was soaked with perspiration which had cooled in the icy room, perhaps a blessing in disguise to cool his fevered body. She was sure he must be thirsty and rose to get him water before attempting to prepare a meal.

As she turned to move away, Mike's hand shot out and grabbed her wrist. His eyes flew open wide, and Jana didn't like what she saw in the depths of them. Peering at her through a red, glazed, fear-filled place, his mouth moved as though he meant to speak but couldn't. Mike seemed to be unaware of what was going on, or even who she was. Jana gently pulled her arm from his vise-like grip, never taking her eyes from his and gingerly laid his hand back on his chest. As she did so, he slumped over and fell back into a fitful, disturbed sleep.

Hurriedly refilling her pot to boil more water, she pulled Mike's blanket back to get a better look at his wound. Her actions and the noise she was making in the cave didn't seem to reawaken him and that was a concern, but might also be another blessing considering the next steps she would take could be very painful for him if he were indeed awake.

The area around the slash was bright red and angry looking, swollen to the point of bursting open. Rivulets of puss oozed between stitches, and swelling caused those stitches to pull at the flesh until it looked ready to tear. A rotten smell emanated from the wound. Having been through a similar situation recently, Jana knew an infection had set in, and she recognized she would have to work swiftly to save him. Just then, Mike began to mumble and thrash around. Jana stroked his hair in an effort to calm him.

Trying to keep him included in the process, so she could do what she needed to do while he was in this delirious state, would be a challenge. She spoke softly to him, preparing him for what she desired to do to help him.

Of course, she didn't like the fact she'd have to reopen and clean the wound. This was a feat which would be difficult enough under normal circumstances, but almost impossible while Mike was in his current noncompliant state. The situation was dicey at best, but Jana knew it would be up to her to try and save the man she'd so severely injured.

Collecting her knife, small scissors, a clean cloth, some gauze and tape, soap and more suturing material from her kit, she prepared. Noting there was very little sulfur powder remaining in her kit, she hoped and prayed it might be enough. Hydrogen peroxide, alcohol, and some of her last few aspirin rounded out her surgical first aid supplies.

Thankfully, Mike didn't stir as Jana began to cut the stitches she'd made only twenty-four hours or so before, but when she proceeded to clean the wound with gauze and soap, he once again began, though in a weakened state, to fight her every move. Holding his arm down with one hand and continued to clean his wound with the soapy gauze in her other hand, she used tweezers to gently lift cut and torn tissues to take a look beneath. Checking to see if anything else was left behind, she found several more small pieces of fabric she'd missed in her initial attempt to close his wound the day before. Cursing herself silently, she removed shreds of material and hoped this was the last of it. After she'd picked out the offending pieces of cloth, she thoroughly rinsed the area with cooled sterile water.

The next steps would be very painful, so Jana began to talk to Mike in soft, reassuring tones and found she was comforting him with the words of some of her newfound favorite scripture: Psalm 62:1–2. "I am at rest in God alone; my salvation comes from Him. He alone is my rock and my salvation, my stronghold; I will never be shaken." Mike's discomfort seemed to subside somewhat, and he calmed down enough for her to finish sewing him up and resterilizing the wound.

Once the injured area was safely covered, she glanced up to see him looking at her again with wide, feverish, and confused eyes, but the message garnered from the look they exchanged seemed to answer all of his questions and a flicker of recognition flashed in his gaze. For that moment, at least, he was at ease. When Jana was done tending to Mike's wound and after he'd fallen again into a fevered sleep, she got up to clean the mess which she'd made while ministering to his injury and to take care of a few housekeeping chores.

Mike slept, after the crude surgery, for a full forty-eight hours, without waking. During his recuperation, when she was able to serve him, Jana helped him sip cool water and broth made from her latest successful hunt, kept the fire going, placed cool cloths on his forehead, and changed his bandages. She had only a small amount of her treasured aspirin remaining, so she rationed them carefully until they were gone. Mike still had a high fever when he awoke intermittently, so she could only hope all would be well.

In her search of the area during her latest hunting foray, Jana discovered a stunted willow tree growing from the side of a small cliff. Scraping some of the bark, she'd use it later to brew a pain-relieving tea. Her survival guide recommended this might be a good alternative to aspirin, and since it didn't list any negative side effects, she was willing to try it in an effort to give Mike some further relief. The book listed many trees and herbs, which could be used in cooking and for medicinal purposes, complete with pictures, so her cooking and first aid arsenals had been growing each day until the recent colder temperatures threatened to finally put a stop to her foraging.

Oddly, she thought, several days after Mike's surgery, Jana found herself praying earnestly for Mike and for their difficult situation. She'd never been a praying person, though she'd seen her parents, her grandmother, and Josh praying many times. In those days, she'd sneered, and silently made fun of Josh when she witnessed him in prayer and that thought came back to stab her in her conscience. But things were different now, weren't they? The more she read, the more she was beginning to receive small glimpses of truth, and praying didn't seem as ridiculous as it once did to her.

There were many things Jana regretted and so much she wished she could go back and do differently. She wondered if the feelings of guilt and deep regret would ever stop plaguing her and then wondered if she wanted them to. After all, she'd done some horrible things in her past. Perhaps she should suffer for all the evil she'd thought and done in her lifetime. Maybe paying for her sins should be her penance after all? Even then, though, it wouldn't change the outcome. Jana knew she could never pay for all the wicked she'd done, but didn't have a clue as to how to resolve all the feelings of remorse which coursed through her and the guilt which plagued her with its constant feelings of condemnation.

16

J ANA MADE HERSELF useful during Mike's recuperation hunting and preserving a vast wealth of meats, collecting what remained of the season's herbs, digging roots, harvesting nuts, and drying the last of the withered berries available on the mountain. Cutting and stacking six cords of wood, which easily covered the longest wall of Mike's spacious cavern quite nicely, would take care of the winter's fuel needs as well. A natural vent in Mike's cave let the smoke from their fires out far from their physical position and would help to dissipate that smoke somewhat before emptying it out into the cold mountain air. She figured this might help in disguising the specifics of their location if anyone out there was still looking for either of them.

Jana took great pains to hide the information which had been entrusted to her. Figuring if she didn't tell Pastor Mike where any of it was, he couldn't be tortured for information he didn't possess in the event they were captured by enemy soldiers.

When Mike finally awoke, after two frightening, fever-filled days, he saw his cave filled with strategically positioned branches which Jana was using as drying racks. Strips of squirrel and rabbit meat in different stages of preservation covered the makeshift racks. Laundry was caught up too, so the rock fire ring was virtually covered with articles of clothing in various phases of drying and laundered cloths which she'd used to scrub and bandage Mike's wounds hung in diverse places around the space.

Eventually, when his mind cleared enough for him to open his eyes without the excruciating pain caused by a high fever, he saw Jana across the room stacking additional fire wood. As he laid in silence watching her move around the cave tending to the everyday chores which would make them both comfortable throughout the winter months, snippets of the past few days came flooding back to him. He was embarrassed to think of the trouble he'd been to her. Though, he reasoned internally, she was after all the culprit who'd injured him.

As she moved with a grace which made her beautiful to watch, he found his mind wandering and then his face blushing red. Just then, Jana turned to see his eyes open. Smiling, she said, "Hi, sleepy head.

How are you feeling?" Mike tried to speak and found his throat so dry only a small croak came forth. Jana's smile turned to a look of concern as she rushed to his side of the cave to give him a drink of cold water.

Jana knew personally what a long, involved process a recovery of this magnitude could be, so as much as she hated the idea of postponing the final leg of her trek to find the ARM encampment, she'd settled her mind that she would stay with Mike until he was fully able to care for himself or travel with her. "After all," she reasoned with herself, "I am the one responsible for his injuries whether or not I was defending myself, and I can't just leave him to fend for himself at any rate."

Anyway, the days she'd lost here in the cave tending to her friend had already been enough to see winter beginning to settle in and the first measurable snowfall of the season now covered the mountain.

Several separate dustings of snow prior to this last event had been her prompter to finish collecting provisions to see them through. She'd taken the seasonal warning to heart and decided, with events shaping up the way they were, she would be required to cover the supply of both their essentials for winter instead of hers only; and taken care of them she had!

Spending some time brushing up on her archery skills, while she was passing time waiting for Mike too awaken, she'd picked up her old skill level pretty quickly and was pleased with her current degree of accuracy. Her lightweight bow was an excellent source of defense and proved to be a great new hunting tool. Jana used the bow in several of her most recent hunting forays with great success.

Outside temperatures were much colder on the mount already, but Jana stacked enough wood to get them through the mountain's harsh winter, and she collected enough food to keep them both sustained for months as long as they were careful with the supplies she'd stored. Having a fresh water spring inside the cave was a blessing beyond imagination in this rough terrain. To have access to water during the freezing weather would be a lifesaver. And Jana knew as long as she rationed some of the dried meats and roots to make soups and stews the food should last until they could move out and on to the ARM base when snow began to melt in spring.

17

EVENINGS, WHICH HAD been a painful enemy all these months since Josh's death, had recently become Jana's favorite time of day. An odd sort of peace filled her heart where tears and desperate longing for her husband had taken up residence before. During Mike's long recovery, she'd begun to spend many of those evenings near the fire, reading and studying until she couldn't keep her eyes open anymore.

Her Bible was fast becoming her best friend, advisor, and source of strength, and as she read more and more of the grace of Christ and His sacrifice for her, she found her heart softening toward the God of the universe who she used to imagine was out to destroy her. Scripture after scripture touched her heart with love and acceptance where, prior to this, she'd mistakenly felt shame, condemnation, and distance for the better part of her young life.

One evening during her reading, she stumbled across a passage about Jesus's wisdom in Luke. The passage read in Luke 7:36–50:

Then one of the Pharisees invited Him to eat with him. He entered the Pharisee's house and reclined at the table. And a woman in the town who was a sinner found out that Jesus was reclining at the table in the Pharisee's house. She brought an alabaster flask of fragrant oil and stood behind Him at His feet, weeping and began to wash His feet with her tears. She wiped His feet with the hair of her head, kissing them and anointing them with the fragrant oil. When the Pharisee who had invited Jesus saw this, he said to himself, "This man, if He were a prophet, would know who and what kind of woman this is who is touching Him-she is a sinner!"

Jesus replied to him, "Simon, I have something to say to you."

"Teacher," he said, "say it."

"A creditor had two debtors. One owed ten thousand dollars and the other one hundred dollars. Since they could not pay it back he graciously forgave them both. So, which of them will love him more?"

Simon answered, "I suppose the one he forgave more."

"You have judged correctly," He told him.

Turning to the woman, He said to Simon, "Do you see this woman? I entered your house; you gave Me no water for My feet, but she, with her tears, has washed My feet and wiped them with her hair. You gave Me no kiss, but she hasn't stopped kissing My feet since I came in. You didn't anoint My head with oil, but she has anointed My feet with fragrant oil. Therefore I tell you, her many sins have been forgiven; that's why she loved much. But the one who is forgiven little loves little." Then He said to her, "Your sins are forgiven."

Those who were at the table with Him began to say among themselves, "Who is this man who forgives sins?"

And He said to the woman, "Your faith has saved you. Go in peace."

As Jana read, she knew her own life was a reflection of that debtor who owed ten thousand, or perhaps much more. She had plenty, which needed forgiving.

The book of Romans was amazing and spoke to her of a Grace whose love she could scarcely understand. She read in Romans 8:1–3:

Therefore, no condemnation now exists for those who are in Christ Jesus, because the Spirit's law of life in Christ Jesus has set you free from the law of sin and of death. What the law could not do since it was limited by the flesh, God did. He condemned sin in the flesh by sending His own Son in flesh like ours under sin's domain, and as a sin offering.

And in Romans 5:1–11:

Therefore, since we have been declared righteous by faith, we have peace with God through our Lord Jesus Christ. Also through Him we have obtained access by faith into this grace in which we stand, and we rejoice in the hope of the glory of God, And not only that, but we rejoice in our afflictions, because we know that affliction produces endurance, endurance produces proven character, and proven character produces hope. This hope does not disappoint, because God's love has been poured out in our hearts through the Holy Spirit who was given to us.

For while we were still helpless, at the appointed moment, Christ died for the ungodly. For rarely will someone die for a

just person—though for a good person someone might even dare to die. But God proves
His own love for us in that while we were still
sinners Christ died for us! Much more then,
since we have now been declared righteous by
His blood, we will be saved through Him from
wrath. For if, while we were enemies, we were
reconciled to God through the death of His
Son, then how much more, having been reconciled, will we be saved by His life! And not
only that, but we also rejoice in God through
our Lord Jesus Christ, through whom we have
now received atonement.

Also, in John 3:16–18:

For God so loved the world that He gave His
One and Only Son, so that everyone who
believes in Him will not perish but have eternal life. For God did not send His Son into the
world that He might condemn the world, but
that the world might be saved by Him. Anyone
who believes in Him is not condemned, but
anyone who does not believe is condemned
already, because he has not believed in the
name of the One and only Son of God.

Reading these passages filled Jana with a hope she'd never known; and soon, she found herself sitting and studying with great joy in the dimming glow of her fire, with tears of growing understanding and joy sliding silently down her life wearied face.

Time she'd spent with her grandmother so long ago, even though it'd been filled with church and religion was a time which settled painfully and uncomfortably in her soul. That whole religious experience felt condemning and hopeless compared to the way these new and revealing passages freed her now. And as she discovered more of the truth of the Word, she understood more about the sad religious world, which her grandmother and so many others inhabited. Added to that hopeless, ruined feeling had been her own anger about the loss of first: her parents, then her grandmother, and later, her husband.

Grandmother's religion was filled with lists of impossible laws and rules to follow, and a sense of ruinous judgment which weighed heavily on anyone who tried to follow those rules in order to measure up. Everything about it made her feel useless and condemned as she'd tried to "earn" her way to heaven in her grandmother's eyes; never succeeding, or even coming close.

Now she was seeing, through reading His Word, that God never intended the sacrifice of His Son to be used in promoting a religion or a practice, but instead to show us we have a Savior to trust in and that He provides us with unconditional love to carry us through all of life's challenges. For so many years in her life, Jana felt deserted by a God who, in her estimation, took everything from her and then failed to protect her from the dangers of the world. She wondered over and over again why Josh's God didn't come to his aid. It didn't surprise her, she supposed, to be ignored. After all, she hadn't followed this God or read His Bible. She knew she didn't deserve His love or protection herself, but Josh? Surely, Josh deserved angels. She realized now that by the time Josh came into her life, she'd been unreachable by any mere human being, and had never so much as given him a chance to help her understand the God of love who was already so familiar to him.

Much of her time had been wasted, throughout her life, in self-hatred. Jana knew she couldn't get those years back, and she would never be able to tell her husband how much his Jesus was beginning to mean to her, but maybe, just maybe, somehow he knew after all.

All the time she'd spent trying to measure up and knowing she never would, never could; all the wasted years of guilt and remorse at the hands of her grandmother. Now Jana was coming to realize she wasn't meant to measure up, that she couldn't measure up on her own, or be strong on her own, that Jesus had lived and died and lived again so she could be righteous in Him and through Him. It was as simple as that. It wasn't about her at all! It was only about Him and the sacrifice He'd made for her. This wasn't supposed to be about religion. It was all supposed to be about a loving relationship with the God of the universe.

Her heart, which had been frozen against the idea of surrender for so long, was beginning to warm and soften toward the idea of a redeemer friend. It was a relief to know she didn't need to try to be perfect anymore, didn't need to try to win her salvation, couldn't earn her way to heaven, but needed only to rely on the Lord of heaven and earth to cover her with His blood and His undying Grace. She understood now that through Him, absolution was hers. He'd already paid it all!

On a quiet, cold wintery night, in a secluded mountain cave, in front of a dwindling fire, she'd built with her own two hands, Jana sat together with Josh's Jesus. Tears on her face reflected the glowing orange and yellow coals of the blaze before her, and her spirit burned now with the joy of one who is truly in the presence of the Lord.

On that still night, Jana confessed the sin of her humanity and her need of salvation, and she gave her heart to the King of Glory. Her circumstances didn't matter anymore as she knew with every fiber of her being she was saved by Grace and loved by the Prince of Peace. He was no longer Josh's Jesus alone, but her Jesus too. Now that she finally trusted in a living Christ, nothing in Jana's life would ever be the same.

18

I T SEEMED TO her that Pastor Mike was finally beginning the long road back to health. Jana had spent many days and nights helping him battle a raging fever with prayer, cold compresses, broth, and willow bark tea, wondering at times if it was God's will that they would win this battle at all.

She'd drained the infection in his side three times in the first few days of his illness, scrubbing and disinfecting everything in sight before at last the wound began to respond favorably to her ministrations. When his body finally began to demonstrate good results from her constant care, she thanked God and began to help Mike get his strength back with more substantial food and as much spiritual and emotional support as she could muster. His recovery seemed to be taking much more time than her own hard road back to health had taken, but she'd used the time productively and had done much reading and studying in the Word since giving her heart to Jesus. Through her study and prayer, she was becoming more and more convinced of God's undying love for her in spite of her own humanity.

When Pastor Mike began spending more time in a wakeful state, he found her to be—much to his surprise—an able and willing Bible student and prayer partner. The time spent together in their cave during those long cold winter nights would do more to shore up Jana's confidence than all the many things she'd learned in the secular world about self-protection and survival, or any worldly knowledge she'd accumulated in college or day-to-day life. As she learned more about Jesus's love for her and discovered more about herself along the way, her mind and heart filled with His peace and rest.

Jana had always been a bright girl, and a quick study and, Mike taught her countless things, including the difference between the covenant of law, which her grandmother had lived under, and the covenant of Grace, which inspired her now. He explained to her that the law was given through Moses, but Grace is a person and came in the being of Jesus Christ.

Showing her how the law is important and necessary as it reveals to us our own sinful nature and need for a Savior. And that if used for the purpose it was intended, it is a good thing. But once the law has served its purpose and has brought us to the end of ourselves, then we should trust God not only for our salvation but also for our righteousness. In Him alone, as He showers us with His unmerited favor and His undeserved Grace through Christ Jesus, we actually become the righteousness of God in Christ through Him.

Mike also taught her how important it is for her to know she is the beloved of God and His favored child. He said to her, "Have you ever noticed that we, in the church, think of John as 'the disciple that Jesus loved'? Yet, if you read the New Testament, you won't see that description of John anywhere except in the book of John. You see, John knew the Lord loved him and that gave him an advantage over the other disciples who were counting on their righteousness being derived through how much they loved Jesus. The importance of this revelation is that during Jesus's ministry, Peter, who we commonly think of as the father of the church, tried to base his own worth on how much he loved Jesus. And John, who never took his eyes off the Lord, based his worth on how much the Lord loved him. While Jesus hung on the cross, He entrusted the care of His mother to the only disciple who stood at the foot of the cross. It is so important that we know how much He loves us. How important we as His children are to Him. We all need to know that our God did not spare His own Son, but gave Him for us, so we can all be His children through adoption if we only accept the free gift of His love."

Jana's strong sense of self hatred, guilt, condemnation, and fear shrank daily, as she succumbed to the all-encompassing, unconditional grace and love of a God who didn't think twice before giving up His life for her. She knew now why Josh had been able to love her no matter how terrible she'd been too him; no matter how much she didn't deserve his love. It was because he knew the affection of an infinite God who loved him when he didn't deserve it either!

And, as she began, step-by-step, to see herself as the beloved of the Lord and His favored child, she became stronger in her desire to share Him with a lost world. A world she was confident didn't know any better either. A world she absolutely believed didn't understand His love and compassion any more than she had until recently. A world who saw God as a big mean bearded guy in the sky with a stick, ready to knock them down for every single moral infraction.

How did she know the world viewed Him this way? She knew because she had been a part of that world view for so many years herself. As she looked back on her life now, she could actually see each and every place in which God held her in His sheltering hand. She recognized specific times in her past where if things had worked out as she would have liked, there would've been chaos. She was sure now that even when she didn't realize it, He'd been there taking care of her and loving her all along.

Reading, she was comforted by Jeremiah 29:11: "For I know the plans I have for you, plans for your welfare, not for disaster, to give you a future and a hope."

And Romans 8:28: "We know that all things work together for the good of those who love God: those who are the called according to His purpose." After all, if God was for her who could be against her? She thought when this ordeal was over she might want to become an evangelist and share this wonderful discovery of a Messiah of love with whoever was willing to listen! Smiling, she remembered all those months ago how upset she'd gotten every time Josh tried to share his wonderful Jesus with her and how hard she'd fought against the idea of an eternal Savior. If only her husband could see her now. Perhaps he could. She still wasn't sure how the heaven thing worked, but she was sure her husband resided there now.

19

MIKE AND JANA became the best of friends, as close as two peas in a pod, during their time in the cave and they were looking forward to celebrating Christmas together. Bible study time had been rewarding and productive for them both, and their partnership grew by leaps and bounds in the process. Mike continued to mend, but the damage to his body was extensive, and healing time would be ultimately longer as well. Jana made regular hunting trips out into the pristine wonderland of winter on the mountain, being careful to move about only in actively falling snow, or to brush her tracks to cover her comings and goings. She intended to stay invisible to the militia whose camp, from the sounds of it, was still very much present on the mountain.

Able to surprise abundant numbers of small game animals while out on the highlands, she filled her larder to overflowing. There was no worry anymore about rationing their food, and she planned a wonderful dinner for the upcoming holiday with some of her most recent acquisitions.

Jana also killed enough rabbits to make a beautiful, long, hooded cape, leggings and mittens for her use from the softened skins. An added bonus was that the rabbits were decked out in their seasonal camouflage, so, dressed in her newly crafted winter garb, she was undetectable in the snowy landscape. With her new disguise working in her favor, she'd begun to venture closer to the PM encampment. Mike warned her to stay away until he was well enough to accompany her, but she'd decided to begin collecting intelligence against his advice. Her trips were sporadic for now, and with the weather so cold, she hadn't garnered much useful information, but hoped to gain some knowledge which might help their mission on future excursions.

As she ventured out on the mount, she felt closer to God than at any other time. The air was clean and crisp, and her mind clear and focused. Jana never stopped missing Josh and wished every day he was here to share her newfound life and freedom, but even without him, she knew she was more filled with joy and peace than she'd been at any other time in her life.

Also aware Mike was falling in love with her; she wasn't born yesterday and was well aware of the look in a man's eye when he was interested. She thought she'd handled the situation well. She really had to give him credit as he was always a perfect gentleman. She'd gone out of her way to make it clear to him she wasn't ready to consider a relationship with anyone, but she didn't think it would have been necessary as he'd never pushed his attentions on her at any time.

Her relationship was growing so strong with the Lord she just sort of considered Him the new man in her life anyway.

20

CHRISTMAS DAWNED BRIGHT and cold. Anticipation of the coming day's events practically exploded in Jana's excited imagination. She'd never looked so forward to a Christmas Day celebration, and she felt childlike in her eagerness for the festivities to begin. Venturing out to see sun glinting off newly fallen snow, which caused ice crystals to sparkle and gleam like rare diamonds, she gasped at the splendor before her. Trees and shrubs, which were clothed in sleeves of hoary frost, glistened from every branch and twig. Shimmering crystallization turned every evergreen on the mountain into a beautifully decorated Christmas tree. "Has there ever been such a beautiful day?" Jana wondered out loud, as she breathed in the cold air and looked out over the mountain—her mountain, her home.

Now that she understood the true meaning of Christmas, this day meant more to her than presents and candy ever had in the past. For the first time in her life, this day of birthday celebration could be attributed to a sole source in her mind. Her head was full of new revelations, and her heart fairly burst with wonder.

Regretting she hadn't been able to find a turkey this far up on the mountain or this far into the season, she was still confident she could make a memorable holiday meal and hurried back to cook several rabbits to a crispy, juicy state of yummy doneness. Their cave filled with the savory smell of roasting meat, and her mouth watered in anticipation. Boiled tubers mashed with dried herbs and wild garlic proved to be a delicious addition to their holiday repast, and reconstituted berries drizzled with some of her prized honey made an excellent dessert. The whole banquet was topped off by steaming cups of mint tea. They agreed this might be the best Christmas dinner of their lives.

Jana made a new hat and mittens for Mike from extra rabbit furs she collected and he'd scrounged enough assorted, dried grasses out of Jana's fire starting materials, to weave a beautiful Bible bookmark for her.

Once dinner was eaten and gifts exchanged Mike sat back against his sleeping pallet with hot tea in hand and began to sing softly in a sweet tenor voice;

silent night, holy night, all is calm, all is bright, round yon virgin, mother and child; his emotional offering beautiful in the closeness of their sanctuary. Jana's heart was full as tears of happiness slid gently down her smiling face.

21

THE DAY AFTER Christmas found Jana and Mike sitting snug in their cave in front of a roaring fire as the worst blizzard of the season, so far, raged on the mountain. Jana was grateful they had plenty of wood for the fire and more than enough provisions. At this rate, they would have ample time for Bible study and prayer, but first there was something she'd been waiting to do for some time.

Digging through her bag for the hand cranked radio she knew was still buried beneath her belongings, she began unloading the pack's contents. Her interest in the outside world had taken a definite backseat to her new relationship with the Lord, as it should, and there'd been lots to do as Mike was recovering, but now he was getting better, and she was curious how things might be evolving back in the world she'd left behind.

Mike watched in amusement as she removed more items, he was sure, than any human being should have been able to stow in that well-worn backpack.

"Here it is!" Jana chirped, pulling the elusive item from her bag. She cranked the radio's handle and switched it on. Fiddling with the receiver knob and extended the antenna to its full length, she finally picked up a faint signal. It came in a bit clearer as she fine-tuned it, twisting the dial this way and that. Listening intently, she was puzzled at first and began searching the airwaves again, listening for additional stations. Now more bewildered than before, she sat back on her heels and looked over at Mike who asked her, "What's going on? Doesn't sound like there's much coming in on that thing."

"That's what I thought too, Mike, but listen closer." Turning up the radio, which only accentuated the sound of static, she turned to him again. "Do you hear? Come closer, here, here, are you hearing this?"

"What? I'm not sure that I hear what you're talking about."

"Listen! I'm only getting one channel to come in at all and it sounds, from the way the announcer is talking, like it might be a government-run station. Listen to this. Do you hear what I'm talking about? Can things have gotten that bad in such a short period of time?"

"Yeah, I see what you mean. Well, Jana, you told me the last reports you listened to were filled with negative news. Nothing but stations airing government sanctioned lists of enemies of the state and information about the martial law ruling. How long did you think it would be before they controlled all the media outlets too? You do know who we're talking about, right?"

"I just can't believe how insidious these people are, or, well, I guess it isn't hard to believe all the things they are getting away with as much as it is hard to believe the American people are letting them do all of this without putting up any kind of a real fight!"

"Well, some of us are putting up a fight, Jana, remember? Not long ago you didn't believe what was right before your eyes either, but we are branded as the bad guys now, at least in the light the government has painted us to the public at large. I'm sure it is getting harder all the time for our people to stay hidden since the government began posting rewards for our capture and for information about our whereabouts. We've lost a number of members due to their own family and friends turning them in to get brownie points as government informants. Do you recall when the government asked citizens to inform them if they heard anyone saying anything negative about the administration's policies, or the health care bill?"

"Yes, I do. I remember Josh talking about that too. I think I made fun of him as usual."

"Well, that policy took a toll on our ranks. You might be surprised at how many people will turn someone in just because they think that person's ideas, which are a little different than their own ideas, are radical. You know, like Christian ideals. I'm sure you'd agree that when you don't see things from a Christian perspective, you see Christians as a bunch of whackos, wouldn't you?"

"Well, yeah, you know I felt that way most of my life, so I know exactly what you're saying."

"It's probably even harder for our ARM members to get anyone to take them seriously anymore since they don't have the proof they need, the proof they know exists, to hold the administration accountable for their actions. It can be pretty frustrating to know the truth and not be able to get anyone to believe you, you know? And there are probably more and more of those now who think turning us in for the reward is a more acceptable idea than siding with us. You do know almost all of the members of ARM are Christians, don't you?"

"No, I guess I didn't. Well, if I'd bothered to think about it, I suppose it would've made sense in the light of everything that's happened. I knew Josh and his parents had begun to figure out most of what was going on in the administration some time ago, and then all the guys at the church got involved, but I really didn't know how widespread the movement was until I talked with you after, well after I stabbed you and all…"

"Jana, the number of Christians involved in the movement is one of the things we have discovered is a big thorn in the side of the administration. Our government has been doing everything within its power to move toward socialism, a 'One World Order' and a 'One World Religion' for quite some time now, and we are putting a major cramp in their style. We discovered through citizens who showed up at the GHO for mandatory implantation that they were given a consent form to sign once they arrived. That consent form didn't just give the doctors permission to implant that individual with a chip, there was also a contract portion attached which ordered the citizen to pledge their unwavering loyalty to the administration. It was worded in such a way that true believers in Christ knew they couldn't sign it, but they were not the only ones who refused. Many conservatives and even liberals of the secular variety were so put off by the wording that they balked as well.

Jails and prisons are filled to overflowing with dissenters these days. We know some of our top operatives have been taken to special holding centers, but we haven't figured out where those centers are just yet. I'll tell you what, the minute the government began talking about implantation through the GHO being a mandatory act, supposedly so they could track our medical information, we knew we couldn't go down that road. But the addition of the loyalty clause to the contract sealed the deal for us. Needless to say, that's made us all enemies of the state now."

"I feel terrible, Mike. If only it hadn't taken me so long to realize the truth! I've probably ruined everything and now the whole organization will be hunted down because they have no proof of the charges ARM was trying to bring against the administration. It's all information I still have in my possession! I've probably singlehandedly destroyed the entire movement!"

"Jana, the longer ARM has been involved in a resistance movement, the more I've been personally convinced there were devious plans of the administration in the works long before we began to be truly vigilant. And, by the way, this has been going on long before any of us started to see what was right in front of our noses, so you are not the only one. There are a great many people working together with those in the administration, many of which we would never have guessed could be involved in something so sinister. It's pretty clear they had all their bases covered from the beginning. Now that we know more the extent of the lies told by the administration, we can better assess the direction we should go with the information Josh entrusted to you.

When we get the information through to ARM, they are going to have to be very careful about whom they trust to share it with. I believe regime officials have paid off more people, departments, and organizations than we could ever imagine. None of these people the government has in their back pocket have any idea who they've crawled in bed with and how badly they'll be hurt the minute the current administration doesn't need them anymore.

There was probably nothing any of us could have done to make all this go more smoothly, so you can stow the guilt trip, okay? We all knew what we were getting into, and none of us really had any other alternatives, unless we wanted to turn ourselves in to the goon squads and be implanted like the rest of the sheep who are being led to the slaughter. We chose the path we are on willingly and now we will be hiding out permanently, or at least until we can get a few things figured out. It is just a fact of life for all of us."

"I guess you're right. Though it's hard to convince myself there is nothing I could have done to make this better. I've been a control freak my whole life. It's hard to let that go. I have a hard time looking back at how I treated my husband. I always felt I had to be in control and have the last word. Knowing what I know now after the reading I've done, I can't help but wonder how Josh put up with me all those years."

"Don't do that to yourself, Jana. Your husband loved you very much. I don't remember him ever saying anything negative about you."

"That's my point, Mike. I don't remember him ever saying anything negative either, but I did enough of that for both of us. I just wish sometimes I could go back and do it all over again. It's too bad I can't erase all the terrible things I've done and give my husband a better life."

"That has already been accomplished, Jana. The day you asked Jesus to come into your life to save you, you erased every negative thing you've ever done. And none of us could ever give Josh a better life than the one he is living right now with the Savior."

"I guess you're right," Jana said in a whisper, hot tears shinning in her eyes. "I just miss him so much. Sometimes, when I'm sleeping, I can almost touch him, smell him, and hear him. It's hard."

"I know, I know. I've never lost anyone who was that close to me, so I have no business telling you how you should feel. I'm sorry, Jana. Forgive me. All of this has been horribly difficult for you. I know that."

"Of course, I forgive you, Mike. I'm fine. Even though it's been so many months since I lost him, I still have a moment here and there where my emotions sneak up on me, but I'm okay now. Wow, I can't believe how much things have deteriorated out there, and it is very scary, isn't it? What are we going to do?"

"Well, for now we are going to stay right here in this cave. There's an awful lot of snow out there you know. Besides, I'm not going to be up to any covert ops for a while. I'm still healing remember?"

"Okay, okay, point taken. I know you still have quite a bit of mending to do. I'm just thankful things are looking as good as they are. For a while, I thought I was going to lose you. I'm glad we're stuck in the middle of winter, so there's plenty of time for you to finish healing before we need to get out of here and meet up with ARM in the spring."

22

T HE BLIZZARD, FINALLY depleted, was replaced with a light, gentle snow falling on the peak. Mike was still sleeping, and the sun was not yet fully risen though it soon would be. They'd been cooped up for three days in their sanctuary as the storm raged on, and after it was over, Jana had a pretty bad case of cabin fever. She'd definitely have to do something about that!

Three days of imprisonment, not able to venture out on her beloved mountain, left her searching for something constructive to do. Digging out her survival manual, she found a project which could be both challenging and useful and decided to tackle it head on. She stripped the bark off several branches and soaked the wood. Once the material was pliable, she separated, cut, and formed it. Finding ample directions in her useful guide, she worked the wood slowly until she had the required shape. Using dried grasses and fibrous leaves, woven together and tied as the guide directed, she designed a tight, strong pair of snow shoes, which would work well enough even in the deepest snow and now she couldn't wait to try them out. Mike, finally awake, kidded her and told her she looked like a rabbit all decked out in her furs with her huge snowshoe clad feet.

Next morning, while Mike slept in, she decided to make her way outside. Forced to dig for quite some time to produce an opening in the snow at the mouth of the cave, Jana finally broke through to daylight. The intense storm created monster drifts in front of the cavern opening, so it was indeed slow going. It was a good thing their cave was supplied with naturally occurring vent holes, or they would likely have run out of air being snowed in this deep. Determined to get out of her weather-imposed prison no matter what it took, now she could finally get out on the mountain.

Decked out in her white, winter gear with bow and arrows slung over her shoulder and knife at her hip, she was looking forward to a little fresh air, knowing it would do wonders for her morale. Emerging from the hole she'd dug and escaping the emotional suffocation of her entrapment, she breathed deeply of the early morning's clean refreshing air. Once free of the confines of the cave, she felt invigorated and decided some fresh meat might be in order for supper tonight. Jana loved the quiet and solitude of the mountain in the morning, and as she walked, she communed silently with her God.

Her new snow shoes worked perfectly. The snow was hip deep at minimum with drifts of ten feet and having the ability to stay on top of the white mass gave her an advantage she hadn't experienced before during her hunting trips. Before long, she'd located and bagged several rabbits which would make a great supper tonight and a respectable stew for tomorrow night as well.

While she walked, she watched the sun creeping slowly over the horizon, lighting the clouds from behind and giving the morning sky a strange, eerie cast. Suddenly, she stopped and looked around, realizing everything looked virtually the same. Covered in snow, the landscape had no distinguishable markers, and she had no way to get her bearings. Not thinking far enough ahead in her eagerness to be rid of the cave, she hadn't brought her backpack, or compass, and now she found herself in a bit of a predicament. So familiar with the mountain under normal circumstances, she hadn't thought she would need any of the extra paraphernalia to find her way home. How could she have been so careless?

Overwhelmed, for just a moment, she stopped to make a plan. "Well," she thought out loud, "if I turn around and go back in the direction I came from, I should be able to see my tracks in the snow. I'll just follow my own trail back to the cave." What she hadn't realized was the lightly blowing snow covered her shallow, snowshoe impressions. Before long, she'd changed directions several times trying to find her previous pathway and was woefully lost.

A light snow was beginning to fall again when she found herself rounding the bend to the PM encampment. Shocked, Jana had no idea she'd come this far and would never have intentionally ventured into the enemy's camp in broad daylight. "But," she reasoned, "while I'm here, it can't hurt to look around a little." Knowing where she was now also took the worry of her immediate situation off her shoulders. She knew how to get home from the camp, so she would be able to find her way back again when she was finished.

Watching from her vantage point behind the rocks, she tried to take in all the details she'd missed the night she'd first arrived on the plateau—the night Mike had been so brutally injured. Mike wouldn't approve of her being here alone; he'd become very protective of her in their time together. But she felt this was an opportunity for her to do a little intelligence work of her own, and since she was already here by some unknown design, she was going to take advantage of her circumstances to their fullest.

Mental notes began as she viewed a series of caves occupying the far side of the plateau. Barred doors covered the cavern openings. That side of the camp was a great distance from where she hid behind rocks in the scrub pine, but she could make out a heavily armed guard in front of what she could only assume were jail cells. The topography of the encampment was such that the base covered about half of the mountain's top plateau. The camp was surrounded by gigantic walls of boulders on two sides with the front of the site open to her present location and guarded by two seriously equipped sentries. From what she could tell, the far side of the mesa ended in a shear drop off behind the barred caves. These had to be the prison cells Mike told her about. The camp appeared to have, by her best estimation, about three hundred troops, and had all the tents, buildings, weapons, and operational equipment a company of this size would require in order to function efficiently. About half way through the camp and to her left was the munitions dump, a medical building was located further to the back on that same side, and to her right hand side nearer to the front of the camp was the mess tent. Various outbuildings and tents, such as a communications structure occupied most of the space, including what she guessed was the commander's quarters.

Watching the day-to-day goings-on of the PM camp caused her to begin thinking. *"Why is this camp still on the mountain? Now that the administration is in control of everything in the outside world, what is the purpose of their hiding an operation here? Who could possibly be left after this much time had passed to challenge any of their evil plans? Surely, they weren't worried about what a group of ARM soldiers might be able to do against a military so large and heavily armed?"*

Jana watched for hours, mentally noting every detail of the camp's movement and schedule. There were some slight differences in the uniforms the soldiers were wearing compared to the uniforms she'd witnessed in her dealings with the militia before this, and she was mystified over that discrepancy. A pole held several flags which fluttered in the breeze. She recognized one of them, but several others including a white flag with a red crescent moon caused her a certain amount of confusion. She realized too that she'd distinctly heard several languages in addition to English being spoken as the day wore on. Witnessing some strange customs, including a Muslim call to prayer which brought several soldiers out of their tents, she was more puzzled than ever.

Two guards carried buckets back to the cells in back and passed what appeared to be bread and other food through the bars. Then they passed empty buckets through the door and received full ones back. Someone was definitely being held prisoner in those caves. How many? She wasn't sure, but it appeared the numbers might be quite high. That had to be it. Mike was definitely right. There was no other explanation. This was absolutely a prison. If only she were closer. If only she could see the faces of the prisoners. She didn't know why seeing their faces seemed so important to her, but something in her gut told her Mike was right and the detainees were very high level indeed. That might be the best and only explanation for the existence of this hidden encampment.

Activity in the enemy's camp was at a minimum, due in part to the large amount of snow covering the plateau. It was probably hard to keep three hundred soldiers busy when their camp was covered in several feet of the white stuff, so it appeared most of the troops were spending time in their tents and respective outbuildings.

Forced confinement would most probably tax their nerves and cause them to be a little out of shape as well. Jana wondered if the observed circumstances would be something she could use to her advantage in order to find out the identities of the prisoners in the caves.

Her stomach began to growl and she suddenly realized she'd been gone for quite some time. She was sure Mike was worried sick.

Crawling away from the rocks until she was out of view of the camp, she stood up and hurried on her way. Rushing back to the cave, Jana noticed the sun beginning to peek from the clouds. As the light revealed itself in earnest, the reflection caused a glare so bright she could barely see. She was relieved she knew her way home from the foe's camp, since she would have only her memories to guide her. With the entirely white setting before her, she had to be careful not to fall off a cliff or injure herself on some hidden obstacle. The landscape was still disguised with the aftermath of the blizzard, but she hoped to make good time getting back to Mike in the cave.

Jana felt good about the intelligence she'd collected, but wasn't at all sure how to use any of it to help their cause just yet. That was a discussion she could have with Mike as soon as he finished scolding her for not telling him where she was going and for getting too close to the PM camp. Picking her way back home and in deep thought about all she'd witnessed, Jana didn't notice the trail she was leaving behind, in the deep snow, that led all the way back to their sanctuary.

"Where have you been?" Mike questioned in an angry tone. "I've been worried sick. I figured you went out to get some fresh air, or some fresh meat, but you've been gone for most of the day!"

"Whoa! Settle down, Mike. I didn't mean to be gone so long. I did go out for fresh air and fresh meat. I brought the meat back with me. I was trying out my new snowshoes, and I wandered off far enough that I couldn't get my bearings in all that snow. I ended up accidently at the PM camp."

"What? I thought we had an understanding you weren't going to go near that camp until I was fit enough to go with you?"

"Well, keep in mind that was your idea. But calm down, it was an accident anyway, just like I said. I got lost, okay? No harm done. I was able to watch for quite a while, and I have their guard schedules down pretty well. Most of the soldiers were in their tents, because of all the snow, but I noticed some discrepancies in the uniforms, compared to what I'm used to seeing. I wonder what the explanation of that is. There were different languages being spoken too, some I understood, some I didn't, and some odd goings on that I couldn't explain. Anyway, I saw the caves, on the other side of the camp, just like you were talking about, and I think you're right. I believe they've got some very high level prisoners in there. I couldn't get a good look at any of them though."

"Okay, okay, so it was an accident. But going forward, you need to let me know when you are leaving, and you really need to take your compass with you, agreed?"

"Agreed. I didn't mean to worry you. I just figured if I was that far out anyway, I should use the opportunity to do a little intelligence gathering. I promise I won't go anywhere again without letting you know, okay, Daddy?"

"Okay, sorry, I do sound like I'm scolding you, don't I? I don't mean to treat you like you have no sense. I know you were surviving just fine up till now and certainly before I came along. I was just worried about you, that's all."

"I know, Mike. I'm not angry. And I know you see I can take care of myself. Perhaps, more than anyone out there ever knew. Your current state attests to that. But I appreciate you are concerned and that you care about me so much. I feel like we've become family, so I'm not out to hurt you or worry you. But I don't want to wait till spring to find out what is going on in that camp! I feel like I've been a constant drain on the future of ARM, and I would like to be able to give something back for once."

"Don't be ridiculous, Jana. Nothing that has happened is your fault. And I agree with you. I feel like you are my family too. Josh was right. He believed in you, and he knew if it came down to it, you would do the right thing. You have proved to be more capable than even he believed, and I sure as heck wouldn't want to go toe-to-toe with you again. As far as other languages, I was sure I heard the same thing. I'm not sure what that means, but I know some of the intelligence the guys collected confirmed that several other countries were involved with ours in attempting to form a one world government, so I wondered if those were foreign troops. We all know the president is friends with some rather unsavory characters and that could explain it too."

"I saw a white flag with a red crescent moon on it. I'm sure that flag belongs to a Muslim nation, though I can't be sure which one. I never paid much attention to any of that, but I'm sure I heard the Muslim call to prayer playing over the loudspeakers, and I saw several soldiers come out of their tents. Do you really think the forces are from all countries? I guess that would make the most sense, and it might explain why some of the troops are still hidden in the mountains out here."

"I'm sure that explains much of what we're seeing. It would certainly fit in with the theory of a one world government constabulary force, wouldn't it? I wish I'd noticed that in enough time to pass it along to ARM before I was laid up."

"Well, I took care of your data collecting days. Sorry about that, Mike."

"Don't be ridiculous, Jana. Think of all the fun I'd be missing if we hadn't met the way we did!"

Jana pulled rabbits from her pouch and got to work cleaning them for supper. She would save these skins too. Finding more uses for the pelts every day, her game pouch was made of furs, and recently, she'd sewn enough hides together to make another great cape which would give her one more layer of warmth in the ever declining mountain temperatures.

Mike and Jana sat together and ate a hearty meal of roasted rabbit and baked tubers. Jana also made a nice broth with some of the rabbit bones, dried onions, herbs, salt and pepper from her stores. After eating, she washed the supper dishes and built up the fire, so she and Mike could sit together and study. Life was good for now. She knew they couldn't stay in this cave forever, and she wanted to find out more about the odd goings-on at the PM encampment on the other side of the mountain, but for now, this was good and she believed herself very blessed.

23

THE SUN WOULD be up soon, and Jana was anxious to get going as usual. This time, she had her backpack, with its new handmade camouflage fur cover, all stocked and ready to strap on plus she'd remembered to clip her compass to the outside of the bag which would surely make Mike very happy.

He'd asked her to be more prepared for whatever might transpire if she was going to go out on the mountain, especially if she was going to go it alone. Trying to please him, she supposed it made sense to be sure she didn't end up in the same frightening position she'd found herself in only days before. Jana planned to do some hiking and hunting, and so she'd packed plenty of jerky, along with dried fruits and nuts for her lunch. Her water bottle, and canteen, was full, and she was outfitted with her new snow-shoes and camouflage clothing as well as her rabbit pelt cape. Snug as a bug in a rug, she was prepared for whatever the weather might bring today.

Handgun loaded, just in case; additional ammo in her bag; trusty knife razor sharp in its sheath at her side; she'd even spent additional time making new arrows and attaching arrowheads so she could get some good use out of her bow. Josh had showed her years ago how to harden wood for the shafts, check for straightness, attach the fletching and nock the ends, so she had a rabbit pelt quiver full of new arrows for her outing. Her snowshoes were strapped on tight, and she was more than eager to get out on the trail.

A nice rabbit stew with root vegetables and herbs was simmering on the fire for their supper. Mike was awake to see her off, so she said her good-byes and out into the cold she went, ready to face the day.

Walking through the pristine pre-dawn, Jana felt more at peace hiking the mountain than she'd ever felt in her tumultuous lifetime doing anything else. Warm breath formed small clouds, in the frosty air in front of her face, and she could already feel the moisture freezing on her nose hairs. Smiling, as ice crystals formed in and then tickled her nostrils, she wiggled her nose to dislodge them. She was exhilarated at the prospect of an entire day to herself. Blood surging in her veins, she started off, and as she walked, she knew without question this was the life—a day on her mountain with God and her deepest thoughts, how could anything be more beautiful than that?

Trekking over snowdrifts, her heart soared and newly learned scripture began to flow through her mind.

Lord our Lord, how magnificent is Your name throughout the earth! You have covered the heavens with Your majesty. Because of Your adversaries, You have established a stronghold from the mouths of children and infants, to silence the enemy and the avenger. When I observe Your heavens, the work of Your fingers, the moon and the stars, which You set in place, what is man that You remember him, the son of man that You look after him? You made him little less than God and crowned him with glory and honor, You made him lord over the works of Your hands; You put everything under his feet: all the sheep and oxen, as well as animals in the wild, birds of the sky, and fish of the sea passing through the currents of the seas. Lord our Lord, how magnificent is Your name throughout the earth! (Ps. 8:1–9)

Jana knew in her spirit God was right here with her, that He was watching over her, keeping her safe, and He would never leave her or forsake her. What a beautiful feeling indeed. This new way of living and thinking freed her in a way she could never have imagined as she thought back to her old, twisted way of observing life and what it had to offer. This was the abundant life He'd promised her, and she knew it started by trusting Him to take care of it all, by casting all her fears on Him. She praised Him and loved Him with all her heart, soul, mind, and strength, knowing He'd loved her first, and she couldn't be happier than she was at this moment.

As the sun began to rise above the horizon, in a cloudless sky, a kaleidoscope of colors danced across brightening heavens in one of the most gorgeous sunrises she'd ever seen. Jana felt as though the beauty of that moment was a special gift from her heavenly Father to shower her with favor and demonstrate His love for her. The world was a soft blanket of white, glittering with hope and promise. Soon Jana had bagged several squirrels and a number of rabbits. After field dressing them to save room, she stored the skinned animals in her hunting pouch, saving the furs, and burying the entrails in the snow, so as not to leave a trail.

In her explorations, she spied the unmistakable silhouette of a willow tree and decided it wouldn't hurt to relieve the tree of some bark to replenish her first aid kit. Scraping what she needed of the bark, she stored it in her backpack. She'd run quite low on the miraculous substance and figured they'd need it again at some point. Mike's recovery was taking much longer than either of them could have imagined it would, and the willow bark, when made into a tea, proved to be a great fever reducer and pain reliever. Jana was having so much fun on her day out that she forgot to keep track of the time, and pretty soon, her stomach began telling her lunch time had certainly long since passed.

Finding a comfortable spot to sit at the base of a mountain pine, she pulled jerky and nuts out of her bag to munch on while she rested. After eating, she took a long pull on her water bottle and leaned back against the trunk of the conifer with eyes closed. Smiling outside and in, she sighed and breathed deeply of the woodsy scent. In her old life, stress had been her constant companion. She'd never known a life without fear and striving. How magnificent to sit at the base of a tree with no thoughts but love and contentment in her surroundings flowing though her mind.

Sun shone down through the trees, and with today's total absence of wind, it left her feeling warm even in subzero temperatures. Before long, she'd dozed off and in what seemed like only moments, woke again with a start. Noticing upon waking the sun had moved significantly in the sky, she realized she'd probably slept for several hours. Not recognizing she'd been so tired, she got up, dusted the snow off her camouflage and got back on her way, hoping she could get back to the cave before nightfall, so she wouldn't worry Mike again.

The sun had already set by the time Jana rounded the last boulder on their side of the plateau which led to the cave. Immediately, when she saw the darkness of the cavern interior, she knew something was wrong. She should have been able to see a faint flicker of firelight through their entrance and smell her rabbit stew still simmering. After all, when she left before sunup, Mike had been fine and the world was as it should be. Instead, now, everything looked cold and forbidding.

Heart revving in her chest, and chills shimmying their way down her spine, she crept closer to their hiding place and stooped over far enough to look inside the cave opening. The place was badly trashed, and Mike was nowhere to be seen. Jana looked quickly throughout the sanctuary and saw her stew had been dumped on the fire. All Mike's things were strewn about and the fire pit was ice cold, indicating the fire had been out for at least a couple of hours. If only she hadn't fallen asleep, maybe she would have been here to help Mike. Jana had carried most of her own belongings with her in her pack, including her Bible, so there wouldn't have been much if anything here which might connect her to Mike.

Thankfully, if the soldiers were looking for her, the contents of this cave wouldn't have given her away. She wasn't even sure yet if the goons were the perpetrators. "Well, who else would it be?"Jana thought out loud. "I can't believe they found us. How? I know I was careful when I went out. How did they find us?"There wasn't time to kick herself now. Jana knew she had to move fast. So far, she believed she was undetected in the dark, but they could be back at any moment, and for all she knew, they might have guards keeping a look out for anyone who might come back to the cave or be working with Mike.

On second thought, the sheer amount of wood and food in the shelter might have been a dead give-away to the enemy that Mike was not living alone in this cave at least not in his current semi-handicapped condition, so they could already be tipped off as to her existence. Jana hustled to her hiding place in the rear of the cave, the area she had not revealed even to Mike, and retrieved the papers she'd hidden there. Then she scavenged through the cave for anything else which might be salvageable and useful to her on the run; loading as much jerky, nuts, and dried fruits into her pack as she was able to safely carry.

Grabbing Mike's canteen and the other water bottles from the cave, she filled them and then hung them from her already loaded pack. Looking around at the total destruction in the cave one last time, she slipped out into the night. How many times in her life would she leave her home after political thugs destroyed everything she'd worked for? But Jana had no intention of leaving Mike to the mercy of those tyrants. First, she would need a bivouac shelter. She wasn't tired, and she couldn't have slept if she tried, so she already knew she'd be up all night working on a way to save her friend.

Sure that if Mike was still alive he was at the enemy's encampment, she could only guess at what they might be doing to him. Happy she hadn't shared information with him on the whereabouts of the documents she was sure they were after, she patted her pack as if reassuring herself they were still safe.

Not knowing for sure if the militia was aware of her presence in particular, or her relationship with Mike, she was at least fairly confident they knew someone had been helping him. Jana was pretty sure they weren't going to let up until they were certain they'd sufficiently contained the situation.

Finding out exactly where the troops had stashed Mike would be important, but setting up a secure home base was imperative too, perhaps more vital since she would need a place to plan her strategy. Jana was relieved she'd been given an opportunity to gather intelligence beforehand. She knew from her day outside the camp that the soldiers were in possession of an enormous munitions depot, and she knew the precise location of that ammo. She meant to use every bit of the information at her disposal to her advantage.

This operation would take some planning in order to be successful. That was okay too. She felt badly it would mean Mike was going to have to wait longer for his rescue, but to move too quickly would be fatal for them both. Sure the terrorists would be expecting Mike's roommate, whoever that might be, to come to his aid sooner rather than later, she decided later might be a better approach anyway. So, that was reason enough to take her time and plan every detail of the rescue accordingly. Jana spent a good part of the night looking for a place to rest—a place which would be invisible to the armed forces in the camp—and thanking God for the full moon that was providing light with which to do it.

Searching the mountain for anything which might give her an advantage, she found the back side of the behemoth, behind the PM encampment, was an almost sheer drop off for what looked to be thousands of feet. It definitely wasn't formed with the same intermittent wide stair-like ledges which comprised the geography of the front of that mountain. Looking intently, with the help of moonlight and a long stick, she discovered a very narrow sill on the back side of the monolith, which was under the tree line about eight feet below the surface of the plateau where the militia camp was located. The narrow shelf appeared to be obscured from view, from topside, by an overhang on the butte. This was just what she was looking for.

She inched her way down the eight-foot incline behind boulders and then along the newfound ledge, by the grace of God, using only moonlight and fingertips, completely aware of the vast space below her. Convinced the shelf would be undetectable from the plateau above, she determined to forge on. Looking up to the militia's camp above, one could only conclude that when looking over the cliff the back side of the encampment did indeed end in a very steep abyss, for it seemed the outcropping of rock and twisted roots which overhung the rock face by two feet or so completely masked the shelf on which she stood.

Feeling her way along the ledge, she found a very small cave etched into the backside of the cliff wall and decided it would serve nicely as her base camp. Estimating the cave, which was a four-foot deep by six-foot wide by three-and-a-half-foot high hollow, to be directly below the best access point to the plateau where the rear of the enemy's camp was located, she unloaded her gear and hunkered down for what remained of the night. Sitting in her small cave, she knew she was quite literally right beneath the area where she believed Mike was held captive. From this vantage point, she'd be able to gather additional information and plan her attack with no worry of being detected by anyone from above. Wishing she could get a message to Mike somehow, instead she prayed and handed the entire situation over to God.

Jana had already decided she would be attacking the militia's army. This approach might seem foolhardy to some, but she knew without question that she serves a mighty God and that He is on her side. She absolutely isn't going to give up and let them win, but she's also decided she won't try to sneak in to this heavily guarded camp to take an injured man out from under their noses entirely by stealth; there would be far too much risk involved in that. No, God had given her a better idea and she was stepping out in faith.

Jana had recently been reading the story of Gideon in Judges 6, 7, and 8, and was inspired by God's intercession in the workings of Gideon's army to bring him success against all odds. She'd begun to discover in her life, little by little, that God, her God, was a God of the impossible, and if He could bring deliverance to Gideon and his army of three hundred against tens of thousands of Midianites, then He could certainly deliver her and Mike against an army of a mere three hundred.

A backpack full of jerky, nuts, and berries would come in handy during this time of planning. The location of her small cave made the building of a fire out of the question, but she took care to shape the ledge's snow up high and tight around the opening of the cavity to keep the wind and any possible stray animals out, though she doubted there would be many living things brave, or stupid, enough to walk the route she'd taken. The wall of snow would also help to shield her more adequately from any possible prying human eyes. Though she also doubted that would be necessary, as a grown man would find it difficult to find stability on the narrow ledge she'd navigated to get here. A snow wall might help keep her from rolling over in the middle of the night and falling off the cliff, so it would be a good use of her time.

Thankful for her hand cranked flashlight, it would allow her to read and plan without a fire. She certainly wouldn't be as warm in this shelter as she'd been in the lodging she'd shared with Mike, but it would have to do for now, and the enclosed accommodation she'd constructed at least kept some of her body heat inside. Figuring the enemy would never suspect she was camping right beneath his back door, she had to admit it was a pretty daring move, downright gutsy even for her, but that thought coupled with the fact she knew God was with her gave her all the confidence she needed. The sun would be up soon, so Jana decided to get a little rest and drifted off to sleep in prayer.

Consciousness and the realization of where she was sleeping came floating back to Jana in the predawn cold of her tiny cave. Stretching elicited groans of sincere and acute pain. Her pack had been her pillow and the cave floor, even covered by her sleeping bag, was a very hard bed. She'd been spoiled with her mattress of soft pine boughs in the cozy cavern she shared with Mike. Last night, she'd been warm enough in her rabbit pelt outer garments, and her cape made a nice blanket, but it would take some moving about to revive her circulation enough to do the things she needed to accomplish by the end of daylight today.

Breakfast was dried fruits, nuts, and jerky and probably would be until she was able to build a fire again. Braiding her thick, auburn hair had gotten harder for her since it'd grown quite long in these past months, but she managed to complete the task in the small space available to her and then tied the thick braid back with a strip of leather from her pack. She drank from her bottle then relieved herself over the edge of the precipice, being careful not to lose her balance in the process.

Leaving her backpack in the small cave made sense for now, so she took inventory to be sure she had all the supplies she needed while she was out and about on the stone ledge. Her handgun and ammo were coming with her on the reconnaissance mission. Her prior hunting forays had not taken her as far as the small shelf on this particular side of the mountain, so she wasn't at all familiar with her surroundings; after all, it had been dark by the time she arrived on the narrow walkway last night.

She did know though that if she climbed the rock above her, the climb would take her to the plateau which held the PM camp. If she remembered her previous surveillance accounts correctly, the munitions would be to her right and about half way across the encampment, because it had been located on her left looking from her vantage point on the other side of the plateau. If she waited till dark, she would have a better chance of moving undetected on the butte, so for now she would walk the back side of the mountain on this lower level and look for various access points to the higher mesa.

As she walked, she didn't spy any footprints, besides her own, for obvious reasons. The ledge was not particularly wide in any given area and was practically nonexistent in some places. There were stretches so narrow she was forced to hug the rock wall and hold on with the toes of her boots and fingertips in order to keep from plunging to her death hundreds, or thousands, of feet below. On several occasions, Jana lost her footing and came so close to falling into the abyss that she was literally sick to her stomach, vomiting over the cliff's edge. Needless to say, her level of concentration was fully engaged all day.

Sure that the militia believed themselves safe from attack on this side of their camp's plateau, she felt comfortable she wouldn't be detected. From her position, she guessed the narrow ledge on which she traveled ran along the entire back of the mountain and wrapped about half way around the far side. Later she would discover it circled almost three quarters of the mount and though it was no more than two and a half feet wide in any spot, it gave her access to most of the PM camp above.

Certainly, she would agree, no significant attack could be amassed from this side of the mountain, even with the advantage of the tiny ledge on her side. But Jana wasn't making plans for an army on her side, she didn't have tens of thousands, or even three hundred, she just meant to make the soldiers think she did.

Spending her day edging along ledges and climbing rock walls was exhausting. Twice before the sun went down, Jana sat on the ledge to rest her body and drink her fill of water. It took all that was within her not to spend any significant time looking over the ridge to focus on the negative of her situation; instead, she focused on her Lord and prayed over and over, Philippians 4:13: "I can do all things through Christ who strengthens me," as she acclimated to her situation.

Climbing to the plateau above would require a feat of sheer strength, and will, due to the maneuvering she'd have to manage in scaling the overhang. But she knew her strength was in Christ and felt sure she could depend on Him to see her through that particular accomplishment of power. She hoped too that she could find boulders large enough topside to attach ropes for future access to the highland, as she would have to return to set up and would also need to revisit for the upcoming battle. Thankful for her recent months of extreme physical activity, she was sure she would be up to the challenge with God's help.

25

WITH NIGHT QUICKLY sweeping over the gorge, she was ready to begin the next chapter of her mission. Waiting until around three in the morning to start, Jana prepped for her climb. The moon was almost full and very bright, so her foray into the armed camp would be dicey at best, but the chosen time frame would put her between guard changes and would certainly weed out any chance of random discovery by soldiers walking about the camp.

Several important factors were in her favor. First, she was outfitted in gear which blended well into her surroundings. Second, she had surprise on her side. No one knew she was here, and she was coming from the back side of the mountain where the PM soldiers would never have expected a prowler to emerge. Third, she had a pretty good idea about the layout of the camp and knew which direction she needed to head. Fourth and most important, she had the God of the universe on her side, and if He was for her, who could be against her?

She'd found a better access point to the PM camp plateau. It was down the ledge a short way from her cave. Discovering that and other pertinent bits of information while she was gathering intelligence this morning, she headed there now. Inching her way along the rock wall so as not to fall into the ravine below in the dark of the night, she reached the area she'd marked earlier and began her frightening and perilous climb to the encampment. As she'd expected, the going was tough. Wind picked up, and there were moments when she feared she might be plucked from the wall and cast to her death in the crevasse below. At one point, she found herself holding on, by gnarled roots, to the underside of the overhang, swinging back and forth like a dry leaf on a branch. Her faith held, and she climbed the obstacle using what felt like every ounce of her strength and energy. Fervent prayer and the grace of God held her, and pretty soon, she was lifting herself over the last bit of rock and twisted vegetation to the flat of the plateau. Trembling almost uncontrollably and breathing hard, she looked around quickly, taking in every detail of her surroundings. Needing to rest and get the power back in her unstable legs, she sat for a moment contemplating her next move.

Examining the landscape of the plateau, she found she was indeed behind the string of caves, which allegedly held prisoners, just as she believed she would be. The caves blocked her sudden appearance over the cliff edge and gave her a vantage point with which to launch her recon mission. First tying her rope to a large boulder, which was attached quite firmly to the back outside wall of the prison caves, Jana hunkered down to watch the goings-on of the camp.

Peeking around the outside of the caves, she saw an armed sentry. From what she was able to observe, the night watch consisted of only one guard as she'd witnessed in the daytime. This would make her job much easier and so she began to monitor his every movement. Identifying the sentinel's patterns and actions, she gathered he wasn't particularly concerned about the possibility of his camp being attacked, especially at night and from this angle.

Like so many who do the same thing day after day, or in this case night after night, he appeared to have become quite complacent. She could almost read his mind. "The base has never been attacked; therefore the base will never be attacked." This obvious smugness on the part of the soldier would work in Jana's favor as well. After a while, Jana saw the guard go to the farthest end of this series of caves and lean against the outside wall there. It didn't take long before he looked to be very relaxed, and she decided this might be her opportunity to act.

Moving quietly, quickly, and keeping a low profile, Jana maneuvered between the tents and outbuildings until she reached the munitions dump. She saw much of the larger ammunition in the penned in area around the tent, but she had a feeling the smaller items she was looking for specifically would be inside that tent. Jana looked high and low for signs of a munitions guard, but didn't see one. She did see two heavily equipped lookouts clear up at the front of the camp. From what she was able to ascertain, these guards seemed to be on the ball and very much awake, but she was half an encampment away from them and knew without doubt God would see her through this entire plan.

It seemed apparent whoever was in charge thought his camp so impenetrable, two guards in front and one guard in the rear at the prison caves was enough, so the rest of the camp was sound asleep and oblivious to any possible danger. That arrogance, or lack of information, would help in their future undoing. In their defense, there was only one obvious entrance to the camp and that front entry was protected by fifty-foot boulders on either side of the ingress. Slipping under the unfastened tent flap of the munitions shelter, Jana took one more look around to be sure she was not followed, yanked the canvass shut behind her and pulled out her flashlight.

Looking for specific items might take a little time, so Jana was resolute in her objective of attaining all the supplies she'd need for tomorrow night's attack on the camp and not allowing her nerves to get the best of her. Every gust of wind ruffling tent walls sent her heart into overdrive, but she also realized the wind would cover any small noises she might make and cause her to be less noticeable to anyone who might happen by. After months of studying her Bible and immersing herself in the Word of God, Jana had become less worried about events in her life and relied more on the Scriptures she'd learned to steady her heart and mind, so she began reciting some of those Scriptures under her breath now as she searched for the ammunition she'd need to make her rescue mission a success tomorrow night.

"No weapon formed against you will succeed, and you will refute any accusation raised against you. This is the heritage of the Lord's servants, and their righteousness is from me. This is the Lord's declaration" (Isa. 54:17). She would need eight of the claymore mines with wireless remote detonation. She loaded the claymores into a carry bag along with wireless remotes for each of the mines.

> The Lord is my rock, my fortress, and my deliverer, my God, my mountain where I seek refuge. My shield, the horn of my salvation, my stronghold, my refuge, and my Savior, You save me from violence. I called to the Lord, who is worthy of praise, and I was saved from my enemies. (2 Sam. 22:2–4)

She picked up boxes of shells. Wanting to put several hundred rounds in each of the eight prearranged locations, she read the outside of the boxes to determine the number of units per box. The ammo was heavy, but she'd do what she had too. Four thousand rounds into a reinforced canvas bag from the back of the tent ought to do it.

> May the Lord be praised, for He has heard the sound of my pleading, The Lord is my strength and my shield; my heart trusts in Him, and I am helped. Therefore my heart rejoices, and I praise Him with song. The Lord is the strength of His people; He is a stronghold of salvation for His anointed. Save Your people, bless Your

possession, shepherd them, and carry them forever." (Ps. 28:6–9)

Next, she found a spool of fuse material and an M16 with multiple ammunition clips. A large container of thermite was last on her list so she loaded that and the M16 clips along with a butane lighter and two pairs of gloves into the top opening of a stack of eight heavy, steel buckets.

There was no way she could carry all this gear by herself, especially in one trip, so she determined to make three very heavy trips. Stowing her spoils behind the munitions tent she made her way back across the camp and past the lightly dozing guard with her first load without being detected and quietly praising God all the way.

Leaving her first haul in the small level area behind the prison caves, she headed across the camp's impromptu obstacle course on her way back to the rear of the munitions tent and retrieved her second batch of cargo. When she arrived at the last covered stop before a span of encampment which would put her in full view of the prison guard for a split second, she heard a shout. Leaping quietly behind the nearest cover, her heart jumped in her chest, and she struggled to catch breath. Was she discovered? Setting her steel buckets down gently and reaching for ammunition, she slammed the M16 clip home; then turning slowly, she realized there was no one there. Visually probing the open space from the protection of her hiding place, she saw the jail's sentry straighten up and take a step forward.

Her breathing regulated a little when she saw a second armed sentinel walking toward the first. It seemed his nightly relief had come, had she been in the camp that long?

Waiting for the changing of the guard to complete, which included some animated conversation, a few jokes, and a cigarette or two, she hunkered down in her furs.

Forced to linger, cold and fidgety for over an hour before the second watch finally began to relax and let down his defenses, she was running out of time to get her last payload moved. The sun would be coming up in less than an hour as she rounded the far side of the caves to stow her second and third loads of borrowed munitions.

Much of her upcoming ambush would be launched from the vantage point of her narrow ledge, below the encampment's plateau, and she figured she could work on that project throughout the day today, but first she'd transfer her supplies from the plateau before they were accidently discovered.

Four trips up and down her rope, with buckets strapped to her back, was what it took to move the heavy munitions. Her arms and legs felt like Jell-O by the time she shouldered her last batch, and Jana knew that only God held her as she shimmied down to the ledge. She pushed the spoils into her shallow cave, covered them with her tarp, and buried the whole thing in snow. Sun was just peeking over the horizon in a clear blue and pink sky when she closed herself up in her tiny, crowded cave to get a little shut eye. This day would be a time of hard labor and could culminate in an amazing night of redemption for many, if she played her cards right.

Jana once again spent her sleeping hours in the comforting arms of Jesus, and His words to her right before she woke were: "Know that I will never leave you or forsake you my child." She awakened from her nap with a deeper resolve and an even keener sense of purpose. Plans had been made and solidified for the ambush to come.

Her strategy, which had become even clearer to her as she slept, dictated that each steel bucket would contain one cup of thermite and five hundred rounds of ammo. Fuse running to each bucket would ignite the thermite, which would burn at an incredibly high temperature setting off the rounds in such a way as to imitate automatic machine gun fire.

She spent the day distributing steel buckets to their designated locations, attaching them firmly to the ledge so they wouldn't dislodge during combat, connecting fuse to the handles and winding additional fuse around the inside bottoms of the buckets to insure contact, then loading the rounds of ammo into each container.

Next, she rigged the claymore mines, alternating them with her steel containers. The buckets were placed on the ledge below the plateau, since they would be nothing more than glorified noise makers, but the mines were set up on the edge of the plateau itself for maximum effectiveness. Placing the mines was a challenge as she had to find toe and hand holds at each placement site in order to climb the eight feet to the mesa and then reach over the edge, undetected, to set the charges.

Once she'd arranged her ammunition on the narrow shelf and anchored each bucket to the ledge, she checked their stability. She reasoned the action in the buckets might jar the vessels from their positions if they weren't adequately attached, and she didn't intend to lose any of her special effects over the edge and into the precipice below in the middle of the battle to come.

Checking her M16, she determined it to be in good working order. She'd have to trust her instincts on that one since she wouldn't have opportunity to try the weapon until the night's warfare ensued. Jana filled her pockets and her pouch with shells for her handgun and clips for the M16 and then sat down to eat some lunch. Jerky and dried fruits might have gotten boring if she were paying attention, but her mind's eye was going over her plans for tonight and what she was putting in her mouth was the least of her concerns.

No amount of preparation could put her mind and heart at ease the way time with her Lord would, so she pulled out her Bible and began to read. She was planning to take another short nap before dark, knowing tonight would take every bit of concentration and strength she could muster. Once she began to read and pray, she calmed down measurably and knew deep within her spirit that God would be her foundation and power throughout this entire ordeal. She read 1 John 4:4, "Greater is He that is within me, than he that is in the world." And 2 Timothy 1:7, "God has not given me the spirit of fear, but of power, and of love, and of a sound mind."

Lying down to rest, Jana turned the upcoming night and the outcome of the eminent battle over to her Lord, and drifted off to sleep, the peaceful sleep of His beloved. The time for trials would come soon enough. For now, she was once again in the arms of Jesus.

Rested, Jana woke determined and ready to go. It would be dark soon, but her ambush could not begin until she was sure the camp was tucked in and sleeping for the night, as she would need surprise on her side. Sure this night would be a surprise for many she was anxious to get going! Using the waning light to her advantage by making one more check of her munitions layout, she deemed everything well prepared and good to go.

Sitting in her small cave waiting for the moment of her testing, she began to reminisce. Her years with Josh had been the happiest years of her life, until recently, though she regretted she'd not made his days a fraction as joyful as he'd made hers. One by one, images of wonderful times they shared filled her mind, and if there had been a witness in the small cave, that witness would have seen tears and smiles accompanying the faraway look in her eyes. If Josh could see her now, he wouldn't recognize her as the woman he'd married and known for all the years they'd been together. She chuckled under her breath when she thought of his smile, his dimples and the way his face looked as he slept. If she had those years to live over again, they would be different, but that could never be. Knowing there was a very real possibility she would see Josh tonight in heaven when she let loose her attack on the camp above; she could say in all honesty that death no longer frightened her.

Mike loved her. Of this, she had no doubt. But her feelings for him were ones of platonic friendship and that was all. He was her teacher and her mentor. She'd always love him for the revelations of God's Grace he'd shared with her, but she'd taken care of him, like one would care for a small child, for a very long time and she knew he would never be more to her than a dear friend. No man could ever fill Josh's place in her heart. Perhaps she would spend what remained of her life alone, well, if she survived this night anyway, but Mike would not be a romantic part of her future.

She'd already determined she was willing to give up her life for the mission tonight. But if God chose to save her life, she'd spend what remained of it sharing the Gospel. She'd already decided nothing in her life was more important to her than her Lord Jesus, and she had a need she couldn't explain to share Him with everyone who didn't know His love and who might consent for a moment to listen to her testimony. Loading her pack for her last trip over the plateau's ledge later that night, she secured her Bible and zipped the pouch.

A cold front moved in throughout the afternoon and evening, bringing clouds and more frigid air; both could be an advantage for her. The clouds would make the dark of night seem even blacker covering her movements, and the frigid air might likely keep the soldiers covered up snug in their nice warm bunks.

One o'clock in the morning and Jana was ready to get things started. Shrouded in a peace she couldn't explain, she knew God was with her, that she was His beloved and that He would be her strength and protector this night. "Okay, Lord, I know you're with me, so let's get ready to rock and roll!" Loading her gear on her back and climbing the previously secured rope to the encampment, Jana pulled herself up and over the twisted roots and rocks to the flat terrain above.

Breathing deeply after the arduous climb, she stopped to center her mind and quietly recited Isaiah 41:10, "Fear not, for I am with you; don't be dismayed, for I am your God; I will strengthen you; yes, I will help you; yes, I will uphold you with the right hand of my Righteousness." As she recited, she felt her whole body and mind come to rest in Him.

Looking around her launching area in the murky darkness, she took stock of her surroundings and got the plan straight in her mind. Jana had her numbered mine remotes lined up in the rabbit pelt pouch along with her ammo, and once she knew exactly where she stood on the plateau, she felt along the rear of the caves to find the bundle of fuses she'd stashed there earlier. More than ready to begin, she said a quick prayer. "Father God. You are my Lord and my protector. Give me favor and success and let all I do give you glory in Christ Jesus."

Lighting the bundle of fuse, Jana waited in anticipation as the fire crept slowly along the cord to the nearest bucket, loaded for bear on the ledge. She took the first wireless remote from her pouch and readied herself for the ensuing conflagration. Her second remote was near at hand, and her M16 loaded with the first of many clips she would use on this night of combat's fire.

Moving cautiously to the far back side of the prison caves, Jana watched the sleepy guard at the other end of the stone cells as she waited for the party to start. Detecting a slight chemical burning smell in the air,

Jana hunkered down, and suddenly, the air erupted with the sound of machine gun fire. The soldier, who seemed almost comatose in his state of relaxation only seconds before, leapt to attention waiving his weapon at nothing and everything at once.

Pushing a button on the first remote, the ensuing detonation rocked the plateau sending steel balls, nails, and metal shards in every direction from the exploded claymore mine.

Screams of fear and pain started immediately, as metal flew through the air and tore through canvass tents. The guard, now wholly confused, ran forward into what he imagined was the fray leaving the prison cells unguarded. As troops emerged half-dressed from their tents into the freezing cold, some with weapons and some without, Jana chose her targets judiciously.

She wasn't ready to give away her position, so her bow helped her dispatch several of the half-dressed soldiers silently. Unarmed combatants didn't represent as much of a threat in her estimation, so she concentrated on those she saw who seemed more prepared and armed for battle they assumed was already taking place.

By now, the second bucket was bursting with the rounds it contained and the confusion became more rampant. She pulled the second remote from her pouch, and upon pushing the button, the situation was once more filled with an outburst of deadly objects, taking out all those unfortunate enough to be within a hundred yards of the firestorm.

Jana knew she needed to be careful when exploding the claymores, going forward, so she and the guys she was about to release, wouldn't be within range of the flying metal. Intending to time her moves and the release of the prisoners accordingly, she saw enemy soldiers running toward the front of the encampment and decided the chance was at hand to free those in the prison caves.

Reaching for the third remote, as the third bucket erupted into the darkness, she listened as militia soldier's screams filled the cold night air. The plateau sounded to be engaged in World War III as she pushed the third button. More shrapnel filled the sky and more PM fighters fell to the already bloody ground. In the fear and uncertainty surrounding the noise of battle, Jana saw combatants emerge from their tents shooting and witnessed militia killing their own in the confusion that filled the horror of that dark highland.

Using the butt of her M16 to knock the lock off the first cell, she motioned the captives forward and gave instructions to open the remaining cells. Intending to explode the fourth mine in a way which would give prisoners additional time to regroup, she held her finger over the trigger. Once all the detainees were free, they were instructed to run to the munitions depot to arm while she laid down more cover fire. She'd wait to explode the fifth mine until she had a signal from the men that they were armed, under cover and ready to join the fight.

Jana ran from her position in front of the caves to a location behind one of the nearest outbuildings. As she reached cover, the fourth bucket's contents joined the excitement, and she pushed the button on her fourth claymore remote. More enemy soldiers joined their comrades in the gore-soaked snow.

Prisoners were all released now and those who were able made their way across the camp to the munitions tent. Intense confusion and all-consuming terror in the camp allowed them to move relatively unhindered, and within minutes, they were fully armed and ready to leap into the ongoing battle.

One of the captives had the foresight to light the ammunition tent on fire as they were leaving the area, and once they'd reached the cover of a nearby building, the entire munitions dump blew in a deafening explosion, engulfing half the mountain's mesa in a ball of fire. Jana assumed this was her sign, and she pushed the button on her fifth claymore as the fifth bucket began its rat-a-tat, tat tale.

Jana hadn't time to ask after Mike and didn't know if he was still in the caves, or with the men who had armed themselves. So far as she knew, there were no fatalities on her side of the battle, but from the looks of it, there were 150 to 200 enemy troops laying on the ground of the encampment, many of which had been killed by their own confused comrades.

Now that the ARM soldiers were armed, the night's battle grew in intensity, so she gave her contact a sign to warn his men, and when they were under cover, she pushed the button on the sixth claymore. Again, corpses joined the growing numbers in the gruesome mess on the mountain plateau. She blew the last two mines in rapid succession, and the air virtually filled with flying steel as the former hostages crouched down and the bodies of enemy combatants began to stack one upon the other. Released hostages began rounding up those few remaining enemy soldiers to take back to the caves in the rear of the camp. Hunters had finally become the hunted.

As the skirmish wound down, Jana realized she'd been running on autopilot through the entire encounter. Her knees began to shake, so she lowered herself to a large, flat rock near the building she'd used for cover, while tears of relief ran slowly down her ice cold cheeks, leaving salty tracks of warmth in their wake. Jana praised God as she cried, "Glory to God, thank you Lord, all glory to God," and rocked her exhausted body back and forth in the cold night air.

Released captives were finishing up the work of searching militia soldier's tents and outbuildings, filling up the caves with new prisoners in the process. Previous prison occupants who'd been too injured to join in the fight were brought out into the nighttime air. Jana saw two men helping a third out to a nearby rock where he stood leaning against the mainstay for support. She recognized Mike right away, so she stood and started toward him. "Mike, I'm so glad you're okay. I was so concerned they'd hurt you worse than you already were."

"They tried to, Jana. But nothing they did to me could have made me tell them about you, or the ARM location."

"I knew you wouldn't break, Mike. I'm sorry it took me so long to come get you. I had a few plans to make."

"I would never have guessed you arranged all this, but I don't know why, it really has become your style to come in with guns blazing, hasn't it? How did you do all this, Jana?"

"It was God, Mike! I used the story of Gideon, and He showed me what to do every step of the way. Really, I wouldn't have had a clue what to do, but He guided me through every piece of the ambush. It was like He was in me and working through me for the battle. All the credit goes to Him!"

Noise of gunfire, which had filled the air on the plateau for the better part of the night, was finally exhausted, and the darkness seemed almost strangely quiet. The mountain was still, but for the sounds of ARM soldiers taking care of a few last pieces of business.

Mike looked at Jana with delight. "I'm so proud of you, Jana! But I have a surprise for you too. After the militia locked me up, I found a protector in the caves. I didn't know if I would ever see you again if the bad guys had found you too; if you were in one of the other cells along with the additional prisoners; or even if you were lying dead in the snow somewhere. I should've known better. You're a firecracker, and you really can take care of yourself. But now, I want you to put the gun down for a minute, because I have something to show you."

Jana was puzzled by his request, but she moved to set her M16 on a nearby stone ledge and quickly turned back to Mike.

No one saw the enemy soldier hiding behind the flap of a nearby tent until it was too late. A single shot rang out. Jana, an expression of total bewilderment on her face, looked down at the spreading discoloration on her chest, just as two recently released prisoners reached the lone gunman and tackled him to the ground.

Watching as the bloodstain bloomed and rapidly saturated her furs, she reached up to touch her chest, as if not quite sure what the red color might be. She heard Mike scream from somewhere in the distance, "Jaaaaaaanaaaaa," as her legs gave way, and she slumped to the snowy ground.

Lying in the icy cold, eyes wide open, yet seeing nothing, her breath ripped from her chest in short painful gasps. Eyes closing slowly, she was on the brink of consciousness until strong arms picked her up and cradled her tight. Opening her eyes, with great difficulty, she was puzzled at the hazy appearance of her surroundings; her head cocked sideways, she saw Mike standing next to her with a frightened, desperate look on his face and eyes filled with tears. Strangely though, she wasn't a bit afraid.

"Jana, Jana, you can't leave me, not now." She turned her eyes slowly to see the face, which belonged to this beloved voice from her past.

She was losing blood quickly, and her foggy mind was not quite able to grasp the perplexing truth which was before her. Just as her spirit slipped away, she gasped, "Josh?"

PART 2

1

SCOTT WAS A young man certainly accustomed to feelings of rejection. It was safe to say for the majority of his childhood he'd felt insignificant and unwanted. Ugly emotions, true, but they contributed a great deal to the person he'd become and sadly would continue to play a significant role in many of the future outcomes of his troubled life.

When he was five years of age, his father, who'd routinely and mercilessly beaten him on the occasions he was home, finally packed up his things and left for good.

Both saddened and relieved by his father's departure, he knew it must be somehow his doing. After all, those things were usually his fault, weren't they? At least that was what his mom had told him. And at some point, he always paid for the things which were his fault. That was just the way of it. Scott had been informed all throughout his young life, by both his parents that he was a very bad boy, that he didn't deserve to be loved, and that they should've gotten rid of him when they had the chance.

He'd also been led to believe that bad boys went to jail where there was very little food to eat, and that if while there he didn't give his food to the large rats which would be sharing his space, they would be forced to eat his fingers and toes in the middle of the night to stay alive. He knew now, of course, that the story was a lame attempt at keeping him in line, though he'd seldom if ever given anyone the impression he'd needed that sort of graphic motivation.

He often had nightmares which centered on the choice of starving to death, or being eaten by large ravenous rats. Of course, this left him in a constant state of panic as he tried very hard to be "good enough" to deserve their meager protection in an effort to avoid becoming rodent food.

He realized upon his father's departure and after much careful consideration, he was actually a bit thankful for his dad's abandonment. And though he was only a small boy at the time, he imagined he might even be a bit better off. At least with his dad gone, the almost daily beatings by the dejected, angry man stopped.

If only there'd been a way for young Scott to know his circumstances were about to get a whole lot worse.

True, his father had been a hard man, but while he was still in the picture, they'd been better off financially; they'd lived in a tiny but adequate house and had enough necessities for survival, if just barely. The man was a drunkard, but managed to keep at least a menial job, drunk or not, most of the time; and Scott grew up to be a hard and willing worker due in part to that example from his father.

The neighborhood where they'd lived in his early years was not a good district, but not the poorest or most violent part of town either. Scott had his own bedroom then, with an old mattress for sleeping and a small area in which to play with a few toys passed down to him by older cousins. The amount of space afforded by living in a single family home, however small, offered him a little privacy and a way to stay out of the path of inebriated, angry parents when necessary. Their house was not clean, by ordinary standards, as his mother did not tend to be much of a homemaker, but was at least usually warm enough. And though they didn't dine like kings, he customarily had enough to eat, unless of course he was being punished.

Due to his parent's uncontrolled drinking and constant abuse, Scott learned to be almost entirely self-sufficient at a very young age. He was a pro at staying out of sight even in the small house, learning all the best hiding places and when to use them.

Before leaving permanently, his father spent a period of time in and out of their lives at will, creating an unpredictable existence of mayhem and uncertainty. The extreme insecurity and violence of their day-to-day lives, in the year before his departure, often left Scott physically ill and unable to attend his kindergarten class. Plagued with stomach aches and vomiting, which was a constant annoyance to his mother and caused his father to consider him a weakling; Scott was very introverted and had an especially hard time making any friends. He wasn't well known, or liked, and was never asked to play outside with neighbor kids, or sleep over at a mate's. In fact, many of Scott's beatings were tied to his father's contempt of the pale, sickly, and frightened little boy.

When his dad was around, he could be counted on to be intoxicated, and when he was drunk, he was a scary sight to behold. It was quite common for him to go into a temper and beat Scott with a belt, but he was also apt to use whatever other devices were available and within easy reach to thrash the child within an inch of his natural life as he lashed out in a drunken rage.

Scott's body bore many odd scars from the multitude of beatings he'd received at his father's hand. It was also a regular occurrence for Scott to go to bed without supper if he was "naughty," sometimes going without food for several days at a time, depending upon his father's pleasure and the severity of his supposed offense.

When Scott's dad was finally out of the picture for good, his daily routine lightened up some, at least for a while. He was no longer forced to find ways of avoiding his father's wrath, and eventually, the constant tightness in his small chest lessened a little. Even his stomach aches diminished which helped with his school attendance. Gratefully, for a time, young Scott enjoyed a short-lived relative peace.

Then quite out of the blue, another awful shift occurred. Stress of his father's absence began to take a strange, weighty toll on his mom. From necessity, his own daily pattern began to include creative ways to steer clear of his exponentially more drunken mother. She'd not particularly been a force to reckon with in the past, leaving most of Scott's discipline to her heavy-handed husband. But the trauma of the man's absence had changed her lazy, disengaged attitude to one of veritable loose cannon; a woman whose moods grew more dangerous daily and whose temperament vacillated between clinginess and unstable, explosive anger.

Scott and his mother were forced to move to a more affordable dwelling after his father's permanent departure. This new apartment, which consisted of a small living room furnished with a sullied, fold out couch on one wall; a tiny kitchenette and even smaller bathroom, left him few places to hide from her growing ire. His new sleeping assignment was a dirty cushion placed on the carpet beside the sofa where his mother passed out mumbling and crying herself to sleep every night.

When his mom was high and feeling lonely, which happened frequently now, she draped herself on Scott, sobbing and slobbering about things he didn't really understand. This disgusted him and his loathing became overwhelmingly apparent as he grew older. He felt smothered by her fetid, wet kisses and hated the way her stinking breath heated his face as she groped at him in her desolate state. But when she became irritated, which was an extremely more common occurrence these days, he trembled with fear at her inventive new ways of torturing him. It seemed to him somehow, looking back, as if her need to cause him pain and her ability to do it lessened her own agony even if only during the execution of the cruelties.

The boy suffered greatly at the hands of his mother, and his memories were filled with symbols of that torment. Future nightmares would forever revolve around a dark closet where he remained locked for days at a time, with only a bottle of water and a bucket in which to relieve his bodily needs; and bloody beatings with her red-handled wooden rolling pin—the same rolling pin which broke many of his young bones when she wielded it against him in her fits of fury over his aggravating, persistent lack of perfection. The secret place in his head, where he fled for escape, became very important during those years. In his secret world, where he could rock to protect himself from her wrath, he felt a small, if false, degree of safety.

Since his aforementioned broken bones were not tended to properly, they mended badly resulting in conditions which plagued him even into adulthood. He could neither sit, nor stand for long periods of time without intense agony in his back and legs from those ancient injuries. Remembering an episode from his troubled childhood, when he'd committed some unremembered, but evidently unforgivable infraction on her long list of unpardonable sins; he recalled she'd forced him to remain for hours in a bathtub filled with ice cold water. During this particular punishment, she sat drinking and then sleeping against the bathroom door, barring any possibility of escape from his frozen agony. He'd wished over and over to die that day, and sadly many times on many similar dark days of his strange, wretched childhood.

At the conclusion of the ice water episode, he'd subsequently become very ill and developed problems with ear infections which would plague him for the rest of his life; further infuriating his mother, possibly due to feelings of guilt that she'd caused the very ailments which were creating more aggravation for her now.

Tragic memories, too many to recount, filled his twisted, fledgling soul. He was saturated with white hot hatred toward his parents and grew to know he couldn't depend on anyone, so young Scott looked after himself; there was just no one else to do it. He fed, dressed, and bathed himself from as early as he could remember. No one hugged him, cooked for him, read to him, or waited with cookies for his arrival home from school. He'd never experienced a single instance of shared nighttime prayers, a kissed and bandaged knee, a birthday party, Christmas stocking, or Easter basket. He never knew a moment of being loved or cherished.

On one especially memorable Monday morning, Scott was making his cereal as he prepared to leave for kindergarten. Filling his bowl with Cheerios, he poured milk without realizing it had soured. After taking a bite and realizing his mistake, he spit the inedible mouthful into his small hand. His mother seeing what he'd done leapt up and came at him, "You ungrateful brat, we don't have food to waste, and I'm not gonna watch you throw away my hard won money, you hear me?" First shaking him till his head snapped painfully back and forth, she then forced him to lick up the spat-out food and eat the whole bowl of cereal complete with sour milk as she looked on with an air of haughty superiority.

After eating the meal, his stomach rebelled and he threw up all over the floor, his clothes, and his worn-out tennis shoes. Livid over the incident, and in her normal drunken state even that early in the morning, she grabbed his spoon, scooped up the vomit, and shoved it back in his mouth chipping his front tooth in the process making him eat every bit of his own puke as he gagged and retched through each mouthful, ultimately vomiting again and being beat over and over until he just couldn't remember any more. Eventually passing out in his own mess, he woke against the wall in his closet prison, covered in vomit, urine, blood, and bruises; knowing for certain no one would ever be there to help. He knew without question he'd always be alone. He was five years old and already felt so lifeless inside that he didn't care anymore if he was alive or dead on the outside either.

After a few months of his father's absence, his mother grew more desperately lonely and longed for male company of any kind. In a misguided attempt to assuage her isolation, she began to pick up men from a local bar and bring them home with her. Beatings from his mother soon began to include additional violent acts by random strangers as many of the men seemed to have mean streaks of their own and came up with new creative torments to add to the list of cruelties Scott already endured. Beatings were usually followed by more drinking, laughter, and unbridled sex on the couch between her and that night's suitor as Scott curled up on his stained cushion licking his wounds and trying not to hear sounds of copulation occurring above him.

On one especially loathsome night, she brought a man home, who knew, through earlier conversations in the bar, she had a young son in her household. His motives were more heinous than the rest. The stranger spent the first part of that evening laughing and drinking with Scott's mom until she fell into a stupor on the sofa. Once she was asleep, he sought the boy out. Scott was wakened, attacked, and used throughout that long night as his mother lay unconscious only a few feet away, too smashed to hear her son's cries for help.

Left in a bloody heap in the corner of their tiny bathroom, his mother found him whimpering and shivering on the cold restroom floor the next morning. Angry that another new boyfriend had left her alone, she blamed her son and kicked him in his back and stomach over and over until she was too exhausted to lift her leg anymore. Scott suffered with kidney pain and blood in his urine for weeks afterward. His loathing grew with each passing episode of violence. He hated her, he hated himself, and he hated his life.

Scott had no way of knowing most of the civilized world didn't live the way he did. Life was rough, but as he grew older, he toughened up considerably, in part due to the abuse and mistreatment; and in spite of his circumstances, he made it through somehow. He knew in every fiber of his being he couldn't count on anyone to take care of him now or later, so he learned as best he could in every situation to do it himself.

He despised school, the authority, the confinement, and the strict schedules. As he grew older, he detested it exceedingly more. Scott wasn't a stupid boy by any means, but without a proper place to study, or any of the fuss parents usually make over their kid's education; at least parents who care whether or not their children grow up prepared; it just didn't seem important or worthwhile to him. He decided if he was ever going to make anything substantial of his life, he'd need to take control of his own destiny and stop counting on the idiots at the school to direct him. He wasn't going to let his mother, or anyone else for that matter, tell him what to do ever again; not if he could help it. Knowing innately he would be wasting his time with people in positions of scholastic power, since they didn't begin to teach the things a guy needed to know in order to make it in the world of real business today, he began skipping classes.

Instead Scott fought. He fought almost every day, and because he fought, he got in trouble just about every time he turned around. Teachers and principals told him he was no good and would never amount to anything. His mother heartily agreed with them at every available opportunity. Pretty soon, Scott agreed too. Having established the assessment of his worth, he learned to dull his pain with drugs and alcohol. He decided no drug was off limits to him, so he gladly, and often, used them all.

Deeply and irrevocably entrenched in troubles too deep to ignore by the time he was in his junior year of high school; Scott was hopelessly addicted to several readily available street drugs, and he'd taken to stealing money from his mother's purse on a regular basis to buy them. He reasoned that she owed him something for the years of hell she'd put him through, so he refused to feel guilt over any possible distress he caused her when she found her precious funds missing. Before long, the pittance he was able to rip off from her welfare check wasn't enough to cover the expense of his continually growing habit, so he graduated to more profitable endeavors.

A force to be reckoned with in the neighborhood, Scott wasn't a pale frightened little boy anymore. He'd become a very strong, exceedingly angry, young man. Not afraid to fight, he didn't care who he hit or hurt. He'd been beat and battered by the worst his whole life, and he became accustomed to using his fists to bend many a differing will to his own.

Scott knew most of the crooks in the community and worked with them eagerly doing whatever despicable things might put a little loose change in his pocket. His mother hated his choice of friends, his choice of entertainment, and his long hair. In continual rebellion, he grew his blond mop well past his shoulders often pulling it back in a sloppy ponytail.

Mom learned, finally, not to take her frustrations out on the boy anymore, because now that he was older, he gave as good as he got, and she ended up on her butt more than once after trying to push him around.

At only seventeen years old, Scott was swathed in tattoos, starting with large skull and crossbones on his chest and advancing to broken angel/devil wings covering his back. His favorites were sleeves made up of legions of intertwined winged demons covering his scarred, but well-muscled arms. One hot summer night, during the premeditated armed robbery of a local convenience store, he was caught, arrested, and carted off to the local jail. A judge who'd dealt with Scott on numerous occasions, for everything from assault to petty theft and who'd finally grown tired of the young hooligan's errant ways, sent him away for five years to pay his debt to society and learn to be a productive member of the community, sincerely hoping Scott would see the dire need to straighten himself out before he killed someone, or lost his own life.

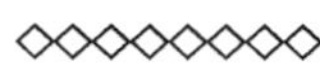

Scott learned many things while incarcerated, none of them good and certainly nothing productive. He got into more fights than he could keep track of, created quite a reputation within the prison walls, and spent more than his share of time in solitary confinement. By the day of his release, which didn't include any time off for good behavior, for obvious reasons, he was well schooled in all manner of illicit activities and quite able to hold his own with any hoodlum in the jail or local civilian population.

Compassionate pastors, visiting the prison throughout his confinement, tried to reach out to young Scott, but he wasn't having any of it! As far as he was concerned, this Jesus guy they all raved about was full of crap. If he was so great, so loving, where was he all those years when Scott needed rescue from his abusers?

It didn't seem to Scott that Jesus had been very worried for his situation at any given time in his seventeen years of existence, so Scott decided he had plenty of other better ideas about how to spend his five years of lockup in this place rife with valuable information to glean.

Finishing high school, getting his GED certificate, and then taking on a few college courses, Scott decided he would take full advantage of the State's dime. He was using his knowledge to make some pretty serious plans about his future before his time of internment was up. He knew he would also need a way to support himself once he was released back into unsuspecting society.

Leaving his prison term at twenty-two years of age, feeling sufficiently prepared with inventive ways to make money if his job search didn't go as well as he hoped, Scott set out with jaw clenched and a bigger chip on his shoulder than he'd had when he was first sent up. In addition, he was in possession of the names of several new drug contacts and had two very excellent, new tats on his already abundantly inked young body.

Scott's foray into freedom lasted a mere six months. Upon release, he'd contacted his parole officer who helped him with some job leads. He searched for work, but sadly, his reputation preceded him. Frustration grew and he found himself doing the very things which had gotten him in trouble earlier. Slowly at first, but then more increasingly, he began going to all the places of which his PO had warned him to stay clear.

Contacting his mother after his release was not an option. He didn't want anything at all to do with her, deciding long ago both of his parents were to be eluded at all costs. Concluding he would probably never be able to forgive either of them, it would be more than foolish for him to have contact with her now.

While living in freedom, he met his future wife Virginia. Gin, who fancied herself the consummate dancer, was plying her trade in a local strip bar. Outrageous and raucous, dressed scantily and oh so enticing to a man who had been locked up for five years, a night of wild abandon led to an indiscretion and an unplanned pregnancy. She seemed so vulnerable, perhaps even needed him. Intent on doing what decorum would dictate to be "the right thing," Scott proposed to her. He and Virginia were married when she was three months along, and Scott was still very much unemployed. Her parents, who were terribly angry over this surprising turn of events, and only after their suggestions of abortion had been flatly turned down, planned a small, private ceremony for some friends and family in their rather less than average backyard.

Gin wore the long yellow gown which had been her prom dress just three years before. Her mother helped her let out the waist a couple inches to allow room for her slowly swelling middle. Carrying a bouquet of daisies from the garden, tied with yellow ribbon and lace, she wore her long blonde hair swept back in a stylish chignon.

As Scott watched Virginia sashaying slowly down the aisle—an aisle created by strategically placing groups of chairs on the family's freshly mowed lawn and covering the space with a long piece of staked down white cloth—he choked back tears of joy thinking perhaps, just perhaps, this could be the start of something wonderful in his life. Maybe having his own loving family would be the cure for his sadness and the extinguisher of the suffocating depression which so often enveloped him. He hoped this marriage might help to quench his inexhaustible anger at the world, at his past, and at his parents. He thought, if just briefly, he might really be able to do this marriage thing. He could have a family, a real family. He'd get a decent job, and if he tried real hard, maybe he could even be a good husband and dad for Gin and the baby.

Virginia's grandma made the wedding cake. Neighbors brought all the components necessary for a nice potluck supper, and her older brother supplied two kegs of beer along with a case of champagne. Scott, as usual, lacking any self-control, had way too much to drink and woke up the following morning splayed out on a couch, downstairs in his new living quarters, located in the in-law's basement.

Scott began the day with a headache. A headache he was sure he deserved, since he knew he'd started drinking shortly after the wedding ceremony ended and didn't remember much of anything after seven in the evening. Virginia and her mom had a few things to say about his lack of propriety on their wedding day. He figured he deserved their sarcasm and decided he could deal with their nagging for a day if he had to. It turned out though that Virginia's vitriol was constant and degrading day after endless day. She, sadly, seemed to take after her mother and Scott felt almost as sorry for Gin's dad at the viciousness of his woman's mouth, as he did for himself over the hatred spewing from his own wife. He found himself on the receiving end of her cutting tongue more and more, and he came to the realization, although he was aware he messed up quite often, he didn't have to do much at all to incur her constant wrath.

Scott, who found himself still unemployed two and a half months after the wedding and still unable to provide for his new family, was getting desperate.

Gin's parents had offered their basement for the time being, but they sincerely believed their daughter could do better with her life than the ex-con living in their cellar. When Virginia wasn't riding Scott, it was a pretty good bet her mom was doing her best to make him feel worthless. He soon discovered he had nowhere to hide from their criticism and growing viciousness.

Their temporary borrowed space consisted of a small bedroom, tiny bathroom, and a sitting area furnished with an old blue couch, which smelled faintly of cat urine, a red chair with the back cushion missing, and a snowy thirteen-inch black-and-white television set still outfitted with bent rabbit ears. Meals were taken with her parents upstairs in the kitchen and came with a good dose of advice, criticism, and reproach three times a day.

Any time Scott was out looking for work, or hanging out with friends, Gin was suspicious, texting him with her qualms and wanting a step-by-step accounting of his day, but when he was with her in the basement, she seemed annoyed by his presence and they argued until heated conversations brought unwelcome involvement from her parents upstairs. He just flat out couldn't win.

Scott resented the continual feeling of failure which comprised most of the waking hours of his existence these days. He thought more than once of taking his own life, but couldn't endure the thought of his child growing up feeling deserted the way he had. He hoped to be a positive force in the life of this little child he'd helped to create.

Finally, when he felt all other avenues of supply had been exhausted and working together with two of his new outside contacts, he solidified a plan—a plan which had been conceived in prison. He believed this job just might solve his money problems and get Gin and her parents off his back for good. If he could pull this one off, he and his little family might be set for years, they could buy a house, which would get him out of his current hell, and he would have the resources to take care of his baby. It was important to him that Gin's parents see him as an adept, skilled, and competent man. He knew this job could make a difference. They'd all see he was capable. He would show them he could take care of his wife on his own, and he'd prove he was worth their respect after all.

2

WHILE IN THE pen, Scott had become acquainted with some pretty interesting characters. One of these previously worked security at a bank located in Scott's hometown. While employed there, the gentleman in question secretly cased the bank, took measurements, and noted every detail of the layout of the establishment for future reference. That same gentleman, however, was sentenced and incarcerated shortly before the day of Scott's discharge on a well-deserved aggravated armed robbery charge. This offense, being his third, caused the judge to sentence him severely though appropriately for forty years to life, and subsequently, he wouldn't need the information garnered from casing that neighborhood bank any time soon.

Scott got to know the man before his own release and they became fast friends. He passed the bank details on to Scott with certain provisos. Upon completion of a successful heist, one third of the proceeds would go to the gentleman's wife and children at a previously agreed upon address. Scott was a felon, but he would never mess with a guy's family, so he'd approved of the terms and took the information with him for possible future use.

Certain that upon his release he'd be able to make a go of it in the outside world he hadn't contemplated using the squirreled away information until now. But what else could he do? The populace at large wasn't going to give him a break; that fact had already been firmly established time and again by his existing circumstances. His in-laws and his wife had run out of patience with him, and he had a baby coming in less than three months. He didn't really have a choice, did he?

Secret meetings began in earnest to plan the upcoming robbery with Frank and Larry, his new partners. Their preparations included a well-timed plant on the inside of the target. Frank's wife applied for a job at the bank, and after an entirely incompetent back ground check by her new employers, was hired as part-time teller. From her new position, she would be able to offer help when they decided the time was right. Most of their composite plans revolved around a newly revamped schedule at the bank and the information collected by Scott's prison acquaintance. After a couple of weeks of arrangements, the trio was ready to pull off the biggest operation of their collective careers.

Scott quickly agreed with his two associates, none of them would tell their families and friends of their approaching plans for the job, so he spent two weeks with knowledge of the upcoming event gnawing at his gut, not able to share his fears. Not that anyone he knew would have cared one way or another if something was bothering him, but his sense of foreboding about the upcoming robbery grew every day.

Meanwhile, Virginia and her parents continued their incessant insults and emotional torture. The night before the robbery was scheduled to go down, Scott decided he couldn't take it; no, wouldn't take it anymore. During an argument, in which Virginia got so belligerent and out of hand that she began throwing lamps and ashtrays, Scott finally shouted back in self-defense. His anger at the treatment he'd endured for the past few months was intense, and he didn't care who heard him. "I ain't a loser! I ain't! Shut up, Gin, you hear me? Shut up! We'll see how your parents feel when I'm the richest man in town next week! You can all just shove it!" Storming out of the house and down to the local bar to drown his sorrows, Scott had no idea those words would prove to play a part in his eventual undoing.

Frank's old lady, though she was as dumb as a box of rocks, managed to keep her job at the bank for the time required and successfully unlatched a window in the women's restroom before she left work that fateful night. Having someone on the inside proved to be an invaluable piece of the plan. Larry picked up ski masks and black sweatshirts at a local sporting goods shop. Scott was in charge of munitions and found a new contact who'd hooked him up with three unregistered guns and ammo for all the weapons; an altogether terrible idea. They were set. That night, Scott made excuses to an angry and suspicious wife and went off to meet the guys.

Waiting impatiently till dark and watching closely for all bank employees to be cleared from the premises, Scott and his associates hid out in Frank's van across the street from their target. Once they were sure the coast was clear, they donned disguises and checked their weapons. They were hoping the guns wouldn't be necessary, but they'd use them if they had to. They were all pretty desperate by this time.

Getting in was easy due to the unlatched bathroom window. But once inside, things got a little messy. Every bit of information, which had been supplied by Scott's prison mole, was inaccurate. The bank added an additional alarm system, and Scott saw there'd been extensive renovations as well. He was angry with himself that they hadn't made Frank's wife part of their planning sessions. As stupid as she was, they'd thought it best to keep her out of the loop, so she couldn't inadvertently spill the beans, but she might have noticed the discrepancies in the floor plans if she'd been present at the meetings. Knowing their job would be infinitely more difficult now, Scott was understandably frightened. All the feelings of foreboding he'd been experiencing made sense now. However, he'd come too far to back down, so he plowed on.

Somehow, in all their stumbling about, one of the guys tripped a silent alarm and Larry dropped the handgun unseen, from his pocket, onto the blue and green lobby carpet. With the bank's new security improvements and renovations, there was no way now they'd be able to get into the vault, and Scott became suspicious about the revamped alarm system so they decided to wrap it up and cut their losses. The guys located and bagged up a minimal amount of dough from the petty cash drawer and vacated the premises just before the arrival of a sheriff's car whose occupant was investigating the bank's recently triggered, silent distress signal.

The three offenders hightailed it back to Frank's van and took off before they could be detected by the local cop, but they left angrily cursing their luck. The piddly amount of cash they'd gotten away with was a drop in the bucket compared to what they'd expected from the heist. After spending so much time planning the robbery, the few measly hundred dollars they'd split didn't amount to a hill of beans and certainly wasn't worth risking their freedom.

Worse than that and unbeknownst to any of the guys, the bank's camera caught their whole bumbling escapade in its digital memory card, right down to waving guns and clumsy escape. The boy's identities were still unknown, due to the ski masks, but when detectives were brought in to collect evidence, they found the previously unlatched window in the lady's room and lifted a print. Tracing the print back to Frank's wife, who'd run afoul of the law at some point in her checkered past, they pieced together events of the previous night. From there, it didn't take long for the authorities to arrest Frank and his wife for the failed robbery.

Scott and Larry felt bad, but not bad enough to turn themselves in for the heist. Frank would understand, especially since he'd been caught solely on his wife's incompetence. Scott felt bad for Frank's small children though. All three would wind up in foster care, with both parents in jail awaiting trial.

Local investigators found Larry's lost firearm and were able to lift a print, though it proved too smudged to be of value. Larry was safe for now. But Scott's luck was about to run out. When the local television station ran the bank film of the three bumbling, armed gunmen over and over, he knew it would be just a matter of time before someone put events together enough to identify them all.

Throughout the day and evening of the video's airing, Gin's parents became suspicious, believing they recognized the build and mannerisms of one of the culprits. One day, while Scott was out looking in futility for work, Gin's mom went downstairs to their small apartment and rummaged through his personal things. She found the black sweatshirt and ski mask he'd worn the night of the theft, confirming her suspicions. His in-laws never liked Scott, so for his mother-in-law, the choice was an easy one to make. When Scott got home later that day, police were quietly summoned and arrived shortly thereafter. Scott wasn't able to supply an alibi for the night of the robbery and couldn't deny the items were his, so with a sigh of regret, he placed his hands behind his back allowing the officer greater access to his wrists. He was promptly arrested and jailed to await his upcoming trial date.

Larry was never fingered for the botched heist. Both Scott and Frank were offered a reduction in charges if they'd give up the name of the third accomplice caught on film, but they knew the kind of karma which might be released by an action such as that and the retaliation a squealer could expect in lockup, so they decided to spare their collaborator.

No one was going to give these two guys a break though. Not the first offense for either marked felon, the prosecuting attorney was out for blood, and the judge intended to make an example of them both. Scott imagined they'd be in for the ride of their lives and was he ever right.

The trial lasted a mere four days and the jury took only two hours to deliberate in order to agree on a guilty verdict. Sentencing was scheduled for bright and early the following morning. Publicity for the case caused an outcry for swift justice. Virginia wasn't present for the trial due to her delicate condition, and her mom was there only to testify for the prosecution, but the whole family was in attendance, glaring at him from their seats across the room, to witness his sentencing. Once again, by the sheer stupidity of his own hand, he would pay the price for his failure, he felt very much alone.

3

FROM BUNGLED ROBBERY—THROUGH agonizing, short trial—to incarceration, took less than a month. The judge meant to make an example of Scott and Frank, and he succeeded admirably. They became the prosecution's new poster boys for multiple offense felons, and they were a laughing stock among criminal circles nationwide.

Film of the botched robbery went viral, and both their bumbling inadequacy and unflattering pictures were plastered, in vivid living color, on social websites and front pages of newspapers around the country. The three inept, armed robbers were an official running joke with every late night talk show host in America for weeks afterward. And they would thankfully be gone for ten long years, due to the unfortunate use of the unnecessary weapons, visible on the video tape; which might be enough time, they hoped, for people to forget everything about them and the embarrassment of their very public failure.

Scott was devastated that he'd thrown away his freedom and even more distraught at the thought he wouldn't be present for the birth of his child in less than two months. He lamented out loud from his cell. Frantic, he threw things and beat his head on the wall over and over till he drew blood. "What've I done? Crap, I can't believe what a giant screw up I am. Maybe I should've killed myself while I had the chance! My parents were right. I am worthless. Now my baby's gonna feel worthless too. Oh god, what've I done, what've I done?" His jailers, who heard his tortured words, put him on suicide watch to make sure he couldn't accomplish anything which might deprive them of the opportunity to torment him to their hearts desire. You see, these guards remembered Scott from his previous visit and wanted nothing more than to seek revenge on him for the trouble he'd caused them during his first prison term.

Scott knew this period of confinement would be much more torturous than his previous detainment, but not for the same reasons. His torture would be derived from the thought of his little family getting on without him. Plus his regret and remorse for what he'd done ate at him continually. Rocking himself to sleep thinking about the baby he wouldn't know and condemning himself for his monumental stupidity caused him to fall asleep night after anguished night sobbing into his pillow.

Guards, who'd plotted torture for Scott when he first arrived at the prison, came to pity him in the next weeks. He didn't seem, to them anyway, to be the same scrappy, rebellious kid who'd given them so much trouble during his first stay in the pen.

Instead, Scott appeared tremendously tortured already. There was no fun in tormenting the kid now, not when he was already so obviously miserable. Those same guards actually began watching out for him as if he were a kind of kid brother, and when they got word in a couple months through the grapevine, Scott's son had been born, they shared the news with him gladly. Even Gin's own family hadn't bothered to report the baby's birth to her incarcerated husband, though he couldn't blame them. Through the kindness of the officers, Scott discovered he had a baby, a son, and his name was Christopher.

He swore to himself that when he got out of this place, he'd do his very best to be the kind of dad Christopher deserved. Scott knew he had to stay out of trouble now and work on getting home to his boy no matter what trouble this place, or its inhabitants tried to throw at him.

He wasn't exactly sure how to be the kind of dad his son needed, but he knew full well the kind he didn't want to be. If only he could go back and do everything differently. He'd give anything to be able to tell Gin how sorry he was, but he was pretty sure she didn't want anything to do with him, not now, not after everything that'd happened. If she'd cared, she would have been in touch with him way before this, wouldn't she?

Christopher was six weeks old when Gin finally came to see him. It was a Sunday afternoon during regular visiting hours. The guard announced to Scott he had a visitor and puzzled at first he followed the officer to a room set apart for those purposes. Not knowing who might actually be wasting their time spending it with him, he was sincerely surprised to see his wife walk through the door. Immediately, his eyes misted and relief flooded his soul. Perhaps there was a chance to save things after all?

She couldn't bring the baby this time, she explained; her parents forbade it, but she did bring pictures. It was a long drive to the prison, and her folks were watching Christopher for her. Scott looked through the photos of his tiny son with tears glistening in his eyes and a heavy heart, knowing the pain he'd caused them. "How's he doin'?" Scott asked tentatively.

"He's doin' real good, Scott. He was up every couple hours for the first few weeks, but my mom helped out, so it was okay. He's sleepin' all through the night now like a big boy. He's a real fine baby, Scott. He smiles all the time, and he's got your green eyes and them sweet dimples."

"I'm so sorry, Gin. I'm sorry about all this mess, and I'm sorry about landin' in here when I oughta be home takin' care of my family."

"Yeah, you know I was pretty ticked off at you. I hated your guts when I was at the hospital screamin' my lungs out havin' our kid, and you wasn't there with me. I was cussin' you out pretty good the whole time. But serious now, it was sad you know? Then my parents started talkin' like I oughta divorce you, and I told 'em to back off and get outa my face! It's my life, and I'll darned well be with whoever I wanna."

"What do you mean? I figured you'd wanna divorce me. I wouldn't of blamed you. Ain't you still livin' in their basement?"

"Yep, I'm in the basement for now, but if they wanna see their grandson, they know they better toe the mark, or I'll go stay somewheres else, and they'll have a heck of a time gettin' any grampa and gramma time with CJ."

"CJ? I got the Christopher part, but what does the J stand for?"

"James, for my grampa. I woulda asked you, but you wasn't around to ask, so I did as I pleased. I'm still kinda pissed at you, and I hate you're gonna be in this place for ten freakin' years, Scott. What was you thinkin'? How could you do this to us?"

"I know, Gin, I know. I'm plenty mad too. I was scared. I couldn't find work. Nobody'd give me a break and our baby was comin' soon. Your mom wouldn't let up on me. She kept callin' me a loser, you know? I just didn't know what else to do, so I did the only thing I knew how to do, and I didn't even do that right. And yeah, I know it was stupid. I screwed up as usual. But I'm gonna get outa here early, Gin. I'm stayin' outa trouble, and I'm gonna get out early. I promise."

"All I know is I feel like a single mom, like I'm gonna have to do this all by myself, and I don't like it one bit. I hate my parents thinkin' they was right, I hate CJ not knowin' who his daddy is. And I especially hate I gotta listen to them cause I'm livin' under their roof."

"I hate it too Gin, but I'm gonna make this right. I promise, really. I'm so glad you came to see me. I didn't know if I was ever gonna see you again, and

I didn't know if my kid would know who his daddy was. I just wanted to curl up and die. Now I feel like I got somethin' to live for, and I will make this up to you and CJ. I'm gonna be a good husband and a good daddy for you guys. I promise, you'll see."

"You better. I'm gonna hold you right to that, and I mean it! I'll be back to see ya. I don't know when my folks'll let me bring the baby, but I'm gonna be gettin' my own place when I get approved for the section eight housing, and they can't keep me from bringin' him then."

"What's section eight housing? Is it like gettin' welfare or somethin'? I don't want my wife and kid bein' on welfare!"

"Scott, you don't got a lot to say bein' in here and all, and with you in here, I don't got much to say about it either unless I wanna live with my parents for the rest of my life and that ain't gonna happen, my friend! This is a chance for me to get away from 'em and be on my own, and I'm gonna take it."

"Just promise me you'll keep in touch, Gin. I'm so lonely for you." Just then, the guard signaled their time was up and motioned for Virginia to follow him. As she was led away, she nodded at Scott, kissing at him with pursed lips, bringing a small smile to his. For the first time in months, Scott felt something akin to hope springing up in his spirit. Maybe he wouldn't lose Gin and CJ after all. His wife left him several pictures of the baby, and he spent the afternoon and evening gazing at his beautiful son, imagining the fun they would have when he was free from this place, and he could watch him grow and learn.

On her monthly visits, Gin continued to bring pictures of CJ and news of his development. She showed CJ pictures of his daddy too, hoping he would get accustomed to Scott's face, and she continued to battle her parent's control over her life and over the life of her son.

Virginia and CJ moved into their very own apartment the same month Scott's little son turned one year old, so she threw him a birthday party complete with Mickey Mouse cake, ice cream, presents, games, and brightly colored balloons. Her parents came grudgingly to the shindig, and several of her friends showed up with their own children to play and eat cake. It was her first independent function in her new place, and she was proud of the fact she was finally on her own even if it was at the expense of the state welfare system.

Gin brought CJ with her to see his daddy for the first time on the Sunday after his big birthday party and every month after, once they'd moved from her folk's basement. Father and son hit it off immediately. Visitation rooms in the prison were constructed of reinforced concrete walls and floors, replete with chained down heavy steel tables and chairs, cracked pleather couches and surveillance monitors in every corner of the dingy spaces. But sounds of laughter filled the place while Scott tickled his baby, and for two whole hours, once a month, he came really, really close to forgetting where he was.

Because on his Sunday visitation days, Scott was actually able to touch, hold, and kiss his wife and son. Those times became of utmost importance to him, and he agonized over every moment which passed from 4:00 p.m. on the fourth Sunday of the current month, when his visitation ended, until 2:00 p.m. on the fourth Sunday of the next month, when his time with them could begin again.

During a specially prearranged conjugal visit, Virginia became pregnant with their second child, a baby girl, and Angela Faith was born at the end of Scott's second year of a ten-year prison term. She was a beautiful, golden child and just like her brother was graced with her dad's green eyes, blonde hair, and dimples.

Scott ached to be with his family, and when he wasn't able, he worked in the facility's laundry for as many hours as he was allowed to fill the lonely time between visits. His hands smelled perpetually of bleach, but there were many worse jobs at the prison, from scrubbing toilets to kitchen duty, so he didn't mind. And the small sum of money he was paid for working in the laundry would add up, so he'd have a little something to take with him upon his release.

While working in the laundry, Scott met another con named Dan. They became friends in almost no time at all. After talking for hours, they realized they had a great deal in common. Both were incarcerated for aggravated robbery and each had two kids, a boy and a girl. Ironically, Dan's wife was a parole officer. He'd met her on release from his first prison term, and after falling in love rather quickly, they were married in a small ceremony conducted by the local justice of the peace. Her parents were about as happy with their marriage as Virginia's folks had been about their daughter marrying Scott, and they had come down on Dan in a similar negative and repetitive fashion.

Dan had a hard time finding a job, after being released from his first prison term, just as Scott had. He tried it straight for many months, but one monumental frustration after another left him feeling completely impotent. He finally gave up, and in a moment of desperation, endeavored to knock off a local convenience store. His attempted armed robbery was as much of an unfortunate mess as Scott's own botched burglary had been, and he was left feeling just as sorry for the situation he'd created as his friend.

The one big difference between the two men was Dan had finally come to the end of himself. After the selfish life he'd led previously, availed nothing; he was sincerely trying to go down a different path. Dan recently began studying with one of the multitude of well-meaning ministers who made regular visits to the prison, and the time he was spending with the pastor seemed to give him some inner peace. He tried talking to Scott about Jesus, heaven, hell, and some crap about outer darkness with wailing and gnashing of teeth, but Scott wasn't buying any of it.

It was all Scott could do to refrain from punching Dan in the mouth every time the name "Jesus" came out of it. He wasn't sure why that name made him so uncontrollably angry, but his mind raged at the gall of a God who wanted to be part of his life now after so much time, pain and trouble had passed. Eventually, Scott asked to be moved to a different section of the laundry in order to avoid his former friend's regular attempts to share his religion. He didn't need any god in his life. He was doing just fine on his own. Now though, he couldn't seem to rid himself of the tiny voice in the back of his head which was desperately and continually searching for some kind of truth.

On a cloudy day, which seemed to be filled with a darkness Scott couldn't pinpoint, after his duties in the laundry were done and he was back in his cell lying on his cot, Scott saw the postal trustee, who'd never in all his time at the prison darkened his door, approaching his cell. The officer held what looked to be a letter in his hand; though it couldn't be, could it? Scott had never received a dispatch of any kind, besides bills, in his life; and the one and only positive thing you could count on, while you were locked up, was that no one bothered to send you a bill for anything anymore.

Actually, he'd seen the trustee passing out letters to other inmates on a daily basis, but no one had ever written him a message at any point in his lifetime, not even a birthday card. He didn't have false hopes that this particular situation would change even as the man made his way closer to Scott's bars. Then he wondered if there was a mistake of some sort, as the officer advanced to his door looking as if he was about to deliver the foreign object.

When the guard handed him the previously opened and inspected item, Scott looked at the return address and was instantly filled with revulsion at the name he saw there. He hadn't heard from his mother since being sent to prison for his first incarceration, and it would have been fine with him if he'd never heard from her again. He'd seen an odd expression flicker across the trustee's face as he handed over the piece of mail, but dismissed it, thanked the man, and turned back to his cot.

Scott tossed the communiqué on the end of his bed and lay back down. Rubbing his eyes to hinder the headache, which was slowly filling his skull to the point of explosion, he tried to stop the parade of painful memories that began marching through his mind. He attempted to extinguish feelings of anger and worthlessness, which seemed to surround him whenever he thought of his mother. When that was unsuccessful, he rolled over and forced himself to rock, hard and repeatedly, as he'd done when he was a boy, until he fell into a short tortured sleep.

After Scott awakened from his well-needed nap with the residual soreness of his earlier headache still lingering in his temples and once he'd finished eating his supper, he glanced at the rectangular, white reminder still on the end of his bed covers. Picking it up, he turned it over in his hands and debated upon whether or not he cared enough about what was inside to investigate the unexpected parcel further.

For the first time, he noticed the address looked to have been written by a very shaky hand. His mother always possessed a very strong, clear penmanship, even when she was stumbling drunk. He'd seen her handwriting on many notes to his school, which she'd written in that particular state of inebriation. He also knew she was capable of fooling most people into thinking none of his instability problems stemmed from her, or her suspected drinking problems.

Curiosity finally getting the best of him, he ran his finger under the opened flap of the envelope, slicing his digit in the process; and cursing under his breath, he pulled the folded sheets of paper from their sheath, sucked the blood from his cut finger and began to read:

Dear son,

I know it probably feels strange to you that I'd call you dear. In your young life, I've never treated you as if you were dear to me at all. I am sorry for that, for both our sakes. I'm writing to share some truths with you which I personally fought tooth and nail for most of my life. I'm sincerely trying to save you the years it took me to discover those truths for myself.

First of all, I wanted you to know I received correspondence recently, informing me of the death of your father. I know the two of you never had a particularly close relationship, but I thought you might want to have the information regardless.

I was told he suffered a stroke and spent over two years in a nursing home, unable to speak, before he passed. Apparently, he remarried at some point over the years, and his new wife found some papers after his death, referencing you and me and the child support which he never paid, so she was kind enough to contact me.

I also wanted you to know I was diagnosed last year with stage four cancer of the pancreas and have been told by doctors I have very little time left to live. I thought of not contacting you at all because I assumed my death, quite understandably, wouldn't mean much to you, but then I knew I had to write. You've been deserted and left to your own devices so many times in your life that I couldn't bear to be the one to do that to you again.

I'm not asking for your pity, your money, or your mercy. I was not a good mother to you. I am fully aware of that. I also don't expect your forgiveness, though I would sincerely love to receive it.

Scott threw the offensive letter across the room; furious she could suggest he might forgive her after the pain and anguish she'd caused him all his life. How dare she even think it? Hating her with every fiber of his being, he was glad she was dying and could only hope she'd suffer as much as she'd wounded him. For the first time in his life, he sincerely hoped there was a hell and that she would go there to burn in it!

Lying back on his bed, heart pounding painfully and head feeling ready to burst, he knew he should calm down. He'd never had a stroke, but thought he might just change that now if he wasn't careful. A part of him, deep down in his soul, felt confused. He wasn't sure exactly what was causing the odd sensation, but he wondered if it might be sadness over the loss of his dad.

Yes, the news of his father's death had thrown him for a loop. Somehow, strangely, he'd always thought there would be a great reunion somewhere. His father would show up, see him, and tell him he loved him, had always loved him; maybe even tell him he was proud of the young man he'd become. Then perhaps they could go off together to do the things they never got to do while he was growing up. They could fish, throw a football around, all the guy stuff he'd longed to do with his dad when he was just a boy. As an adult, he'd given up the idea any of that fantasy would come true, but learning of his father's death closed the door on the obscure hope with a finality which hurt to his core. Tears came to his eyes, and he squeezed them shut hard, as he took a few shaky breaths to calm himself.

Lying in his cell, he thought of the hatred he felt for his mother and wondered why his loathing of her was so much more overwhelming than any hostility he'd felt for his dad. With clenched jaw, he slammed his fist into the bed over and over and knew. Of course, he knew why he despised her so. He abhorred her for bringing men into their home and allowing the sick bastards to attack him mercilessly. He hated her for not protecting him even when she knew full well she, his mother, was all he had left in the world, his only protection against the evil which surrounded them. He hated her too for causing him to hate himself when she should have been his biggest cheerleader. And he thought her the most despicable of women for not loving him unconditionally, even when he messed up as a kid. Of course, he hated her most! Coming to this understanding gave him the strength of conviction to continue, so he picked up the letter and began again to read:

> Forgiveness was something I had a problem with most of my life, Scott. As a small child, I was beaten and abused by my parents and molested repeatedly by my father from the time I was four years old, until I was twelve. You would think these facts might've made me more sympathetic to your plight, but, I guess I simply didn't know any other way to live.

He gasped. Scott never knew any of these facts about his mother. They shocked and surprised him. A portion of his heart cried out for the little girl who would grow up to be his mother, and that cry caused him to instantly rethink the degree of anger and hatred he felt toward this woman who'd given birth to him. No wonder she was a monster. This information didn't make his past circumstances any better, but empathizing with that little girl whose life was rife with pain, as his own had been, became more of a possibility as he regretted his past feelings toward the woman who'd suffered so many of the same things.

When I married your father at sixteen, I thought I was escaping the pain of my childhood, until I realized I'd married a man just like my dad. I loved your father and was deeply hurt by the way he treated me and then later, you. But I suppose I cared more for how he viewed me than about my own son's welfare, so I played into his anger toward you and took part in the torture until it became a part of who we were as a family. I became the mother I hated. Especially devastated when he left us, I didn't know how to deal with the idea of being alone.

I'm afraid, son, that you suffered at both our hands, and I know now that I took my frustration, anger, and loneliness out on you even more after he left. For all this and more, I am sincerely sorry. I hope you will find it in your heart to forgive me some day. I should've been protecting you, and if I could go back and change things, I would do it all differently now. I was so busy being miserable and hurt, I didn't bother to see your pain.

I have another truth to share with you. I was visited by a local pastor, whose name is Mike, a couple of years ago and after many conversations and much soul searching, I asked God for forgiveness of my sins. I've accepted Jesus's free gift of salvation and asked Him into my life as my Lord and Savior. For what remains of my existence, I chose to live in faith believing what my God has to say about me instead of living in fear believing what Satan has told me all my life.

A huge weight has been lifted from my shoulders, and my life is truly changed. I know now when I leave this place I will be in heaven with my Jesus, and I am no longer afraid to die.

I know it's probably hard for you to see me as anything but the monster that made your life a living hell when you were a child. And it would be understandably hard for you to see a "just" God being able to forgive me for the things I've done, although I've come to understand my forgiveness is not based on my own performance, but solely on the sacrifice my Savior Jesus made on the cross when he took my sin upon Himself.

I want you to know He loves you too, Scott. Nothing you've ever done in your life is bad enough to keep you from His love if you ask Him to be your Lord and Savior.

Yes, I know, listen to me talking about the bad things you might have done when my own life has been filled with selfishness and evil. Thank God, He has not only forgiven my sins, but He's forgotten them as well, so I don't ever have to feel guilty again. I praise God that His own sacrifice for me makes me worthy.

I want you to know son the moment I realized how much He loves me, I began to learn how to love you. I only wish I'd been able to show you in person how much you mean to me and how deeply I care for you.

I can only hope you don't allow the anger and hatred, which was born of your suffering at my hand, to smother you for as long as I allowed my pain to wreak destruction in me.

God bless you, Scott. I will love you forever son.

Mother

Scott held the pages in his hand for a moment. Shock over what he'd read causing him to feel as though someone had kicked him hard in the stomach. Then he realized there was more and turning to the last remaining page, he saw a very different hand-writing. This was another, shorter letter and it read:

Dear Scott,

My name is Mike. I've been visiting with your mother for some time now. I'm the pastor she mentioned to you in her letter.

I am grieved and sorry to tell you we lost your mom yesterday. She died quietly with her brothers and sisters in Christ by her side. I was with her until the very end and her last loving words were of you. She told me of this letter she'd written and asked me to forward it on to you. It was painfully written and addressed by her own hand.

I would like you to know your mother was a very tortured human being until she came to know Jesus a few years ago. Not only tormented by the treatment she'd endured in her life, but tortured by the way she'd treated you, her son, in your painful childhood.

She stopped drinking the year you were first imprisoned at seventeen, and she sincerely worked at improving her own life by going back to school, getting her high school diploma, taking some college courses, and getting a secretarial job which paid enough to support her simple lifestyle. She also began a few years ago to worship the Lord with us. Her biggest regret in life was the loss of communication with you, but she didn't think you would want a relationship with her after your shared past.

Your mother made peace with her Lord, and I know she is at rest, in heaven, in the arms of her Savior.

When I tried to find out where to send this letter, I was saddened to find you are again incarcerated. I understand you are married and have two small children. Your mother wasn't aware she was a grandmother, and I didn't find out any of these details until after her death, so I wasn't able to share the wonderful information with her. She would have been delighted to know about the two little ones.

I hope you will be comforted by the words of truth which Paul shares in 2 Corinthians 5:8, "We are confident, yes, well pleased rather to be absent from the body and to be present with the Lord." Your mom is in a better place, and she finally knows for herself the full meaning of the true love of our Father.

God bless you, Scott. If you ever need a friend, or wish to talk, please contact me. The prison can supply you with my number.

Your servant in Christ's unending Grace and Love, Pastor Mike Anderson

Scott folded the letter, slipped it back into its envelope, curled up on his cot, and cried until he had no more tears. He cried for his mom and the pain she had endured as a little girl. He felt as if he knew her a little better now and was saddened by her lonely and tortured childhood. If only he'd known these things before it was too late. He cried for his dad and for the relationship he would never have, with the man he'd never really known. And he cried for the little boy he'd been, who'd endured so much at the hands of people who evidently never really knew any better themselves.

Once he was finally asleep, he dreamed, and in his dream, his mother came to him, wrapped her arms around him, and rocked him like a baby. He woke with mixed feelings of regret and relief vying for dominance in his mind. His heart was heavy with grief and yet lighter with the knowledge that his mother had reached out to him before she died; a heart and soul which were broken and yet somehow more at peace now.

Scott had never experienced a single moment in his life where he felt loved by either of his parents; and today, he felt that love from his mother for the first time. To have found and lost his parents all in the same day was more brutal and devastating than anything he'd endured as a child. But for the first time in his existence, he didn't hate them, not at all.

A burden was lifted from his shoulders—a burden which weighed heavily his whole life. And for the first time, he was more than a little curious about this Jesus his mom had spoken of in her letter. Was this the same Jesus Dan had come to know? Maybe there really was something to this Savior of the world character after all.

Scott found he could hardly wait the two whole weeks till his next visitation, with such great news to share. Anxious to tell Gin of the letter from his mother, he was almost bursting at the seams. He hadn't talked much about his parents, or his tragic childhood to Gin in the past, but the little he had said was all negative, and he wanted to tell her of the wonderful things his mom had said to him in the letter he'd received. Maybe even talk to her a little about this Jesus his mom had come to know and trust before her death.

Scott regretted that his parents died without knowing their daughter-in-law or their grandchildren and wished he'd done some things differently, but there was nothing to do about it now. All he could do was revel in the feelings of healing which had finally begun in his soul. When visitation day arrived, he was almost beside himself waiting until 2:00 p.m. By two thirty, he was a little bothered his wife and kids hadn't arrived yet, and by three, he was sick with worry. He got permission from the guards to call Gin, and when no one answered, he was even more concerned. "Where are they? What's going on?" he wondered out loud.

Scott had no visitors that day, or the following month. He tried calling Gin several times throughout that period and got no response. When the third month with no visitors came and went, he fell into a deep depression. He still didn't know if his wife and children were okay and had no way to find out.

The guards, seeing how distraught Scott was, sent one of the young volunteer pastors, who haunted the halls of the penal institution each day, to see him. Scott didn't know how this man might help, but was grateful for any source of assistance in the matter. Pastor John prayed with Scott, which made him feel extremely uncomfortable, since he was all too aware of the many sins which filled his own life. With all the evil surrounding him, for as long as he could remember, how could God possibly care enough about him to help? After a few days, the pastor was able to get hold of Virginia, and when he came back to talk to Scott, the news was difficult and very confusing.

Virginia told Pastor John she wouldn't be coming to see Scott anymore. She'd decided to move on with her life. She underwent a recent surgery to have her tubes tied. She didn't want any more children and said she didn't want to spend the rest of her life waiting for a man who'd thrown his own life away on a botched robbery.

Scott didn't know quite what to make of this strange information. Things seemed so good between them the last time he saw Gin. She'd laughed, told jokes, and shared with him all the updates from back home. Besides, his children were always so excited to see their dad! His son loved him, and they had fun playing together in the visitation chamber. His baby daughter, his little Angel, was finally getting to know Dad; smiling all the while they were together and even falling asleep in his arms before they'd left to go home on their last visit.

How could he endure the idea of never seeing his family again? Overwhelmed with thoughts of grief and hopelessness, Scott cried for hours. He tried to sleep, but couldn't. Then, in the wee hours of the morning; exhausted, hurt, and too depressed to care anymore, Scott sat in his cell, staring at nothing, feeling more dejected than he could remember in his life. He'd never been a man of faith, and the only hope he'd ever known just walked out of his life taking his babies with her. Knowing he just didn't have what it took anymore to get through a life in this place without them, he slowly honed a salvaged metal spoon to razor sharpness and used it to slit his wrists wide open. When the prison guards discovered him entirely by accident on the floor of his cell in a large pool of his own blood, he had no pulse. Scott's last tortured thoughts before he knew no more were filled with the loss of his parents and the children he'd never know.

As his life slipped quietly away in a river of blood, he was enveloped in a void of obscurity which grew to cover his world and conscience. In his dying, he didn't witness a Hades of fire and brimstone with devils with pitchforks, but he knew, without question, he was teetering on the brink of hell. This total blackness was so completely and entirely devoid of any light, love, or music that somehow he knew an eternity here would be an eternity without the God of the universe, an eternity of regret and insanity. This must be the place Dan talked about where there was wailing and gnashing of teeth, the outer darkness. As much as he might have scoffed at this idea of hell in all the previous years of his life, in death he was terrified beyond imagining. Suddenly, a voice, like a melody, filled the space. "Scott, it is not your time, but your time will come, son. Only believe on me."

4

WAKING IN A fog, white hot pain throbbing through his head; Scott tried to move his arms and realized they were heavily bandaged and strapped to the cot where he lay. Panicked, he yelled for help. The nurse who responded to his shouts was stern and told him to quiet down or she'd be forced to medicate him for his own good.

Nancy was her name, and once Scott settled down, her demeanor changed for the better. Explaining she was only there to help him and knew he was puzzled, she offered to get the doctor. When Doc entered, Scott could tell right away, from the drained look on the man's face and his hooded, bloodshot eyes, he was harried and overworked.

"I'm Dr. Baker," the man said, as he held out his hand.

Scott, with a look of consternation on his face, proffered, "I'd shake your hand, Doc, but as you can see, I'm a bit tied up."

"I'll loosen the straps on one condition. I would like you to tell me what caused you to try to take your own life, son."

Scott looked down to his stocking feet at the end of the cot. He was ashamed of himself for trying to take the easy way out and realized he wasn't any better than his father who'd left a five-year-old boy to fend for himself. Considering the current circumstances of his life, and his knowledge of how his suicide might have affected his kids, perhaps his sin was even worse than that of his dad. "I don't know, Doc. I just didn't feel like I could take it anymore. First, the letter from my mom, findin' out she and my dad was both gone and today findin' out my wife was leavin' me. I might never see my kids again. I just couldn't deal with it, I guess."

"Scott, you said you found out today that your wife was leaving you?"

"Yeah, Pastor John talked to her, and she said she was movin' on with her life. I guess that means there ain't room for me anymore. The crummy thing about that is, the only way I could see my kids before was when she came to visit, so now they're gonna forget their dad. I just couldn't handle the thought of it, that's all, Doc."

"I'm sorry to hear that, Scott. I'm sure you were very hurt. I have an additional concern though. I don't think you're aware of how long you were unconscious. The guards found you on the floor of your cell over a week ago. You lost quite a bit of blood. I ultimately gave you six pints of the red stuff, and usually at five, you'd be a dead man. If the guards hadn't found you when they did, you would have certainly bled out completely, and we wouldn't be having this conversation. I would say your being alive is quite a miracle if I've ever seen one, and that you must have someone upstairs looking out for you."

"Well, if I do, Doc, I ain't met him yet. I can't figure out why he'd wanna keep me around anyway. I ain't doin' anybody any good here, that's for sure."

"Well, Scott, the situation now is that I can't let you leave the infirmary until we're sure you won't be a danger to yourself anymore, my friend. So, you and I are going to have a bit of time together to try and figure some things out, okay?"

"That's okay for me, Doc. I don't got any plans I can't change, if you get my drift."

"Yeah, Scott, I get your drift." Doc removed the straps from Scott's arms. "Like I said, we're going to have some time to get to know one another a little better, and I for one will enjoy that quite a bit."

"I think I might like that too, Doc." Scott commented as he gave his sore, bandaged arms a gentle rub. "I'll be lookin' forward to it."

Over a period of time and through many long conversations, some of which lasted far into the night, Dr. Baker and Scott talked and shared. The doc discovered much of Scott's dark childhood and sad past. The information he recorded, besides making an excellent case study, would go a long way in convincing a parole board of the original root of Scott's problems and in showing them the possible positive directions his life could be guided.

Currently, with counseling to help his mental outlook, his new desire to be a productive member of society and his desperate willingness to be a good dad to his kids when the time came for his release; he would have some good information to provide the board for a parole hearing.

Scott spent over a month in the infirmary talking to the doc and giving his arms time to heal. He'd cut them up pretty badly, and it took the doctor a long time and much expertise to put him back together again. Once returned to his cell, he saw the floor had been bleached clean and the room searched for any items which might be used to cause him future harm. He felt a moment of panic when he didn't immediately see the pictures of his kids on the wall, but after some searching, he found the precious items stacked with his other personal objects on a back shelf.

CJ was two and a half and his little Angel only six months old the last time he'd seen his kids, but he looked longingly at their pictures every night and hoped that if there was a god in heaven somewhere, he would look after his babies and make it possible for him to see them again. Doc Baker's words resonated in his mind. "I would say that your being alive is quite a miracle if I've ever seen one, and that you must have someone upstairs looking out for you." Who knew? Was it possible? Maybe he did.

The dream he'd had while unconscious, after his blood loss, resonated in his mind and caused him to wonder if he'd been hallucinating or if someone in that dark frightening space had actually been talking to him.

5

Two and a half long years after the day Scott tried to take his own life, he was called before the State Parole Board for his first hearing. He'd been a model prisoner for his entire four plus years of detention, excepting of course for his attempt at suicide, so there was a real good chance the outcome would be in his favor. The fact that prisons were currently at an all-time state of overcrowding might also factor to his ultimate benefit.

After his interview and the subsequent testimony of prison guards, his doctor, and counselor, he was told by the parole board he would hear something regarding his plea within six months. Scott might have been more anxious about the results of their findings, except he really had no place to go upon release. He didn't care anymore, not one little bit, if he achieved freedom; not since his wife's pronouncement that she'd decided to move on with her life.

In the exercise yard, on the same day as Scott's parole hearing, he met a newly processed inmate who introduced himself as Jake. The con was more than a little arrogant and seemed full of a desire to hurt anyone who messed with him. Scott wasn't looking for trouble, so he quickly stood down even when the wise guy got right in his grill, red faced, sputtering, and spitting. After some time passed in close proximity to Scott, Jake realized his new acquaintance was not a threat to him, so he settled down; and they worked out together in the prison yard for over an hour without incident. Jake actually turned out to be a nicer guy than he'd first appeared. He was simply filled with fear as any new convict would be; and the swagger was just a phony self-defense mechanism.

While talking with Scott that day, Jake confessed he felt like a real jerk because he'd left his lady and two babies high and dry when he was sent up. Charged and convicted of second-degree murder for killing the guy he punched in a bar fight, in addition to the fact that this conviction was his third offense; he would be in the joint for a minimum of twenty-five years before he was eligible for parole. Jake had always battled a temper problem he confessed, but, he shared, "The other guy was comin' on to my ol' lady. He put his grubby hands on her, so what's a guy supposed to do?"

Scott felt real bad for the guy. He knew what it was like for a man to be away from his family. They made arrangements to meet the following day back in the exercise yard with pictures of their families and stories of their kids. Scott looked forward to the opportunity for some meaningful interaction. He spent the night tossing and turning thinking of Gin, CJ, and his sweet baby Angela.

His meetings with the shrink were great. The prison's psychiatrist gave him good advice, helping him deal with the pain of missing his kids and the loss of his parents. However, it wasn't the same as talking with a guy trying to manage in the same less than desirable circumstances. And Scott really hadn't made any new friends since he'd transferred positions in the laundry to escape conversations with that religious nut Dan.

Next morning, Scott gathered his pictures of CJ and Angel to take to the exercise yard and directly after breakfast headed outside to meet Jake. The two men smiled sheepishly as they approached one another. "Hey, man. How ya doin'? How was your first night?"

"It was tough goin' if I'm gonna tell the truth. I mean I ain't slept in the same bed with my Ginny since the arrest, but even the cots in the local jail are better'n these."

"Ginny? Man, that's weird. My lady's name is Virginia. I call her Gin too. That's somethin', huh? But I ain't seen her in a long time."

"That is weird, man. My lady is Virginia too. I call her Ginny, but her given name is Virginia."

"What about yer kids? You said you had two kids?"

"Well, Ginny had two kids when we met, but CJ is five and little Angel is three. They are cute as the dickens and real good kids too."

Scott's whole world tipped upside down and began to spin out of control as he stumbled sideways, first grabbing at and then sitting on a nearby concrete bench slowly gaining back control of his senses. It took him a few minutes, for all practical purposes, to achieve the use of his voice again. "Man, those are my kids."

"Whatta you mean your kids?"

"I mean those are my kids. Here, here let me show you my pictures."

"Wow, Scott, yeah, I...I got some pictures here too," Jake said, as he fumbled through his stack and shared his photos, which further confirmed their families were indeed one and the same. Jake suddenly seemed very uncomfortable, but Scott just sat shaking his head from side to side as he tried to wrap his mind around the irony of the whole situation. "You okay, man?" Jake asked.

"Yeah, I guess I'm okay. I ain't seen my kids for over two and a half years. Those pictures are great, man."

"Two and a half years? That's how long Ginny and I've been together. You know, she never got a divorce from you, don't you? We was just livin' together. Boy she just can't catch a damn break, huh?"

"Yeah, I know what you mean. She ends up with one loser after another. Oh, no offense intended guy."

"None taken. If I was you, I would've punched me in the nose by now."

"Why? It ain't your fault. You didn't know me. Were you a good guy to my kids? I mean did you treat them right?"

"Yeah, man. The kids are great. CJ is a real little man. He's in kindergarten this year. Real smart, you know? And little Angel is a doll with those big green eyes and dimples. Hey, just like yours man. You're a real lucky guy."

"Well, lucky wouldn't exactly be the word I'd use. Remember, I ain't seen them for over two and a half years. CJ probably doesn't remember me, and I'm sure little Angel has no clue. Tell me, man, do they call you, Daddy?"

"Sorry. Yeah, they do. Wow, I feel so bad right now, but I ain't sure who I feel worse for, you or me. I wish there was somethin' I could do for you to fix things. I feel like I've really messed up your life."

"Don't worry about it, Jake. I messed up my own life a long time ago, you know. It is what it is. When I get outa here, I'm gonna see my kids whether Gin wants anythin' to do with me or not. They can't keep me from seein' my kids, can they? I mean they're my kids."

"You won't get a fight from me. You got every right to see them kids. When I asked where the kid's dad was, Ginny made me think you was some sorta monster you know. I never knew who you was, so I was just trying to do the best I could for them little guys. Trying to be the best kinda dad I knew how to be. It ain't like I had a good role model myself when I was a kid or anythin' like that either."

"I know what you mean. We must've had the same kinda dad, and I appreciate you bein' good to them."

"Hey, it ain't like Ginny is ever gonna wait for me, and I don't blame her. I'm gonna be in here for a long, long time, and you and her is still married, ain't you? Like I said, I don't think she ever divorced you."

"As far as I know, I ain't got papers or nothin'. Even if she don't want nothin' to do with me she can't keep me from seein' my kids."

"I wish ya luck, man. Them kids need a dad around, and you loving them the way you do is a good thing. I mean it, man. Good luck."

The following month, on visitation day, Scott was informed he had company for the first time in recent memory. The guard led him to his usual meeting space where the elusive Gin and his kids were waiting for him. His heart leapt in his chest at the sight of his children.

"Hey, Scott,"

"Hey, Gin, long time no see. You look real good."

CJ and Angel cowered behind their mother. And if Scott were to have been asked how he felt at that moment, he would have said that watching the abject fear in the eyes of his little children was like being kicked in the gut. Sitting down at the metal table, in the center of the room, with his hands folded in his lap, he waited until Gin sat across the table from him. She made herself comfortable while the kids skittered to her far side, still using their mom as a human shield from the somehow familiar, yet vastly strange, man across from her. His kids looked questioningly at their mom.

"It's okay kids. This here's your daddy." More puzzled looks from the kids.

"So what've you been up to, Gin? Why ain't you been out to see me for so long? I tried to call you."

"I dunno, Scott. You glad to see us now, or should we go?"

"Course I'm glad to see you. It hurts to see my kids so scared of me is all. I just feel like I missed so much. They got so big. It's been over two and a half years, Gin."

"Listen, maybe this was a big mistake. Maybe I shouldn't have come. I thought you'd be more excited to see us is all."

"I am excited, Gin. I missed you all so much. It's been lonely in here that's all I'm sayin'."

"I was thinkin' I wanted to move on with my life back then, but things didn't work out the way I wanted. I decided when you get outa here, you can come home if you want to."

"It might be sooner than you think, Gin. I had a meetin' with the parole board last month, and I think it went pretty good. I'm hopin' I'll be gettin' outa here real soon."

By the end of their visit, the kids were beginning, slowly, to warm up to their dad. He didn't mention his conversation with Jake to Gin. There was no reason to embarrass her. And during the times, in future visits, when the kids accidentally spoke of their other dad, Scott pretended he didn't know who, or what they were talking about as he watched Gin look uncomfortably down at the concrete floor, color rising in her face. He actually even felt a little sorry for her uneasiness.

Over the next few months, Gin and the kids came for regular visits just like the old days. The children grew more comfortable around their dad and even began calling him Daddy again. Scott saw Jake in the exercise yard a couple times, but he just waved and walked on by. Jake understood. He knew he'd gotten off pretty lucky. If it'd been him, he didn't know if he would have let the other guy live. Of course, it was that temper of his that got him thrown in the joint in the first place.

6

WHEN SCOTT RECEIVED notification from the parole board, they'd ruled favorably in his case; he cried with gratitude and relief. His personal effects and the small sum of money he'd earned working in the prison laundry were signed over to him. He left the prison on a grey, rainy day, after saying good-bye to the doc, his counselor, and the many guards who'd been kind to him during his time in lockup. Then he took the long bus ride home.

Scott had Gin's address in his wallet, but the township had grown considerably since his incarceration and was mostly unfamiliar to him. Not sure where her apartment building might be located, he asked for directions. Strange looks from the gentleman at the bus stop and a woman in the market caused him to wonder if it was so painfully obvious he was a recently released ex-con. Those looks continued to seem odd and uncomfortable to him clear up until he flagged a cab and rode through a vast new area of slums in order to find the correct address.

Scott was sure the enormity of the poverty-stricken area he was witnessing had not existed, at least to this extent, before he'd been sent up. He chalked it up to the economy and lack of jobs in the area. News reports he'd seen while in the joint were chock full of talk about high unemployment, national debt, and rising unrest over the state of the country for quite some time now, even from the usually liberal media. But seeing it hit home to this degree was pretty unsettling, and he could only hope it wouldn't jeopardize his efforts to find a job.

Located in this less than desirable part of the city, Gin's complex was a towering mess of graffiti; mismatched building materials; decade's old patches and windows which were boarded over with particle board and two by fours. Scott figured the building's owners must currently be in violation of dozens of city codes. The outer hallway of the structure reeked of sweat, sour wine and urine, and was littered with cockroach and rat-infested garbage and the half-eaten carcass of an unfortunate tabby cat.

Scott's discharge, at least this soon, had been a surprise even to him and had occurred in between his scheduled monthly visits with his family, so he hadn't expected anyone to pick him up on the day of his release. Arriving at Gin's apartment and rapping twice on the door, he saw her peer through the peephole with a shocked and then irritated look on her face while she slid back the deadbolt to let him in. After what she'd said during their last visit, he'd expected a warmer welcome from his wife, but wasn't surprised by the cool reception, she was a continual mystery to him.

He'd not seen her apartment yet, since she and CJ had moved into the place while he was still locked up. They'd lived here, eventually adding baby Angela to the household, for the past four years now, and as he looked in the door, he wondered if the place had been cleaned properly, even once, in all that time.

The door was flung wide by his eager kids as they ran out to greet Dad. He knelt to catch them in his arms, but was knocked back on his rear instead. They all laughed while he hugged them; as hot, salty tears streamed down his scruffy, unshaven cheeks. Scott vowed silently in that moment he would be a good dad to these little ones, and that his kids would never feel deserted by him again. There was no way he could know what his future might hold and absolutely no way to know he wouldn't be able to keep the promise he made to himself that grey, rainy day.

Gin's place was furnished with stained, damaged odds and ends she'd picked up at various flea markets and garage sales. The living room carpet was soiled and ripped in several places, and the walls were dirty, gouged, and badly in need of a fresh coat of paint. Scott was shocked at the filth and disrepair in the apartment where his kids were living. It made him sick to think of them growing up in a place like this and caused him to think back to his own dysfunctional childhood.

With lingering aromas from the outside hall following him into the living room and adding to smells of kitchen garbage and a dirty bathroom, the apartment was pretty hard to stomach. Scott thought it kind of ironic he would think the prison he just left didn't smell as bad as Gin's place. Nevertheless, he was glad to be here with his family, so he would make the best of it for now.

Gin was currently working part time as a cocktail waitress, and since she wasn't aware of Scott's release until he'd showed up at her door, she obviously hadn't secured the day off. The sitter would be coming any minute now, so Scott told Gin to call the girl and tell her not to bother. He couldn't think of a better welcome home gift than to spend some time with his kids.

While Gin worked that night, Scott had a great time being a dad. He fed the kids, bathed them, played games, read stories, and put them to bed a little later than Gin had ordered him to. He was giving Angel a big hug and tucking her in when she wrapped her tiny arms around his neck and whispered, "I love you, Daddy," causing his heart to swell with emotion for this small bit of his own flesh and bone.

"I love you too, baby."

"I love you too, Dad. Are you gonna be here when we wake up in the morning?"

"Yeah, little man, I'm not goin' anywhere, son. You sleep tight now and have a good dream." He tousled CJ's hair, kissed his forehead, and tucked him in, leaving the door open a crack in case one of his children should need him in the night.

After the children were sound asleep, he found he was too excited and restless to relax, so he scrubbed the bathroom from top to bottom and cleaned up the kitchen including dozens of dirty dishes and pans. After mopping the floors, something that apparently hadn't been done in years since it turned five shades lighter with a little soap and water, he picked up the toys in the living room and took out the garbage. Finally, after locating an ancient vacuum cleaner in the hall closet and outfitting it with what appeared to be the last existing bag, he vacuumed the carpet, being careful not to unravel the whole mess by catching loose threads in the machine's beater bar. When Gin walked in later that night to the smell of a much cleaner apartment, sleeping kids, and her husband snoring lightly on the couch, she smiled and felt glad she'd decided to let him come back home. He would be pretty handy to have around, and she could save lots of money on child care.

Scott met with his parole officer for the first time since arriving home. She had some good job leads for him, and he hoped his luck would be better this time than it had been after his last release from prison. They went over her expectations for him, and he left for an interview with one potential employer. Known for hiring former convicts, this shop supervisor seemed down to earth and fair. He asked Scott to take a welding test the very same day. Scott had never welded a day before in his life, but he'd seen it done plenty of times, and after his test, the boss said it was one of the cleanest beads he'd ever seen laid down. Who knew he had skills which could actually earn him an honest living; certainly not Scott!

The position paid extremely well and came with impressive benefits, which would kick in after only thirty days on the job. The best thing was he'd be able to take care of his little family. Maybe in a few months he'd have enough saved to get Gin and the kids out of the little hellhole where they were living and into a decent place. For the first time in years, Scott felt a surge of hope infiltrate his previously defeated soul, and he found himself whistling all the way home to tell his wife of his good fortune.

Working opposite shifts, Scott and Gin didn't see much of each other until her nights off on Sunday and Monday, but that didn't bother Scott, and it meant one of them could always be with the kids. She still hadn't admitted her affair with Jake, so Scott was having a serious problem trusting her intentions or whereabouts when she left the apartment. A tension, thick enough to cut with a knife, hung in the air whenever the two of them were alone for any length of time.

Aware the restaurant where Gin worked closed at 10:00 p.m. caused even more suspicions to rise in Scott's mind since Gin was not arriving home until three, four, or even five in the mornings. What she might be doing that late at night he could only guess, but really didn't want to. When he tried to talk to her about the situation, she refused to hear any questions from him, reminding him instead of his own failures and telling him she didn't answer to him or anyone else in this world.

Scott discovered he was far more forgiving than he'd known, after examining his own previous reaction to the letter from his mom. The revelation had been a pretty big shock to him. Thinking himself a tough guy for a long time, forgiveness didn't fit into that imagined reality. But the way he figured it, he'd screwed up so much in his own existence on this planet he didn't have much room to hold a grudge toward anyone else, especially if they'd been willing to apologize. All it'd taken for him to grant mercy to his parents is a bit of the truth, some history, and an admission of guilt. He figured Gin didn't know him well enough, or trust him with the truth enough, to give him a chance to forgive her.

Wanting an opportunity to show her the many ways he'd changed as a person, he tried to encourage her, but found she wouldn't open up to him. He became more frustrated with their relationship, or lack of one, each day and grew more steadily weary of her constant and ever growing put downs and insults. As she railed at him each day about how worthless and useless he was, it took everything in him not to throw her own infidelities in her face.

In only two short months, Scott saved enough money to move his family to a small house in a vastly better neighborhood. He hoped this new home might make a real difference for his wife and give her a feeling of stability. His dream was to heal their relationship and have a happy family.

The house was a little run-down, but Scott didn't think any of the improvements which were needed would be too difficult to handle on his own, mostly cosmetic stuff. After signing the lease, he bought supplies and scrubbed the place clean as a whistle. He washed windows and shampooed carpets to ready the place before moving their belongings on the upcoming weekend. Painting the walls and making some minor repairs helped a great deal too, and before he knew it, the house was almost good as new! Some of the guys at work offered to help, and he thought he just might take them up on their generous offer.

Scott and Gin bought some secondhand furniture, which was in much better condition than the stuff from Gin's former apartment. The new house had a small fenced area in the back where an old tire swing hung from an ancient, maple tree, so Scott bought a used lawn mower and spent two days mowing, weeding, and cleaning up the yard. That small plot became his favorite place on the new property to spend time with his kids. They had great fun playing in the little backyard, and he knew in his heart he was doing exactly what he was put here on this earth to do. His old resentments began slowly to heal as he took every opportunity to be the kind of dad he'd never had as a boy, hoping he could somehow break the terrible cycle of abuse which had plagued his family for, evidently, generations.

Scott got to be pretty good friends with most of the guys at work. Lately, they'd all been talking about their anger over controversial amendments to the health care act, which had been passed one holiday weekend in the middle of the night in twenty twelve. The last of the mandatory phases of the bill had been implemented a couple years back by the administration, and the general populace was becoming more displeased daily by promises not kept and lies perpetrated by those government entities running the program.

No one bothered to read the health care bill before they voted on it, and once passed, it seemed to be full of surprises which even the most liberal of legislators found disturbing. Rumors abounded of the compulsory implantations being done in local Global Health Organization offices nationwide, and it seemed everyone had a story about a friend or family member who'd suffered greatly at the hands of a secret government constabulary force called People's Militia, for simply not showing up to their implant appointments.

Friends from work were worried about what they considered to be the continuing "'Destruction of American's rights and ideals', obliterating the Constitution and the country as we know it." The health care bill wasn't the only mandate they unanimously despised. Recent gun bans left many feeling as though their beloved country was living in the clutches of nineteen thirties mindsets; the same mindsets which left Germany wallowing in communism after spawning the Third Reich. Some of the guys were talking about taking off with their families to avoid the government-mandated implantations. Gun bans meant they had no way to defend their families against government tyranny and many decided to try their collective luck with the ARM movement in the mountains.

There were admittedly many strange and unexplained things going on in the public and political arenas. New laws seemed to spring up every day out of thin air—laws which were not voted on by congress or the people, nor were they sanctioned by individuals of good moral conscience, but simply dropped in place by "Executive Order." These were laws which applied to everyone other than the present administration and those in power. These laws were being thrust on the country by an unethical and tyrannical government and clearly pushed society farther and farther off the dangerous cliff to a social-ist/Marxist end.

With all the new information to ingest, not least of which was the existence of the new "Goon Squads," Scott wasn't sure in what direction he was inclined, but he didn't like the idea of the government telling him what to do, or threatening him. As an ex-con, he didn't have the right to own firearms, but he also didn't like the idea of the recent gun bans because it was one more right denied to the law-abiding citizens of the land. While he was incarcerated, he'd heard a federal law was shoved through congress requiring folks to register their arms, after a couple of loons had shot up another school, and once the administration had the names of all the law-abiding gun owners, it wasn't a stretch for them to write new laws demand-ing those guns be turned over to the authorities.

Most citizens were opposed to losing their sec-ond amendment rights, but it was no use avoiding mandatory firearms collections, due to lists compiled during compulsory registration. This new madness did not lower numbers of weapons carried by crimi-nals, as those individuals had not registered their arms, so the statistics of violent crimes skyrocketed higher daily and resulted in citizens being afraid to leave their homes. The administration's militia squads didn't mind this side effect, because it made their job of subjugating the populace much easier; and around and around and around it went.

Scott tried several times to talk to Virginia about his feelings on the subject, but she'd made up her mind. She and the kids were getting their implants regardless of his suspicions and forebodings. He was having a difficult time understanding her feelings on the topic now that he could easily supply his family with health insurance of their own, and it looked as if the government's health care plan was a huge failure, costing taxpayers billions of dollars.

One morning, as Gin was sneaking in at 5:00 a.m., Scott sat up on the couch and confronted her. "I don't get it, Gin. Why did you tell me you wanted me to come home? Is there someone else? Where do you go so late every night?"

"I already told you, Scott, you lost your right to know what I'm doin' when you got yourself stuck in the pen."

"But I'm home now, Ginny."

"What? What'd you call me?"

"Ginny. Does it bother you for me to call you Ginny?"

"I just don't like it, that's all."

"I don't know. You didn't seem to mind it when Jake called you Ginny."

"How do you know about Jake?"

"He got sent up right before my parole came through. We had a few chances to talk, and he told me his old lady's name. I thought it was just a coincidence 'til he told me his kid's names too."

"Why didn't you say somethin' when I was comin' to see you?"

"I was so relieved to see you and to see the kids I thought I could just live with it, but I'm feelin' like there's more stuff goin' on now I should know about. Is there somethin' you might wanna tell me about, Gin?"

"I shoulda known there was somethin' goin' on when you was cleanin' and takin' care of the kids. There ain't no man out there that's doin' all that without expectin' somethin' in return. And you know what, Scott? We was better off before you got out of the joint. We had plenty of money and food stamps comin' in from the government, and I was makin' extra on the side, so we was just fine. Now here you are makin' just enough for us to barely pay the bills and then we're broke all the rest the time. We woulda been better off if you'd never come back. I mean it, Scott!"

"So is there someone else, Gin? I deserve an answer even if I don't deserve anythin' else."

"There's lots of somebody's, Scott. I make better money after work than I make at the restaurant."

"What do you mean, Gin? Are you turnin' tricks?"

"Oh, don't get all uppity with me, Scott. I ain't doin' nothin' wrong. I can take care of myself and the money's good. After Jake left, I had to do somethin'. A friend set me up, and I been doin' pretty good so far!"

"Gin, you don't need to do all that. I can take care of us now." There was some piece of Scott that was almost relieved to hear Gin was turning tricks instead of being in a serious relationship with some other guy. He knew it wasn't an ideal situation, but in his vast experience, it could be worse. After all, she could be in love with some really great guy, and he didn't feel as though he had enough good personality points to compete with anybody who was worth too much.

"Take care of us, Scott? You can't even take care of yourself."

"Come on, Gin. I mean it. We argue all the time now. That ain't good for CJ and baby Angel. Please stop what you're doin' and let me try to do what I'm supposed to be doin', okay?"

"Okay, Scott. You think you're so great, such a big man. You really think you got what it takes to do right by your family? We'll give it a try for a month. But if you can't make things work I'm outa here. You hear me?"

"Yeah, Gin, I hear you. Thanks, really. I'll make things right, I promise."

"Yeah, Scott, you make plenty of promises. Let's see if you can keep this one!"

Over the following month, Scott worked as many overtime hours as he could manage to pick up. He was making plenty of money now and was determined to prove he didn't need any help at all to take care of his little family.

Gin quit her job and stayed at home with the kids just as she'd agreed to do. However, it became more evident each day she wasn't cut out for the housewife and mommy role, as she was getting pretty antsy being with two kids all day. Gin's lack of any real attempt to keep the place clean throughout the week meant Scott spent his weekends keeping up on the household chores. He even made an attempt to cook, though he'd never claimed to have any talent whatsoever in that area. He wanted Gin to be happy, and he tried everything he could think of to accomplish that end, but nothing worked. He gave her money to shop with from every paycheck, and he watched the kids while she went out on her sprees and partied with her girlfriends. Even that, though, didn't seem to help. She was miserable all the time, and when she was miserable, everyone in the household was miserable. Scott couldn't seem to win with her and began to wonder if it was worth it.

The letter Scott was dreading for months finally came. The whole family was scheduled for implant at the local GHO in two weeks.

Arguments between the two got worse, and as a result, Virginia plunged wholeheartedly back into her old habit of degrading her husband every chance she got. Now though, she was doing it in front of his kids as much as she could manage. With their mother treating Daddy in a demeaning way, the children no longer felt they had a responsibility to listen to their father even during the hours when Mom was out, and he was the only adult in the house. Lack of respect had become such a major issue among the grown-ups; it was creating repeated discipline problems between Scott and the kids during their time together. Scott regretted ever getting back together with Gin. He might have been better off divorcing his children's mother and having the kids for visitation, at least then they wouldn't have to hear Mom talking to him the way she did now.

Scott and Gin contended about everything these days, and they clashed about the current government administration most of all. Gin liked every new law and policy the regime put in place, even when they unfailingly used less than honest means to accomplish their ends.

As long as it meant, she got "free stuff," she was all for it. Scott on the other hand didn't trust the president, or his cronies, one little bit and was suspicious of every new piece of legislation they passed by hook or by crook. He thought it odd too that the people who seemed to like this administration the most were the ones who thought the government owed them something and those that thought government should take care of everyone's needs and desires. Scott knew this way of thinking, from all he'd learned lately, was socialism at its worst and he also knew no one should be taking care of him and his little family, but him.

Watching the news more closely, talking to cow-orkers, and doing his research caused him enough worry, however, to get him attending meetings at a work friend's church on the west side of town. The guys over there were getting together frequently. They were also coming up with ideas to move people, who were opposed to the idea of implantation, out of harm's way of the government, and the ever growing PM squads. Since every attempt to change the law had failed, going into hiding was definitely becoming a more popular solution to the problem for many conservative citizens.

Pastor Mike Anderson, the man who'd written him a letter after his mom died, was heading up the nightly meetings along with a big fella named Josh Conyers and his best friend Mark. Josh was a huge guy, in physic and personality, with an engaging smile and the greenest eyes Scott had ever seen. His handshake was firm enough to make Scott wonder how hard it would be for him to break a guy's limb in an arm wrestling match. It was great to finally meet Pastor Mike and put a face with a name. He was a younger man than Scott imagined he might be for all the wisdom he'd displayed in his correspondence, but on the subject of what the government was doing to our country, he was all business and maturity.

On one of his first visits to the church, the lead speaker at their weekly meeting was a retired brigadier general with lots of experience in foreign affairs and some pretty strong opinions. He was talking to the men about the methods by which a government puts its citizens in a downward spiral toward Marxism and socialism, explaining there are six major steps involved in that process. He'd witnessed the procedure many times in his work as an antiterrorist operative and in his dealings with oppressed people around the world, including the downward spiral of the country of Venezuela. His oratory went on to cover those steps. The first step in that course is to nationalize sectors of the economy. Our current administration accomplished this with huge bailouts, taking over businesses and industries as well as appointing czars to govern every area of the private sector.

The second is redistribution of wealth. That step was accomplished by taxing and fining of private citizens to pay for an unsupportable health care bill and by forcing businesses to purchase health care in order to provide entitlement programs for those who refuse to work, and illegal aliens, in addition to many other fiscally irresponsible entitlement programs. Rung three in the progression is for the government to discredit its opposition. That is done by the administration pointing out to the populace which groups they believe are the biggest threats to society. This had already been done by reporting, in a recent Homeland Security memorandum, they should watch out for threats from returning veterans, right-wing Christians, promoters of the second amendment, and pro-life groups. Nowhere at any time did they point fingers at government oppression, militia squads, Islamic terrorists, or jihadist groups in that same memo.

Censorship is fourth. With recent hate crime legislation passed, government had targeted pastors and conservatives in an all-out attempt to tell people what they can and cannot say. Many were arrested for quoting Scripture from their pulpits, which pressed other pastors into submission through fear. Dangers of fundamentalist Islam, homosexuality, premarital sex, and even abortion were taboo subjects these days. Number five in the process is gun control. Government mandates to register guns and ultimately confiscate citizen's weaponry led to the takeover by the Third Reich in Germany and the deaths of millions. Even the imprisonment of Japanese citizens here in the US in World War II started with the confiscation of weapons after gun bans.

The general told them if they looked back at our past and the pasts of many oppressed countries, they'd see history rife with cases of government tyranny and the confiscation of private weapons. The general went on to explain the founding fathers knew from experience a government could easily become tyrannical and citizens needed to have the ability to protect themselves from their own government. The sixth and final stage in the evil course is to establish a constabulary force. The president already accomplished that with the ever popular People's Militia—a force which was answerable only to him. The meeting was informative and frightening. Scott became even more determined not to be made a puppet of this wicked regime.

Later during a short conversation between Scott and Pastor Mike, the pastor asked Scott how he'd been doing since his mom passed away. "Pretty good I guess. Things've been kinda messed up with the old lady. She don't think the government is up to nothin', and I can't seem to get her to listen. I don't know. I've screwed up so much in my life. Maybe I don't deserve a happy ending. I have to say it don't ever seem to work out that way for me anyway."

"Scott, I'd like you to know something. God isn't mad at you. He's not disappointed in you. He knows who you are, what you're about, and loves you with all His heart. He knew you before you were born. He loves you so much He sent His Son to die for you and wants nothing more than for you to accept His free gift of salvation. He wants to forgive you and make you free if you'll let Him. All you need to do is invite Him in, Scott."

"Oh, I don't know, Pastor. I gotta say he sure ain't ever done anythin' for me. It's okay though I don't expect nothin' from anybody any more 'cause then I don't have to worry about gettin' disappointed if you know what I mean."

"I do know what you mean, Scott, and just so you know none of us is good enough. But that's okay too. That's why Jesus died for us. His sacrifice two thou-sand years ago, and His death, has already paid the ultimate charge for us—the whole price, every bit of it, for all time. Heck, I'm not nearly where I want to be, but I thank Him that I'm not where I used to be. I like to think I'm a work in progress, and I'm grateful God will never disappoint His children."

"Pastor, I gotta get goin'. Thanks for everythin', but I'm runnin' late now. Thanks again." Scott was feeling uncomfortable and making any excuse he could think of to leave. He didn't know why the mere mention of this Jesus fella was still enough to make him want to escape, but he couldn't walk fast enough. As he was getting in his truck, he paused. There was something about the way Pastor Mike told him God wasn't mad at him that caused him to stop and sit behind the wheel of his white Chevy truck; with his head down and his hands clenched tightly on the steering wheel for a good long time. First, Dan, then his mom, and now Pastor Mike had said things which opened his awareness to a loving God just a little bit at a time. They all told him things which nudged his heart, but he didn't feel ready to give in, to trust, at least not yet.

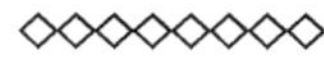

One day, two full months after their agreement was struck, giving Scott thirty days to prove he could take care of his family, he came home from work and slammed in through the front door.

"Hey, Gin, you home?"

"Daddy, Daddy!" his two little rug rats screamed as they abandoned their afternoon cartoons and rushed at him from the living room.

Smiling at them, he squatted down to give them each a big hug before turning back to his wife.

"No, Scott. I ain't here, left this afternoon for my trip to the French Riviera. Course I'm here! Where else would I be? It ain't like I got a real life anymore or anythin'!"

"Okay, okay, so I wanted to tell you the guys at work been talkin' again. One of them told me his sister in-law and her old man were supposed to go in to the GHO last week, but they didn't go. When they didn't show up, a militia squad came and arrested the whole darned family! I told you before what I been hearin'! I just think we oughta get outa here is all. More of the guys from work left last week with their families. We oughta go now too, before things get any worse. The more I think about it, I don't want nobody puttin' nothin' in me that ain't natural. The whole thing just freaks me out! I don't want the government, or nobody else, trackin' me."

"Oh for god sakes, Scott, nobody wants to track you! And if you hadn't done so much stupid crap back when you was a dumb kid, you wouldn't have to worry about it now. You're just paranoid is all. The president told us he just wants to give us free doctor care, and I ain't about to turn down nothin' for free! Those people gotta track everybody's medical information somehow. What else do you want em to do? I don't know where you get these fool ideas, but if we don't show up for the implant, they'll just come and arrest us anyway! We're supposed to be goin' in next week and the kids and me is goin' whether you do or not."

"Hey, I don't want them government people puttin' implants in my kids either, you hear me? I'm their dad, and I got some say in this too!"

"You ain't got anythin' to say to anybody, Scott. I can call that government number and report you like the commercials on TV said, and I will, you hear me? They'll come get you before you can do anythin' to stop us. And you know what, Scott? I'm gonna fix all this right now. The kids and me is gonna go to my sister Becca's house. We'll go to the GHO from her place so you can't do anythin' that'll get us in trouble. Do whatever you're gonna do, Scott, I can't stop you, never could, even if I'd a mind to."

"Well, Gin, you're gonna do whatever you're gonna do no matter what I say either. I ain't ever been able to talk reason to you. I can't believe you're getting sucked in to all this socialist crap like everybody else, but I'm gonna get outa here. I wanna take my kids too. I have a right to those kids. And I guess I knew somehow you'd end up at your sister Becca's house. You've been tryin' to work that out for a long time. You're only doin' it now, so you two can run and act like a couple a single gals again. I can't keep you from doin' that, but I want to take my kids with me. Why do you wanna put them through all that?"

"Scott, if I'd known what a prize catch you was before I married you, I could've saved us both a lot a trouble and told you to get lost, but you ain't takin' my kids anywhere. I told you I'll call that number and they'll come get you so fast it'll make your head spin, so leave us alone Scott, you hear me?"

"Okay, okay just drop it, Gin, and yeah, I gotta say bein' married to you has been a real picnic too! Just do me one favor, okay? If you're gonna go, at least promise me you won't let my kids forget who I am."

"Scott, every time you're gone, they forget you. It ain't like you've been here most of their lives anyway. You think you've been a real dad to them? One they can brag up to their friends? Well, I'll tell you what. The whole time you was in jail last time, the other kids made fun of CJ and picked on him for his daddy's sake. He was cryin' all the time! You're just a real forgettable kinda guy, Scott, and most of the time, they just wish you'd stay gone, so they don't gotta deal with all the drama that goes along with havin' you for a daddy."

Scott thought he might like to die at that moment. He knew Gin had grown to hate him more, but the new creative ways she manufactured to hurt him, using his kids against him and making him feel like a worthless jerk became further varied and harsher every day. Scott knew he would miss his kids, but he thought he could probably go the rest of his life without Gin's slamming remarks and he'd do just fine.

Gin and the kids left for her sister's house the next morning. Scott hugged and kissed his children before they left, but as they walked out the door, he felt as if his heart was crumbling into a million pieces. He knew full well he might never see them again, and the knowledge left him feeling undone. All the promises he'd made to himself to be a better dad than his own father was to him were about to be scattered to the wind.

Planning to leave for the region's ARM camp over the coming weekend, he would first finish out the three days left of the work week and pick up his paycheck on Friday. His previous week's wages had paid the rent and utilities and of course supplied Gin with her shopping money, so he was a bit strapped for cash, and he still had a few items to pick up for his trip.

For the next two days, Scott woke up and went about his schedule in a tortured fog. He missed his kids, but when he tried to call Gin's cell phone, she didn't answer, so he left several voice mails for the children. At this point, he doubted the kids would ever get to hear any of the messages he'd left. Trying her sister's number too, he got only the answering machine and left more messages. Scott was beyond angry and confused, but he knew if he didn't hear back from Gin before he was scheduled to leave on the weekend, he just might risk going over to her sister's place to say good-bye. The more he thought about his position, the more he knew he couldn't live with himself if he deserted his babies without a word.

Planning before to say his farewells via phone, to keep things easier on everyone, Gin was no longer giving him that option, and he knew his absences in the past were hard on the children, so he didn't want to leave them without a good-bye. Wondering what Gin might be capable of now that she'd left him for good, would she continue to keep his kids from him, perhaps even report him to the GHO authorities if he pushed the issue?

Not positive the woman he knew was malicious enough to turn him in to the officials, he had to admit he had a pretty good idea it would be a piece of cake for her. He supposed her decision would be determined by just how miserable she was willing to make his life. Part of him wanted to stay behind for his kids, but he knew he couldn't help anyone else if he allowed the government to implant him with their control chip, so he was determined to follow through with the plans he'd made.

Stories abounded at work and around the neighborhood about people trying to remove the implants by themselves and dying in the process. Somehow, the GHO had concocted a way to booby trap the mandatory inserts. Embedded transplants emitted a signal which tied in to the host's normal brain and heart rhythms, and those were programmed into the GHO health care computer. If the implant was tampered with in any way the government's computers were alerted, and a signal was sent out which interrupted those normal brain and heart rhythms causing instantaneous death. Scott had been told the administration was willing to kill its citizens to obtain total control, and it looked as if that was indeed true.

There wasn't a doctor in the land willing to defy the government's implantation mandates in order to help, at least no doctor who wasn't already on the run with ARM. And as far as any of the guys knew, the doctors who would be willing to help didn't have the answers they needed yet. Unless a way was discovered to disarm the medical implants, the only choice for freedom-loving citizens was to refuse implantation of the device in the first place. He hated the thought of his kids walking around with tiny time bombs in their little bodies, but he didn't have a solution for that either. Their mother was bound and determined she was going to get all she could for "free" from the administration's organization.

7

THURSDAY EVENING SAW Scott coming in from another hot, grueling day of welding, dirty and exhausted. He tripped over his backpack, still on the floor by the back door, a reminder he hadn't finished packing yet. He'd be leaving the next evening right after he cashed his check and picked up a few more supplies and knew he had only a few items ready to go with precious little time to get the rest together. Leaving on Friday, before the militia soldiers could be dispatched on Monday to arrest him for blowing off his appointment, was imperative, so he decided he'd finish his preparations right after a shower.

Not able to get hold of Gin and the kids by phone for days now was eating at him, so he left another rather stern message for Gin on voice mail telling her he expected to talk to his children before his departure. Tired and hungry, he grabbed some clean jeans, a T-shirt, socks, and underwear and headed to the bathroom.

His heart ached over the fact that he hadn't been able to make his life work this time. He'd tried, really tried, but nothing ever seemed to go his way for very long. He was a giant screw up, of that he was darned sure, and it seemed he couldn't do much of anything right. Blaming Gin for finding someone else while he was locked up wouldn't have helped, he didn't fault her for that, but couldn't she see how much he wanted to make things right between them now? Didn't she see how hard he'd been working to take care of their family? This little house, the effort he'd put into making it nice for her. How was it she couldn't see how much he cared? Well, he couldn't go back and change things from the past now; it was what it was after all. It seemed to him there was probably too much water under the bridge for her to get over those things which seemed to be eating at her. He felt empty and so very tired.

Ignoring his scheduled appointment at the GHO today, he knew that meant the administration's thugs would be coming for him. From all he'd heard, that conclusion was inevitable. Positive, Gin had taken his children for their appointment today, he knew surely they'd all been implanted hours ago. That knowledge was like a knife twisting in his gut. He finally had to admit to himself once and for all he couldn't take the kids with him even if he was able to contact them, not with their newly installed tiny GPS systems set and ready to go.

As far as he was concerned, it didn't take a rocket scientist to figure out the implants had never been intended just to store medical and financial information, but also to track personal facts which the administration didn't have any right knowing. Aware that an implant meant you carried not only a tracking device, but a ticking time bomb, implied the government meant to intimidate its citizenry into submission. Let's face it, they wouldn't get much resistance from a fella who knew he had a loaded bomb in his body, and that the administration had the only remote control with which to detonate that explosive device at will.

Heck, once you were implanted, the administration would have the ability to eliminate you just for disagreeing with them and make your death look any way they wanted. Scott knew he wasn't the brightest guy in the world, but if he'd figured this out, why did it seem to be escaping the understanding of the general populace? How could they have been so naive throughout this whole illegal process? Were people really that stupid? Well, it appeared his Gin was and she had many, many gullible friends.

Aching for tomorrow to come so he could just leave this empty house where, in his mind, he could still hear the sound of his children's laughter ringing through the halls, he closed his eyes and rubbed his throbbing temples. Done with the pain of this situation, he wanted to start anew and take his mind off the pointless mess his life had once again become. Would it be possible to go far enough to forget the torment of this most recent loss? Well, that was what he wanted if it was achievable. Bone tired, mostly he just didn't want to worry about it anymore. He could only hope Gin hadn't said anything to the officials when she was at her GHO appointment earlier that day.

As he stood in the shower, hot water pulsing over his sore muscles, he thought about his parents, his wife, and his kids. A shiver of grief, like icy fingers, ran the length of his back. Salty tears mixed with soap and warm water as he broke down, racked with pain and defeat. Would the losses ever end? He didn't know how much more he could take. If there was a god out there, what was He doing, trying to see how much more Scott could handle before he'd crack? Well, he had news for the dude; whatever cruel deity in the universe might be watching, or even instigating this painful torture, the answer was that he couldn't take much more, not much more at all.

Would he get the chance to say good-bye to his kids, he didn't think so, and that prospect broke his already aching heart. He also didn't know what Gin was saying to the children about him, and the thought she might be turning them against him made him feel even more lost and angry. Though, he had to admit as he reasoned it through, it might be better for the kids if they did hate him. Perhaps his absence wouldn't break their little hearts as badly if they despised him as much as he'd loathed his own absent father.

Stepping out of the shower, he began rubbing his body briskly with a stiff towel. So tired he didn't know if he could eat, but aware he ought to take in the calories for his upcoming trip; he decided some of that meatloaf leftover from last night might do the trick. He'd eat something and then finish packing for his journey. Dressed and about to leave the bathroom, he heard a noise outside the window. Parting the bathroom curtains, ever so slightly, he peered through and saw an SUV there, which seemed oddly out of place in this neighborhood. It was a sleek dark number with tinted windows, the type of transportation you might expect to be filled with secret service agents following the president. He saw the door open and two black clad mystery men stepped out. Now he was certain. These men were members of a PM squad, come to collect him.

Watching for just a few seconds more, he saw the men pull out their firearms and sidle sideways up the walkway with barrels pointed skyward. He didn't have much time. As the administration's soldiers made their way up to the front door of his house, Scott ran for the back. Jumping into his boots, grabbing his jacket and his backpack, he slipped out the rear exit quick as a flash.

The front doorbell rang, but Scott was already pushing his Harley down the alley to the main road beyond. His doorbell rang a second time and was followed by a loud boom as the door came crashing in. It was already getting dark as Scott hit the main road and made his way out of town toward the mountain. His trip would be starting a day early and under circumstances he'd not foreseen. Now he knew for sure he would never see his babies again. Chill fall evening wind dried the tears on his face as he set his jaw and made ready for the ride of his life.

8

S COTT KNEW HE couldn't take his Harley all the way up the mountain, but with any luck he meant to get as much distance as possible between the death squad and himself before daylight.

It was pretty cold, much too cold to ride, but his white Chevy pickup would've been easy to spot against the dark surroundings of these empty, back roads, and he couldn't risk being located by the search parties. Riding without a headlight, his only illumination was that small amount of light which the moon provided intermittently from breaks in a cloudy sky, and his nerves were raw and frayed as a result of watching intently for any debris which might lie on the roadways waiting, as it were, to wreak havoc on his journey.

Coming to the end of paved roads, he continued on gravel, then dirt. Moving fast, way too fast for safety's sake, he couldn't slow down now for fear of being discovered. As he distanced himself from civilization, his path snaked through stands of trees decked out in the gold, oranges, yellows, and reds of autumn's vibrant hues. Twisted scrub pine, tall buffalo grass, and miles of rough hill country stood between him and the base of the mountain. He trekked as far as he could manage with the motorcycle before deciding he might do better going forward on foot.

When Scott reached the base of the monolith, he unhooked his pack from the back of the Harley and laid the bike down behind a stand of dwarfed conifers. Covering the motorcycle with brush and debris, he disguised it as best he could, hoping its dark color would help conceal it from searching eyes in the night.

Gathering his pack out of the dirt, he pulled the straps over his shoulders and headed off for higher ground, hoofing it quickly through what remained of the tall grass and up to the large rocks at the base of the mountain. Stopping for a moment to listen, he heard the distinct sound of a helicopter approaching from the city and then a searchlight appeared out of the blackness of the western sky.

Assuming it was a patrol out scouring the area for him, his suspicions were confirmed as the sleek black aircraft came into view, so he moved quickly to get out of sight of those oncoming troops.

Pressing his muscular body tight against the shady, back side of a nearby boulder; he knew his black leather jacket and dark jeans could aid in his camouflage in the gloom of night. Wrapping his leather clad arms around the back of his head in an effort to conceal his mop of blonde hair, he made himself as small as possible in the rocky crag. The copter came closer, circling the area and shinning its spotlight far down into the rocks below. He hoped he'd hidden the bike well enough to keep it from view of the guards, but knew there was nothing he could do to change it at this stage of the game.

Dirt and gravel kicked up by helicopter rotors and hurled through the night became a veritable storm of projectiles. Small stones pelted Scott's body, stinging his exposed flesh as they flew through the air like tiny, granite bullets. Many hit hard enough to remove chunks of skin and soon, the mass of wounds on his neck and hands were bleeding liberally as he stood unyielding against the cold boulder.

Every nerve in his body screamed at him to take flight and run for his life, but he fought the urge to flee and remained motionless in the rocks. After what seemed like an eternity, the helicopter turned tail and started back to the city, perhaps believing him to have escaped already up into the shadows of the dark mountain.

Shaking with fear and breathing so hard, he worried he might black out, he began his climb up the steep mountainside. The guys in his welding bay at work had been telling him for months that the region's ARM encampment was up on the dark monolith directly ahead of him, but no one had given him a map, so he'd be on his own for this one. Many of them had headed there with their families already, and he wanted nothing more than to join them.

As he rose higher on the face of the behemoth, the angry wind blew cold and hard. He regretted he hadn't been able to grab his gloves on the mad dash from his house. His fingertips were raw and bleeding as he fought to hold on to the rough, cold rock ledges in howling, powerful wind gusts.

After climbing for some time, Scott spied what appeared to be a ridge just yards above his head, and relief surged through his shivering body. He climbed those last few meters, pulled up and over the ledge and stopped to catch his breath.

Searching the area for a place which would provide adequate shelter for the night, he found several tiny caves before he finally stumbled on one which looked sufficient for his needs. Gathering dry branches to use for firewood, he also took out and filled, the two empty water bottles from his pack, in a nearby fresh water stream. After gaining entrance to the cavern, pulling pine boughs in to the entrance to block the way of possible intruders and unloading his supplies, he saw some things which seemed oddly out of place.

It appeared he wasn't the first one to hole up in this cave as it looked to have been recently used. What remained of a store of firewood, a carefully placed stone ring, and an article of discarded clothing were obvious clues. Upon closer examination, the cast-off article proved to be a ladies jacket, stiff with dried blood. The shoulder of the jacket was punctured and torn. Scott couldn't begin to imagine what the story might be behind the coat he'd found, wondering what became of the mystery woman who'd worn it, but he had to admit its presence filled him with an unknown dread.

Determining to better search the cave, something he probably should have done before moving in, he carefully explored every nook and cranny and found it to be clear of wildlife. Digging through his backpack, he located fire-starting tools and soon had a good blaze going. Jerky from the front pouch of his bag would do for supper, so he leaned back against the closest rock wall with thoughts and fears of the unknown filling his mind. What was he doing? He hoped he hadn't done another stupid thing which could be added to his list of life's regrets. There were already so many of those in his past.

He missed CJ and Angel with a pain which threatened to crush his heart, and as he sat on the cold floor of the cavern, slowly chewing his jerky, tears of sorrow flowed relentlessly down his unshaven cheeks. "Maybe I should've gone in for implantation," he thought out loud. "What's so bad about the government knowin' where I am all the time? It's not like I'm doin' anythin' illegal anymore. Who cares what they know about me?" But Scott knew that wasn't true. He knew that what the administration was doing constituted a major step toward legitimizing slavery of the American people and just one more stride on this president's forced march to socialism. He'd never stand by and let these people take over his life, his decisions, and his independence, he couldn't. Living without his personal freedoms for much too long already, he'd certainly not just hand it over to some clueless idiot politician now. He only wished he'd been able to figure out a way to talk Gin into allowing him to include his kids in this new life. His heart ached for the future of oppression they'd be forced to endure and the fact that he wouldn't be a part of developing them into strong loving adults.

Building up the intensity of his fire to deter visitors of the four-legged variety and to keep the cave warm throughout the night, Scott tried his best to get comfortable in order to achieve some much needed rest.

It seemed years since he'd arrived home that evening. "Wow," he wondered out loud, "has it really been less than a day since the goons kicked in my door? Are you even out there God?" Scott questioned. "My mom believed in you, but you sure haven't ever been there for me. How do you expect me to trust you when you never answer me? He lay back against the cold stone wall, contemplating a God who could supposedly see all that was transpiring in the world today and yet didn't bother to come forward and offer His help. It didn't bother Scott that this God, if He truly existed, seemed to be absent in his own life. After all, he'd never really spent any time searching Him out either. But what about all those people who claimed to be His followers? Why wasn't He at least there for them?

What difference could any of His so-called all-powerful omniscience make if He didn't even love and take care of His own followers? Yet, there had to be some redeeming value to this strange, confusing God, he reasoned. What had Scott's mother seen in this Savior? Why would she have trusted Him with her eternity when she'd only just barely met Him herself? He didn't know if he'd ever have the answers, but he did know he was terrified so, shaking with fear and cold, he prayed. "God, if you're here please help me. I don't know who you are, what to do, or where to go, and honestly, I don't know if you even care. But if you do and you want me to know you, then please show me some kind of a sign. Make a way for me, please."

Scott lay in the dark cavern, light from the fire's flames dancing on his face. Transfixed by the leaping conflagration, he waited expectantly for the sign he'd requested. When no sign of help was forthcoming—within the predetermined period of time Scott had set down in his own mind—he drifted off to sleep disappointed but feeling singularly vindicated in his own conscience concerning his opinion about this uncaring, seemingly absent god.

Scott was a city boy. He always had been. He'd never camped out, hadn't been a boy scout, and he'd never read a single book on how to survive in the wilderness. The fact that his backpack contents included two micro-filter water bottles, a multi-tool with knife, fire-making tools for dummies kit, and a jumbo bag of beef jerky was total happenstance. The gentleman at the large sporting goods outlet, where he'd bought his pack, insisted these would be necessities if he indeed intended to camp out in the high country. If he ever saw the gentleman again, he'd have to thank him for tonight's supper, but at some point, he would necessarily have to figure out how to rustle up some grub on his own. When he woke the following morning, stiff and sore from sleeping on cold stone, he wasn't at all sure what his next step should be.

With nothing on the menu but jerky, he threw some water on his face to rinse the sleep from his eyes and then chewed on a couple pieces of the spicy, dried meat, washing it down with long draws of cold water. He'd been hearing a low pounding noise coming from somewhere farther up the mountain and assumed he must be close to his destination, though with no expertise regarding the distance sound travels through rock and no real sense of direction, it still might take him a while to reach his journey's end. Anticipation of the unknown caused his heart to pound in a way he'd never experienced, but he thought he just might like the feeling this newfound freedom released in him. Obviously, he'd broken parole by running off, but the alternative was undoable, so he hoped he'd fit in to this new life with relative ease.

Scott didn't have much gear, so packing up for the trail consisted of putting his bag of jerky away and refilling water bottles. He had no map, but up was up, so he proceeded on to find a path, or access point, to the next ledge on the behemoth.

Scott's trek up the mount continued painfully throughout the day; he was in much worse shape than he'd imagined. The muscles he'd grown in the prison yard and cultivated further in his work as a welder certainly didn't help where plain old endurance mattered.

He heard the pounding, which he'd noticed earlier in the morning, growing louder as he made his way higher, ledge by ledge up the massif. Puzzled by other sounds he heard, including those of distant gun shots, which was something he was a bit more familiar with due to his checkered past, he wondered what would make the people in the ARM encampment so careless as to give away their position to the outside world. But then, he reasoned, they must be much more aware of how far away their adversaries were located than he would be. Perhaps their lookouts knew the enemy troops had stopped their mountain search, which would absolutely make his path safer.

Noticing the weather going from cold to colder as the altitude increased, he was grateful that, for the time being, the sun was still out and shining on his head. He plodded on almost mechanically until the sound of gunshot rang out very close by. The first blast was followed closely by a second, and every hair on his body stood on end. Scott threw himself behind a patch of evergreen shrubs, hoping he'd be out of sight, should whoever was on the other end of that gun venture past. When no one appeared, he slowly relaxed and eventually went back to his previous trek, though not without a more wary mindset. Not knowing who might be shooting on this level of the mountain, he guessed they might be hunting. He'd try to be more careful going forward.

Two more nights of small caves, cold stone floors, and jerky left Scott feeling exhausted and surly, but giving up now would certainly not be an option, so he trudged on.

After three days of incessant climbing, he became less conscientious of his surroundings, just wanting the whole mess to be over; he rounded a steep rock wall and patch of scrub pine and came upon the bloody remains of a lone wolf. Dry foam on its muzzle was a fair indicator of the reason it was killed. He found himself grateful to the hunter he'd probably never meet. Without a weapon, he would've been fair game for the rabid wolf.

Pressing on, Scott figured he was getting closer to the camp. Pounding noises had gotten exponentially louder, and he could smell the smoke of campfires in the air. Stress was replaced by relief as he heard sounds coming from a plateau above where he stood and climbing the last bit of distance before that final access point, his sense of fear left him to be exchanged with a sense of peace. He threw his leg over the last ridge and hauled himself over the ledge.

Standing up, he raised his arm to signal the soldiers there, while instantaneously seeing movement to his left out of the corner of his eye. Glancing quickly from side to side, he realized he was surrounded. Relieved, he turned to the guards, believing they were simply ARM soldiers here to check out their visitor. Turning, he was struck from behind. The soldier's weapon hit him at the base of his skull and his weary, worn body fell in a heap at the feet of the grinning PM guards.

9

SCOTT WOKE IN the dark, head aching clear down to the soles of his feet. He tried to sit, but the quick movement caused bolts of lightning to streak mercilessly through his skull, so he lay back down gently. Not sure where he was, he lay still assessing the situation. Cold stone beneath his body and soft snoring from several other unknown persons across the black space were dead giveaways. He'd shared enough jail cells in the past to know a prison when he was in one, and he was now even more confused than he'd been when he was struck down in the plateau clearing.

Vaguely remembering reaching the plateau and seeing soldiers, he didn't remember anything past the point of an object connecting with the back of his noggin. Trying again to move, the ensuing migraine caused a wave of nausea to surge through him, and he moaned as he fought the urge to retch.

Suddenly, a cool hand was touching his forehead and a deep voice asked him, "You okay, buddy?"

"No, actually, not at all. Where am I?"

"You're in a prison cave in the People's Militia camp."

"People's Militia. I thought this was the ARM camp."

"Wow, not even close. No, you've managed to wander into the enemy's highly secret prison camp, fella."

"Well, I didn't wander. I walked right in like an idiot. I didn't even know the militia had a camp on the mountain. I've been plannin' this trip for weeks. Guess I didn't plan to good, huh?"

"You aren't the first one to say that, believe me. Who are you?"

"Oh, yeah, I'm Scott, Scott O'Fallon, how about you?"

"Josh Conyers. Glad to meet you, though it would have been nice to meet under different circumstances. Sorry, it's so dark in here. They don't give us light, so we won't be able to see each other until morning, which should be happening in just a few hours, and then only as much as the light gets in through the bars in the door. Sorry, it's so cold in here too. The enemy doesn't exactly treat us like royalty."

"Josh huh? The name sounds familiar. But, no, don't worry about it. It's warmer in here than it was on the side of the mountain, so I'll be okay. Wish I had somethin' for this headache though."

"Sorry, I can't help you. You've got quite a goose egg on the back of your noodle. I noticed it when I was checking you over after they dumped you in here last evening, but I'd imagine it'll get better in time. They didn't let us keep any of our gear, except our coats, when they threw us in here, so my aspirin is probably in the pocket of some soldier out there by now. I'd guess they didn't leave you anything either. And, yeah, your name sounds familiar too, but I'm not sure why. You should really try to get some sleep. We'll get it all figured out tomorrow, or, well, this morning anyway."

"Thanks, Josh. I guess I'll see you when it's light." Scott tried again, without success, to get comfortable on the chilly rock slab. He couldn't have slept if he tried, not with so many questions swirling in his aching head, so he laid in the darkness of the cave missing his kids and wondering what kind of mess he had gotten himself into this time.

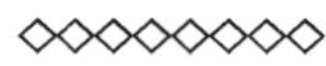

As light filtered over the plateau and crept slowly into the cave opening, Scott took mental notes of this most recent prison cell. The cavern was about twenty feet wide and around ten feet deep. A natural stone ledge, about two and a half feet wide and two feet above the cave floor, ran the entire inside edge of the cave walls and looked almost as if it'd been carved into the rock. He was one of six prisoners in the space, most of who were still sleeping. The moment he saw Josh's eyes watching him from the sleeping space nearest his, he knew he'd met him before. This was the big guy from the church meeting he'd attended a few times back home.

By the look on Josh's face, he could tell he was recognized as well. "How's your head feeling now, Scott?"

"A little better I guess. I feel like I been rode hard and put away wet, if you know what I mean. Worse hangover ever, and I never even got to drink the booze."

"Nope, don't know what that feels like, but if you say so, I believe you."

"Yeah, sorry, I forgot I met you in a church. You probably think I'm some sort of heathen or somethin'."

"No, Scott. No preconceptions here. I try not to label anyone, and I'm not here to judge you. I believe none of us is perfect, except in Christ."

"Well, Josh, I'm not sure your Jesus is too interested in me. I never saw Him go out of His way to do nothin' for me even when I was beggin' and pleadin' out loud. But I gotta admit, I probably wouldn't have gone out of the way for somebody like me either. I ain't ever done anythin' worth anybody's notice with this life, and I've done plenty to be ashamed of especially over these last ten years or so."

"Well, Scott, you're alive, aren't you? That should be proof enough He loves you and still has plans for you. If He didn't care about you, He would have let you kill yourself in one of your self-confessed, destructive moments and then Satan would have you for the rest of time. None of this is a surprise to God, Scott. He knew you and I would be here, at this moment, and that I would be more than willing to tell you that He loves you like a son and that He isn't one single bit mad at you."

"How do you know what He's thinkin', or how He feels about me, you ain't God or anythin'." Scott crossed his arms over his chest and took on an insulted tone.

"No, I'm not God, but I am the next best thing. I am His beloved son, Scott. And, so are you if you trust Him and seek Him as Lord and Savior. I read the Word and that Word is His Word to us, so we can know what He says about things and what to tell others about His love and grace. It really isn't a big secret, Scott, we have to have faith that He loves us and that He is always interested in providing us with the best of everything, His best.”

“Like I said before, I’ve never seen Him workin’ in my life. How am I supposed to believe in somethin’ I can’t even see?”

“That’s exactly what faith is, Scott! Hebrews 11:1 tells us, “Now faith is the reality of what is hoped for, the proof of what is not seen.” If we could see it, we wouldn’t need faith, would we?”

“So what good is this faith then? Why should I trust Him to take care of me? When I was a little kid and I really needed Him, where was He then?”

“I don’t have all the answers, Scott. I don’t know what the path might have been for you if you hadn’t experienced the things you did, or even if it might have been worse for you in another direction. I also don’t know what you needed to learn in order to follow Him, Scott. But God doesn’t let anything that happens to us go to waste. Romans 8:28 says, “We know that all things work together for the good of those who love God and are the called according to His purpose.” He can use anything that’s ever happened in your life to help you grow, to teach you things that will help make you stronger—things which will help you make better decisions and will even equip you to minister to someone else. With all you've survived in your life, He must have a great purpose waiting for you."

"Yeah and how am I supposed to know what this great purpose is? You're trying to convince me that God has some big plan for my life, but how can I even know who your Jesus is, or what He could ever be to me?"

"Hey, man, no one can create a relationship with the Lord for you. Your connection with Jesus has to begin by you believing He is the Son of God and asking Him into your heart as Savior and Lord. By confessing your sin and accepting the fact that He died and rose again to give you eternal life, you're assured an everlasting home in His presence. However, He didn't just rise again to give you a life after this one, but to give you life worth living here, an abundant life, life filled with health, healing, prosperity. That's the first step, then comes the faith and the seeking."

"Seeking?"

"Yep, first we need to know He has already done all that was needed when He hung on the cross and said, 'It is finished,' then if you want to know more about Him, it's all about the believing and the seeking, Scott. You said you don't know who He is, or what your purpose is, so you seek. Hebrews 11:6 tells us, 'Now without faith it is impossible to please God, for the one who draws near to Him must believe that

He exists and that He rewards those who seek Him.' I believe our greatest purposes in life are to discover how much He loves us and desires for us to be whole and then to share Him with everyone we meet. He does the work of bringing those people into our lives if we will just open our eyes to those around us. We just have to step up and remember He is always with us. I am not ashamed of the Gospel of Christ, Scott, and that has kept me and strengthened me my whole life."

"You know, my mom tried to tell me some of this in a letter she wrote to me while I was in prison. Some of the chaplains gave me stuff to read too. Does that shock you I was in prison?"

"No, we're all in prison until we meet the Savior, Scott. Once you meet Him, your life starts over, just like mine did. You become a new creature in Christ and part of the family of God, which makes you my brother. It doesn't matter where you were before you met Him. It only matters where you're going. Just know He laid down His life for you, and I would gladly do the same. Once you are His, you learn to fight from victory instead of always fighting for the victory. He is our victory, as simple as that."

Scott felt a weight slowly lifting off his shoulders and realized he had tears streaming from his eyes, but he wasn't ashamed. This was the first time in his life he'd ever felt truly accepted by anyone, and it just so happened that it was by a relative stranger. It was as if all the people who'd been trying to reach him, all the prayers, all the words of encouragement culminated in the very revelation, which filled his spirit at this moment. No one had ever really explained God's love so perfectly. If this Jesus could make Josh into the kind of man Scott admired most and cause him to feel loved and valued in a way he never had before, then maybe he should give Him a real chance. "So, what do I have to do to know I'll have Jesus in my life forever, I mean if I want to?"

"That part is as easy as saying a prayer. Would you like to do that now?"

"Yeah, I think I would. Can you help me?" It was as if all the years of introductions from Dan, his mom, Pastor Mike, the other chaplains, and now Josh came together, and he knew God was calling him, holding him and forgiving him.

In a prison cell, unlike any prison cell he'd ever occupied before, Scott bowed his head and surrendered to the King of the Universe. As he opened his heart to the Prince of Peace, he felt the bitterness and anger of years of abuse and neglect melt away to be replaced with a sense of serene joy. When the prayer was complete, his new cellmates cheered.

Scott, unaware he and Josh had an audience for their conversation found, strangely, he wasn't uncomfortable at all with the idea that others had witnessed this momentous moment in his life. A cellmate exclaimed, chuckling, "We didn't know we had another roommate, but leave it to Josh to get to you first. He's an evangelist of the first order, and he's gotten to quite a few of the brothers when they initially arrived, at least to the ones who didn't already know Jesus."

The guys all shook hands with Scott, some even hugging him and slapping him on the back, by way of congratulations for his recent acknowledgement of, and surrender to, their Lord Jesus. For the first time ever, Scott felt as though he was truly where he belonged, a part of something much bigger than himself, in this place of brotherhood in Christ. Prison or not, cold or hungry, this dwelling felt more like home than any place he'd ever lived in his life. Trust in a God who had brought him to this place at this time, and for purposes he had yet to discover, would change his life forever.

10

ALKING TO THE other detainees, Scott discovered confinement of prisoners in this People's Militia camp was neither happenstance nor any small undertaking for the PM soldiers. There were a total of eleven caves lined up on the back of the plateau where the enemy camp was positioned on the mountain. Each of the caves contained ten to twelve captives. Any newly acquired prisoners would naturally be bunked in with Josh's group since they were only currently housing six hostages. Information garnered from his comrades, in addition to bits of overheard dialogue from the guards, led him to the awareness that the militia didn't believe it was necessary to post sentries behind the caves, as there was but a narrow strip of ground behind the holding cells which preceded a sheer drop off down the back side of the mountain.

Hostages were taken from their cells for only two reasons: scheduled interrogation and body removal following death. Detainees were fed once a day through the iron doors where cold wind blew in continually. They relieved themselves into crude containers, which were then passed through the same openings in which their daily rations were delivered, and for the most part, they were left to their own devices to create exercise and entertainment routines in an attempt to stay in shape, sane, and ready for anything.

Scott also learned very quickly how strong their appointed leader was. Josh was taken away for questioning every morning. Colonel Cage, the base commander, was an expert in interrogation and believed Josh knew the location of some vital papers implicating important government officials in plots against the American people. He came back beaten and bloody every day, but never lost his joy, or his desire to share the Word of God. Colonel Cage meant to break him and became more frustrated each day with his lack of success in obtaining the needed information; therefore, the beatings and torture grew worse as time passed without results.

Cage was a hard man, feared by his subordinates and looked to by the administration to get the job done, no matter what that task might be. He took personally Josh's lack of fear and refusal to cooperate, and sincerely wished his instructions had not ordered him to keep this man alive until he had extracted all the vital knowledge he held. Simply put, in moments of anger over his detainee's noncompliance, he sorely wanted to strangle Josh with his bare hands.

Each afternoon, the prisoners finished their meager meal and then Josh sat with his brothers to share Scripture. It was apparent to Scott that his friend had memorized the Bible, but not only because he could quote scripture and verse. It was something in his eyes and something that radiated from his heart when he talked about Jesus. Well, that and he surely had an answer for just about every question which arose from the guys.

As time passed, Scott respected his mentor more and more. He was clearly a man who loved his Lord and was not ashamed to share Him with anyone who would listen for a minute or two. He'd not met a man so committed to anything in his lifetime and his commitment had helped to save Scott's life and sanity. Not allowed Bibles in this place, Scott vowed to himself that when they were freed, he would invest in a Bible of his own and begin to seek the Lord more intimately. Who knew, perhaps his life would be dedicated to evangelism as Josh's was.

Scott still had plenty of questions of his own though. After weeks in captivity in the PM camp, he was becoming more frustrated and wondered why God hadn't come to save them, or at the very least,

Josh. Surely, the Lord knew how worthy this man of God was? Josh explained to him he was satisfied to be wherever God put him and was equally happy no matter what the circumstances surrounding him. "Just like Paul, Scott, I've learned to be content whether I have plenty, or nothing. God never promised being a Christian would be easy. He just promised if we trust Him, we would be filled with His Spirit and His joy forever, and we would spend eternity with Him. He also never promised we wouldn't have trouble, but He did promise He would be with us through the trouble. Psalms 138:7–8 tells us, "'The Lord will work out His plans for my life.' And, I truly believe all of that or I couldn't go on."

"I know Josh, but you keep tellin' me He'll take care of us, and I see us still sittin' here in this damned hole."

"I know it can be hard to see past circumstances sometimes, brother. But we have to learn to live by His promises instead of by our feelings and life's changing situations. Sometimes, what we think would be the best for us is the very thing which would cause us most harm, or at the very least would not be best for our spiritual growth. So, if we are His, God intervenes in our lives and causes doors to close, which would have led us in the wrong direction and opens another way where there was no way before to lead us in a direction which will be more profitable for us.

He sees the big picture, where our own vision can be quite limited. When I look back over my life, I see many times where I didn't get what I was praying for, but things turned out much better than anything I'd asked for in my prayers.

Ephesians 3:20 says, "Now glory be to God who by His mighty power at work within us is able to do far more than we could ever dare to ask or even dream of—infinitely beyond our highest prayers, desires, thoughts, or hopes." We must learn to be patient and to recognize that God loves us and has our best interests in mind. He really is in control, Scott, even after all we've seen here in this prison and elsewhere."

"Okay, Josh, so let's say I really wanna share Jesus with people. If I decide to be an evangelist like you, how do I get anyone to take me serious? Anyone who's ever known me knows my past, the things I've done, and that I spent time in the joint. Who's ever gonna believe I changed, or that I'm worthy of any kinda' respect?"

"Well, first of all, they will see the changes in you, Scott. I've seen changes in you myself, and I haven't known you very long. You've been learning the Word, and I know you feel differently since you've asked Jesus to be your Savior, so He will honor that. Secondly, this isn't about us. None of us is worthy except through Christ. He makes us worthy through

His sacrifice. Since we are doing the work of evangelists, He will make a way and provide us with the tools needed to get the job done.

"You know, even Jesus ran into people who wouldn't listen to Him. There were those who'd known Him as a child, even family members who didn't believe He was Savior until after He died and rose again on the third day. You will always have to be careful around those who knew you when. It's just a fact of life for those who want to share the Gospel, Scott. Mark 6:2–6 even tells of a specific time like that in Jesus's ministry. It says,

> What's this wisdom that has been given Him that He even does miracles! Isn't this the carpenter? Isn't this Mary's son? And they took offence to Him. Jesus said to them, "Only in his hometown, among his relatives and in his own house is a prophet without honor." He could not do any miracles there, except lay His hands on a few sick people and heal them. And He was amazed at their lack of faith.

So, you can see ahead of time you'll be in for lots of trials and persecution if you choose this path, but you'll also be in some pretty amazing company." Josh chuckled lightly and shook his head as he recalled many times in his life and ministry he'd been forced to stand firm for Christ, even when he stood quite alone.

The weather continued steadily colder and the inside of their prison became more unbearable with each passing day. The guys watched, through the bars of their stone cell, light snow falling often now, but there was no attempt by their captors to equip them with any means of heating the cave. This could prove to be a very hard winter.

Colonel Cage refined many types of inventive new tortures; he'd been an exemplary student, absorbing all manner of tutelage in that particular subject, and had been feeling out Josh's weaknesses for some time now. He'd worked on the prisoner with torments which brought most men to their knees begging for mercy. Additionally, he'd deprived him of common necessaries to the point he wasn't sure how the man continued to survive, but still no results!

His superiors were counting on him to break Conyers and break him he would. The one area he felt might be the young leader's Achilles' heel was his men. Their welfare, their safety, their well-being seemed to be his only concern. He held staunchly to the belief that his "Jesus" would miraculously deliver him somehow, so he was never concerned for his own physical comfort, or future. Cage knew he could use Josh's weakness against him. His trust of this Jesus he looked to would be his eventual downfall. With winter coming on quickly, there were many ways to make these men's lives very difficult indeed!

11

"Jana, no!" Josh cried out in the darkness of the cold cavern; his whole body shaking with wild emotion carried over from this most recent nightmare.

"Hey man, you okay?" Scott was concerned for his friend and reached over to touch Josh's cold, trembling arm.

"Yeah man, sorry, I didn't mean to wake you. I've been having some crazy dreams for the past couple months is all. Why, what did I say?"

"You yelled a name. Sounded like Jana. Who's Jana?"

"Jana is my wife. She probably thinks I'm dead, and I don't know where she is or what she might be doing these days. Heck, I don't even know if she's alive. But, somehow, down in my gut, I feel she is. I've been having lots of weird nightmares lately. This one was really strange. I saw her in the middle of a huge firestorm, bodies falling all around her and explosions like you'd see in some kind of action movie.

You know, I haven't seen her since I was grabbed and shipped here on the night my friend Mark and I were taking a family to the ARM drop-off point. It's odd though. You know, I think about her almost constantly, and I pray for her all the time. It feels like we have a stronger connection now than we had when we were together, and somehow, in spite of all that's happened, it seems like we're still communicating. Does that make any sense?"

"Yeah, I think I know what you mean, man. I've never had that kinda connection with anybody in my life, but it's something I've always dreamed about."

"You know, Scott, she still didn't have a relationship with the Lord when I last saw her, but I have faith God will reach her somehow. I think one of the things I feel the worst about is that I didn't do a very good job of reaching her myself, in the years I had that chance."

"Wow, Scott, you just got more information from Josh than any of us have been able to squeeze out in all the months we've been together in this hole," one of the fellows from across the shared space commented.

"Sorry guys, I wasn't trying to be so closed. It's just hard to talk about some things. I really miss her, so I hate to sound negative. You guys are like a family to me, and I didn't mean to shut you out. Mark knows my Jana. Do any of you remember Mark? Some of you met him before they moved him to one of the other caves. I just didn't want to talk about things from back home, you know? Not when there's nothing I can do about it but pray. Scott, you'd like her. You would all like her. Jana has a lot of spunk. No one could ever tell her what to do, not even me. She's a tiny little thing with a short fuse and more anger and hurt than any one person oughta have, but I knew we were meant to be together from the very moment we met.

"From that first moment, I could see there was something in her nature that was special, and my gut told me her heart was the biggest thing about her. I always knew if I could reach her for the Lord, she'd be a mighty force indeed! She has a lot more in common with most of you than you'd think. Her life was a tough one when she was growing up, and she definitely felt like she had something to prove to the world, a real chip on her shoulder, but she put her whole self into everything she cared about, that's for sure."

"You're right, Josh. She's probably more like me than I'd like to admit, especially the anger part, but I think I'm gettin' a little better about that these days, don't you? She sounds special, and I'm really sorry you don't know where she is. It must be hard, not havin' any closure or anythin'. I know where my old lady is, and as much as I don't like that she ain't with me, at least I know where I stand. The part that hurts the most for me is, she took my kids with her and I couldn't do anything to keep them safe."

"Hey, Scott, I'm sorry about that. Have they been implanted yet?"

"Yeah, the day I went missin'. I was supposed to go in that day too, but I decided that ain't' happnin'. She wasn't listenin' to me and went to stay with her sister Becca a couple of days before, so I couldn't stop them. The rest is history. I hate the idea I couldn't even save my own kids, you know?"

"It doesn't sound like you could have done anything about it. It wasn't your fault, buddy. God will watch over the little ones."

"That's a tough one for me to count on, but I'm still workin' on that too, Josh. I didn't feel much like anybody was watchin' over me when I was a little guy, if you know what I mean, and the trust has gotta build a little at a time I guess. I pray every day for Him to help me trust Him."

"I know Scott remember God has promised you double for your trouble and beauty for ashes. I believe you will have more joy than you could ever imagine when all is said and done. Keep believing in Him and trusting Him, you won't regret it. And your prayer is a great one by the way, because He is the only one who can help you build your trust and faith in Him, Yeah, even faith is a gift from Him."

"Like I said, I'm workin' on that one too. I know He did it all and I know He loves me, but this is all pretty new. So far here we are in this godforsaken place, and I ain't seen a whole lot of proof about anybody's love for me except for you guys right here in this cave. I'm trustin' though."

"Good, trusting is good. Faith is what it's about. You're on the right track, Scott and God will reward that belief, I know He will."

"I'm counting on that Josh. More than you know. I'm countin' on it for me and for my babies too. I miss them somethin' fierce."

12

TEMPERATURES CONTINUED TO fall and with more snow on the ground, it was pretty clear winter had officially come to the mountain. The prisoners in Josh's cave took to grouping together to share body heat, placing the weakest among them in the center of the circle and they were surviving, if only barely.

Several emaciated bodies had been removed recently from other holding cells while the prisoners watched in horror, and the guys knew their overall numbers were dwindling. As the weather deteriorated, it could only get worse. Josh grieved he wasn't able to encourage the guys in the other cells. The captives were fighting to maintain their weight and health on one meal a day, in the freezing cold and with terribly unsanitary conditions, and he prayed God would intervene somehow.

Calories needed to keep a man's body going in freezing conditions are significantly higher than those needed under normal circumstances, so the lack of food was taking a bigger toll as temperatures dropped. Morale was slipping away too, as the death toll rose and the bleakness of winter hid whatever small bit of sunshine had previously shone through the iron bars of their prison.

Josh kept close track of his days of imprisonment though, and by his calculations, Christmas was near. He announced to the other inmates he would like to rejoice with singing and a service to celebrate the birth of Christ. Scott had never done much celebrating for Christmas. He hadn't been a follower of Christianity, and his family never had money for presents, so he found himself experiencing a strange sort of child-like excitement about the upcoming holiday event.

Christmas dawned bright as sunlight glinted off newly fallen snow. Crystals of ice, like diamonds, captured the sun's rays and sent bits of brightness dancing through the caves and onto the walls. Josh started their celebration off with a prayer and then the guys sang every carol for which they could remember all, or even part, of the words. They laughed and cried, and Josh recited the history of the Nativity while the other fellows listened with wonder to the story which had started it all. His ability to remember the biblical account word for beautiful word was a gift and caused them to respect him a great deal.

Scott felt himself encased in a cocoon of warmth, even in the midst of the cold cavern. He'd never been more filled with joy than he was in his new relationship with the Lord and with these special men who loved Jesus more than their own lives. He was truly beginning to understand what Paul meant when he said in Philippians 4:11–13,

> Not that I speak in regard to need, for I have learned in whatever state I am, to be content: I know how to be abased, and I know how to abound. Everywhere and in all things I have learned both to be full and to be hungry, both to abound and to suffer need. I can do all things through Christ who strengthens me.

Scott was sitting in a cold cave in the enemy's camp and yet was filled with the peace and joy of Christmas for the first time in his life. If only he could've shared this joy with Gin and the kids. If only his mom could see him now. Maybe she could.

13

J OSH'S MEN WOKE on the day after Christmas to the worst blizzard of the season thus far. Snow was so deep outside the iron bars that no one bothered to bring their daily rations, or empty their waste containers the whole day. On the other hand, the cold gusts of wind through the door were greatly diminished for the height of the drifts, and the cave actually felt minimally warmer. The snow lasted all day and into the night, so for the present they were entirely on their own.

With the end of the storm came new rations and a few scratchy, but very welcome, blankets. The guys were excited beyond belief at their good fortune. Soldiers even supplied the guys with some wood and matches to start a fire for the first time since their collective imprisonment. Warmth was a commodity highly underrated and taken for granted in the civilized world, and the guys felt like they were in heaven with the light from a fire and the magnificent heat which accompanied the blaze.

They praised God for their good fortune and laughed at the idea that, even a year ago, none of them would have had an inkling of how important a little thing like firewood and a match could be. It didn't take long before the cave was toasty warm, and they all noted that from Christmas day to today, three whole days had gone by without anyone coming to get Josh for his routine torture sessions. He was less bloody and beaten than the fellows had seen him since their incarceration began. God was infinitely good, and the world was as it should be.

14

ON THE FOLLOWING evening, after their gift of firewood, as Josh was leading his nightly Bible study, they heard a loud commotion outside their cave entrance, and suddenly, their iron bars were swung open with a crash. Guards with M16s tramped into their space stomping the snow off their boots and carrying a man on a makeshift stretcher. Josh recognized the man immediately, but held his tongue. He didn't want his friend to be relocated to another cell as Mark had been, just for knowing him. However, once the guards left, Josh hurried to the pastor, "Mike?"

"Josh?" Mike couldn't believe his eyes. How long had they all thought the man dead?

"What are you doing here, Mike?"

"Well, it wasn't exactly my idea, but those gentlemen insisted. Wow, Josh, we all thought you were dead! How long have you been here? We thought they were keeping some high level prisoners in these caves, but I had no idea they had a scoundrel as frightening as you under lock and key," Mike tried to sit up and grimaced, holding his abdomen.

"What happened to you, Mike? The stretcher and everything, what's going on? Where did they pick you up?"

"Actually, they picked me up during a surprise home visit."

"They picked you up at home? Hey, what are you talking about man?"

"Yeah, I had a nice little thing going on in a cave on the other side of this great big mountain. I was left to gather intelligence and to wait for somebody who hadn't shown up yet. And, as to how I got in this condition, you will never believe who I ran into, Josh."

"Who you ran into, what are you talking about? Who could you have run into on the side of a mountain?"

"Actually, Josh, I was outside this very camp when I saw someone about to give themselves away by walking directly into the enemy encampment. She thought this was the ARM camp."

"Well, there seems to be a whole lot of that going on lately."

"Huh?"

"I'll explain when you're done, Mike."

"Okay, anyway, I grabbed her, we wrestled and she cut me open pretty good."

"Cut you open, who cut you open, man?"

"It was Jana, Josh, I grabbed Jana as she was about to announce her arrival to the goons. She's become quite capable of protecting herself, by the way, and proved to be very strong! I was out of it for some time as I healed. She took care of me, hunted, and kept the cave stocked and warm. One day, as I was waiting for her to get back from a hunting trip out on the mountain, the militia soldiers showed up and took me. I don't know for sure where she is now. I have no idea if she's still alive or captive, and I'm sorry I don't have more info for you on that. But, Josh, you will be so happy to hear this; she has given her life to Jesus! We were sharing Bible study every day in the cave."

"She asked Jesus to be her Savior? Oh my soul, Mike, that is the most wonderful news I've ever heard, she was reading the Bible. I can't believe it. Well, of course, I can believe it. God is awesome! I've had so many dreams about her lately, Mike, but the dreams are full of explosions and fire raining down all over the mountain. If she's trusted Jesus for salvation, why would I be dreaming about her in conjunction with a rain of fire?"

"I don't know, Josh, but when you see her, and I'm sure by the grace of God you will, you will hardly recognize her. She's such a different person. Still talks about you all the time, even though she thought you were dead, just like I did, just like we all did. She talks about you like she believes you're watching over her. It's as if she thinks of you as her guiding star or something."

"Pastor Mike, do you recognize me? Scott O'Fallon, we met at a church meetin'? You led my mom to the Lord and you wrote me a great letter? I'm the other one who walked into the enemy camp thinkin' it was one of ours."

"Yes, Scott, I do remember you. So why were you walking into the enemy camp?"

"Well, I guess I didn't notice the difference in the uniforms and thought I was walkin' into an ARM camp, but I'm not sorry it happened. I wanted you to know I asked Jesus to be my Savior too, and Josh has been teachin' me lots about the Lord. I would've never met either of them if I hadn't mistaken the camp the way I did."

"That's wonderful, Scott! You know this whole situation has proven to me once again that God can use everything that happens for our good. We serve a great and wonderful Creator!"

15

FOR THE NEXT two evenings, the guys in Josh's cell could be heard sharing stories, studying the Word, laughing, crying, and becoming closer than ever around a warm fire. Also, for the next two nights, Josh's dreams grew worse as he saw Jana in the middle of a firestorm he couldn't explain. He woke gasping for air, clutching at his exploding chest, and in the process, woke Scott and Mike who listened, reassured him it was only a nightmare and stayed up with him talking softly in the dark till he could sleep again.

Josh's torture sessions with the colonel resumed after the mess from their last major snow storm was cleared from the cave openings, and he began again to come back to the cavern beaten and bloody every day. Mike was shocked at what the others had come to accept as daily routine. Cage hadn't gone soft when he'd authorized the fire building materials and blankets; he'd simply been given orders from his superiors directing him, in no uncertain terms, to keep their precious assets alive. It seemed they were a bit upset about the recent rash of deaths due to the cold. Cage was enraged at the idea of "going soft" on the prisoners, as he saw it, but orders were orders. He would figure out another way to get through to Conyers.

Josh assured the fellows he was fine, but they could see the lack of sleep and food and the constant torture beginning to wear on him. His eyes were ringed with dark circles, and they'd lost some of their usual confident gleam. Neither Mike nor Scott thought Josh could handle very many more days of this constant abuse to his already ravaged body. Josh was ever Josh though, positive and encouraging to everyone else around him, and they continued to have Bible study each night without fail.

Two nights after Mike's surprise imprisonment, Josh woke at around one in the morning with his usual puzzling dreams of Jana and the coming firestorm. He was awake, praying, when her first planned explosion rocked the mountain and woke the other fellows in the prison. He knew instinctively the blasts and gunshots he was hearing were related to the dreams he'd been having. He hollered to the guys who'd been inextricably drawn to the iron door by fire raining from the sky, "Get back from the door, guys, or you'll be caught by shrapnel." His comrades dropped to the floor of the cell and stayed there through what seemed like hours of warfare. With no concrete idea of what was going on outside the cavern, they waited for instructions from their leader.

During a relatively quiet period between bursts of gunfire, a detainee from one of the other cells showed up outside their door and broke the lock off their cell with a large rock. "Get low and follow me, guys. We're supposed to wait for her signal and then go to the munitions tent and arm ourselves."

Josh knew the man was talking about Jana, and the knowledge birthed a smile on his face so big it quickly spread from ear to ear. He turned to Mike and said, "You stay here, Mike, just until we figure out what's going on. We'll come get you when it's safe."

"You already know what's going on, Josh! I can't wait till she sees you. Go get her, man!"

16

JOSH WAITED FOR a signal from the other released captives and ran to arm himself, poignantly, with his enemy's ammo. Once he was sure all the freed prisoners were equipped and ready to go, with all the ammunition they could carry, he set the munitions tent on fire and ducked for cover as quickly as his legs would carry him to safety. The ensuing blast from the camp's stock of explosives was a huge distraction and would further aid in the battle they waged against the PM soldiers. It took very little time for the loosed hostages to get control of the skirmish, and before Josh knew it, they were locking those few guards, who'd survived the conflagration, in the caves they'd recently vacated.

Gazing around at blood-soaked snow and heaps of enemy corpses lying on the ground, he, for obvious reasons, expected to see at least a few of the legions of ARM soldiers who'd come to liberate them mixed in with the PM dead and wounded. It appeared though that they were it. His fellow captives were the only friendly forces on the mountain, and they remained untouched to the one by the late night combat.

Then, Josh spotted her. How had she done it? Was she really by herself? How could that be? Two of his fellow ARM prisoners helped Mike out to a nearby rock, as they continued locking new enemy captives in the caves, and she had her back to Josh as she walked hurriedly to meet Mike. Josh's heart pounded in his chest as he thought even from behind she looked wonderful. Her auburn hair had grown quite long and was pulled back and tied in a braid. She was clothed in a coat of white furs and held an M16 almost as long as she was tall. He couldn't help but smile at the vision she presented even in these circumstances. He stood watching her, animatedly telling Mike her story.

Mike, in the meanwhile, was smiling and glancing in Josh's direction over and over, as he waited for his big chance to disclose the secret they shared. Josh could tell by the look on Mike's face that his presence was about to be revealed and that caused him to begin walking slowly in Jana's direction. He was filled to overflowing with love as he strode her way, ready to sweep her into his arms, and his eyes filled with hot tears as he got close enough to hear her familiar voice telling Mike her exciting tale of ambush. Mike said something, which made her stop chattering, and she turned slowly toward him. Suddenly, a single shot rang out. He watched in horror as Jana, obviously surprised, looked down at her chest. He stood looking, in shock, as her furs become quickly stained with a growing circle of blood. Jana's face contorted in a look of confusion, and she slumped to the ground. Meanwhile, the shooter was tackled to the snow by recently released hostages.

He ran to her as his mind quickly switched into overdrive. "Oh my Lord, my Jesus, please save her. Oh Jesus, she can't be dead, not now, not after everything you've done to bring us back together."

Josh reached Jana and gathered her limp form in his arms, hugging her to his chest as he pleaded with her not to die.

17

"JANA, JANA, YOU can't leave me, not now," the voice annoyingly persistent, but familiar somehow, whittled away at her inner resolve. Jana wasn't ready to open her eyes just yet. Her head ached and her body throbbed with white hot pain too excruciating to speak. "It's cold here, so cold in this place," she thought drifting, drifting. She roamed somewhere, everywhere, nowhere in the thick fog, neither here nor there.

Wanting to lick her dry, cracked lips to moisten them, but lacking the energy to complete the task. Longing for a cool drink of water to sooth her parched throat, she tried to speak, but produced no sound. *Did my lips move?* she wondered silently. *Can anyone in this place hear me? Hello? Is anyone there?*

She vaguely remembered a face or perhaps it was a dream from long ago and far away. She couldn't quite recall, but something was haunting her, is haunting her still.

Was it the voice? That voice, his voice. It hurts too much to think about it, and breathing has become a chore—a chore much too difficult, too unbearable to endure.

"Oh, Lord, why does my chest hurt so?"

Darkness surrounds her. Lost in the void, not belonging to this world, but absent are her ties with the last. Should she be afraid? Jana feels something, but isn't sure if it is fear. Then she wonders in her darkness, what has she to be afraid of? He is not the author of fear. She moves on. On to a place where there is no pain. Thank heaven, no more pain.

A glowing mist forms in the dark, and suddenly, the void is filled by an energy illuminated from within the haze. Light grows and becomes brightness; brightness more beautiful and peaceful than mere sunlight. Brilliance has now permeated the place and filled her to overflowing with, what? With life, is she alive even now?

Suddenly, a voice, big as the universe, fills the bright space with love like a tangible thing. This is a voice she remembers from her dreams; the voice of her Lord.

Jana is excited, anxious to see His face again. She's never wanted anything so much before in her life. "Am I alive?" There is no more pain. "Am I dead? Is this heaven?"

"Jana," she hears the sweet voice again.

"Yes, Lord?"

"Jana, child, your time has not yet come."

"Lord, please, I'm so tired. It hurts so much back there, and I miss my Josh. Please just let me come home to be with you."

"Jana, your time will come in due course. For now, I need you to share my love and the power of my unwavering grace with the world. So few of my children understand the true rest which can be found in me and the healing peace I offer. I need you to go and share. I will never leave you, little one. Come with me, my child. It's time for you to go back."

Once stilled lungs abruptly suck in huge gulps of cold night air; Jana, shocked awake, finds herself looking into the eyes of her beloved Josh. His strong arms hold her tight as grateful tears stream down his handsome, trembling face. "Josh," she croaks.

"It doesn't matter, Jana. You're home now, and I'm never going to let you go again." Josh declares, as he holds her gently in his strong arms and rocks her on the cold, snowy ground.

As her eyes closed again, Josh, sobbing, shouted, "Help her, somebody help her! Mark, Mike, Scott, I need you!"

PART 3

1

"MARK, MIKE, SCOTT, I need you! Help me get her into the infirmary. See if you can find me a medic somebody, NOW!" Josh, shaking so hard from shock and cold he can barely breathe, picks up the limp body of his injured wife; holding her tight to his chest, her blood soaking through his coat feels wet and sticky against his skin. He rushes her through the metal door Scott has swung open to the base infirmary, as fast as his legs will carry him.

Mike, who'd seen their ARM comrade and mutual friend, Mark, being released from the cells earlier that night, already reconnected with him as the gunfire from the wild skirmish on the mesa slowed down. He discovered while talking with Mark that Dr. Rose was also here on the mountain, the same doctor he and Josh thought dead for many months now. Josh wasn't yet aware, they had one of the finest medical experts and surgeons in the country with them here on the highland, but he soon would be, because Mark was now busy searching the plateau for the famed physician who would be Jana's best and only hope.

Dr. Rose, still on cleanup and lockdown maneuvers with other ARM soldiers, was scouring tents and outbuildings for possible enemy stragglers and operatives, not aware his expertise was needed on the other side of the mesa. But once the good doctor was located, he hustled off to the infirmary to see what help could be offered.

Doc was housed in the prison caves longer than either Josh or Mark and his skills proved invaluable during sickness and injury for other inmates on numerous occasions during his extensive time of incarceration. As the boys knew, he'd originally gone on the lam with his family rather than allowing the government to implant him, and they'd all thought him lost, just as Josh and Mark had been thought dead and gone. But as it appeared, he'd been nabbed and imprisoned all those months ago by the administration's forces before he could find ARM's secret camp.

Militia had also taken the doctor's wife and kids, and sadly, he didn't know where they were, or even if they were still alive. But he was undaunted in his desire to do the right thing and intended to help his new resistance movement family wherever and whenever he could. Staying busy helped assuage feelings of anxiety over the whereabouts of his loved ones if nothing else.

When first captured, Josh and Mark had been housed together, but when their obvious bond was observed by guards, they'd been split up for fear they would concoct a scheme of rebellion more easily together than they could alone. For several months before the night's battle royal and his subsequent reuniting with Josh, Mark knew the doc was still very much alive but had no way to share that great news with his friend, so he was anxious to do that now.

Once Josh safely transferred Jana to a stainless steel gurney in the base's bright, white infirmary, he began gently peeling the handmade rabbit fur garments from her limp form. Only her shallow, labored breaths and an occasional, pained moan let him know he wasn't disrobing a corpse. He continued talking to her as he worked, in part to calm her and in part to calm himself. "Jana, I'm right here, baby. I'm not going anywhere, ever again, and when we get you all better, we're going to catch up on the time we've lost. I can't tell you how much I've missed you sweetheart. When Mike told me you were alive and that you'd asked

Jesus to be your savior, I cried like a baby. Nothing in my life, well besides my own salvation, has ever made me happier than hearing that beautiful news." As he peeled away the last layer of clothing to reveal the destruction to his wife's petite body, he gasped and paused, then took a deep shaky breath and continued talking without allowing his voice to convey the fear which suddenly filled his burdened heart and racing mind.

Searching the room with his eyes as he labored, he was looking for the means to mop Jana's gore-soaked chest, so he could better assess the injury there. Spotting what he needed, he motioned to his friend Scott who retrieved the needed items. Working almost mechanically as he spoke reassuringly he employed a box of tissues, and then alcohol-soaked cloths, in an effort to clean up the blood he'd found covering her decimated ribcage. The sniper used a hollow point shell, and the bullet had indeed done its job for all the destruction he saw there. "You know, I'd been having some strange nightmares for the past few weeks, Jana. I even shared the dreams with Scott. Oh, you'll like Scott, Jana. He's a regular guy, and he just recently asked Jesus into his heart too, so you'll have lots to talk about. Anyway, the dreams were about you, honey, and some crazy fire-storm on this very mountain. I wasn't sure what all the nightmares were about. I mean, how could I have ever guessed you'd figure out a way to arrange all this? This is hardly the Jana I left back home if you get my drift; there've obviously been lots of changes in your politics and your training regimen since the last time we were together." Josh laughed nervously and then continued to chatter, in a voice becoming more and more choked with emotion, as he fought to keep his composure and even harder to keep Jana with him.

Scott stood by helplessly, watching Josh weep silently and talk endlessly as he ministered to the needs of his unresponsive wife, with tears of compassion in his own eyes. The desperation he saw in the face of this godly man he respected above all others, who'd been a mentor and major part of his life since his own capture was tearing him apart, but he didn't know how to help, or what to do. Shifting from foot to foot in exasperation, with the day's pent up energy and caged sorrow bursting to escape, he watched what seemed to be a hopeless scenario playing out before him, and he knew too how this would likely end.

Sure, these forthcoming circumstances would probably crush the optimistic, positive man he'd come to know and love as a brother, he racked his brain for a way to make a difference.

As Josh talked to Jana, throat constricted with feeling, causing the pitch in his voice to waver; Scott thought he barely recognized his friend, as the strong man who'd been the backbone of their group all these past months. He'd never seen his hero so broken, so vulnerable, not even after hours of torture, cold, and starvation. He ached for a way to help in some way, any way he could. Just then two men came crashing through the hospital door. Mike limped in, holding his wounded gut, right after Mark and the doc cleared the entrance; and a flicker of hope flashed over Josh's tear-stained appearance when he recognized the face of the doctor he'd thought dead long ago. Dr. Rose checked Jana's fluttering heart rate and practically, nonexistent pulse and jumped into action. "She needs blood, Josh, what type are you?"

"AB, Doc, does that help?"

"Only if you know what type Jana is. Please tell me you do, because we don't have time to cross match even if this place has the equipment."

"I don't, Doc. I wish I did. What can we do now?"

"What about you Mike? Mark?"

"Sorry, Doc. Type A."

"Yeah, me too, I'm type B. Sorry, Josh."

"Hey, I'm O negative, Doc! I think that makes me a universal donor, don't it? I ain't ever had a chance to give blood before, and I think I'd like to do that now if it's okay with everybody here!" The look of gratitude on Josh's face, as he looked at Scott said it all.

"All right, guys, your friend will be the donor, but I'm going to have to get in there and repair a lot of damage, or we can pump all the blood we want and it just won't stay put! I'll need some instruments, and I'll count on all of you to help me out here today. Is it a deal?"

"It's a deal. And, it's Scott, Doc, the blood donor is Scott. Just let us know what to do and we'll get it figured out. What do you need first?"

Dr. Rose rattled off a list of implements he'd require for surgery, and for the essential blood transfusion, as Mike wrote everything down on white paper covering the office's second gurney. Ripping the list off the metal table, the guys headed to the back and searched every cabinet, shelf, drawer, and cupboard in the building, in record time, until they had all the items on the list, or reasonable facsimiles thereof; loading the appropriate instruments into the infirmary's sterilizer. Pulling the second gurney alongside the one occupied by Jana, Scott tore off his coat, boarded the table in a leap and rolled up his shirt sleeves. Mark swabbed Scott's arms with alcohol as Josh held Jana's hand, and the doctor prepared her for the lifesaving surgery. Things were moving quickly, which helped to keep the degree of anxiety to a minimum, since the pace meant there simply wasn't time to think or worry about all the things which could go wrong.

Josh trusted the doctor's medical expertise, but he was laying his life and Jana's at the foot of the cross. He knew with the blood his wife had lost, the only one who could save her now was Jesus. As he comforted her and held her hand, he was in an attitude of prayer, praising God for the miracle he believed had already been performed.

Inserting an IV line in Scott's right arm and one in Jana's left, Doc jerry-rigged a means of transfusion, which would accomplish the task, and clamped the tubing off until they could safely proceed. He wouldn't begin the transfusion until sufficient repairs had been made in Jana's ravaged chest to keep the transfused blood where they needed it, as he was all too aware, Scott didn't have unlimited supplies of the red stuff flowing through his mortal veins.

Preparations for that necessary lifesaving step complete, they could now get down to business. Scott was ready and willing to help, just to see the look of helplessness leave the face he admired so greatly. Mike found a bottle of ether in a back cupboard, a drug which had been used as a general anesthesia in years long past, and Dr. Rose decided using it would be ultimately better than having nothing at all to keep his patient asleep while he worked. As Doc began to place the mask over Jana's pale face, Josh stayed his hand, leaned down to kiss her cold lips, then helped to guide the cover to its destination. Mark would hold the mask, two drops of ether, and one more at a time, when instructed, should be sufficient to keep her under for the required amount of time, though Dr. Rose wasn't an anesthesiologist by trade and was only making a more than educated guess. Surgery to mend Jana began quickly. Doc cut into her chest and found more mutilation than he'd expected due to the despicable choice of ammo the sniper used. The mess would have been enough to thwart most surgeons, but his talent was unrivaled, and he knew full well God was guiding his hands.

Doc was forced to harvest several veins from Jana's legs, to replace ones in her torso, too badly damaged to repair. But by the Grace of God, with unrivaled proficiency and tireless work, pretty soon sufficient repairs were finished to allow the transfusion to ensue without wasting the precious blood supply available to them. Completing the surgery, down to the finite, took several more hours, as the devastation was monumental, but the men could see Jana's condition improving as soon as adequate blood flowed from Scott's body to hers. Josh knew God had kept her breathing, had kept her heart beating, and had brought her back to him. There was no other explanation which made sense.

Doc explained it would take some time for her to recuperate, not only from the chest wound but also from the amount of blood she'd lost and from the veins which had been taken from her lower extremities. Though due to the speedy way her injury had been treated, he hoped and prayed for a full recovery. Jana was scrappy, young and strong, so those things would work in her favor too. Now all they could do is wait to see what God would do. Scott began to sit up on the adjoining gurney and fainted dead away, tumbling off his perch and onto his head. The guys scooped him up and laid him back on the metal table. His contribution was greater than he'd imagined, and it would take him a while to get his strength back as well.

2

ANESTHESIA WEARING OFF, Jana, still more under than not, began moaning as she started her assent to consciousness. Josh held her head, stroking her hair, as she retched into a bedpan in reaction to the after effects of ether. Mike, who watched over Scott after his considerable blood donation and subsequent topple to the floor, left him long enough to bring cool cloths for Josh to bathe his wife's face. Still in significant pain, Jana hadn't yet come fully awake, but began thrashing in confused hurt until Doc administered one of the few doses of morphine he'd found when he broke the glass door of the meds cabinet earlier that day.

He'd also located codeine with acetaminophen tablets to help alleviate her discomfort later, but he was sure it wouldn't help much with the intense pain she'd experience during these first few hours and possibly days. Scott ate graham crackers and drank juice Mike scrounged from the mess hall, and he was slowly recovering from the lightheaded nausea plaguing him since trying to sit up shortly after Jana's surgery.

Rushing to the infirmary, Mark brought bad news. He and several ARM soldiers, who were currently controlling the communications building, received a disturbing message through the base's communication network. Purely by normal rotation, new recruits were on their way to the mountain. They'd be arriving in less than twenty-four hours. Jana's attack was a huge surprise to the unsuspecting militia camp, and they'd not been able to convey word of their demise to headquarters before the raging battle was complete, and they were imprisoned in their own caves.

Colonel Cage, well known for his arrogance, had been so sure they couldn't be vulnerable to a raid, considering the sheer drop on the backside of the behemoth and the heavily guarded front side of the PM camp; hadn't taken nearly enough precautions to keep the base safe. No sentinels in the communications building last night meant no one at headquarters knew today that the encampment was overtaken. Nevertheless, Josh and his troops would need to head out and be clear of this part of the plateau before reinforcements arrived. And they would have to move Jana, whether she was ready to go or not.

There'd be many days of travel over rough terrain in order to locate ARM's newest base position. Josh built a simple travois in which to transport his injured wife. This conveyance wouldn't completely protect her from the bumpy ride to come, but he could at least try to take the brunt of the trip for her.

Doc raided the medical stores in the camp's infirmary for all the antibiotics, pain relievers, bandages, and small medical implements he could find and loaded them into several large duffle bags, passing the bags out to various resistance troopers to carry on the next morning's journey. ARM soldiers also got busy relieving dead enemy combatants of guns, ammo, boots, and any other useful articles they could appropriate with relative ease and carry on their upcoming journey. Lastly, the mess tent was rifled for provisions—dried fruits and meats, bread, dried herbs and seasonings, powdered milk, and any additional food stuffs that might travel well. They would, after all, have many mouths to feed on their journey, and with no way of knowing how long their march might last, they wanted to be as prepared as possible.

The following morning dawned bright and cold as Josh's band of warriors made last minute adjustments to supply packs and finished up final preparations to head out of the enemy camp. Compassionate enough to supply their recently acquired prisoners with blankets, the means to build fires in their cells and enough food to last through the next couple days, which was infinitely more kindness than they'd been shown under the same circumstances, they felt no guilt about leaving their enemies behind bars.

Josh knew the base's new recruits would arrive sometime late the following day, so he had no worries the prisoners would perish for lack of supplies in the caves. Their own trip, however, would be far more perilous as they traveled the length of this mountain range to find the nearest ARM encampment. He knew they would be doing all this in subzero temperatures, with injured comrades in tow and somewhat limited food supplies. Josh had no doubt God would lead them, his confidence was sure, and for all intents and purposes, they should be warm enough after availing themselves of additional outer wear, tents, tarps, and blankets from the store rooms on the host base, so he refused to worry about the road ahead. They would simply do what they could do knowing God would do the rest.

Jana was packed securely on the travois, in layers of blankets under and over, for warmth and cushioning, and Josh would spend almost as much of the long excursion to come looking back to the comfort of his passenger as he spent looking forward to his footing.

Mark and Scott would expend much of their energy spelling Josh for short periods, or lifting the back end of Jana's stretcher over especially rocky and craggy surfaces, making the going more agonizingly slow for the entire group but doing what was necessary under the circumstances. The guys would also assist Mike, still healing from his prior injury, as this trek would prove to be a lengthy, arduous trip for their friend to endure as well.

Jana drifted in and out of consciousness throughout the next few days. Her body unremittingly racked with pain, which the meds Doc had access to did little to deter, rebelling with every twist and turn of the bumpy ride. Lying flat on her traveling stretcher, she could see only where they'd been, on the occasions she opened her eyes, not where they were going. But she couldn't be bothered by wondering over the destination. Due to her extreme level of discomfort, she longed only for the voyage to be over. Time and again throughout the day, Josh stopped his forward progress long enough to check on her well-being, but once she was finally able to communicate, she hesitated to tell him the truth of her pain; sure there was nothing he could do to help. She suffered terribly, actually experiencing moments of resentment toward a God who hadn't allowed her to die, rather than endure the torment of this endless expedition.

Dr. Rose checked in with her frequently. He'd taken the time that first morning after surgery to make introductions before they'd loaded her and all her blankets on the travois, but Jana didn't remember the introduction, which was made during the fog of post surgery.

Doc, who became more concerned each time he examined Jana, saw her surgical sites seeping and inflamed from jarring she underwent with every step of their march. Additional irritation from fabric covering her injuries and rubbing her already inflamed wounds only added to her deteriorating condition. In an ideal situation, she would have spent a minimum of a week in the hospital, under sterile conditions without excessive movement, after such an extensive surgical procedure. He was deeply fearful now over how this journey was affecting her overall recovery. Jana had many people praying for her, and she was spending a great deal of her own time conferring with her Lord. Even in her often semiconscious state, she knew God loved her and would protect her against any and all foes, but the pain was so intense she had to remind herself of His love often as the distress of this horrible crossing raged on. She found herself mumbling over and over that passage from Isaiah 53:5, "But He was wounded for our transgressions, He was bruised for our iniquities; the chastisement for our peace was upon Him, and by His stripes we are healed," knowing from experience that even when she didn't yet feel the healing, Jesus had already done everything needed. All she must do now is believe, agreeing with that truth, and the physical manifestation of her healing would soon appear. Of this, she was sure; she had to be, or she wouldn't make it. After all, hadn't He already delivered her from impossible scenarios on several occasions since her adventures had begun all those many months ago?

Josh felt a responsibility for all 117 souls traveling with him through this frozen, mountain range to the elusive ARM encampment, and with the weather currently so severe, shelter and food would be their greatest priorities, in that order. He delegated officers, who in turn selected their group's self-declared best hunters to supply meat for the larger group, using bow and arrow, instead of guns, to draw less attention to their whereabouts. It was a bit difficult to "lay low" with 117 bodies, but they would do their best. Where possible, on their way, they found caves and natural barriers against the cold nights and mountain predators, which gave them more leeway to light fires for warmth and protection. On occasion, when ordinary shelter wasn't available, they found themselves crowding into the tents they'd procured from the base supply depot. Due to number of tents versus numbers of bodies, this made for some pretty tight quarters and offered less protection from the cold nights and wild animal populations, causing a few close calls along the way.

As leader of their resistance faction, Josh assigned runners to go ahead of the larger group and scope out the terrain for easy passage, scouting as far ahead as possible to locate the new ARM camp location for which they were searching. Those runners also located water sources and possible sheltering sites for the upcoming nights where available. So far, they hadn't been tracked by militia soldiers, at least as far as they were aware. Josh knew the new PM recruits, back at the camp, had their hands full. Once they'd arrived on base, he fully expected it would take them at least a few days to gather enough soldiers and working munitions to launch any sort of counterattack, but after five days of travel, he realized retaliation became a bigger possibility with each passing moment. He also recognized his own slow momentum, as he dragged his injured wife, was hindering the whole group, and he suggested on several occasions that the rest of the soldiers go on ahead and leave him to find his way alone.

Of course, the guys refused to desert him, and his best friends seemed deeply hurt he would even suggest such a thing. Mike, Mark, and Scott all voiced the same thought. "We go together, or we don't go at all!"

Evenings saw the group stopping to set up their improvised camp and settle in for the night. While Josh and the doc gathered supplies to clean and re-bandage Jana's wounds, hunters unloaded the day's assortment of game, which was slim this late into the winter, but infinitely welcome in whatever amounts. Soon kettles of soup were simmering around the campfire, filled with portions of meat, dried pota-toes, onions, herbs and carrots, and anything else from their previously seized supplies as might add to a well-rounded pot. So far, at least no one was starv-ing, and Josh counted on God to continue dividing the loaves and the fishes. Before the group sat to eat their supper, he offered prayers to a Lord of second chances; a God who continued unwaveringly to show them favor and protection from all harm.

Doc was feeding Jana antibiotics three times a day along with as many painkillers as he felt safe offer-ing and he wondered, as he examined her, if the meds would ever kick in. He'd become more seri-ously alarmed for her worsening condition each day. For the first five nights, Jana vacillated between life and death as her husband and doctor ministered to her spirit, mind, and body, and infection did its best to overwhelm her immune system. But on the sixth night, she began slowly to show signs of better health and lucidity. These signs, increasing daily, finally saw her sitting up, and eventually, after twelve days, walking for very short periods of time, giving her husband a break from his duties as her designated pack mule.

Josh and Jana reveled in the moments they could walk side by side in the beauty of the mountain, even though the circumstances, as of yet, were not optimal. Jana knew she had a duty also to talk to Mark about his wife Tina and her suspicious demise. How often Jana had longed to share her mountain home with the man she loved, but never thought it possible for having lost him so long ago, and she couldn't leave their beloved friend Mark in that same limbo of uncertainness over his own wife's situation.

That evening, as they shared time around the fire, Jana told Mark of the death of his lovely Tina and held him as he cried. She reminded him that to be absent from the body is to be present with the Lord, and that someday he would be reunited with the woman he loved. She also reminded him that his children were safe with Tina's sister at an ARM base, probably somewhere on this very mountain range.

Josh was amazed at the woman who sat beside him now. He'd always thought her physically beautiful and full of passion, but now, hearing her comforting others and talking about the Lord filled him with awe. He knew they could truly begin again and could start dreaming of a future together—one they'd previously thought impossible, and to his mind, that was more wonderful than anything he'd ever imagined, or hoped for. He found himself more grateful to God than ever for his life, his salvation, and his beautiful wife.

As they walked the heights the next day, Jana related stories to her husband of the trials she'd faced in her journeys, including the mountain lion attack and Mike's nearly fatal wounds, Josh marveled at the capable woman she'd become and grew to respect her more than he'd thought possible. Josh shared stories too, from his months in the prison caves, leaving out the fact that he'd suffered daily torture at the hands of Cage, and she admired his strength and evangelical boldness, hoping one day to be so unflinching in her own growing Christian walk.

Doc found himself relentlessly watching Jana for signs of exhaustion and pain while she took her daily walks with Josh. When he saw evidence of discomfort, he corralled her, overrode her stubborn reasoning and excuses, and made her board her travois for the rest of the day. Josh and Jana could continue to talk while she rode in relative comfort, and he worked all the harder for it, but she found she would much rather walk beside her husband than ride behind and the doctor's job, of keeping her contained, became harder as her strength improved.

More than two weeks on the road saw the small resistance group stronger than ever despite the cold temperatures and many, countless hours of hiking they were forced to undergo. Assigned hunters had managed to find a steady supply of small game to add to the provisions they'd commandeered from the base, which meant they were eating better than they had while incarcerated, and the roving group had been relatively unbothered by aggressive wildlife on the behemoth due to their numbers. Each night of their journey, Josh held a Bible study by the fire, attended by most, and they hadn't heard anything from the militia, a condition they knew would likely not last forever.

Meanwhile, back in the enemy camp, preparations were reaching a fevered pitch as soldiers completed plans to track and kill the escaped resistance prisoners; anger over the demolition of their home base, as well as a good dose of wounded pride, caused Colonel Cage and his surviving militia officers to plot revenge against the feisty group of ARM troops who'd bested them so easily. They had no intention of recapturing the escapees, no matter where those orders originated. They wouldn't risk resistance warriors getting so far as to have boasting rights against them, so upon the location of their foes, they planned unthinkable tortures and, ultimately, execution. Too much time had passed though for this mission to be a quick and easy one, as the escaped prisoners had gotten quite a head start on them, and many of the base's weapons and supplies unfortunately left with the renegades.

Cage was forced to wait for arms shipments as well as replacement troopers to carry out his mission in any kind of thorough way, but carry it out he would. The commander lay awake at night imagining new methods of torment for Josh and his group of soldiers. He'd make sure they all suffered accordingly, for shaming him the way they had, before he joyfully put a bullet in each one of the damned traitor's heads.

Cage had waited long for a command of his own. He'd trained for years, in the hidden mountain camps, at the behest of the president. Long, long before the general populace began to see evidence of a People's Militia, it'd been training in the high wilderness. Much earlier than the infamous comment by the president stating that he would have a military force, a people's militia, to rival all militaries, which would answer only to the White House; they were training in multitudes of concealed camps ferreted away in the heights. This being the idea of mentors who'd ultimately trained and funded the current administration to do their socialist bidding.

Cage knew the Commander in Chief had been slowly adding Islamist fundamentalists, Marxists, and terrorist sympathizers to his cabinet since the beginning of his first term. And also that he'd ultimately planned to call for martial law long before the GHO started implanting American citizens with GPS locator chips, all he'd needed was an excuse. Those same chips, which eventually drove the people to rebel against all-out governmental control, proved to be the excuse he'd needed. That rebellion finally handed the administration its perfect opportunity to achieve total power.

Cage knew too that the end was already imminent the moment mandatory health care was forced down the throats of unsuspecting citizens. Stockpiling of weapons and ammo, bought up by the administration, as they were stripping America's citizens of their second amendment rights was no surprise to Cage. He was fine with all of that. He'd been won over by the administration's ideas of a socialist regime long ago, so long as it meant he could exercise his own sick brand of justice and play war with the big dogs. Why should he care about the abuse perpetrated on innocents? As long as he was on the right side of the inevitable battle, what difference did it make?

No one ever cared about him—never in his twisted life—and he was exactly the type of man the administration sought out to lead their bands of People's Militia goons. The mercenaries' legions were filled with men and women who'd been brainwashed into believing America didn't stand for anything anymore, and that the American people were too stupid to govern their own cities in any effective way. Sick individuals who thought nothing of torturing women, children, and the elderly to get what they wanted and then killing them without remorse. Somehow, these disturbed individuals believed their president had the only valid answers to the questions, and they were willing to do his will, no matter the consequences. Cage, among many camp and base leaders, had been handpicked by the president specifically for his past affiliations, liberal bent, and especially cruel streak. The leader of the country believed he would be more likely to get the results he needed from these men if they'd had certain specific trainings and beliefs.

Cage, and the rest of his ilk, was loyal to the administration and particularly to the president, and he yearned to prove his worthiness for the appointment he'd received from this, self proclaimed, world changer he admired beyond words. If he could just prove himself to this great man, he knew he would accomplish grand things. He aspired to the position of Western Regional Commander, but he'd never get there if he allowed his plans to be thwarted by the likes of Josh Conyers and his ever interfering band of resistance fighters.

3

I T'D BEEN FOURTEEN days since resistance fighters battled PM troops on the mountain's plateau. Fourteen days since Jana was critically wounded and saved by surgery and miracles. Fourteen days since PM base Commander Cage and his men were overcome and locked in their own prison caves. Fourteen days had passed before sufficient arms and troops were gathered and all was prepared to begin a search for the escaped resistance group. Cage, who was beside himself with rage at the incompetence of individuals at every level of preparations, swore vengeance on the men who'd humiliated him, and he was beyond ready to get on the trail.

The commander was an evil and manipulative man. Arrogant and abusive to the soldiers in his command and to prisoners housed on his mountain base; Josh had sadly been on the receiving end of his malevolent imagination during endless hours of torture sessions throughout his imprisonment, and knew more than anyone else, the depths of Cage's sinister soul.

The commander's main responsibilities on the People's Militia base were prisoner interrogation and overseeing the base's overall security. He'd excelled at the first, well, with most of his prisoners; though Josh had never given him a shred of information for the pain he'd inflicted. Cage hated him. He hated him for the humiliation that the man's courage and strength of character had caused him, and he hated him for being a better man. And, he'd obviously fallen flat in regard to his second, perhaps more important duty. He had not kept the base secure. He would never, however, take responsibility for the lack of security which had led to the capture of the camp. Instead, he blamed every bit of the incompetence on members of his staff who'd not survived the battle. It was an easy enough fix, as those unfortunate individuals weren't present to defend themselves. The overwhelming death toll would ultimately come in handy for him after all in escaping the blame for his own incompetence.

Search for the escaped prisoners could not include helicopters due to the peaks and ridges on the behemoth and wind gusts, which could certainly slam pursuit vehicles into the mountain walls during winter's drastic wind shears. Therefore, the hunt would take place entirely on foot. Commander Cage's arrogance would once again play a part in the outcome of the expedition. Cage enlisted one hundred men for this emergency expedition. He felt confident his one hundred highly trained soldiers would be more than sufficient to quell the insurgents. Each PM soldier had a week's ration of food and water in his backpack along with ammunition and emergency essentials. Cage was again so confident of his abilities he knew he could overtake the resistance fighters quickly, especially since they were dragging that useless, wounded woman on a stretcher; that he left the base, for his assignment, tremendously undersupplied and without a clue as to the dangers this particular mountain chase entailed.

Josh's fighters had several advantages. They had a fourteen-day head start; most of them had prior experience on the mountain so they'd brought sufficient supplies, and they knew their lives depended on their swift progress in finding the elusive ARM camp.

Knowing the commander would certainly be mounting a search, Josh started sending scouts backward, as well as forward, a few days prior to Cage's troop launch. Those sent forward were still searching the mountain for likely campsites, water, meat, and the obscure, ever moving ARM base; the guards he sent back were watching for the advancement of PM troops, which Josh was sure would be forthcoming. Six days after Cage and his men deployed on their mission, and twenty days into the journey undertaken by the resistance group, one of Josh's backtracking scouts came to him with bad news. Cage and his men were only about six days behind the slow moving group. This meant they would cover in fourteen days the same ground that it had taken Josh's group twenty days to manage. Unless they found the ARM camp soon, the math would play out and they would be discovered.

There was another consideration as well. If they were getting close to the ARM headquarters, they certainly didn't want to lead Cage and his men right in through the front door. That evening, Josh sat with Jana, Mark, Mike, Dr. Rose, and Scott and discussed their options. Josh's tracker told him Cage had one hundred troops with him, so obviously the man had underestimated the power available in Josh's band of freedom seekers. After only a week on the trail and considerable rationing, Cage's men were low on supplies and would still have to make it back to base when their mission was concluded.

Josh's hunters kept his group in fresh meat, and though taking time out every night to set up camp, cook, and conduct a prayer and Bible study meant they were not making as good of time as their pursuers, Cage's men would be tired, starved, and morally insolvent by the time they caught up.

Josh didn't mind the odds of one hundred famished, exhausted men against his well-rested, well-fed, and well-armed soldiers, regardless of the difference in levels of experience. He didn't want them to be sitting ducks, however, and so they devised strategies which would continue leaving rear guards to track the progress of the enemy as well as scouts to search out the upcoming route—a strategy which had been successful up to now. Jana became stronger with every passing hour, and soon she was employing her bow to help with the demand for fresh meat in the camp. She'd become quite a skilled hunter during her time on the run and proved to have a more proficient handle on the use of her weapons than many of the men assigned to the hunting team, so even those who'd not previously known her grew to respect her skills.

Jana praised God for bringing Josh back into her life and intended, with everything in her, to be the wife he deserved going forward. She thought it strange that she could be so filled with joy when their lives were so devoid of material possessions, considering how hard she'd worked in her former life to attain those very things which now seemed to hold so little significance. All she knew was she felt more alive now than ever, and each time she turned and saw her husband's face, she felt gratitude toward God she couldn't begin to describe.

4

DAY TWENTY-ONE OF Josh's search for the DARM encampment began early as he received important information from his recently arrived recon soldier. The bad news was that Cage and his men would overtake them in a mere three to four days, much sooner than Josh had anticipated, as they were moving pretty quickly through the rough terrain. The good news was that Cage's numbers had dwindled. Without enough supplies, proper shelter, and much needed experience in this mountainous environment, he'd already lost thirty of his troops to extreme weather incidents, accidents, and lack of appropriate mountain training. His loses would continue to multiply as his trek continued; it doesn't matter how well your troops fight if they aren't familiar with the surroundings in which the fight will take place and Cage's men, mostly brand-new recruits, were not at all prepared for the extreme temperatures and conditions they faced on their hurried march.

What remained of his ragtag group was a hungry, tired, cold, and weakened militia. Though Josh knew he could never discount Cage's hatred for him, or the fuel that hatred seemed to add to his desire to see Josh destroyed, he also felt the threat Cage and his army posed had so greatly diminished that his own more rested, fed, and prepared troops would be at an advantage with God's ever present help.

Day twenty-two of their mountainous trek brought more good news. Forward scouts had found evidence of ARM's last location and felt confident they would soon find the group they sought. Now the question remained. Should they continue to seek out ARM and risk exposing their comrade's location to the enemy, or stand their ground and defeat that enemy before they could become a threat? After Josh, Jana, Mark, Mike, Scott, and Dr. Rose, who had together become an impromptu council of elders, assessed their alternatives and the condition of the troops, they decided they would stand and fight! Preparations began immediately.

Their new well-chosen location was naturally equipped with several caves and large outcroppings of rock, which would provide good cover. On their side of a self-imposed demarcation line, they had a fresh water stream. In the area through which the enemy must travel, an area they had previously trekked, there were shear drop-offs, no easily accessed fresh water, and little to no cover, so after setting up an infirmary in one of the caves, for the treatment of possible injuries, and checking weapons and ammunition, Josh and his resistance army were set for whatever Cage might throw at them. Several of the men began preparing pots of stewed meats and vegetables as they readied themselves for a night of prayer and sleep before what could possibly be the fight of their lives. They'd approach this battle physically, emotionally, and spiritually prepared.

5

COLONEL CAGE WAS also sending scouts ahead to seek out Josh's group of escaped prisoners of war. Pushing his men to the brink of their physical strength, with no emotional or spiritual bolstering and a deep and growing resentment for their commanding officer, they began, though minimally at first, to push back. Mutiny was becoming a common thought in the minds of his abused troops.

Most of those newer recruits in the People's Militia camp were pressed into service in their hometowns after forced implantation. They didn't have a choice in the matter to serve anymore than they'd had a choice about the chip in their hand. Fed lies first by the administration and then by their trainers and military superiors, they were now seeing, to what depths of depravity the socialist regime was willing to fall firsthand, and many didn't want to be a party to the corruption they were witnessing.

Many of these boys were average Americans who'd just not seen the trouble coming until it was too late. They were blind to the power grabbing and manipulation of their government as long as their own needs were met. After their forced draft to service, they'd been led to believe the purpose for which they fought was a noble one, and the people they hunted were traitors to their homeland. After all, hadn't they been taught for years that terrorists lurked around every corner and that the clash would eventually come home? Now, though, they were seeing first hand that the people they hunted were just Americans, regular Americans, trying to be free.

More and more, they were seeing their commander as the arrogant, cruel, tyrant he was, and they secretly blamed him for those men they'd lost on this march. Those friends and comrades who'd fallen, and been injured, those who'd been left behind along the way, and the four who'd been shot as "traitors" when they questioned commands from Cage which were dangerous to the whole group. This left those remaining frightened of what the maniac they followed might do to them if they spoke up, but seeking how they might escape.

Of course, there were those officers in Cage's command who fully believed in their colonel and the lies they'd been fed, and they would follow him to the death. There were also still sprinkled through their numbers foreign troops who were supplied by the coalition of One World Government, sanctioned by the United Nations. With those who were faithful to Cage scattered among those who were not, there was enough room for suspicion in the troops to keep them from forming a full on mutiny.

Josh's soldiers were set for battle as the militia rounded the bend and came in full view on the plateau. With nowhere to hide, Cage and his men were sitting ducks. Rifle shot echoed through the high places and men fell, their blood staining the new fallen snow. Cage, who hid behind his troops, was not badly injured. When the colonel's remaining men threw up their arms in surrender, he shot two of them for treason before Josh could wing him, causing him to drop his weapon. Josh's strategy worked and though there were many casualties in the militia camp, the resistance fighters fared even better than had been anticipated. Their few minor injuries could be easily treated in the infirmary by Dr. Rose. The bigger challenge would be what to do with their prisoners.

Cage, seething with hatred, sat bound and spewing threats at his captors. His injuries tended to, he was back to his bitter, hateful self. A quick meeting with the resistance group of elders led to the conclusion that they couldn't, in good conscience, murder their captives and they certainly couldn't try to take the remaining forty-five hungry and wounded prisoners with them on their trek. There was only one solution. They'd turn one of the larger caves into a makeshift prison, leaving their captives enough food, firewood, and blankets to last until a rescue mission from the PM camp could be launched. Josh's group knew it was the only thing they could do, though they knew they wouldn't have been treated so kindly if current roles were reversed. Cage's radioman would be allowed to contact base after all preparations had been made, and they would therefore be assured help was on the way.

Supplying forty-five men with supplies for two weeks would make a significant dent in their own rations, but again Josh knew God would take care of them and honor their compassionate decision.

Several in Cage's group begged Josh to take them with him, to free them from their commander's grip, but the implants in their hands wouldn't allow that. Josh, with heavy heart, had to refuse their requests for the safety of all those he already led; knowing full well that their requests had been witnessed by their evil commanding officer and would likely end their lives.

When the prisoners were sufficiently secured and supplied, Josh stepped forward and offered a prayer for their safety and for his resistance fighter's continued good fortune, and they set out again.

Cage, beaten once again, and filled with hatred so intense he thought his head might explode, screamed through the bars of his new prison. "I'll get you, Conyers! There's no place you can go, no safe place. Do you hear me? I'll find you, and I will kill your sweet little lady while you watch, before I put a bullet in your worthless, traitor head!"

Josh smiled, slowly shaking his head. He had no doubt he and Cage would meet again, but he knew he served a God who would watch over him to keep him safe. He knew too that his new life with the woman of his dreams was a gift from God, which he had no intention of wasting. He had his beautiful Jana back in his arms, and he would never let her go again. They were indeed blessed. He wrapped his arm around Jana's waist and turned his face to hers. "Ready to go, wife?"

"More ready than you know, husband, more ready than you know!"

www.ingramcontent.com/pod-product-compliance
Lightning Source LLC
Chambersburg PA
CBHW071423190726
48292CB00001B/93